The Eyes of the Heart

RICHARD A. HACKETT JR.

The Eyes of the Heart

For more information about the author and other novels or books he has written, please visit the author website at:

www.rhackettjr.com

The characters and events in this book are fictional, and any resemblance to actual persons or events is coincidental.

ISBN-13: 978-0-9856743-2-8

Acknowledgements

To Pete for planting the seed for this story,
for helping me to see this powerful and unseen world around us,
and for his eternal friendship.

To John for the endless hours of editing, insight,
and unconditional friendship these past years.

To my wife who has encouraged me to write and to follow my dreams
and to my children that I hope will learn from life's truths
that are hidden in plain sight all around us.

Prologue

He took a deep breath and smiled as he turned in a slow circle, taking in the beauty that surrounded him. It had taken thousands of years for the small river to carve this massive gorge out of the mountain and the end result was spectacular. The river gradually grew in size and speed as it gathered more of the melting snow that had started as a trickle at the head of the gorge from the higher elevations and carried it to its final destination in the valley beyond. He could not help but admire the beautiful groves of quaking aspen, sage and wild flowers that were growing everywhere. It had been an incredible fishing trip; one that he knew was now almost over. He was somewhat melancholy that this incredible journey was coming to an end.

As the bright sun reflected off the water of the small river, it reminded him again of his reason for being there and with careful steps; he began his methodical final trek down the river. Carrying his fly rod, small tackle box, and large stringer of fish at his side, he followed the dirt trail that paralleled the river as it wandered through the valley. As he had done the entire trip, he stopped briefly to survey each deep pool, protected boulder, fallen log, or undercut bank that he came to, and then he carefully selected the best location to cast from. With each cast or flip of his wrist, the line would float across the distance, placing the fly perfectly on the water, allowing the river to carry it across to the desired location. The result of each cast was different, sometimes the native brook trout would rise to the fly and at the last moment turn away, others would gently break the surface and carefully nip at it, and some would attack the fly with such ferociousness that it would take his breath away. Inevitably, those that took the fly would begin their unique dance at the end of the line. He would play the line out, letting the fish run, and then when he felt the time was right, he would carefully begin to reel it in. He loved catching fish.

From the moment the fish grabbed the fly, he knew how well he had hooked it and whether he would be able to land it or not. But in spite of that foresight, he would still strive with all of his heart and with all of his skill. Those that managed to break the line or shake the hook free would turn and swim downstream. He would smile sadly as he reeled in his line, knowing that all he could do was would hope for another chance at them, even though it would be far more difficult the next time. Those that he did reel in he would hold and admire, as if memorizing each part of them, before letting them return to the river.

He heard the sound of the splash upriver, just past the bend where he had previously cast. He knew the sound and what it meant. It was the same sound he had heard each time he left his prior fishing hole victoriously, but this time the sound was much closer. Knowing what was coming, he waited as the river eventually carried the dead trout toward him. As the torn body of the fish floated by, he reached in with a heavy heart and pulled it out of the river to add to his growing stringer of dead fish. The wolves were closing in.

Not only were the wolves upstream getting more aggressive, he could tell by their howling and increased activity that they also were gathering in mass downstream. It was becoming clear that the closer he got to the exit of the gorge, the more aggressive and numerous they were getting. Initially, they were small packs that preyed mainly on the fish he had caught. But as he got closer to the exit the fishing had become more difficult. Instead of crystal clear water, the wolves had muddied it with their continual traversing back and forth across the river. Where the fish earlier in his journey were much easier to catch, they had become far more skittish and difficult to attract to his flies. He knew it would not only be very difficult to catch anything from that point forward, but also very dangerous.

As he picked up his fly rod he could sense the pack circling the area, remaining just out of sight. He knew there were far too many of them to just ignore and that the time had come for him to do something drastic if he wanted to keep the path clear. He looked down at the stringer of torn and lifeless fish on his belt and then at the river as it disappeared around the bend, *it's time* he thought and then sighed.

He walked a little further and stopped in a small clearing next to the river. He stood next to a massive boulder that had long ago rolled down from the walls of the gorge and had come to rest near the river. He reached down and unhooked the stringer from his belt and laid it on the boulder above him. Then he sat down next to it and closed his eyes. The sun felt good on his face and the gentle breeze carried the smell of the fish that were now warming on the rocks down the gorge towards the wolves. He knew the smell and opportunity would eventually be too great for them to ignore. It was only a short time later, with his eyes still closed as he leaned against the boulder, that he heard them cautiously approaching the clearing. He initially followed their approach from the faint sounds of twigs breaking, but the sound of their breathing and the uncontrollable lapping of their tongues not only made it easier to place them, but it revealed how close that were getting. He waited. They were being very cautious those last few steps, fearing a trap, but he knew that the sight of him so vulnerable with his fish close by would be too much for them. It was not until the breeze carried the overwhelming smell of their dank, musty, almost putrid breath to his nose that he finally opened his eyes in time to see them lunging toward him. With their ears laid back, a wild rage in their eyes, and their fangs exposed, they lunged for his throat.

With a scream, Luke threw his arms out in front of his face as he jerked upright in his bed.

Chapter 1

The green glow from the digital clock cast just enough light for him to see the ceiling that he had been staring at for hours as he lay in his bed. No matter how hard he tried, he could not find a way to fall back asleep after being awakened by that nightmare of a dream. *What an idiot*, he thought as he remembered the stupidity and horror of letting the wolves just walk up and attack him. He wrestled with the whole dream the rest of the night and could almost remember the exact display of numbers for each of the endless times that he checked the clock from about 2:37 a.m. until now at 5:29 a.m.. He knew that at any moment the radio would click on, letting him know that it was 5:30 on Monday morning and time to get up. He reached to shut the alarm off, thwarting the impending intrusion and noticed his hand was shaking. He paused and stared at it in the glow of the numbers and the day that was before him and knew exactly what had brought that nightmare on.

Luke, there's nothing to worry about, he told himself, or more correctly, that's what everyone had told him over and over again, yet the thought of a "business trip" to Baghdad, Iraq set his mind churning with visions and images of suicide bombings, kidnappings, beheadings and assassinations. Looking back on it, he was pretty confident that he would have never taken this job in the first place, had he known that he would be asked to fly to Iraq. He still did not fully understand why he was chosen to go on this trip. He barely knew the product that the company wanted him to field demonstrate to the military. He thought he had taken a job with a leading game development company, not a company that was developing military equipment that would require him to travel into a war zone. The fact that his immediate boss was traveling with him, someone who was not prone to take personal risks, made him feel somewhat better about the business trip.

As the alarm clicked on and the sounds of the morning news around Los Angeles began to fill the room, he reminded himself how much he needed this job. When he looked beyond his misgivings about this trip, the truth of the matter was that the job was a great opportunity. He had nearly quieted his thoughts and the feelings that kept him awake for most of the night when his attention focused on the words that the newscaster reported in the background. *"...Another roadside bomb attack killed three American soldiers and wounded four more during a patrol just outside of Baghdad."* His stomach knotted as he listened to the news and thought of the terrible impact that this would have on the families of those soldiers. *"In a related item, the headless body of the English contract worker who had been held captive for the past several weeks was found along the Tigris River this morning..."* He had tried to push the 'off' button on the radio alarm before hearing the latest item in its entirety, but it was too late. The mental damage had been done.

In spite of all his worries, Luke allowed his mind to disengage and shift into autopilot and simply follow his daily routine, the same routine that he had followed the majority of his life. Shower, shave, teeth, hair, dress and breakfast. After finishing the first items on his daily checklist, he went to grab the morning paper to read while he ate breakfast. As he opened the front door of his apartment to retrieve his morning newspaper, he looked down to see a folded headline about Iraq. Leaving it where it lay, he closed the door and decided to toss out the "reading the newspaper" part of his morning routine. As he put his rinsed cereal bowl and coffee cup in the dishwasher, he glanced out the window to confirm that the cab he had scheduled last night was there waiting to take him to the airport. He was almost disappointed. With his bags already packed from the night before, he grabbed his jacket, suitcase and laptop and headed out the door.

As he neared apartment 310, he overheard raised voices of the newlywed couple beginning their daily barrage of angry verbal assaults at each other. *They're starting a little early today,* Luke thought as he got closer to their door. Suddenly the door jerked opened and an angry-faced, blond woman stepped out in her bathrobe, apparently to grab the newspaper that was lying in front of her door. She was obviously just as surprised as Luke as she saw him passing in front of the door. In less than a second, her angry demeanor transitioned to a smiling and beautiful young woman. "Oh, hi Luke," she said with a smile as she turned and stepped back into her apartment. He had returned the smile and a "good morning" and then shook his head once her door closed. It was a typical interaction with them. They were all smiles and bliss when they were in public together, the perfect California professional couple, but behind closed doors the truth could be heard playing out almost every morning and every night. Choosing the stairwell instead of the elevator, Luke headed down the steps. *You need the exercise,* he told himself as he completed the last flight of stairs, passed the security door and stepped outside into the warm air of a summer morning.

The first sound that greeted him was that of a police siren in the distance. The cab driver seemed rushed and agitated in spite of his well-practiced greeting and false smile as he loaded Luke's luggage in the back trunk and jumped in the driver's seat. The cabby stepped on the gas and proceeded to weave in and out of traffic in his private battle against the city streets. Luke reached down and found the seat belt and snapped it on, *just in case,* he thought. After quickly merging into freeway traffic, it didn't take long for his driver to become even more agitated and begin yelling and cursing at other drivers, who were quick to return fire with a counterattack of honks and other well known hand gestures.

Whenever Luke sat in the back seat of a cab, he always seemed more aware of his surroundings. Without the distractions or concerns of having to drive and navigate a vehicle, he felt like he was just an observer of events unfolding around him instead of an active participant. As they drove the 20 miles to the airport in stop and go traffic, he witnessed the recent results of several freeway accidents sitting alongside the shoulder. An assortment of shattered glass, plastic tail lights, twisted metal and ambulances for as far as he could see. Looking down the side streets of the city, he saw police cars with lights flashing and someone handcuffed in the back seat of the closest car. One of hundreds of tragic stories and events in this big city that more than likely would never even make the evening news, yet Luke knew that each and every one of these events would have tragic impact and pain for someone's friends, parents, or children.

They arrived at the terminal and Luke paid the driver who had unloaded the luggage a bit too quickly, undermining his plastered on smile. While checking in at the airport, Luke could feel the tension. Strict security measures and constant warnings over the intercom made people edgy. Frustrations from those rushing to meet connecting flights, long lines with understaffed check-in counters, and a mother yelling at her kid who was throwing a fit on the airport floor, while the disconnected father remained distant to the whole situation created a thick fog of anxiety for Luke.

"Who am I kidding? I live in a war zone," Luke mumbled to himself.

As he approached his gate, he could see his boss pacing back and forth and glancing at his watch. "Apollo" was not his real name, it was Stanley Walpole, but everyone knew better than to use it, instead they would use the mythical nickname he seemed to prefer. No one knew where he got the nickname, but it was strictly enforced. He was the lead developer and the self-professed "savior" of the company since coming on board seven years ago. At least that was the scuttlebutt around the office. Even the CEO of the company called him Apollo. Not quite the "geeky" type that you would normally expect from a programmer that devoted nearly every waking hour to writing code, at least not from his outer appearance. He was short in stature, slightly heavy, and his blond hair was never out of place. He wore only the best in designer clothing and drove the nicest car in the employee lot. In spite of the impressive outward appearance, Luke felt Apollo matched the stereotype of a programmer on the inside; distant, non-relational, methodical, calculating, and unemotional. *Ugh. I'm being a little overly judgmental about him again,* he thought, as he walked toward him with a smile.

"Luke, you're late!" Was the greeting Apollo used without offering a good morning, or returning the smile. In reflex, he glanced at his watch and realized that in spite of leaving early, that he was indeed 4 minutes later than the 7:15 time they had agreed upon last night. He thought about tossing out the usual "bad traffic" or "security check-in" excuses, but then realized that it would do no good. And besides, Apollo had made it on time so he had no reasonable excuse. Then again, he'd probably been here for an hour already just to relish in this moment.

"Sorry about that. How was your morning?" he returned instead.

"Uh… Fine," Apollo responded, with almost an off-balance edge to his voice as if he was prepared and expecting to deliver a far different response. Not missing a beat though, Apollo jumped right back into business mode, "A lot is riding on this field presentation, are you ready?"

"Yep, I'm just not sure why we need to spend 28 hours in airports and on planes to go to Iraq to demonstrate it to the military bigwigs there. Why not Camp Pendleton for a test area, or some other facility located on the mainland?" he joked sarcastically, emphasizing the last word.

"They want to see it in a real environment. Apparently, they would like us to test it on a few prisoners for them," Apollo responded without looking at him, apparently not realizing Luke was just being sarcastic and already knew the answer. Or maybe he did, but chose to ignore it.

Luke could not help but remember the images of the highly publicized prison abuse scandals that had plagued the military early in the war and he couldn't stop from glancing at his trembling hands again. "What, do they want us to determine if they are happy to be prisoners or not?" he joked. He understood how their "product" could benefit them in that environment, but he just couldn't help being flippant as a result of his stress.

"You were hired as the Psych analyst expert, you tell me." Luke just nodded, knowing that Apollo did not want for him to answer that question.

From Los Angeles to London they went over the presentation process for the tenth time in the last three days. Apollo made it clear that he would do all the talking except when it came to explaining the color data spectrums generated by the software and the generic hardware view. Looking at their tickets, he was initially relieved to find that he had the good fortune to not be seated next to Apollo on the evening flight from London to Riyadh, Saudi Arabia, but then he realized that the reason was that there was only one first class seat available and Apollo graciously took it. *Oh well, maybe I can finally get a little sleep somewhere along the way*, he thought.

After typing into his laptop the highlights of the earlier 7 hours of personal lecture notes he received from Apollo, he saw the soft yellow card hidden in his notebook case. It was a card from Danielle. Danielle was always so thoughtful and encouraging, and beautiful. Until now, he had totally forgotten that she gave the card to him at the end of the day on Friday before leaving the office. She presented it to him with a "Don't open it until you're on the plane" request and a kiss on the cheek. Feeling a little guilty about forgetting, he tried to find a good response if she were to ask him if he had followed her request. An eyebrow went up and a smirk etched onto his face as he thought, well she didn't say which plane to open it on, so he felt he could tell her that he did indeed open it on the plane.

"From your wife?" a voice with an English accent asked. It came from the passenger sitting next to him in the window seat who had asked it over the humming of the planes engines. He was a rather big man who had his eyes closed as if sleeping when Luke first got on the plane in London.

"No. I'm not married," he replied and tried to return to reading the outside of the envelope as he prepared to open it.

"Girlfriend?" The large man interrupted him again with the question and this time followed it with a smile and a wink that made Luke feel uncomfortable. "Yeah." Luke replied and then angled away from the man as he proceeded to open the envelope and remove the glossy card inside, but again he hesitated and drifted off in thought. *Girlfriend,* is that how he would describe their relationship? Two weeks ago he would have said yes in a heartbeat if asked that question, but now, he was not so sure. A little "strained" would be the way he would describe their relationship the past few weeks. In all the prepping for the trip and the stress involved with the location of the field test, Luke felt there had been way too many discussions about life and purpose and personal character for his comfort. What used to be fun and crazy nights on the town with Danielle that included dinner, wine, more wine, dancing, more wine and then back to his place for the night, had grown less physical, involving less drinking and way more self-control on her part than he preferred. He had been racking his brain as to what he might have said or done that would have caused her to pull back, but nothing came to mind. He didn't think he had changed, but there was something definitely going on with their relationship and he felt getting away might be a good thing, although he would have preferred someplace other than Iraq.

As he pulled the card out of the envelope, he saw a scene with a scorching desert and a camel looking, well, like a camel. No words, just the picture. As he opened the card, again no pre-typed words, just a hand written note to him from her.

Luke,

They say a camel can go a long time without water, but I'm not sure how long I can last without seeing you. It has been great growing closer to you these last nine months and I will be missing our late night coffees and ice cream runs until you return.

Please be safe and know that you will be in my prayers.

Love Danielle

He wanted to feel encouraged and grateful, but his face gave his thoughts away as he sat in the seat holding the card with a furrowed brow.

In my prayers. That was an expression that he had never heard her use before. The more he thought about it, the more he was not sure how to take it. Did she think that something bad was going to happen to him while he was in Iraq? Something so terrible that she felt he needed some sort of divine intervention to save him? From what he had learned about her in their conversations, she was not religious as a kid. In fact, not even close: as she could party and curse with the best of his friends. *In my prayers…*

He tried to search his heart to understand why the statement bothered him so much. He didn't have anything against someone saying that they would pray for him, it just didn't seem right coming from Danielle. Maybe if some priest or pastor or even his mom had written it, it would be different, but coming from Danielle, well, it had the same "you're kidding, right?" feeling that he had when his buddy in college would wake up every Sunday morning after partying, cursing and chasing women all night to say he was "heading to Church". It just seemed so hypocritical to Luke. Not that he was any better than his college buddy, but if being "on good terms with God" was a measure of good deeds versus bad deeds, then he felt he had as good a chance as most of the religious people he knew to get through the pearly gates, if not better.

Luke remembered going to church with his family when he was just a kid, but deep down he wasn't even sure he still believed that there was a God. He somehow felt he wanted to, perhaps for selfish reasons, but the world was such a mess and it was often the "people of religion" who seemed to be behind a great deal of it. Cover-ups of pedophile priests and pastors, mega church leaders and TV evangelists professing their righteousness while sleeping with prostitutes, living in extreme wealth and comfort, all while duping and manipulating their destitute, desperate and good hearted members to send them their money. It all made him sick.

Then there are the radical fanatics within the Islamic believers like the Osama Bin Laden types. Organizing and directing horrendous acts of terror against innocent civilians (most of which were even directed at fellow Muslims), radical Shiites and Sunni's killing each other in Iraq, the Taliban in Afghanistan condemning and executing school teachers for teaching women to read, while at the same time growing and selling Heroin to pay for their regime and ideology. What a joke. Not that Christians fared any better in this measure of hypocrisy, with Catholics and Protestants spending decades killing each other in Ireland, David Koresh and Jim Jones type groups sacrificing their members, then there was the Crusades and Inquisitions of the Middle Ages, and the countless wars and acts of horror all in the name of religion. The leaders of Judaism, Hinduism, Mormonism, Buddhism, and every other "isms" that he could think of all had their "skeletons in the closet" of history associated with them as well.

In all fairness, Luke conceded that the acts of extremists within those religions didn't represent everyone within those groups. In fact many amazing works of art, science, technology and acts of kindness have come from religious people. Still, if those "leaders" and their actions were what the people were willing to follow, then as far as he was concerned, they all deserved each other. He didn't want any part of it.

Luke had to take several deep breathes to clear his mind and calm down from the mental rant that was running through his mind, the same one that seemed to come every time he tried to discuss the topic of religion. At least he didn't start chewing on the whole "politics" side of the forbidden topics as well. He closed his eyes and took another deep breath and smiled at the thought that the technique of 'breathing' probably originated with some religion, but he didn't let it stop him. After several more minutes, the angst he felt slowly began to clear away and he began to drift off into sleep. He had nearly nodded off when her words, *in my prayers,* crept back into his mind and started the whole thinking process all over again. It wasn't until several hours later that he finally dozed off with that phrase still fluttering around in the recesses of his mind like a bird that can't see, trying to find a branch to perch on.

A sudden, bright light brought him out of the sleep he had fought so earnestly for but it was a peace-less sleep that left him as tired as when he had drifted off. As his eyes adjusted, he saw that the English gentleman sitting next to him had lifted the window shade. It just so happened that the sun was positioned on the left side of the plane and the angle of the plane as it turned to change direction had placed Luke's face in the direct light of the sun through the window. He hated being in the center seat on plane flights as he was at the mercy of the people on both sides. As the plane leveled out and his eyes adjusted to the light, he glanced past the shoulder of the man that had raised the window shade and saw the yellows and browns of the desert colors below him. *Were they close,* he wondered? The stewardess confirmed the silent question with the traditional and this time multi-language rendition of the "seat backs and tray tables must be returned to their full, upright positions" routine that they went through just before landing.

As he stepped off the plane onto the enclosed gangway that lead them into the terminal, he felt the desert heat forcing its way through the openings. He was suddenly thirsty and was relieved as he finally entered the air-conditioned terminal. Being first off, Apollo was waiting impatiently for him with an expression on his face that was saying that his delayed exit from the plane was somehow Luke's fault. Luke was getting really tired of dealing with Apollo's attitudes, but he knew that voicing those feelings would not be a good career move.

At the baggage claim terminal they were greeted by two men in civilian clothing who came up to them as if they knew them, both were Caucasian and had short hair, one brown haired and the other blond. The blond haired man was taller and slim, maybe late forties, while the brown haired man was a little shorter and stockier and Luke guessed him to be in his late twenties. They introduced themselves as Cliff Jackson and Steven Lampkins and flashed some badge that as far as Luke was concerned, could have been a membership card to the Mickey Mouse Club, but it was official looking enough and they augmented the flashy badge routine with some impressive title that Luke couldn't remember more than a few seconds after it was stated.

"Mr. Walpole and Mr. Baker, your three bags and two boxes of equipment have already been removed from the conveyor and are on their way to the awaiting aircraft. We have already cleared you through customs as well." Cliff said to them as they shook hands. Luke smiled at the thought of these men not using the nickname "Apollo" when speaking to them. *How did they know we had five items?* he wondered. Heck, he didn't even know how many bags Apollo had brought with him. The statement did make him feel a little better about the chances that their escorts were indeed who they said they were, but who really knew in these times. The fact that they and their bags had been cleared through customs was either pretty impressive or very concerning. They asked Luke and Apollo to follow them to a waiting car, to which both he and Apollo, without any show of great concern, simply nodded and walked after them. *Lambs to the slaughter,* Luke thought, as they walked with the two men.

As they stepped outside the terminal, the heat of the day slammed into him as if he had walked into an invisible wall. A few short strides later and they stepped into a waiting sedan that had the air conditioning fans blowing on high, giving him a momentary respite from the heat. Except for a few courteous statements, there were few verbal exchanges and the sedan quickly delivered them to another nearby terminal less than ten minutes away. As they drove, Luke watched from the coolness of the sedan and thought that the large number of turbans and veils were the only things that gave away the fact that he was in Saudi Arabia and not Los Angeles. Well, there was the heat to deal with, but not from inside the vehicle. As they passed through several security checkpoints, each with high fences and walls, he felt a little more reassured and secure. The sight of American troops on the tarmac preparing their gear and loading onto awaiting planes that had American insignia on them helped to soothe his fears a great deal.

There were more introductions with other soldiers as they exited the sedan and walked toward a building next to the tarmac. Once inside, a sergeant Patterson escorted them toward a waiting room where he strongly suggested that they take a moment to use the restroom one more time before they boarded the transport. Both Apollo and Luke took advantage of the offer. At the same time, Cliff and Steve momentarily excused themselves and came back in military fatigues and sporting side arms.

"Things will be a lot more military in appearance now that we will be leaving Saudi Arabia," Cliff said to them in response to their expressions and glances at the firearms on their sides.

"They don't like their people seeing American troops walking about," Steve added.

"They feel it will also be a little harder for the bad guys to target us as well if we try to look like average citizens." Cliff ended the statement with a smile. Luke could not help but smile as well as he looked at Cliff's blonde hair and blue eyes.

"Yeah, I could hardly tell you apart from the locals," Steve chuckled at Luke's response and Cliff also smiled. Humor always helped to relax him in stressful times.

Luke sat in a folding chair and for the most part, looked out the window and watched the people coming and going. Everyone seemed relaxed, which in turn, helped him to relax. Apollo on the other hand seemed extremely nervous and continued to pace back and forth in the waiting room. Slowly he would walk to one side of the small room, look out the window, then turn and walk to the other side and do the same. Each time he completed the cycle, he would check his watch and look out the window and into the sky as if checking to see if the weather had changed. *Rain Man*, that should be his nickname, Luke thought to himself as he watched Apollo repeat the same actions over and over. *I'm an excellent programmer,* he imagined Apollo would say at the end of each turn. After watching about 30 cycles, Luke just closed his eyes and tried to think about something other than being here. Danielle entered his mind quick enough and he smiled. It was not long before the words she wrote in the card *In my prayers* popped back into his mind. His face formed a frown and he tried to grasp her reasoning for using those words again. He did not want to slip back into that circle of thought, so he opened his eyes and decided to watch Apollo the "Rain Man" pace back and forth as he wondered what horrors awaited them in Baghdad.

Chapter 2

Three hours later they were finally boarding the military transport. Luke had watched them load what seemed like an endless number of huge, plastic wrapped pallets into the back of the airplane. The sun was well into its afternoon arch as they headed toward the transport and stepping into the heat reflecting off the asphalt of the runway was like stepping into an oven.

They climbed a set of stairs and entered a side door of the transport, on the opposite end from where the pallets had been loaded. The seats were hard and faced sideways instead of forward. Luke was very happy that he was sitting next to one of the few windows available with Cliff sitting next to him. It was loud and there was no air circulating other than the hot air blowing in from the open back loading door. He looked down at the 3 bottles of water that he still held and was grateful he did not decline them when Cliff was handing them out in the waiting room. In spite of Cliff's brief training course on the importance of drinking a lot of water, Apollo decided adamantly that he only needed one as they were leaving the air conditioned waiting room and as usual, he essentially "dismissed" Cliff when he refused the other 2 bottles that Cliff encouraged him to take. As the last of the soldier passengers boarded, Luke noticed that Apollo had already consumed over half of his bottle.

The rear loading ramp was raised by heavy hydraulic arms. It closed with a thud and the still air and the heat were stifling. "It'll cool off a bit once we get airborne." Cliff almost yelled over the noise of the engines as he watched Luke wipe the sweat running down his face. "Your body will adjust after a few weeks." A few weeks! Luke smiled at the thought; *I'm only planning of being here a few days at most.*

The transport, as if feeling the same lethargy caused by the heat that Luke felt, seemed to take its time as it lumbered toward its planned starting point on the runway. It turned and paused, as if to catch its breath, hesitant to make the final sprint down the runway. Finally, with a deafening roar, it lurched forward, the engine whine increasing in pitch as the plane labored to pick up speed. Luke thought about all the huge pallets of materials loaded in the back of the transport and wondered if they had miscalculated the gross weight and overloaded the plane? Or worse, how many of those crates could "detonate" if they were bounced around too much. The whole transport vibrated and rattled, its very frame straining like the rope in an epic tug of war battle between the enormous load and the power of the huge engines. Luke was positive they were running out of runway and would crash in a ball of fire. He imagined it would be the lead story in a folded paper on his own doorstep the following morning. Then he felt the nose of the plane suddenly angle up and he could see the ground begin to drop away, taking his stomach with it. The vibrations settled down and the hum of the tires on the runway faded leaving only the roar of the engines. Luke swiveled his jaw to pop his ears and breathed a little easier. He was relieved to feel the temperature inside the cabin gradually drop as they gained altitude. Although it was still hot, at what he guessed to be 90 degrees, it was much better than the 115 degrees they had left below.

Twenty minutes later he was handing one of his water bottles to Apollo. Apollo had nervously downed the last of his bottle within minutes of getting airborne. In all fairness, Luke realized that he personally had also finished the majority of his first bottle, but he knew he had two more bottles for the remainder of the trip. Just like two kids, Luke knew Apollo wanted his other bottle but he was determined to hang onto it. At first, Luke pretended not to notice

Apollo "eyeballing" his water and simply sat back and closed his eyes as if resting. Apollo countered by yelling small talk across the seats toward Cliff about how hot it was and how thirsty you could get in such a short time. Luke was pretty sure that Cliff also got Apollo's hint about needing more water, but he just answered "yep" and smiled.

After awhile, Luke started to feel pity for Apollo and ignored his earlier arrogance and pride. He yelled across the engine noise "Here you go!" and tossed one of his remaining bottles to Apollo. It did not surprise Luke that there was no "thanks" or nod, or even a smile for the kind gesture. Apollo just opened the bottle and drank the top third of it without a word. Maybe that alone was worth giving up his water, but it still irked him to no end.

"He'll have to pry my last one out of my dead hands." Luke mumbled lowly to himself as he glanced out the window, but apparently it was loud enough for Cliff to hear. Cliff chuckled in response, "He's not getting mine either."

After about an hour, Luke felt the vibrations and heard the sound of the engines change. He looked out the window again and Cliff half yelled "Iraq" and then nodded as Luke stared at the land of Iraq below. The city that he had seen off in the distance from an earlier glance was now right below them.

"It looks so peaceful from up here," he said, but Cliff barely smiled in response. Almost on cue, the plane suddenly banked and went into a sharp dive toward the ground. Luke could not help but look toward Cliff with questioning and concerned eyes. Seemingly unaffected by the events unfolding around them, Cliff casually leaned toward Luke and spoke to him in a low voice.

"Not to worry too much, the pilots do it to reduce the threat of any air to air missiles; the shoulder fired anti-aircraft missiles that the terrorists can use." Luke exhaled at the explanation and realization that they were not about to crash, as he first feared. Looking across the aisle, Apollo had what must have been the same look of terror written all over his face as he tried to grasp what was happening. *Knowledge is power,* came to Luke's mind as he met Apollo's eyes, so he just gave Apollo a smile and pretended that the sudden dive didn't bother him at all.

At the very last minute, and just before the breaking point of his own façade of calmness, the transport leveled off above the ground and landed onto a runway that appeared out of nowhere. Once the plane had touched down, the engines reversed and the brakes engaged slowing it down before it angled off the runway and taxied over to the hangar. Once again, the heat filled the cabin as the transport came to a stop and the engines were turned off. For several minutes, a ghostlike humming roar from the engines continued in Luke's ears. It reminded him of the humming sound he heard after the last rock concert he attended, except worse.

"Welcome to Baghdad!" Cliff said to them as they unbuckled from their seats. Luke gathered his empty water bottles and the two Apollo left on his seat and put them in the same bag that Cliff had placed his empties. As he stepped off the transport, in the waning daylight, he looked around at the airport. Unlike Saudi Arabia, there was a very strong American military presence in every direction. They had barely reached the hangar when he saw that men were already unloading the transport and four soldiers were carrying their bags and equipment, right behind them.

They entered the terminal where a Captain Stevens and two lieutenants greeted them and offered them each a bottle of cool water. They gave the same "drink lots of water" speech that Cliff had given them in Saudi Arabia. This time Apollo took two bottles, one for each hand. He quickly opened one of them and began drinking from it. The new members to the group escorted them to several waiting vehicles that had been mentioned in the introduction. As he walked through the terminal, Luke could not get over how out of place and vulnerable he felt. Men around him were in flak jackets and helmets and all he had was a light cotton shirt and a pair of slacks, both of which were sticking to him. As they exited the terminal, there were two military Humvees waiting for them.

They split into two groups, Cliff, the Captain, one lieutenant and Luke in one and the other consisted of Steve, Apollo and the other lieutenant. As they slid into the back of the hot vehicles, Luke noticed that there was a driver and a soldier in the front seat. Their vehicle had a rather intense fracture in the front windshield. The fracture showed how thick the bulletproof glass was that surrounded them. Although he felt better about it, he also remembered the scenes on TV of the twisted and burning remains of similar vehicles that had driven too close to an improvised exploding device or had been hit by a rocket propelled grenade. He pointed to the window?

"IED or RPG?" He asked the soldier, using a few military acronyms in a sentence. The soldier just shook his head.
"We'd be dead from those," he replied and then smiled. Even with the smile, the thought did not ease Luke's mind.

The two truck convoy wound its way through the streets of Baghdad at high speed. The drivers raced down the roads, completely ignoring any apparent speed zones. Iraqi civilians were out in the streets as they drove by. Some were shopping, some drinking coffee and smoking cigarettes, and most appeared to not care about the Americans driving past in their vehicles. Others, however, stopped what they were doing and just watched the Humvees pass by with cold stares. Those were the people that made Luke nervous.

After thirty minutes, they arrived at a military checkpoint outfitted with sandbags, machine guns, and barbed wire protecting both sides of the gate. The defenses and barbed wire wound gradually out of sight in both directions. After they came to a stop and exchanged documents and salutes, the gate was opened and they drove into a walled complex filled with nicer buildings that were in contrast to those outside the complex. Somehow, Luke felt safe again.

"This was one of Sadaam's favorite residences prior to his removal," Captain Stevens shouted over the engine noise. "We appreciated him taking the time to build these for us prior to our arrival." He smiled to Luke as they pulled up to a half circle drive landscaped with potted plants and a small fountain. As they stepped out of the Humvees and stretched, Luke went to gather his bags that were being unloaded.

Captain Stevens shook his head as he saw Luke reaching for the bags.

"We'll take care of the bags and equipment. Your bags will be delivered to your rooms and your equipment to the briefing room for tonight. Lieutenant Simmons will show you to your rooms and acquaint you with the facilities. We will meet for chow at 1900 hours and then head over to the briefing room to take a quick look at what you have to show us."

Luke knew that Apollo and another employee had already given the military officials in Washington an overview of the product. The past three months had been dedicated to building an "easy to transport" field demo unit as well as hiring and training Luke on the unit's operation and using his area of expertise to interpret the readings and create a training module for it. He shook his head thinking back to the interview. When they said "potential travel", it seemed exciting and attractive. He just wished he had asked then, where they intended to have him travel to.

The brick and cement of the structure kept the air inside much cooler than the outside temperature. The rooms were attractive in design, but held only the basic amenities. Cliff explained that the place had been looted by the people of Iraq prior to the military's arrival and occupancy of the building. After several minutes of walking around and inspecting various details and views from the windows of his room, he put his clothes away and changed for the meeting. Once changed, he decided to visit the briefing room to set up the equipment, but when he arrived he found Apollo already there with most of the gear in place.

"Where have you been?" he said as Luke entered the room. "I want to run a full system test and do a dress rehearsal before dinner." They spent the next hour preparing and positioning the presentation charts, handouts, equipment and screens for maximum visibility and impact. Apollo repeated himself over and over detailing how he wanted the meeting to flow. Luke got it the first time and, although he was not in full agreement with Apollo's approach, he took the easy road and nodded each time. Based on the number of seats, there would be less than twelve people attending this demonstration, which seemed less intimidating than a large crowd. They each took one last look before they headed to the mess hall.

They filed into a "great room" near the kitchen with military-issue tables and chairs placed around the room to accommodate the maximum number of people at each meal. The chow line was pretty self-explanatory so they grabbed a steel tray and utensils and shuffled down the line, stopping at each station where a young man or woman plopped something onto each plate. Luke smiled and thought it reminded him of a military "Club Med" minus the bikini's, ocean, pool and large quantities of alcohol. Knowing the dangers and location, he was sure the troops stationed here felt that his comparison would be far from their minds.

He sat down at the end of an empty table and looked around the room at the soldiers who were filing in and out or sitting and eating. Many were laughing or talking loudly with other soldiers. In contrast, others were quiet and stoic. It seemed strange, but although some sat at a full table, they acted as if they were sitting by themselves. The other troops did not seem to feel the need to intrude on their space, but instead respected it. As he looked around at the soldiers, it hit him as to what made America so unique and special compared to other countries. There were people of just about every color and with every racial trait sitting, laughing, and serving together. "Our greatest challenges are our greatest strengths" he had read somewhere about America and the extreme racial diversity among its people. While the civilians seemed to find the negatives of such diversity, those in the military seemed to exemplify the positive of it. In spite of Apollo talking incessantly about work to fill the time, Luke felt somehow moved by the observation. He mentioned it to Apollo, interrupting him in mid sentence as he was going on and on about the handouts. Apollo seemed perturbed, but he took a moment to look around the room as if he needed to confirm or overrule Luke's random observation. "Yeah" was his only reply before reengaging his mouth about the handouts.

Luke was surprised that the meal was not all that bad. After the terrible stories he had heard about military food in the movies and books, he had very low expectations. Then again, he remembered that he had not had a decent meal in nearly 24 hours. Even though, he still felt he would happily eat the same meal again if offered to him. "It's just fuel" is the way he looked at most meals. He loved a good meal, but eating was never an obsession for him. For Danielle on the other hand, each meal seemed to be an exciting experience of flavors and textures. She was always the adventurous one when it came to trying new food, where he preferred the "sure thing" on the menu. Over the past few months that they had been dating, she had definitely expanded his eating and social horizons.

Apollo tapped his watch to let Luke know that the meal was over and they left the mess hall and headed to the meeting room a little early, only to find it already full. The room went silent as the two of them stood in the doorway waiting for direction or clarity on the next course of action they should take. Cliff seemed to read the uncertainty and let them know that they would call them in when they were ready for them. In the meantime, they were asked to take a seat down the hall in the lounge area. What was supposed to be a fifteen minute pre-meeting turned into almost an hour. During that wait, Luke could see that the jet lag and lack of sleep had started to take its toll on both Apollo and himself. No matter how much caffeinated soda he drank, he could not get his mind and body back on track and he became more and more inwardly focused and quiet. Apollo's response was the opposite; he became more critical and short with Luke and would not shut up. About the time Luke had his fill of it and was ready to snap back, one of the lieutenants finally came out to escort them into the briefing room.

As they entered the room, Luke saw that there were eleven men and one woman sitting around the conference table. Although he recognized five of them, the rest he had never seen before or if he had, he could not remember their faces. With quick introductions flying around the room, Luke missed the majority of their names and instead tried to focus on their ranks. After the introductions were completed, a hand signal and nod was given from the major sitting at the end of the table toward Apollo. Without hesitation, Apollo launched into his canned product presentation with a vengeance as the others turned pages, trying to keep up.

He started with a PowerPoint presentation which gave a generic overview of what the product was designed to do. A simple, straightforward presentation that he felt almost anyone who was paying attention could follow. As Luke watched Apollo distribute the handouts, he remembered that most of the guys on the design committee proposed skipping the basics and going straight into the technical stuff to save time. They felt that since all those attending would have received the classified handouts of the product days before the presentation began, rehashing it would not be necessary. Luke disagreed and was able to change their minds by asking them a few questions.

"How many of you have thoroughly read the color spectrum handouts I gave you last week?" Knowing confidently that they hadn't, they still all slowly raised their hands as if to let the managers in the room see that they were doing their jobs. "Anyone care to explain how reactionary reads can affect the color spectrums?" No one took the bait, so he drove home the point. "Just because you are given a handout does not mean you will read it. We are all busy with other things so we can't assume that they will not be busy as well. We have to ensure they have a basic understanding of the product first, or we will lose them or intimidate them with all the 'techno jargon' we use. It may all make perfect sense to you, but the end-user will have no clue as to how it works." His appeal seemed to convince them to save the statistics and hardware explanations of the product until after they confirmed the audience had a good understanding of the purpose of the product and its benefit to them. Apollo's words brought his mind back to the room.

"Our company has been a game developer in the US and international markets for the past six years. We recently began developing a new generation of game technology that would take the user from sitting in front of the TV and out into the real world. We plan to do this by adding a thin video display membrane to the outside of eye glasses which is then connected to a portable system module that can easily be carried on a person's body. This would allow the end user to easily transform standard glasses into a video display platform that could go anywhere they do."

"There's a fifty car pile-up on a freeway waiting to happen," one of the members interjected which brought a laugh from the others sitting around the table.

"People will be walking into poles and walls all over the place," another person said as the laughing grew a little louder. But just as another individual started to join in on the fun, the major sitting at the end of the table held up a hand and everyone immediately calmed down.

"Let's let him continue," he said with a smile, while at the same time apparently appreciating their humor.

Apollo seemed a little flustered by the laughing and glanced at his notes as if trying to figure out how to get started again. Seeing the situation was heading down a precarious path, Luke decided to buy Apollo some time to gather his thoughts by interjecting himself.

"We understand there will be challenges in the civilian world, but in a more controlled and disciplined environment like the military, we don't believe such concerns would be an issue." That seemed to bring the group back into a more professional attitude and environment, where Apollo continued the presentation again.

"Yes, and such social concerns are still a long way from reality due to the current technology gap. My initial efforts to develop this membrane are still far short of a full video display. But in the initial development phase, I designed a software program that takes advantage of current on-shelf technology that will revolutionize how the military can wage urban warfare. We call it 'Cat Eyes' and this incredible advancement is what we are here to present to you today." Apollo nodded toward Luke who opened the small carrying case that was in front of him. Luke removed the glasses and system module from the case and set them on the table. Everyone seemed to have a different visual response to what they saw sitting in front of them. Apollo continued as Luke closed the case.

"As you can see, the production model is small, lightweight and unassuming to the casual observer. But to the wearer of the glasses, it is a visual guidance system and a personal database and classification system for determining the hostility potential and threat level of an enemy." Apollo looked toward Luke. "My colleague is one of our lead designers and holds a master's degree in psychology and has advanced software development skills. He will explain and demonstrate the functionality of the product." Apollo then looked down at his notes as if he was preparing to follow along in case Luke lost his place. Luke smiled at everyone as he glanced up from his prepared presentation notes. 'Lead designer' that was the first time that title was used to describe him. He felt nervous as he glanced down at the canned presentation notes Apollo had created, but for some reason he made a decision to change things a little in hopes of personalizing the presentation to the audience.

"How many here have emotions?" Luke raised his own hand as if to show it was okay to participate and a few others did as well while the rest nodded. Apollo on the other hand immediately looked up at Luke knowing that he was not following the script. Luke kept his hand in the air as he continued. "Anger, hatred, fear, sadness, confusion, frustration, love, lust, like, happiness, joy, contentment," he rattled off many types of emotions. "There are hundreds of emotions that we go through in a day that we cannot control on the inside." He then lowered his hand as he continued. "Now on the outside we can often mask or hide those feelings right? And truthfully, some of us are better at hiding certain emotions than others. Children on the other hand have a difficult time concealing their emotions, but as we get older the majority of us learn to be quite good at keeping our inner feelings masked or hidden from the casual observer. But no matter how good we are at hiding them outwardly, inside, the feelings are still there."

While speaking, Luke strived to make eye contact with everyone around the table, except Apollo, trying to read their reactions. In doing so, he felt his confidence returning and his nervousness easing.

"Our minds can produce all types of emotions as a result of sights, sounds, smells and many other triggers based on the thoughts it processes." He held up a finger as if counting. "We have emotions that are triggered by processing memories of our past history. For example, you can be happily hanging out with your buddies one moment drinking a beer, but when a person that 'did you wrong' walks by, the memory produces an electro-bio-chemical reaction and our emotions can suddenly change dramatically. As that person disappears around the corner and out of sight, your neural activity and bio-chemistry settles and thus your emotions slowly return to where they were prior to the memory. Even our private recollection of our past history can directly trigger a current emotional response. Now a close friend or spouse might have a chance at sensing your changing emotions at the time, but the casual observer would more than likely see nothing change in your countenance." Luke paused long enough to let the concept sink in and then added a second finger to his count.

"Now let's say you're sitting with the same group of buddies, and someone punches you in the arm from behind. As a natural form of self-defense, the emotion of 'anger' is initiated, sending a burst of adrenaline in to your system preparing the body to fight. However, as you turn to retaliate, you see it's another buddy that has come to join you so, the emotion of 'anger' disappears almost immediately. You see, you think, you feel and then you react. We call these reactionary emotions." He paused again.

"But the emotions we often fail to see or recognize in time, and the ones that are the most dangerous to society, are the emotions of 'intent.'" He added a third finger to his count and then opened his hands. "The dangerous emotions of 'intent' can be a deadly combination of hatred, anger, sadness, determination, rage, revenge and many others that can have disastrous endings if the individual chooses to act on them. These emotions are tied to a reoccurring thought process that produces a continuous bio-chemical reaction in the thinker. Similar to a drug addict who keeps a chemical in their bloodstream, as the entrenched thought process continues to cycle, so too does the bio-chemical reaction. We see the final destination to cyclical emotions of intent every day around the world, in premeditated murder, stalking, rape, and even terrorist attacks and suicide bombers." He let the last few words sink in before he continued. "Imagine if we could read, or better yet, see the emotions of people? Instantly being able to classify and evaluate possible threats before a single word is spoken or an action taken and to be able to act preemptively. What tactical advantages would that give to your soldiers in the field? How many lives could it save?" He smiled as he started his next topic and saw that the minds in all those sitting at the table were engaged and thinking as he continued.

"How many here have heard someone talk about their 'aura' before?" He paused a moment before continuing and saw nods and a few fingers in acknowledgment of his question. "I don't know about you, but I usually think of some fruitcake sitting at a table wearing some sort of mystical headgear with crystals scattered around the room, trying to tell someone's fortune, saying 'your aura is very strong.'" Luke said with a B movie horror voice. "But in a more common setting, it can be just a passing statement of someone trying to describe someone's personality to you, 'she just has a great aura about her.' Or maybe it's the emotion that makes the hair on the back of our necks stand up when someone says 'I have a really bad feeling about this guy.' Whatever example comes to mind, the point is that it is scientifically measurable that our bodies generate a continual 'energy field' or 'aura' if you will, that under observation, is constantly changing and unique to each person. The question is; does that energy field or aura tie directly to our environment and the emotions we are experiencing?" Luke picked up the glasses and held them up as if he was going to put them on.

"Would you agree that having the ability to classify an 'aura' into an easily understandable tool that measured threat potential would be a huge breakthrough for science, for society, and more importantly, in your case, for the military?" He stopped and set the glasses back down onto the table knowing that Apollo would to continue the presentation from there. He could see by the facial expressions around the table that mental gears were still turning.

"The 'Cats Eyes' glasses and receiver module accomplish just that." Apollo came in right on cue, although his tone communicated that the presentation was changing from interactive discussion back to a lecture. "The electronic membrane used with the Cats Eyes product continually converts a person's unique but ever changing 'energy field' into colors. It would enable the user to immediately see and interpret those colors and the emotions they represent with just a glance, and then respond accordingly."

Upon Apollo's completion there was a long, uncomfortable pause, as eyes glanced toward the major. Luke got the impression that it was a leadership or respect issue, not necessarily a lack of interest. Luke felt pretty good about the presentation and assumed that Apollo did as well. Finally the major broke the silence and gave his synopsis back to Apollo.

"So by wearing your glasses, my soldiers would be able to easily distinguish the good guys from the bad guys that they may encounter? With one look they would know whether the person is for us or against us, thereby increasing their own survivability in the field?" the major stated more than asked and the rest of the group seemed poised to interject as well.

"Could this also be used to help process the hundreds of Iraqi's we bring in daily for questioning, so that we can quickly determine who is a threat and should be held for further questioning and who is not?" a captain interjected before Apollo could answer the first question. Luke remembered from the introductions that was the captain responsible for a local internment camp.

"In the most generic sense… yes to both questions," Apollo answered them. Luke knew he was going out on a limb with that answer and that there was a lot more to it than just putting on the glasses but he fought back the desire to comment.

"If they work, it would be a great way to help clear out the jails," the captain responded.

The major leaned forward and looked at Luke, then the rest of the table and then finally at Apollo.

"I have listened to a lot of crazy ideas from a lot of different computer jockeys and salesman representing their companies through the years. I've got to say that this one definitely tops the list." He took a breath and held it for a moment and Luke felt his heart sink. "But I've also been wrong in the past with a few of them." He then looked away from Apollo and back to his team, almost as if to subliminally give them permission to speak freely.

"I agree, this reads more like a science fiction novel than reality," one of the men said.

"So did night vision goggles when they were presented," another man replied with a smile.

"It sounds like a whole lot of smoke and mirrors to me," a sergeant interjected and frowned.
"I tend to agree. One bad read on someone and you and your men are dead, then no one would ever trust the glasses again," the female lieutenant replied.

"Yeah, too many variables and the training curve could be high. Most of our soldiers have only a high school education," another soldier tossed in.

"Those same high school boys and girls are trained to operate some pretty technical equipment being used in the field today." The major seemed to be defending his field troops and the young soldier seemed a bit humbled by the correction.

"Good point, but I also agree that unless it's pretty simple and fool proof, it will never be accepted by the men in the field," a young officer replied.

A silence fell over the room, as the meeting seemed to be heading in a bad direction. Luke was surprised how quickly things went down a negative path and knew that he had to find a way to redirect the conversation before the momentum ended the meeting. Another thought for the use of the glasses had entered his mind on several occasions, but the obvious use seemed to always outweigh the one currently bouncing around in his mind. He thought he would toss it out to break the awkwardness of the silence.

"I believe it would also help to minimize the antagonistic view the Iraqi's have toward your soldiers." Luke's psychology background suddenly took over his thinking process. All eyes were on him. "Would you care to elaborate on that son?" Once again, it was the major who broke the silence as he and the rest stared at Luke.

"Well, if your soldiers can quickly recognize a 'threat' from a 'non-threat', for example an Iraqi citizen that they encounter, their initial attitude will be less hostile toward a non-threat correct? Major, your soldiers are trained to assume and plan for the worst in each encounter and for good reason, but in doing so they initially treat all of the Iraqi's as if they are a threat. Unfortunately, the citizens can sense and feel that antagonism and mistrust and they in turn assume the worst of the soldier. Perhaps if your soldiers could more quickly assess the threat level of the citizen and be less harsh in their initial interactions, the average Iraqi citizen would be more at ease and more willing to cooperate?" He took a moment to let it sink in, and then continued as he turned to the internment captain sitting across from him.

"For example, in an effort to learn the motives and/or guilt of someone, you may need to hold them against their will for long periods of time by locking them up, holding them in camps, and keeping them away from their families. As you can imagine, it would not take long for the imprisoned person to build a strong resentment toward the captor." Luke continued to look at the captain in charge of the internment facility, before looking back toward the major. "Imagine if you could avoid generating such emotions, by speeding up that learning curve from weeks or months, to just minutes. If you could, you would stand a greater chance of winning their confidence. Or at least greatly reducing their animosity." The major just stared at him and rolled the pencil he held between two fingers. Luke glanced toward Apollo who almost glared and gave him an 'I wish you would keep your mouth shut' look.

The major looked across the table at the captain sitting across from Luke.

"You seem in deep thought, John. Is this whole thing a waste of time or is there potential?" The major looked at him and waited for an answer. The captain looked up briefly from the handout in his hand and smiled.

"Actually, I'm looking forward to seeing it field tested. Anyone can talk the talk, but can they walk the walk," he said to no one in particular. The major smiled and nodded his head.

"Well, it's my understanding that we are scheduled to do just that on Thursday morning at 0700. Unless anyone feels it is a waste of time, I think these men have made a case for allowing the field test to go ahead as scheduled. We will see those of you there that are scheduled to observe the test. For those unable to attend, we have a briefing that will be held following Thursday's field test. Any questions?" the major asked, but no one interjected.

Luke worked through the math to determine what day it was and realized that it was only Tuesday evening. Two days before he could wrap this up and get back home! As everyone was leaving, he nodded and smiled to those that made eye contact as they left. Once the room was clear, Apollo began to slowly put away their presentation equipment. Luke walked over and began helping.

"That went well," he said in slight sarcasm. Apollo looked up at his words.

"You'll have to do a flawless job to recover from this meeting," Apollo said with his critical tone. Luke was unsure of the meaning of his words. Was he saying that he had screwed up or that the overall presentation went poorly? Apollo stopped and turned toward Luke.

"You need to learn to stick to the primary concepts and script of the product when speaking. Don't waste their time and ours selling the soft potentials of the product. We are not here to win the 'confidence of the Iraqi people.' We are here to convince them that this will help defeat the insurgents which, in turn will help us to sell the product to the buyer, lots of product." Luke fought back the urge to defend his views and the direction he had taken the meeting, and that he did not agree with Apollo, but he also understood that the "money thing" drove most of what businesses were about. He finished putting away the last of the equipment in silence and headed off to bed. He was exhausted.

Chapter 3

The sound of the explosion, or maybe the concussion of it, made him nearly jump out of his bed. Was it real or had he been dreaming? He looked toward the window and saw that dust was drifting down from above, highlighted by the early morning rays of sunlight peeking through the curtains. *"Boom!"* Another explosion detonated close by and brought more dust as it shook his bed and rattled the window behind the closed curtains. *What exactly am I suppose to do in this situation?* Luke thought. He could run down the hallway, but to where? He was definitely not going outside. He realized that this was the same reaction he had when one of the big earthquakes hit Los Angeles. His urge to look out the window to see what was happening was brought to an end when a third crashing *"Boom!"* sent the glass, the curtains and the rod they had been hanging on to the floor. At first he thought it was the concussion of the blast, but then he saw a small hole, the width of a pencil, in the wall across from him that he knew had not been there the prior evening. He just sat frozen with his feet on the floor and the bright sunlight now streaming into his room. As quickly as it started, it was over. There were just the three thundering blasts, spaced maybe three seconds apart and then nothing but silence. No gunfire, no sirens, nothing. *Three,* he thought. All he could think about was some book he read in college about things coming in threes being a bad omen. *'For whom the bell tolls… it tolls for thee'* played in his mind.

He suddenly realized that he had done nothing during all that commotion. He couldn't believe he just sat there on his bed, frozen in place by fear and indecision. All the ideas of what he should have done came pouring into his head. He should have ducked under his bed or stepped into the hallway and put another wall between him and the outside. Instead, he did nothing. Like the wolf dream, he felt like such an idiot. He would have never made it as a soldier. He stared at the glass near the window and followed it to the foot of his bed. The sparkles coming from small pieces of glass had managed to land on the tops of his feet. The previous night he wished that his bed was closer to the window and had even considered dragging it over there to try to catch a cool breeze. He was now very glad fatigue had convinced him otherwise.

He was still sitting in his underwear when Cliff came into his room with barely a knock, yet a sense of urgency and concern was on his face. His concern faded as he saw Luke sitting on the edge of his bed and then at the glass and curtains on the floor by the window.

"Good morning. Hell of an alarm clock wouldn't you say?" Cliff said with a smile. "By the way, you're late for breakfast. You better get dressed and down to the mess hall if you want something to eat." Eat? Food was the last thing on Luke's mind as he stood up and tried to shake off the glass shards.

"Is everyone okay?" Luke asked Cliff.

"I believe so. We get a few mortar rounds every now and then, nothing to worry about." Luke could tell from Cliff's expression and eye movement that the last part of his statement was not entirely true and was meant to ease the worry that must have been written all over Luke's face.

Luke looked around the room and, as Cliff waited by the door, he put his pants and shoes on. He started to pick up some of the broken glass that was nearest to him, but Cliff's words stopped him.

"Don't worry about that. I'll have someone stop by and clean up the mess for you. See you in five minutes?" Luke nodded and with a dazed look on his face, searched the room for his shirt. Cliff shut the door as he left.

Compared to the morning, the rest of the day was relatively uneventful for a civilian. There were several times that the key staff in the command post flew into a flurry of activity, but whatever these emergencies were Luke was not included. For the most part, they left as quickly as they came, and the camp returned to normal. Normal for a war zone anyways. Apollo wanted to meet a few more times that day to go over the plan for the field test at the prisoner facilities. During the meetings, he reminded Luke to just focus on the presentation and let him do all the talking. Luke headed off to his room and spent the early part of the morning re-acquainting himself with the color spectrum charts that they had developed back in Los Angeles. The charts matched the emotions of the individuals they studied and had been created with a great deal of hard work.

He found a comfortable chair that faced an inner courtyard where he enjoyed the shade and some time away from Apollo. As he drank a cold soda from the mess hall, he remembered the long hours he spent when he was first hired, setting up and testing the product. When he first looked through the membrane he felt like he was looking through a very thin sheet of plastic, and things were a little blurry. Despite that, he was amazed at the clarity and definition of the colors displayed. The visual results of the product were the same today as they were then, but the glasses and system unit were much smaller and more attractive than the initial bulky prototypes.

He smiled when he thought about the first set he tested. They applied the membrane to a set of welder's goggles with thick cables running down to a laptop PC. They had made huge improvements on the aesthetics and wear-ability of the design since then; in fact the majority of the work since Luke joined the company had been on the hardware. He had no idea how the membrane was designed (nor was he cleared to know), only that it was thin and easily damaged, which was why they would place it between two clear glass lenses. The membrane and the software code were highly guarded secrets of the company. The only thing he knew was that the information was translated by the system unit which had evolved to be the size of a small cell phone. The bulky wires had been replaced by newly developed cables that connected to each end of the arms of the glasses, just behind the ears and ran down the wearers back to the system unit.

The membrane could potentially be applied to any type of clear glass lens. It could even be applied to corrective lenses without it affecting the prescription. However, they did learn that polarized or tinted glasses could not be used because it distorted the color spectrum and threw off the readings.

They also reduced the size of the membrane so instead of covering the entire surface of a lens, it was just a strip at the top of the glasses. This allowed the user, even those needing corrective lenses, to see normally through their glasses as they walked or read. When they wanted to see through the Cat Eyes membrane, they would just angle their head down and look through the top part of the lense, basically the reverse positioning of bi-focal glasses. It was definitely a distraction to see colors coming through the top of your glasses, but that only really occurred in crowded areas, like at multi-level shopping malls where there were people on upper levels within your view.

While testing the product, Luke had learned to take short glances while wearing the glasses. Then when you saw a color of interest that needed your full attention, you needed to stop moving to really focus on it. Otherwise, much like the military staff in the conference room had astutely joked, the colors would dominate your attention and you could accidentally run into something, fall down stairs, or worse, get hit by a car, which almost happened to him.

They initially started the testing process with employees who had no idea what was being testing on them. They would ask them many questions, have them perform certain activities, and interact with other employees in both standard and challenging environments. Hired specifically for the project, Luke had spent a great deal of his initial training time learning to understand and chart the various color spectrum readings that were generated while using the glasses. Almost immediately, he was able to establish primary colors for each primary emotion. The happy emotions like love, joy, gratitude, excitement, and peace, fell into the blue category; the angry emotions like hate, anger, bitterness, envy, and jealousy fell into the red spectrum; uncomfortable emotions like fear, pain, uncertainty, doubt, and sadness fell into the yellow spectrum; and the last color of black, or what he determined to be a 'darkening' or tainting of the primary colors, was the hardest to read. Those were the emotions corresponding to intent.

The discovery of emotions of intent had come about almost by accident. Luke was trying to understand the mysterious darkening of colors that kept showing up during an interaction between two employees that had trouble working together. In one situation between them, the color darkening appeared in two opposite color spectrums. One aura had more dark blue while the other was more dark red. Even after reviewing the extensive interviews with each of the subjects, he was still unable to point to the differing results. The subjects each had very strong emotions about the other and the points of contention were similar. It was in a conversation around the water cooler that Luke finally realized the difference in shading that led to coining the term intent. In casual conversation, one of the employees, a young woman had stated that although she was frustrated about the situation she wanted to find a way to work through it and resolve it. The young man on the other hand was determined to see the young woman fired. One wanted positive resolution, the other negative resolution. After some blind tests, Luke was able to classify the darkening of the colors and chart them as 'good intentions' and 'bad intentions.' He found that they were often the same emotion, like determination, desire, conviction, and attitude, but what darkened the primary color was the desired end result of those emotions, to either harm or to help someone else. Luke knew he still had a long way to go in understanding the color readings of intent but the initial findings were fascinating.

Watching the color spectrums of test subjects often made Luke feel as if he were watching a ever changing rainbow of colors. The subject's emotions often rapidly changed; levels of fear (yellow) and love (blue) flowed together to make different shades of greens, or when different levels of sadness and anger flowed together to make various shades of orange. Many colors were very beautiful to look at and learning to interpret each color and not get distracted by the beauty of it took intense concentration.

Once they completed the smaller employee test groups, he gradually began field testing the unit in shopping malls and other public areas. He would sit on a bench watching people walk by and take notes on what he saw. Luke used an ear bud device that hunters often use to amplify sound so that he could hear conversations without being so close that he drew attention to himself. Although he felt awkward about eavesdropping, he had written it off as being for the furtherance of science. He would observe men by themselves, men in small and medium sized groups, women by themselves and in groups and in mixed groups. He would then make comparisons between their behavior, conversations and the color spectrum recordings. It was daunting in scope, but eventually patterns were recognizable and the color chart was produced.

Not surprisingly, women had a more active color spectrum and were therefore much harder for him to read than men. The color spectrum for men was smaller and clearer cut to him, but perhaps that was because he was a man and understood how they thought a lot better than how women thought. *Mars and Venus* he thought to himself. He knew that in the near future the company would need to hire an experienced female analyst to work with him to better understand and translate the color spectrums for women.

A chill ran up and down his spine as he remembered the first encounter he had with 'evil intent' while testing in the malls. As he sat on the bench, observing people, a man in his mid thirties walked by and Luke saw dark red hues radiating from him. In spite of the color spectrum, his face was relatively blank and emotionless and he walked without showing stress or frustration. Not wanting to miss an opportunity to learn more, Luke decided to follow and watch him from a distance. After several minutes of walking behind him and observing his actions, he started noticing a pattern in what the man was looking at and his heart dropped to his stomach. The pattern was a focused attention on young boys. At first he had trouble putting it together, initially thinking it was the occasional mother or young girlfriend that accompanied the various boys that drew the man's interest, but it did not take long before he realized that it had nothing to do with the women.

Luke watched as the man's color spectrum would change to a deeper burgundy color as he routinely asked those that he had been following for the time or for directions in the mall. He eventually ended up following the man into a video game store and proceeded to watch him scope out the store for possible opportunities. He ended up observing him pretending to wait for a 'test' game console to become available where two kids were playing side by side. It did not take long for the man to strike up a conversation with the two boys and gradually ask more and more personal questions. One of the two boys either finished his game or decided to leave and the man stepped in to work the other console next to the remaining boy.

Luke realized that had he not been wearing the glasses, he would have either thought the man was the boy's friend, relative, or father and he probably would have ignored the whole situation or passed it off without concern. But with the knowledge gained by the glasses, listening to the man made him sick to his stomach and he could feel the rage and anger beginning to flow through him as the man tried to work his way past the boy's guard and gain his trust. Luke was torn as to what to do, he knew what this man was doing, but he could not reveal to anyone how he knew. He heard the man ask the boy about a certain online game that they both apparently played and suggested that they could 'group up' and he would give the boy some 'weapons' that his online character had. The boy definitely seemed very excited about the offer.

"Why don't you give me your Instant Messenger account name or email and I'll contact you when I go online?" The boy was just about to give it to him when the man looked up and saw Luke coming up toward the two of them and that Luke was looking right at him. Luke had not even consciously decided to approach the two of them. He just reacted and started heading in their direction.

Without taking his eyes off the man, Luke said out loud,

"Never give this man or any other stranger your personal information, or speak to him at all. He is a very sick man that preys on young boys like you." The words just came out of his mouth and he watched the boy's face suddenly go white with fear as he glanced back and forth between the two men before him, each trying to stare the other down. Other kids and adults standing close by stopped what they were doing and turned toward the angry and accusatory voice, and the situation that was now before them. The boy either realized the mistake he almost made, or saw something new and frightening in the eye's of the man he had been speaking with before because he backed away from the two of them and quickly headed toward the exit. The man had recovered from the initial shock of the moment and the words used against him and tried to recover his composure.

"How dare you accuse me of doing... that!" His voice gained momentum and strength with each word until the last word was spoken through clenched teeth. As the man began speaking, Luke had quickly angled his head down slightly so that he could see through the top of the glasses. He watched the color spectrum change from fear and embarrassment to intense anger. Luke held the man's eyes and took another step toward him and interrupted the man before he could continue. Luke's words also came out through clenched teeth and the tone was much more threatening as he looked down at the older, but stockier man.

"We've been watching and filming you following boys all day long and even have your conversations recorded as well." Luke lied to the man as he held his jacket open long enough to show him the test unit attached to his side. When the man looked down he briefly saw the unit and the wires that were running to some unknown location before Luke let his jacket cover it again. It seemed to work as his color changed immediately back to intense fear. Luke continued with his story.

"We have been documenting your sick activities for months and have enough incriminating evidence to file charges against you. Not only will we be turning this over to the police, we will also be notifying and sharing our findings about you with other mall and school security agents as well." Luke thought he might have gone too far out on a limb with that lie but that didn't stop him. He took another step forward and put his face only inches from the other man's face.

"Your sickness has brought you to the brink of ruin and now it is you that will be watched and hunted wherever you go. Your presence is no longer wanted in this mall. Unless you want a personal escort, I would leave now and never come back. Are we clear?" The man's face was red and his eyes were moving in all directions except to look into Luke's eyes. He tried to mouth a few words but nothing would come out as he slowly stepped away from Luke and angled toward the exit of the shop. He glanced over his shoulder at Luke as if to see if he was following him. Luke reached up and put his hand over his ear and made as if he was speaking to someone on the other end of his imaginary intercom and he continued to watch the man briskly walk down the mall to the nearest exit. Luke looked around the game shop and saw that every eye was on him and not a word was being spoken.

"Keep an eye on your kids," he said with a nod and headed out the door toward the mall exit near his car.

As Luke walked out to his car, he realized that his legs were shaking and his heart was pounding. He was not a confrontational type and was very surprised that he had actually stepped in to stop the man. He couldn't tell the authorities about the incident because it would lead to too many questions about the product and chances were high they wouldn't believe him anyway. He took deep breaths as he sat in his car. He felt pretty good about the situation and how the glasses performed, and even marveled at the power that they offered. He smiled as he started the car and backed out of the parking spot and noticed a red sports car apparently waiting for his spot. Luke gave a brief 'thanks' wave to the waiting driver as he pulled away and headed back to the office.

The sudden rumble of gunfire in the distance reminded him that he was not back in Los Angeles, but sitting in an open-air courtyard of a former retreat of an overthrown sovereign leader, in the middle of Baghdad, Iraq. A place that is still very much in turmoil. He picked up the charts again and spent a few more hours training his mind to instantly recognize and translate the colors he viewed on the charts so that he could respond quickly and accurately during tomorrow's field test. The whole idea of putting charts on flip cards sounded strange to him at first but then he realized that the difference between a forest green and an ocean green could be a serious and dangerous error. The difference between a burnt orange and a citrus orange could mean a person's life.

Later that evening, Luke was scheduled to meet with Cliff. When they met they talked about the best approach for the field test. Luke felt like Cliff was probing for weaknesses while at the same time giving Luke some insight on how to make the field test a success. Cliff's approach was pretty endearing and Luke had to keep reminding himself that Cliff was the buyer and was just doing the due diligence work he was hired to do for his client, the U.S. government. Even so, it was hard not to like him. Luke wondered if Apollo was going through the same process with Steve.

Chapter 4

That night, although he had already tested them, Apollo made sure Luke checked that all the battery packs were fully charged and all three demo units were working effectively before calling it a night. Recalling the explosions from the night before made it difficult for Luke to get to sleep. When sleep finally came, it seemed as if only minutes passed and it was time to wake up again.

Fortunately the next day's wake-up call was not more mortar rounds, but instead a soldier who knocked on the door until Luke responded with a "Come in."

"Your presence is requested at breakfast in 10 minutes. Shall I return in 5 minutes to remind you?" the soldier asked from the other side of the door.

"No. No, I'll be there. Thanks," he said and lay still long enough to hear the soldier's boots fade down the hallway.

He looked toward the glassless window and saw that there was no light coming between the newly hung curtains. Turning on the light he quickly dressed in the military clothing and boots they had delivered to his room the night before. Although they were not the standard soldier camouflage, they were definitely government issued. When he asked 'why he had to wear them', the young soldier simply said that it made it easier to tell the good guys from the bad in a firefight. Those were not the words that he wanted to hear.

As he headed to the mess hall, he saw Apollo coming down another hallway tugging at his new outfit as if adjusting it would make it more stylish. Their group was served breakfast in a separate room and four of the original twelve attendees of the 'conference room' group were there as well. Cliff, Steve, Sergeant Doyle and the captain that was interested in seeing it field tested, and a Capt. Tillman. After the introductions and brief morning greetings, Luke repeated their names and titles continually in his mind so as not to forget them. While they ate, Captain Tillman went over the day's schedule.

"Barring any unwelcome interaction with the local populace, we will be arriving at Internment Camp Bravo Three at 0700." *Not another 'three'* Luke thought as Capt. Tillman continued. "Once there, we will proceed to one of the main holding cells where our guests will have the opportunity to demonstrate the Cat Eyes hardware. We will have interpreters present to translate any questions you care to ask of the detainees. At no time will you be in danger while at the camp. We have three hours scheduled. Should you require additional time, let me know and we will try to accommodate your needs. Any questions?" Luke felt like he would throw up if he heard one more three mentioned.

Capt. Tillman glanced around the room and then rested his eyes on Sgt. Doyle.
"Sgt. Doyle has some party gifts he would like to give you before we load up. See you outside in 10 minutes." He nodded to Sgt. Doyle and exited the room. Sgt. Doyle stepped into the place the captain had been moments before and pointed to the corner behind Apollo and Luke. As they turned to look they saw four sets of military gear laid out for them.

"We require all of our guests to wear helmets and body armor when traveling with us, so please put on the appropriate gear labeled with your name. Once you are geared up, we will meet out front for departure." Cliff and Steve were in their gear and outside in a few minutes and, anticipating the need for assistance, Sgt. Doyle stepped into the room to help both Luke and Apollo into their bullet-proof vests and helmets. Luke noticed that while Cliff and Steve were both given side arms, he and Apollo were not. The vests were lighter than they looked, but still heavy enough to be uncomfortable. The helmet however, was surprisingly comfortable and fit well.

He laughed at how he felt with all the gear on and remembered the first time he and his buddies put on their football pads in junior high school. Everyone wanted to test out the protective pads by ramming into each other and banging helmets with other teammates. Somehow the thought of bouncing bullets off each other's chest was not the same, although he did have a strong urge to do a helmet bash with Apollo. Fortunately he allowed his common sense to squelch that urge. Like wearing the football pads in school, he did feel much more secure with the vest and helmet on him, but he also knew they were no match for a RPG or roadside bomb.

Luke and Apollo each carried a case holding a set of glasses and system module; Apollo's was a backup in case Luke's unit had a problem. The nice thing about the Cat Eyes was that it was small and compact enough to tote around. As they stepped outside, Luke realized that it was still almost completely dark. They split up again and entered the three Humvees that were waiting for them outside. Once beyond the gates and past the security check points, they started winding their way through the city of Baghdad. They eventually came to the city's outskirts as the sun started to rise in the east gradually lighting up the sky. The city, which had been still and quiet in the early darkness, quickly became a buzz of activity as the sky grew brighter. They passed several convoys of U.S. and Iraqi trucks, tanks and armored vehicles at various points on their way to the camp. They passed through many checkpoints as well and saw cars and individuals being checked and searched before they were waved through.

Approaching the camp, Luke felt a sense of foreboding emanating from the structure and the surrounding grounds. On one hand he was happy to be behind the walls of a secure structure and protected from the terrorist bombs and snipers, but on the other hand he realized that he had entered an area that had the highest concentration of those same terrorists.

Climbing out of the vehicles, Luke could already feel the warmth of the day displacing the night's chill. He reached back into the Humvee for his water bottle and test case and followed the group through a high fenced gate and into the front doors of the main building. Captain Perez, of the internment camp, greeted them as they entered. Luke recognized him as the one who attended the initial presentation and had such a strong interest in the product.

"Gentlemen, it is good to see you again," Captain Perez said very formally, as if seeing them again was the least exciting thing he had done in months. Luke felt like he and Apollo were just the delivery men for a new toy. They were useful, but no tears would be shed if they were lost along the way.

There was no tour of the facility; they were simply escorted into a dark inner room where they could see through a glass window into an adjoining room. Luke's heart sank as he looked through the window into the room beyond where a desk and chair sat. His hand touched the glass and he could see the tint of the reflective film on the window and knew that the Cat Eyes glasses would not work or at best, would not get an accurate read through it.

"It won't work in here," he said as he turned and looked at the group. "Do you have a room without the tinting or reflective film on the windows?" he asked with a voice that he hoped did not sound as desperate as he felt inside. The group looked back to Captain Perez for the answer. The Captain glanced toward the window and then walked up to it and looked through it.

"No. Unless there are any objections, we will have you sit in the room during the testing and you can ask the basic questions." He glanced back to Apollo who, without looking at Luke, said, "That will be fine."

As Luke listened to Apollo's agreement on his behalf, he looked at the adjoining room with the table and chair and surmised that it would barely hold five people. He would be sitting in a room with potential terrorists that wanted to see him and the rest of America dead. Why should Apollo care? He wasn't the one who was going to be in danger. The Captain's words brought him out of his thoughts.

"I will have you and the translator set up in the room. Once you are ready to begin your questionings, a guard will bring the prisoners in one at a time. Not to worry, we will have the guard stay in the room in case there is any trouble. We'll observe the interaction from here."

All Luke could do was nod his head in agreement. He looked back into the room through the glass and realized that the questioning part of the field test would now be handled by him and not one of the camp guards. He took a drink of his water as he was escorted into the interrogation room. He was allowed to set up his gear and prepare for the interview alone, as they did not want the other staff to get an early peek at Cat Eyes system.

He was glad to see that there were no whips, burning coals or instruments of torture in the room, recalling movies he had watched. There wasn't even a bright light hanging above the table that they could shine in their captive's eyes. Just a room that reminded him of a study area he had used in college. He removed the system unit from the case and attached it securely to his belt. Then he removed the glasses and fed the wires that led from the end of the support arms just behind the ears down the back of his shirt and to the system unit at his belt. He adjusted the glasses on his face and turned on the system unit. He then laid a green folder that he had filled with some of his random papers and set a note pad out on the table in front of him and held his pen in his hand. He took a deep breath and turned to the reflective glass behind him and nodded to the people watching from behind it. Seeing his reflection in the mirrored glass made him feel alone and very vulnerable.

After a few minutes a Middle Eastern looking man entered the room in military fatigues and introduced himself as Sergeant Saeed. Luke glanced at the U.S. flag on his arm and was relieved to know that he was American. As Luke introduced himself and shook his hand, he angled his head up and down to confirm that the glasses were actually working. He saw that Sgt. Saeed was, for the most part, falling into the blue/yellow color spectrum, a green reading.

"How long have you been stationed here?" Luke asked to fill the time and get a better understanding of the feelings he was having.

"My third tour… 14 months, Sir." Luke watched his color adjust toward yellow.

"Is there a wife and kids waiting for you back home?"

"Yes sir," he said with a smile and his color adjusted back toward the blue spectrum. "Two boys, 8 and 10 years old," he responded proudly.

Luke was preparing to ask where the Sergeant was from, when the door to the room opened after a brief knock. Luke looked out the door and saw two soldiers standing on both sides of another Middle Eastern man who was looking, or perhaps a better description would be glaring into the room. Luke focused on the man he knew he would be interviewing and angled his head down just slightly and saw that a strong orange color surrounded him, shifting back and forth toward the red and yellow hues as the prisoner glanced into the room. One of the guards spoke to him in Arabic and Luke watched the color surrounding the man shift to red. One of the guards entered the room with him while the other closed the door behind them.

The prisoner stepped into the room and looked around. His color slowly moved back toward yellow, until he stopped and stared at Luke, still sitting behind the table. A hint of a sneer appeared on the man's face as he glared at Luke. The reds came back and then darkened getting very close to black. Even without the glasses Luke could feel that the man was trying to intimidate him and Luke was sure that the man hated that he was there. Luke fought the urge to stare him down and instead motioned to the chair across from him as he picked up the green file folder and leaned back in his chair. The man continued to stand and stare at Luke. Sergeant Saeed spoke something in Arabic and pointed to the chair, but the man refused to respond.

Luke's mind scrambled, trying to think of a way to defuse the standoff and avoid ruining the field test.

"Please inform this man that I am here to investigate reports of prison abuse and religious persecution at the facility and report my findings back to United Nations General Counsel. I have been granted an audience with only a few detainees to derive the truth in this matter. His help would be appreciated, but not needed if there is nothing to report," Luke asked the Sergeant as he returned a confident look to the prisoner. Luke could see the prisoner's colors change even before the message was translated and the intensity of the reds reduced and flickers of yellow began to appear. Luke decided to take advantage of the prisoner's indecision. Luke smiled, nodded his head and motioned with his hand toward the door.

"Thank you for your time." He then turned toward the Sergeant. "Can you bring in the next prisoner?" As he finished his request he heard the sound of the chair sliding back and watched as the prisoner sat down in it. Although the red hues were still present, the yellow hues were growing stronger. Luke raised an eyebrow as if in surprise and then turned back toward his folder.

"What is your name and why are you here?" he asked the prisoner and watched his colors move toward the red.

"You already have that information in front of you," the man said. His English was heavily accented, but clear enough. In truth, Luke did not have the man's information in the folder he held, he had not planned to be in here asking the questions so he never thought to ask for the personal information of the prisoners. He wondered if they would have given it to him anyways. He decided to continue with the ruse.

"I have been given much information and been told a great deal about you. Should I just believe all of it? I prefer to hear your side of the story before I try to ascertain what is true." He waited for the translator to finish his words before continuing.

"Hakim Raa'id. They accuse me of planting roadside bombs, but I am a simple businessman," he said and his colors moved toward green.

"How long have you been held here?" Luke asked.

"I was brought in 18 days ago." His colors stayed in the green spectrum.

"So you had nothing to do with the bombings?" Luke asked and watched his color spectrum intently.

"No, they lie," he said and his color flashed yellow at the word 'no', and then moved to red when he mentioned 'lie'. In Luke's experience, a yellow flash almost always occurred when a lie was being told; the red was probably the man's hatred coming out again.

"So you are not involved in any way with the insurrection?"

"No." Again, the yellow flash.

"Have you had any contact with the leaders of the insurrection?"

"No." Yellow flash.

"Have you been mistreated while in captivity?"

"Yes." His color went deep red, but no flash of yellow.

"Tortured?"

"Yes." No yellow flash, but it did move more from red to yellow. Was the red from fear of reprisal from the guards Luke wondered?

"Describe some of the tortures you have experienced here." Luke readied his pencil.

"Beatings; Suffocation; Drowning; Sodomy; No food or water; Not allowed to sleep; they made me eat pork; they have done the same to everyone here." Without taking his eyes off of Hakim, Luke jotted a few letters to correspond to each accusation and put a check down next to those that flashed yellow. When he had finished, he glanced down at the results. BT was a lie, SUF was a lie, DRN was mixed, SDM was a lie, NFD was true, NSLP was true, PRK was a lie, as was the last statement.

As Luke was looking at the notes, the door opened and Captain Perez walked in.

"My apologies, but this interview must be concluded. Our time is limited and you have many other candidates to interview." Luke could see yellow and red coming from the Captain.

"I've only just begun this interview. I need more time," Luke responded.

"See, they fear that you will learn the truth!" Hakim almost spat at the Captain.

"Please escort the prisoner out immediately. Sergeant Saeed, can you step outside for a moment?" The Sergeant followed the prisoner out the door and Captain Perez shut the door behind him and turned toward Luke and placed both hands on the table as he leaned forward until his face was in line with Luke's. Red was now his dominant color and his voice came out in strong, pronounced statements.

"You are here to test your product, not start an inquisition of my facilities and men in an effort to destroy their reputations and the reputation of my unit. If you want to continue this procedure, you will honor that request. Are we clear?" He was leaning over the table and looking directly at Luke. Luke fought the desire to debate him before answering.

"Yes sir," he said very respectfully. He paused long enough for the Captain's colors to change from red back to yellow before continuing. "I have no intention of bringing your men or your unit into disrepute. If you remember, when we came here I was planning on just observing, not asking the questions. No one provided me with a list of pre-approved questions to use. I was unable to get a clear read on the prisoner, and the only thing I could read was his intense hatred. I needed to gain his confidence and bring him to a different level to be able to see and evaluate the changes." Luke watched his color begin to move more toward the greens.

"I'm not looking for some prisoner's false accusations to somehow find its way into the media and harm this unit."

"Nor am I," Luke responded and then looked at his notes and continued. "For the record Captain, the accusations of 'beatings' was a lie, 'suffocation' was a lie, 'drowning' apparently had some basis of truth, 'sodomy' was a lie; no food or water was not a lie; no sleep was not a lie, and being forced to eat pork, was a lie. And based on my readings, he IS involved with the insurrection." He glanced up from his notes and saw that the captain was now firmly in the green shades with flickers of yellow. There was a long moment of silence as the Captain just stared at Luke who just returned the look with his head angled slightly down.

"So what am I thinking now?" the Captain asked.

"Unfortunately, I'm not able to know what you're thinking, but based on your color, I do know that you're feeling a lot more secure about my intentions. I would guess you would like to continue, but you're trying to figure out a way to do so without it appearing as if you're giving in." Luke saw the Captain's colors jump to yellow and raised an eyebrow. "Uh oh, now you're mad again," Luke said with a smile. At first the Captain just stared at him with the best blank look he could muster, then a gradual smile crossed his face and Luke could see it return to green, and even a shade of blue. Then he slowly started to nod his head.

"From now on, you take those off when we're talking," he smiled and removed his hands from the table and walked to the door. "I'll trust your judgment, but if at all possible, try to avoid the 'torture' issues. As you can imagine and have now seen, we're kind of sensitive about that."

The second prisoner he interviewed was a shopkeeper from Baghdad that was not a fan of the Americans, but from what Luke could tell, he was not involved with the insurrection although he may have supported it indirectly. He was much easier to question because he did not intensely hate, but rather feared his captors and his situation. The 'debriefing' with the Captain and the others watching through the mirrored window was quick and to the point. The captain simply nodded and listened to Luke's analysis and then excused himself and brought in the next prisoner.

The third prisoner was at first difficult to read and his response colors were hard to understand. He seemed far too comfortable with everything. Luke sat back and thought about the difficulty he was having. Was he tired? Were the glasses malfunctioning? Then the answer dawned on him. He started down a delicate line of questioning that secretly revealed his guess. He took a deep breath as if to say I give up and then thanked the prisoner.

Captain Perez came back into the room while the guard waited outside. Luke quickly took off his glasses, rubbed his eyes and then looked up at him.

"What did you find out about that one?" Captain Perez asked with a look of concern. Luke stared down at his notes for a moment and then looked back up.

"I'm just trying to understand why you would put one of your own men in prison?" Luke watched the captain's expression hold firm, and then he nodded his head and smiled. "What gave it away?"

"Too many conflicting lies, probably the biggest was about how much he hated America." Luke smiled back.

"I have about 700 other prisoners I would like you to meet today. Feel up to it?" he asked Luke who just blinked and tried to find the right answer. Captain Perez saved him by raising his hand to stop him from answering and smiled. "I'm just kidding. As much as I would like that to be the case, I'm afraid I have too many other things on my agenda for the day." He stood and smiled at him. "I appreciate your time and honesty today. Watching you and your product work was a pleasure and I must say very impressive. Thank you for coming and I believe we have a meeting scheduled for tomorrow to discuss this field test further." He shook Luke's hand and nodded to the mirrored window and exited the room.

Luke put the glasses and system unit back in its case and put away his folder of notes. With his case in hand, he exited the room and saw Apollo and a guard waiting by the door to the observation room. The guard led them down the hallway to what appeared to be a breakroom of sorts.

"They want some time to discuss the interviews in private. You are a loose cannon that is very dangerous to the company," Apollo said to Luke and then looked down the hallway. No "great job" or "good work" was offered from him. Fighting back the frustration, Luke just shook his head and looked down the other direction of the hallway until he could get control of his feelings. He felt he had done a pretty darn good job of handling the situation and demonstrating the effectiveness of the Cat Eyes, yet not even one word of encouragement. He took a deep breath and then turned back toward Apollo.

"It sounds like we are here for one more day." Apollo's comment interrupted his prepared rant and it was stated as if Luke was not even in the room. As much as he tried not too, Luke's response of "Yep" still had a frustrated edge to it.

Luke clenched his teeth. What was it about this guy that made him so ungrateful and sour and disconnected from people? He could not remember a single time that Apollo had offered words of encouragement to any member of the staff. 'Never good enough' was the general attitude you got from him no matter how good your work was or how much time and energy you sacrificed to get it done. Never would you hear a 'thank you' or 'job well done' response coming from him.

Twenty minutes later, the few members of the observation group that they originally traveled with to the Bravo Three facility, joined them in the break room. Cliff went up to Luke and patted him on the back.

"Nice job in there. You're pretty quick on your feet." Luke looked over to where Apollo stood next to Steve and saw that the compliment had once again fallen on deaf ears.

"Thanks," he responded, as they started heading out the door to the awaiting vehicles. "Whose idea was the plant?" Luke asked Cliff, as they donned their vests and helmets and climbed back in to the vehicles.

"Well, I guess all of ours. We felt the odds were pretty high that most of the prisoners would be hostile toward us, so we figured we had better mix it up a bit," he said with a smile as their Humvee headed out of the complex behind the lead vehicle.

"And the innocent shopkeeper?" Luke asked in response.

"His son is involved with the insurrection. We were not sure if he was actively supporting him or not, so based on your quick read of the first guy we thought we'd see if you could shed any light on the matter. We actually had eleven potential candidates waiting to be selected; we played it by ear as to whom we would bring in for you to question. We eliminated the six known aggressive candidates after the first interview, we had three passive candidates, one of which you interviewed, and two bad actors," he said with a smile and looked out the window as Luke smiled back.

Luke thought about what Cliff had said and he could not help but be impressed with the depth and detail of their thinking and strategy for the field test. Initially, he had the feeling that things were just being thrown together for their demonstration, but in reality, a lot was going on behind the scenes to ensure the truth was discovered about the product. He started thinking about the other men in the vehicle, where they were staying, their involvement in the testing and what other levels this plot might have that involved him without his knowledge. He wasn't sure if he should feel concerned or comforted about being a pawn in all of this. Cliff reached over as if he was reading his thoughts and patted him on the shoulder.

"Don't worry. You're doing fine," he said with a smile. Luke smiled back but instead of feeling encouraged by Cliff's words, he now wondered what they meant. Luke quickly by them and decided that he could not take anything at face value there. He suddenly felt that he was in way over his head.

Chapter 5

Luke sat in the same conference room as he had two days ago, with nearly the same group of people. He smiled at the realization that nearly everyone sat in the same exact chairs as before as well. *Creatures of habit,* he thought to himself, as Captain Perez completed his overview of the prior day's field test at the Internment camp.

Although the feedback overall was complimentary, the tone quickly changed as Captain Tillman interjected his views.

"I agree with my colleagues that this could be very useful in a secure environment such as a prison camp, or even a checkpoint where questions can be asked and where time is plentiful enough to analyze the responses. But I do not see this as an effective tool for the soldier on patrol needing immediate intel to analyze a situation." Although he said it as if it was a fact, he held his hands up at the end as if asking a question. He looked directly at Luke for the answer to his question.

Luke was hoping Apollo would step in to somehow take the heat, but he realized that he was on his own as usual. He took a deep breath before answering.

"I disagree," Luke said as he leaned forward in his chair and continued. "Today's field test was not about trying to determine if they were hostile toward America. That was easy enough to read. It was more about determining what was actually true." Captain Tillman interjected before he could continue as if to wrap up the meeting and perhaps the sales presentation trip too.

"I appreciate your confidence, but I don't see how it could be used quickly enough to give my men an advantage in the field. My concern is that it would have a greater risk to confuse them or slow their response to a situation instead of speeding it up." Luke at first nodded as if in agreement, and then shook his head before he continued.

"It may seem that way, and I know you probably think we would say that just to secure the sale of our device to the military, but those actually using the device would be able to react very quickly to any given situation," Luke said from a real belief in the product. Captain Tillman, stared at Luke a long moment and then shook his head.

"Sorry son. You've done an admirable job with your demonstration, but I just don't buy into it for the soldier in the field," he said as he gathered up his notes, effectively ending the discussion. Luke could feel the success of the presentation slipping away and apparently Apollo did as well because he finally interjected.

"I believe if you took the time to field test it yourself, you would find it to be very effective," Apollo tossed the words out as almost a challenge to him.
"I don't think any of us have the time to learn or to teach someone how to operate your equipment," the captain said as he scooted his chair back from the table and Luke agreed wholeheartedly with his response.

"There's no need to train any of your men. We can do the field test with them," Apollo said with an almost urgency in his voice. Captain Tillman stopped himself in the middle of his attempt to stand up from his chair and Luke turned his head to look directly at Apollo, totally taken aback by his offer. Luke knew that he was the only one trained well enough to go on such a field test. Was Apollo actually volunteering the two of them to field test this in a combat zone? He would have never guessed Apollo would put himself in harms way for anything. Luke knew that Apollo saw the sale slipping away and was trying desperately to hang onto it.

"I could not risk the chance of putting you and your staff in danger with such testing, though your offer is appreciated," the captain said in response as he sat back down in his chair as if waiting for someone to take the bait. Unfortunately, Apollo bit. "I do not see it as being anymore dangerous than driving back and forth on the roads here. Don't you agree, Luke?" he countered and looked over to Luke briefly. Captain Tillman seemed to hold Apollo's gaze as he silently thought about Apollo's offer and then turned his attention to Luke, waiting for his response. Luke looked around the room and in a flash realized that every eye was now starring at him. There was no way he was going into a war zone for anyone.

"Yes, it seems simple enough," he said and could not believe those words just came out of his mouth. He was too worried about looking bad or weak; that the words just popped out. He was such a people pleaser and his stomach went into a knot as he hoped the captain would stand firm on his earlier conviction about not putting anyone at risk.

"Well, if you're willing to take the risk, I guess I am. You understand that you will have to sign some waivers and that we are not responsible for anything that might occur?" he asked as Luke's heart sank and his stomach lurched to his throat.

"No problem," Apollo said for the two of them. All Luke could do was look at Captain Tillman and then nod his head, as the words failed to come out.

"Do you have an idea on how you would like to test it, John?" The masked Captain Tillman and the words brought the uncomfortable silence to an end.

"Yes, but I will need some time to set this up with the proper equipment and the right squad of men. I will need about three days to put it together. More importantly, I will also need to give our guests a crash course on working in the field with my men. That might take a little longer."

"Does Tuesday or Wednesday of next week give you enough time?" the major asked. The captain glanced back and forth at Apollo and Luke and they both nodded their heads with concerned looks still evident on their faces.

"If you find that you need more time for training, we can adjust the schedule accordingly," the major added.

Somewhere between those last words and the last person exiting the room, there were handshakes, pats on the back, words of encouragement and questions of sanity exchanged. Luke stared at the door a moment and then turned toward Apollo to give him a piece of his mind, but Apollo interjected before he could speak.

"Nice job back there," the first words of encouragement that Luke had heard come from his mouth almost stunned him as Apollo continued with another compliment. "I think you saved the deal for the company." Then he looked away and began gathering his notes.

Realizing that his mouth was still hanging open from the verbal attack he had been about to deliver, Luke paused to let a more controlled set of words come out.

"I did not sign up for putting my life at risk just to sell your product." His face went red as the words came out of his mouth. He could not help but feel embarrassed at his cowardice, knowing that Apollo was willing himself to go through with the field test.

"Luke, they won't put us directly in harms way. I'm sure we have very little to worry about. They know what they're doing." Apollo kept adding words as if trying to build up his own courage as well as Luke's. He patted him on the shoulder as they headed out the door. Luke glanced in surprise at the gesture. Strange as it seemed, he was beginning to feel more uncomfortable from the affection that Apollo was showing him than the thought of going out for a field test on the streets of Baghdad.

**

"You could have been heading home right now if you would have kept your mouth shut. 'I believe if you field test it...'" Cliff said with a laugh as he tried to copy Luke's voice just before he tipped back his Pepsi. Luke had run into Cliff on the way to his room. It was not hard for Cliff to read his rather depressed demeanor. He asked him to join him in the mess hall where they each picked up a soda and sat at a table.

"I did not say anything about joining a squad to field test it," Luke mumbled and shook his head.

"You eventually agreed to it, which technically means the same thing." He winked an eye at the end of his statement but there was a seriousness in his face. Perhaps to ease Luke's mind he gave a soft belch from the carbonation of the soda followed by a smile. Luke shook his head slowly as he replayed the whole event in his mind.

"Are you going?" he asked Cliff hopefully.
"I doubt it. I'm not really needed or have the skill set for that type of thing. Although I would like to see how you do out there. You've handled yourself pretty well so far."

"Yeah, open mouth and join the army," Luke said sarcastically. He took another deep breath and tried to clear his mind, then said goodnight and headed back to his room. He hadn't been able to eat that night and decided just to go to bed in hopes he would wake up to find it was all just a bad dream.

The next morning found Luke and Apollo up at dawn being shown the basic components and how to wear the field gear that they had been temporarily issued. Luke was physically fit enough to carry the extra weight, but Apollo was having a much more difficult time. Sweat was running down Apollo's red face, his breathing was heavy and they hadn't even left the inside of the building yet. They tried to remedy the situation by emptying all unnecessary combat items and belt supplies to lighten his load. Although Luke was fine with the weight,

Apollo was still struggling. Even stripped down to the basics; helmet, protective vest, boots, belts, and army issue fatigues, it was more than Apollo could handle. At least that was how he was making it appear.

Luke felt sorry for Apollo at first, as he struggled with the weight of the gear, but then he started to realize that there was no way that Apollo was going to be able to handle the gear in the field and would end up not going. Luke would be on his own out there. He burned with anger and he could not help but wonder if Apollo's eagerness to sign them up for the field test was based on his knowledge that he never intended to go along. Knowing what he did about Apollo, Luke understood that backing out of it at this point would mean losing his job. He decided he would wait to see what unfolded before making the choice between risking his life and unemployment.

If it was not for the fact that the soldier training them was so fun to be around, he would have stopped without hesitation, if they pulled Apollo out of the training. Private Scott Jacobson of Fort Worth, Texas, was all soldier and proud of it. He was funny, confident, polite and very encouraging. He made you want to do a great job and Luke was actually enjoying the whole thing. He remembered Danielle calling him a "closet soldier" because he loved watching the History and Military Channel back home. While Luke was soaking up all the terminology used in the field that helped soldiers to better communicate with each other, Apollo was soaking up water trying to keep up with the rate he was sweating it out. Directional terminology, interactive terminology, and hand signals: Luke found it all very engaging. Although the training sessions were fun, he knew he would have to make a decision very soon as to what he was going to do.

At the end of the second day, he was sitting outside with Cliff, Steve, Apollo, and Captain Tillman after a briefing by Private Jacobson. Apollo was playing up his new routine of drinking gallons of water and continually asking to be excused to use the bathroom facilities.

"From what has been reported to me, my apologies, but it appears that you lack the physical ability to join us on a field test," the captain said to Apollo and Luke, though his eyes rested on Apollo. "I'm unwilling to endanger your lives and the lives of my men if you are unable to keep up or follow orders should a problem arise. Therefore we will need to cancel the field test," Captain Tillman stated. Luke could see Apollo looking over at him as if waiting or willing him to interject. Luke simply nodded his head in agreement at Captain Tillman's words.

"Does that apply to both of us, or just one of us?" Apollo asked. There it was! Luke knew Apollo would not sit back quietly and let this pass.

"Well, I'm afraid you are our concern Mr. Walpole," he replied. Luke could feel the silence and the eyes of both Cliff and Apollo on him as if waiting for Luke to take the bait. He kept his mouth shut and let the silence sink in, even though it was uncomfortable, waiting for it to happen. Just when he thought that it wouldn't, Apollo spoke up again.

"If just I stayed back, could we still attempt the field test with Luke?" Luke could tell Apollo was very uncomfortable at having to volunteer Luke without really asking him. Luke did not need special glasses to be able to read Apollo's true intentions. Luke never looked up at Apollo, but glanced over at Cliff, who just held his stare.

"Yes we could. But that is for Mr. Baker to decide." Luke suspected that each person wanted him to say yes for different reasons. Captain Tillman wanted the field test to happen so that his men might have another advantage in the field, Apollo wanted it to happen because of the dollar signs attached to it, and Cliff wanted it to happen to somehow strengthen the U.S. Government's arsenal. What did he want to do? He had stopped caring about the "job" part of the equation the day before and couldn't care less about what Apollo thought or wanted. He did care about Scott Jacobson and Captain Tillman and any other soldier that could benefit from this product if it proved to be of value. For those reasons, he made his choice and looked directly at the man asking the question.

"Captain Tillman, I think it's important that we test the Cat Eyes system to its full potential in the field. I will conduct the test and you can determine whether or not it works to your expectations." Captain Tillman held his gaze for a few seconds, confirming his commitment. Then he nodded his head.

"Then the demonstration is still on. I have it set for Tuesday of next week. Private Jacobson says you're doing fine on the basic skills. We'll also get you familiar with the communication equipment and perhaps basic sidearm weapons training. I'm not expecting you to fire a weapon, but if the situation arises, you will need to know how to at least defend yourself without shooting one of my boys in the process." He smiled and held his gaze again as if looking for some sign of regret or fear in Luke's eyes. Then without looking away, he continued,
"I will see you again early next week to go over the field test plan."

Perhaps feeling the attention and importance shift to Luke, Apollo asked, "What would you like me to focus on during this time?" Captain Tillman began to answer but stopped himself before his initial answer came out. He paused and then said, "I will have you work with our communications unit so that you can observe the progress and safety of your employee during the field test. I'm sure that is your utmost concern," he said with just a slight twang of sarcasm and then excused himself.

"Of course," Apollo responded almost defensively.

As Captain Tillman withdrew, Luke watched him stop and talk with Private Jacobson who nodded and then saluted him as he left the area. As Scott was heading over to where they were seated, Luke noticed that Apollo had moved over beside him.

"Sorry Luke, I wish I could join you. I will pull some strings and have a nice bonus waiting for you when we get back," he said with a fake smile. Luke fought back the urge to tell him where he could put his bonus, but instead just smiled back and walked over to meet Scott.

"So you want a little more training do you?" he asked Luke as he shook his hand.

"Yeah. Apparently you're not any good at this, so we have to start over," Luke said with a smile and Scott nodded and just smiled back.

"Then I will see you first thing after breakfast," he said as he walked back toward the quarters. As strange as it seemed, Luke felt at peace with his decision, not stressed or worried about it like he was before. He felt he made the right choice, perhaps because finally it was his decision, not Apollo's or anyone else's.

Cliff slowly moved in beside Luke as he took a sip of his water and shook his head with an incredulous smile.

"Now you did it, no going back. The exit door was wide open again, and you didn't take it, again. You want to explain that one to me?" Cliff said in a humorous voice that sounded more like an approval than a question. Luke looked back at him and smiled.

"Apparently, I'm a closet soldier," he said as they walked to the mess hall for dinner and he thought about Danielle again.

Chapter 6

The next day Scott reviewed the communications equipment that the team would be wearing with Luke. It consisted of an earpiece with a small microphone leading from it, down his chin and ending at the side of his mouth. At first it seemed rather cumbersome in conjunction with the glasses. Luke was also concerned that because they were close together, there may be some distortion between the two units. But testing them together did not show any such effects.

They continued to work together over the next few days. Luke learned hand commands and how to react to the verbal commands given to him. None of it was coming to him naturally and he always felt that he was two steps behind. Instead of just responding, he first had to think about what to do after each command, and then act accordingly. He recalled sitting on the edge of his bed during the mortar attack trying to think of what to do, instead of doing it. They wandered through the camp and Luke would call out hypothetical targets and locations to Scott, who would then correct him and offer constructive criticism on his technique. Luke was happy to see Scott's colors stay mainly in the green and blue hues, although they did shift to the yellow spectrum a few times when Luke was struggling to grasp some of the basic lessons.

Luke had to learn to call out the visuals without using his hands to point. The challenge came when Scott instructed him not to look directly at the visual, but Luke was not able to do so without losing the Cat Eyes reading. So they improvised and had Luke keep his head slightly tilted down when viewing a target. It was not as inconspicuous, but it was less obtrusive than looking right at the target. He was actually thinking he was getting pretty good until the whole unit showed up for dress rehearsal at the end of the week.

Ten soldiers, with Captain Tillman at the lead, came into the training area shortly after breakfast. Luke recognized several of them from the mess hall, although he had never spoken to them. They were fully armed and wearing their headsets as well. Luke lowered his head and scanned them with the Cat Eyes as they approached. With the exception of Captain Tillman who was dark green, all of their auras were firmly in the yellow with several of them moving toward dark orange which signaled that 'intent' was mixed in with their thoughts.

"Good morning, Mr. Baker. Private Jacobson tells me you're a good student and I wanted you to meet the rest of the field team that you will be working with," he proceeded to quickly run down a list of names and ranks that Luke was able to keep in his memory for all of 5 seconds until the next introduction was made which then flushed the previous name out of his mind. He decided to just nod and give a firm handshake to each of them. "I want us to go through a mock field testing with everyone together so that my men will know how your product works and how best to work within your limitations," he stated with a stern expression.

He then walked through the positioning of each soldier and explained each of their assignments. Luke was given the nickname "Ice" because there was another soldier in the group whose last name was Baker and they didn't want any confusion when directing communications. One of the soldiers joked that "Ice" sounded like "Eyes" and after a few musical renditions and dance moves of Vanilla Ice's "Ice Ice Baby" the name stuck. Luke was concerned that the name was actually given based on a comment one of the other soldiers jokingly made that he might "freeze up" in combat, but either way he was officially Ice.

Luke was put in the middle of the squad as they marched around the complex. They quickly tested his field knowledge with brief commands and warnings and found gaping holes in it. On several occasions, a command was given and Luke was the last one standing in the open, not sure which direction to go. Then he went to the other extreme and found himself overreacting and "hitting the dirt" while the other men were just taking a break.

Luke could hear the laughs, sighs, and grunts in his headpiece every time he messed up and felt the added pressure growing with each failure. When one of the men named "Boots" vocalized his thoughts for all to hear, the captain told him to "cut the unnecessary chatter" and moved them forward to the next scenario.

He understood that they were testing him, but he also could see by their hues that they were making fun of him as well. "Boots" was particularly cruel in his words and actions toward Luke and his colors were almost always orange or dark red. Based on his comments and expressions, Luke gathered that he was not at all thrilled about having to work with an untrained civilian and he even turned off his mic once to share within earshot of Luke and the two other soldiers near him that Luke "was going to get them all killed". Later, and again off mic, so the captain would not hear, he shared that Ice was an appropriate name because they would all be on "ice" by the time this was over.

They broke for lunch with most of them heading toward the mess hall. Luke was putting a fresh battery pack on the Cat Eyes unit as an excuse to avoid following the rest of them and to gain a little time to think things through. The "get us all killed" comment really shook him up. As he looked up briefly he was disappointed to see that Jacobson and Captain Tillman stayed behind to wait for him.

"How are you feeling?" Captain Tillman asked seeming to already know the answer to his question.

"It's not every day that you get the opportunity to get people killed if you screw up," he said sarcastically as he purposely fumbled with the battery.

"Is Jezewski starting to get to you?" Tillman asked.

"Is that the big mouthed, Neanderthal jerk they call Boots?" Luke asked.

"Yeah," Tillman responded with a chuckle.

"No, not at all. Why do you ask?" he replied sarcastically and then continued with something that had been on his mind all day. "By the way, why is he called Boots?" Luke asked with a painful expression of his face.

"Because Jezewski is hard to understand on the headset, so he got his name based on his reputation. When he takes off his boots, the smell almost kills you," Jacobson smiled as he shared the story.

"Well his mouth takes after his feet," Luke responded and the other two chuckled.

Luke saw Jacobson glancing down at his com gear, and then looked back up at him with concern. "Ice, you probably should have turned your mic off before making those comments," Luke's heart sank as he thought about the words he just used to describe Boots and the ramifications of them. He glanced down in confusion to see that the com link had actually been turned off. When he looked up Jacobson was smiling and popping his eyebrows up and down. "Psych!" he said with a laugh.

Captain Tillman just shook his head at Jacobson.

"We laugh, but it's happened to all of us." He stood up as if he wanted to head for the mess hall. "In spite of his stinky feet and big mouth, Boots is a hell of a good soldier and I trust my men and my life with him," Tillman said after the smile faded. "I also picked him because he is a hard sell and he represents the typical soldier. If you can convince him of the value of the product of yours, the rest will be easy."

Luke ran out of things to check on the system unit and decided that perhaps a soda and sandwich was not a bad idea after all. He got up and headed into the mess hall with them. The rest of the day was much like the morning with Boots riding him and Jacobson encouraging him. The only difference was that Luke started calling out hypothetical threat targets to the group and getting them to respond appropriately. The soldiers seemed to be much faster at learning his commands than he was with theirs. Although he personally felt he was doing much better by the end of the day, you would not have guessed it from Boots' snide remarks.

They had wrapped up and everyone in the squad exchanged goodbyes and handshakes with Luke except for Boots, who left without saying a word to him. Luke stood with Captain Tillman at his side, and watched them leave.

"Do you feel ready?" the captain asked Luke.

"No," Luke replied.

"I agree. I'm going to have Jacobson train with you again tomorrow with instructions that I will give after I debrief the men this evening. You need to get all the kinks worked out because I intend to make my decision tomorrow." He then turned and looked at Luke. "If you don't feel ready by then, I think the best thing for everyone would be to cancel the demonstration." Luke nodded his head but inside he was frustrated at himself.

"Get your rest tonight and I will talk with you and Jacobson tomorrow at the end of the day." Without looking back, he walked in the direction that his men went. Luke watched him leave and battled with thoughts of either purposely sabotaging his next training efforts to avoid having to test the unit in a live environment or really focusing on getting the commands and reactions down to avoid failure. That night he vaguely remembered eating dinner with Apollo and hearing him ramble about his views and thoughts on everything, but Luke was very distant and did not share with him what he was struggling with. He excused himself early and went to hang out in his room alone. It was not until late in the evening as he stared at the ceiling that he made his decision. Once he did, he fell quickly asleep.

He woke up early and sat and meditated for a while. He mentally visualized all the commands and reactions that were required of him. Essentially, he would be leading this group of men and what he said or did was vital to the success of the demonstration and more importantly to the lives of the men. When Jacobson arrived, he focused intently on his instructions and the subsequent corrections needed as they walked through the multitude of scenarios again. When Tillman arrived that afternoon, he initially met with Jacobson while Luke ate dinner alone. Toward the end of his meal the two of them sat down at the table and joined him.

"I have to tell you that last night I made a personal decision to cancel the demonstration. I did not want to put my men or you at risk in the field," Captain Tillman admitted. He looked over at Jacobson and then continued, "Based on what Jacobson is telling me about your progress, I'm now questioning that decision." Again, he looked over at Jacobson and then back to Luke. "What are your thoughts on this? Yesterday you did not feel ready, nor did it seem like you wanted it. Is it something you now believe you can do?" he asked.

Luke stared at him a moment before responding.

"Sir, I believe this product has the ability to save lives and give you an advantage in the field. I also believe I can demonstrate to you and your men the ability of the unit to be useful in a typical field environment. My only concern is that if your men do not believe it, then it is a waste of time for everyone. I'm ready, but are they willing?" he replied.

Captain Tillman leaned back in his chair and exhaled slowly. They waited for what seemed like hours, but Luke knew it was only a few minutes. He then brought his chair back to the ground on all four legs and softened his expression.

"I know your time is short as is mine, so my plan was to incorporate this squad into a major operation and see how this worked in a live and potentially combative situation." He paused. "But I agree with your assessment. Excluding Jacobson, my men are not ready or confident in your abilities to guide them, nor do they believe in the functionality of the product. That, Mr. Baker, is a recipe for disaster and there are too many lives at stake. But…" He glanced at Jacobson and took a deep breath again. "Jacobson has brought up the idea that instead of canceling the overall demonstration, we test it on a smaller and less intensive scale. That allows us to see it in a live environment without risking lives." Luke was not sure if he felt disappointment or relief at his words.

"What do you have in mind?" He asked.

"I'm going to schedule the squad for a standard security patrol first thing in the morning. We will be in and out in a few hours, far less ambitious and something I should have done in the first place. Unless there are any objections, I will send Jacobson over later this evening with the orders for the day." He stood and held out his hand for Luke to shake. "I appreciate your honesty, Mr. Baker. I look forward to tomorrow." Luke nodded and smiled.

"Great job today. I'll touch bases later this evening for a briefing." Jacobson said.

"I'll be here, unless I can get an earlier flight out," Luke joked as the two men walked away to wherever they went to when they left him each day. As they disappeared, he somehow did not feel the heavy burden that he had felt that morning. He walked back to his room to change clothes and prepare for the day ahead.

That night, he called Danielle. He was not sure just why he felt the urgent need to call her, but to hear her voice added to what had thus far been a good day. He knew that she would have been able to hear the concern in his voice had he called earlier. It was easy to talk with her now. He joked that he had been hitting most of the popular discos in Baghdad and that he had been taking long walks alone through the city to keep his head clear. She laughed and asked if he could bring back a few pictures of him with some of the insurgents he had befriended so she could hang them on her walls. After the joking and teasing was over there was a moment of uncomfortable silence. Filling the void, he thanked her for her card.

"I'm so worried about you being there." She replied in a soft voice.

"They are taking good care of me, besides, Apollo would never allow anyone to put himself in a dangerous position. So as long as I stick close to him, I'm safe," he joked with her in an attempt to keep the truth of the matter hidden.

"Any idea when you will be coming home?" she asked.

"I think we should be finishing up in a few days, and then I can take you out on the town and show you all the new dance moves I picked up in Baghdad," he said with a dry tone.

"Let's just start with a quiet relaxing dinner and see if we can't cool your jets after being in that wild party atmosphere for so long. You might find that I'm not who you remember me being," she replied with a soft giggle.

They continued to quiz each other as best they could without him breaking any security rules or her letting him know too much about what she was doing that was out of the norm. As they said their good byes, she ended it with that same statement that she had written in the card.

"I'll keep you in my prayers."

The words caught him off guard again. He wanted to ask her about her use of this new phrase and its meaning but he hesitated too long and the phone went quiet as the connection ended.

That was twice now that she had used those words. What was she thinking? She knew he was not a religious man. The truth was that he had made it clear that he wanted nothing to do with religion of any sort, so why use those words with him now? Like on the plane, he spent the next few hours going over their discussion and trying to decipher some hidden meaning of what she meant by *"you might find that I'm not who you remember me being."* By the time he finally nodded off to sleep, he had come to the realization that she had not joked about partying while he was gone, mentioned other guys, or even used a hint of foul language or innuendos in their discussion. Although she was not overly prone to foul language, she had always been rather promiscuous in their discussions. Something was up and he was determined to find out about it when he got home.

He wondered if she was interested in someone else?" He felt an urgency to wrap this whole "testing" thing up and get home, but then he reminded himself of the importance of keeping his head clear and focused for the final field test. Lives depended on it.

Chapter 7

Once again, they ate breakfast while it was still dark as Captain Tillman briefed them on the day. The plan was to patrol a ¾ mile stretch of a busy road in the city. According to recent gathered intelligence, the area was reported to be a low threat zone, but even in secure zones, there were always potential dangers. The captain reviewed the basic guidelines of engagement and clarified that the purpose of the patrol was to test the viability of the Cat Eyes in the field. He fielded a few questions and then dismissed the group. They quickly loaded up and headed out.

Luke glanced at his gear as they rode in their Humvee toward their destination. He was wearing the full field outfit with body armor, helmet, communication headset, water, basic field kit and supplies. He looked around at the other soldiers and realized that the only thing he was missing was a weapon and the many clips of ammunition they had tucked away in various pockets. Luke, on the other hand, was carrying the Cat Eyes unit connected to the battery pack by the wires that they had run down the inside of his uniform. He also had a spare Cat Eyes unit packed in his smaller pack.

Luke watched the soldiers loading the molle pouches on their plate carriers with the extra clips and he made a big deal of tucking away his two spare battery packs for the Cat Eyes into his own jacket pockets. Several of them noticed and smiled at the gesture.

"It's always a good idea to store them over your vital areas as extra protection. It could save an arm or leg," one soldier joked in dark humor. Luke thought about the suggestion and started removing them from the jacket.

"Unfortunately, I don't have that many batteries, so the two I have are going to have to save my two legs," he replied and repositioned the two batteries from his jacket, where he already had body armor, and into the thigh pockets of his fatigues.

Although he was still a little nervous, Luke was relieved that they would be patrolling a secure part of town instead of the full-scale insurgency mission they were originally training for.

Their group and the support team traveled in four Humvees supported by two armored personnel carriers, or APC's as they called them. The plan was to travel together until they approached the patrol area, then split into two groups that would secure both ends of the designated street. The group that Luke was in was to take up fixed positions at the east end of the patrol area where they would start. The other group was to up a position on the other end of the patrol route and would take Luke and the soldiers back to the base after they had completed the patrol.

They arrived at the starting area and Captain Tillman positioned the three vehicles at various points in the intersection that would allow them to provide 'maximum field of fire' for each other and for the surrounding area should an attack occur. Each Humvee had a top gunner and a driver that stayed with the vehicle, and each APC had four additional soldiers that were outside the vehicle making routine stops and checks with and one inside manning the communications system. He was the ears and safety net for the mission. Should the patrol call for assistance, they were to come to their location to offer additional firepower and extraction, if required.

The hustle and bustle of the city street was surprising to Luke. Cars and foot traffic filled the street as they grouped up and began to move toward the other end of the road, five blocks away. The patrols were intended to provide the Iraqi citizens with a show of force and security. Although the Iraqi police had been gradually taking on the responsibility for security, the U.S. troops still provided the lion's share of the work.

Luke looked around at the people and was reminded of when he first tested the unit in a shopping mall. The analogy of trying to drink from a fire hose was the best way to describe the visual stimulation. A flood of colors and images flowed together when he lowered his head to peer through the Cat Eyes. He fought off the same feeling of being overwhelmed by it all, especially when red hues came into view. Gradually, he calmed himself down. He was glad he had the time to get adjusted while the vehicles took up their positions. Like a quarterback in a football game, he first took it all in and then focused on just the objectives. His headset, which had been filled with a constant stream of commands, went silent.

"How's it looking, Ice?" The nickname made him realize that those words were for him and he recognized Jacobson's voice.

"Kind of like trying to find Waldo in the picture," he replied. He was happy to hear a few chuckles.
"Who's Waldo?" Luke thought he recognized Cooper's voice behind the question.

"It's 'Where's Waldo,'" one of the guys said.

"Why 'where' instead of 'who?'" Cooper asked in a sincere voice.

"Never mind, Cooper," one of the guys answered and the others laughed as they took up their patrol positions and prepared to head out.

A group of kids came running toward them as they crossed the street. Luke lowered his head and watched the soldiers react to their arrival.

"Ice, any concerns in this group?" Tillman asked as the kids closed the gap on them and began asking the men for candy.

"Not sure. I can only read the oldest kid and he shows, well, I guess I would call it anticipation or desperation. The rest I don't know. Children for some reason do not give off a reading," he replied.

"What! Why not?" Boots complained into his ear.

"I don't know, for some reason it's not until somewhere between twelve and fourteen that you can start getting a read on them. Sorry, but since our focus has been on certain high level applications of the unit, we haven't really invested in the research in the units application to children," he said.

"Well you had better figure it out," Boots continued, "because one of these little bastards blew himself up in the middle of a patrol last month and killed some good men."

"Well that explains why your aura changed to 'fear' as they approached," Luke replied.

"That was 'caution' dirt for brains. What did yours change too? 'Oh how cute?'".

"I don't know. You can't see your own aura," he replied and the group went silent for a minute.

"Why's that?" Jacobson finally asked.

"Not sure. It's just another one of those things that makes you go 'hmmm,'" he said. Luke noticed that Boots' color remained red as they continued down the street.

Luke continued to take in all the colors of the people that they encountered. He managed to ignore the non-threatening colors and focus on isolating those of concern. He found that at times when there were so many people in a moving mass, he could not keep up with them all. He would have to raise his head or look off in the distance to clear his mind. It was easier when he got up close to a person because he was able to distinguish their individual emotions.

"George Bush and Obama number one," a man said to them with a smile as they passed by, yet his hue was that of fear toward them.

There were a mixture of smiles and cold stares from those they passed and from those sitting and drinking coffee at tables outside of restaurants along the street. The hues ranged from being at peace to being angry. Luke would point out to Captain Tillman those that flashed anger. The captain would then approach them and purposely engage them in conversation. Stevens, the group's interpreter would translate his questions and their responses. Tillman was very personable, respectful and kind to them as he worked to defuse their anger. While the captain spoke, Luke would watch from a distance and quietly relay any changes in their color spectrum to him. With almost every case, by the time he was done speaking with them, their spectrum had changed to the better. Although there were those that just sat with their arms crossed with a defiant arrogance about them. If their hues did not change, Luke would tell Captain Tillman who would withdraw with a respectful "thank you" and continue on his way.

"Kill them with kindness," he said as they continued down the street.
"And those that refuse to be our friends, well, we use bullets and bomb,." Boots said sarcastically.

"Stow those comments, Boots," the captain retorted.

After an hour of this interaction with the people they encountered, Luke was getting very comfortable with the whole process as was the rest of the patrol. As he watched the captain work his magic on the next group of citizens at a coffee table, he glanced up to take a quick look around. As he turned back toward the captain, a deep red caught his eye on the far side of the street. He made the mistake of looking directly at the target and he locked eyes with the stranger. The man's color went from dark red, to yellow showing a moment of fear, and then back to a dark red again. Luke's blood ran cold as the man simply smiled and started to walk away, disappearing into the crowd. He realized that he had not said a word to the patrol during the whole experience and now the moment of opportunity had passed.

"Uh, I saw a bogey, but he disappeared into the crowd," he whispered.

"Care to share the location?" Boots snapped back sarcastically.

"Sorry, ten o'clock, far side of the street moving away from us. He was wearing a white shirt, short beard," he said and knew what was coming before he had even finished.

"Wow thanks, that really narrows it down," Boots quipped back on cue.

Luke desperately scanned the area hoping to spot the man again, but to no avail.

"Don't worry about it, Ice. We might get another opportunity at him since were heading his way, so just keep your eyes peeled for him," Tillman said and patted him on the back as he walked past him after leaving the coffee table of citizens.

They spent the better part of the next hour interacting with the civilians in the area, but Luke stayed alert, scanning for the deepredaura. As Captain Tillman disengaged with the latest group, Luke saw another flash of dark red directly ahead of them. This man was walking toward them on the edge of the street in an attempt to avoid the other people on the sidewalk. The man was a good 50 yards away when Luke called out the bogey.

"Bogey, twelve o'clock, teenager wearing a blue jacket zipped up the front, a pair of sunglasses and no facial hair. He is walking straight at us down the edge of the street," Luke called out louder than he needed into the microphone.

"Got him," someone replied quickly and then a handful more confirmations echoed in the headset. The lead man on patrol stepped into the street and pointed his M-16 at the man and shouted at him in Arabic to "stop". The young man in the blue jacket seemed surprised at being spotted and stopped momentarily He seemed to size up the man with the rifle aimed at him that was now less than 40 yards away.

"He's thick in the middle," one of the soldiers said but Luke did not understand what he meant by that.

"Don't let him get any closer and put some cover between you and him," Tillman said and Luke watched the men in the patrol start to move behind walls, cars, posts and benches as they trained their weapons on the man. Luke saw the man's color momentarily change to fear.

"He's afraid," Luke said quietly. But no sooner had he said that than his color went back to dark red. The people in the area were quickly moving away from the man and soon he was left standing all alone.

Looking around, the man decided to take another step toward the patrol but was quickly ordered to stop by those closest soldiers.

"What are you getting, Ice?" Jacobson asked in the headset.

"He has intent and is hostile toward us," he replied.

"Ice, I need you to move back into the store alcove and scan the surrounding area for anymore bogeys," Tillman's voice echoed in his ear. "Do it now, Son," Captain Tillman gave a sharp order when he saw that Luke was not immediately moving. Luke quickly moved the· fifteen feet to the storefront entrance and added the protection of the stone walls between him and the man in the blue jacket. Once there, he remembered he was supposed to be scanning the surrounding area and began searching the crowd of people that were quickly moving in all directions away from the scene. As Luke watched the yellow and orange ocean of fear flow from the area, he noticed spots of red that seemed set against the flow.

"Nine o'clock, far side of the street, man watching everything wearing a brown shirt, leaning against the wall next to the big… jar… by the yellow building." In the urgency of the moment, he couldn't think of the word for "urn".

"2nd target acquired," someone said.

"He's acting strange," said a voice through the headset a few moments later followed by orders and comments about the lone man in the street.

Luke was stunned when he heard Boots say, "If he takes one more step I am going to drop him."

"He's moving!" Someone barked.

The sound of the gunshot echoed across the plaza and made Luke jump. The silence that followed was deafening and he allowed himself a look around the corner to where the man had stood moments before. He was now on his knees looking down and holding his hands over his chest. He slowly looked up and tried to speak but nothing came out that Luke could hear. Unsure as to why, Luke lowered his head to verify that he had read him correctly, but there was no color to read. He glanced quickly to one of the soldiers and saw that the glasses were still working and then back to the dying man, his mind racing. Luke looked away at the sight of the dying man and wondered if his words of warning had killed an innocent man. His heart sank as he slumped back against the wall and stared out into the crowd of people that were now looking back toward the area they had just left, almost as if to see what happened and to determine if it was safe to return.

The look on their faces said most of what he expected, but he lowered his head anyways to see what emotions were coming from them. For many, the hues of fear had been replaced by those of anger and hatred and from others he saw, sorrow. Although the majority continued to move to safer areas, there were some that had stopped to survey what had just happened in their streets. Luke began thinking about what would happen if the crowd decided to turn on them for shooting the young man. What would they do? What would he do?

Along the edges of the crowd and from the alcoves along the street he began to see a scattering of dark red emerge into recognizable shapes as they moved forward and into view. His mind kicked in and he jumped to action.

"We have multiple bogeys behind us," Luke said nervously and then calmed himself and continued. "Bogey three, five o'clock, right side directly under the yellow sign." He heard Captain Tillman issue an order, but was too focused on the armed men he could see behind him to understand it. "Bogey four, six o'clock, he is crouched down directly behind the silver Mercedes, right side as well." He heard someone confirm the target under the sign and then heard someone else call confirmation on the target near the Mercedes as he continued speaking into the headset. "Bogie five, seven o'clock, left side, moving through the crowd toward us, black shirt." Luke heard more orders being issued from Captain Tillman. In the middle of the captain's instructions, Boots yelled something about a hand trigger, but it was cut off by a deafening roar of an explosion from the direction of the man they had shot in the street. Gravel, dust and debris went flying past Luke and rattled off his helmet as he sucked his head down into the neckline of his body armor. His mind felt almost numb from the blast, but he held onto his last thought of the three men with rifles that were either taking aim or moving toward them. There was a high-pitched ringing in his ears yet the noise of the street was muffled like his head was surrounded by cotton.

Luke looked up again and through the dust, he saw that the crowd had now dispersed into the side cafes and buildings, and those that had lingered before, were now running at top speed away from the area. Suddenly a rapid series of dull "popping" noises came from close by. Luke looked over to where a soldier was crouched down behind a wall and was firing at the target by the big jar. He saw the man by the urn go down as the bullets struck his body. Luke wondered how the man by the urn had produced an AK-47 in the midst of all this. More "popping" noises caused his head to turn and he glanced back down the street toward where the other bogeys had been seen. Luke could see that the man who was standing under the sign was now lying under it and not moving. The clear windshield of the silver car was now crystallized from either the blast or bullets. He could not see the third man that was behind the Mercedes or the man in the black shirt that was on the left side of the street.

A distant voice could be heard yelling and Luke struggled to make out the words. Although the ringing continued, the muffling seemed to be fading and the sound of the gunshots was getting louder as he continued to somewhat disconnectedly watch the scene unfolding around him.

The wall across from him suddenly burst into dust that flew back toward him and stung his face and clicked off his glasses. He looked up to see three deep holes in the concrete that bullets had carved out. Then the distant voice again and he thought he recognized it.

"Ice! Get down!" Luke hoped the man was listening to the orders. A cool breeze gently blew past him and then the reality of all that was happening seemed to come crashing into his mind again. This was all real! The bullets hitting the wall were aimed at him and the orders being yelled over the headset were for him. A quick survey of his surroundings showed that he was still standing upright and leaning against the wall just as he was before the shooting began. No sooner did he drop to a crouching position than the wall above him started raining down debris onto his helmet and back.

Luke saw Boots drop down behind a wall near him and then continued firing.

"Ice, get inside the building," he heard Tillman yell into his earpiece.

"Yeah, I think we can figure out who the bad guys are from here," Boots added over the sound of gunfire. Luke stayed low and reached up to the doorknob of the shop and pushed it open. More bullets struck the wall across from him, shattering the windows of the shop that were above him. Glass showered over him as he crawled into the room. A steady stream of orders, voices calling out positions, and gunfire were heard from the men in the patrol as he crawled toward the inside of the shop. It appeared the shop owner sold Persian carpets, rugs and fine cloth as he glanced around and made his way past the various items, crawling over them as he continued looking for a place to hold up. Finding the best place he could think of, he crawled into a gap of tightly rolled carpets that were leaning vertically against the wall and wedged himself as far into it as he could and then tucked his knees to his chest. He tried to figure out a way to spin the two battery packs in the side pockets of his pants around for more protection, but he soon realized that it was impossible and decided to focus on listening to what was being said over the intercom.

Luke took a deep breath of relief when he heard on the headset that the APCs and Humvees that had been listening in were on their way down the street, but he slowly let it out when he heard Captain Tillman order them to stand firm where they were. Tillman explained that he felt the attack was too well organized. He worried that they had prepared for them to call for the support vehicles and might be planning an ambush. He asked the APC to request heavier armor from a nearby base. He added that they currently had good defensive positions, but to be ready to move to them should the need arrive.

Tillman asked for a quick health check and Luke was surprised to hear that during all the gunfire and explosions, no one on the team had been killed or even seriously injured. They had taken down nine insurgents and had five more currently pinned down.

"FYI, there's a juicy RPG laying in the street next to a dead bandit and it's just out of reach of another bandit who wants it real bad," Cooper said softly into his headset as if he were hoping for the insurgent to reach for it.

"Stay on it. It's only a matter of time before he pops out and tries to get it," another soldier said. They continued to call out where the bogeys were and the results of their shots.

"Most of them are just firing wildly over the top of the walls without aiming or showing themselves," another voice stated.

"Stay sharp, they normally would be bugging out by now," Tillman said. "They must be staying put in order to try and draw in the APCs."

Luke stayed tucked in between the carpet rolls. Every so often, random bullets would come bursting through the walls and windows and embed themselves with a "thud" into the various carpets throughout the store. Luke just sat back and tried to be as small as possible while the soldiers did their jobs. Wedged between the two carpet rolls, he found it less stressful to close his eyes and listen to the headset than to watch the bullets strike around his area. Close ones, would make his eyes pop open and he would flinch for a moment, but then he would settle back down and wait for the next one. His heart was racing faster than he could ever remember it beating.

At the end of a long burst of fire, a sound from the back of the shop caught his attention. It did not sound the same as the bullets striking around the area. This sound was more continual and mechanical in nature. As he cautiously looked past the edge of the carpets, he saw that the back door was now open where it had been closed before. He was torn as to what he should do next. He had no weapon and was afraid if he said something that his hiding place would be compromised, yet if he said nothing the patrol outside would be in danger. He calmed himself again and spoke very softly into the mic.

"Possible bogey in the shop with me," Luke spoke so softly that he was afraid no one heard him.

"Armed?" someone asked, but Luke didn't respond because he heard soft footsteps coming toward him from the back of the room.

"Are there more than one? Ice?"

Luke somehow managed to shrink another three inches into the dark recess of the gap, as the steps got closer. The first thing he saw come into view was the tip of an AK-47, then the hands and arms holding it and then the body of a man squatted low next to him. His heart stopped in his chest as he recognized him as the man that he had earlier locked eyes with across the street. The man slowly turned his head toward the gap and gave that same cold smile.

"There you are. I missed you earlier, but now it's you who will see death," he said coldly as he turned the barrel toward him and squeezed the trigger. In that moment, Luke realized that he had wedged himself into the gap so tightly that he could not move or even try to dodge without moving closer to the end of the rifle barrel. As if time had frozen, he stared at the opening at the end of the rifle and waited for the flame and bullet to jump out of it. He felt a cool breeze blow by him at the sound of the trigger release mechanism driving the firing pin into the bullet casing. "Click" but there was no explosion, flame or the pain he expected that followed. He looked up from the gun barrel to see the man's smile change ever so briefly as he realized that he needed to eject the misfired cartridge from the chamber and start again. Luke started to move, but the man was quick and smooth and had cleared the cartridge and chambered another round before Luke had managed to move even a foot out of the gap he was wedged into. The man quickly raised the weapon to fire again. The sound of the rapid gunshots filled the small shop and there was a strange pause as he waited for the bullets to tear into his chest, but instead of pain, he saw the man's body jerk convulsively as he was propelled toward the back door.

As the body hit the floor, Luke saw through the Cat Eyes the deep red color of the dying man swirl into a darkness and then dissipate into nothingness. Luke's surge of momentum in trying to get out of the way of the anticipated bullets carried him from the gap between the carpets to the floor and onto his hands and knees. He turned to see Boots with his rifle still aimed in his direction, looking through one of the broken windows of the shop and a grin was on his face.

"Got him," Luke heard in his headset at the same time as he watched Boots' lips move to the words as he dropped back down behind the window.

"Clear on this side," Jacobson reported through the headset and from across the store at the same time. Seconds later, Boots was next to him and was scanning the store. Luke heard Jacobson moving down the other aisle toward the back door. He just stayed frozen on his hands and knees in silence, reliving the previous moment over and over in his head. He allowed his head to drop down and he glanced at the floor, just inches from his hands, was a single unfired bullet. Then the tip of a boot came into view and gently but expertly stepped on the tip of the bullet, causing it to lift the end of it up to be seen.

"Someone must be looking out for you. AK's rarely misfire," Boots said as his boot released the bullet and he stepped by him and joined Jacobson at the back door of the store. "Back door is secured," Boots confirmed. "I'm leaving Jacobson at the door and I will be moving back out front so don't shoot me," Boots said and chuckled. Luke heard him walk past and out the front door.

Luke continued to stare at the bullet for a moment and although unsure as to why, he picked it up and put it in his pocket. For some reason, Danielle's voice and the last words she had spoken to him *"I'll keep you in my prayers"* was echoing in his mind.

Gathering what was left of his strength, he rocked back onto his heels and fell into the gap between the two carpets. He felt as if all his energy suddenly left his body except for the buzzing at the end of his arms. He lifted his hands in front of him and watched them dance uncontrollably at the thought of what just happened.

Although the firing continued for several more minutes, almost on cue, the insurgents started evacuating their positions. There was one last continual burst from two insurgents AK-47's toward the patrol, probably cover fire, and then it was silent. Luke just sat between the two carpets and continued to relive the last few moments of what could have been a very short life.

The members of the patrol stayed in their positions for the next 45 minutes as additional armor and men were brought in to reinforce the patrol. During that time, they continued to report and chat with each other. Jacobson was watching the back door, but with a click, Boots and Tillman went silent for a while. Luke guessed that Boots must be giving Captain Tillman a report on what happened inside the store. A few minutes later it was confirmed.

"Ice. How are you holding up?" Tillman asked him over the headset.

"Compared to what?" he asked back. He heard Tillman and someone else chuckle in the headset.

"Compared to back home at your desk job?" he replied. Luke thought about the vision in his mind of sitting at his desk writing code or going over reports.

"Well I'm sure glad we didn't have to test this out in a *war zone*," he replied sarcastically and emphasized the last two words. He heard a chorus of chuckles from the team. "Let's just say that I don't envy your jobs," he admitted.

"I just wanted to make sure you're doing okay."

"Actually, I'm rather pissed that Boots shot the guy just as I was ready to put some serious hurt on him," he joked as if to relieve the fear and stress that he was battling inside of him. Then someone replied in a perfect Monty Python "Holy Grail" accent.

"What were you going to do, bleed on him?" he said and more chuckles were heard and various words and renditions of the movie were shared as if it was their way of letting off steam as well. It eventually got quiet again and Luke took the moment to share a thought.

"FYI, he was the same guy I saw and reported earlier that faded into the crowd." He took a deep pause and then continued in a somber voice, "I know this might sound weird, but, I'm pretty sure that he was looking specifically for me. Like he knew why I was here."

"What makes you say that?" Jacobson asked.

"Because he said he had missed me earlier and that it was now my turn to see death."

"It was just talk," Tillman said. Then there was more silence as he could feel the other guys wrestling with it as well.

"Hey Boots," Luke asked.

"Yo." he replied and Luke tried to find the right words to use, but only one word came out.

"Thanks."

"No problem," he replied with an almost uncomfortable voice but Luke felt better in getting it off his chest. Tillman was right, Boots was a good soldier.

"Hey Ice," Boots asked.

"Yo," Luke did his best to imitate his response.

"You and your glasses did all right back there," he said, very out of character. Luke never saw that one coming.

"Thanks," he replied and tried to think of what he could say that would go into a little more detail of his gratitude than just "thanks." But Boots interjected before he could reply.

"Don't get me wrong, you still have dirt for brains, but your product is good. You saved some lives back there and I owe you for it," he continued.

"I love you man," someone said with a faked crying voice.

"I think we need a group hug! Come on everyone, group hug!" another soldier added and laughter and chuckles resounded through the headsets. Luke just smiled as they bantered back and forth. He noticed that his hands were not shaking like they were before.

"You bunch of queer grunts; you're just looking for an early ticket home," Boots retorted.

"Don't ask, don't tell," someone replied and the language and insults quickly escalated. Luke just smiled at the deep bond of friendship these guys had toward each other, forged from war and the daily danger of death. Here they were friends, no matter what race or social background they came from. Here they would die for each other if need be. He greatly envied the relationships they had forged.

Luke stuck his head out of the gap and glanced over to where Jacobson was keeping an eye out the back door. Whether it was the noise he made or he instinctively knew Luke was looking at him, he turned and smiled and nodded his head. Luke nodded back and then leaned back into the gap again.

As they prepared to head back to base, he saw the bodies and the weapons of the insurgents being loaded into a truck. The RPG was still unfired and he wondered if the one insurgent that had wanted it so badly had died in his attempt to retrieve it, or had chosen wisely and instead just ran away? Captain Tillman had apparently made the right call in holding back the APCs and Humvees as Luke heard reports of Iraqi citizens pointing out the locations where the insurgents had been waiting to ambush them had they moved toward the group. A contingent of newly trained Iraqi soldiers and police were on their way to secure the area and pick up the questioning of the locals on where the insurgents had fled to and what support may have been given to them.

As their group drove back toward base, Captain Tillman looked over his shoulder to the back seat where Luke was sitting.

"You passed the test," he said with a smile and looked back out the window. Luke nodded before responding.

"Yeah, I think it worked well leading up to battle, but I'm not sure how useful the glasses were once things get hot." Luke saw that Tillman was shaking his head and stopped talking.

"I meant you as a soldier. I'm putting in a request with the Pentagon to have you drafted into the Army and added to our unit," he said without looking back toward Luke who just sat in silence with his mouth open. Tillman looked back at him again and then smiled. "Just kidding. But if you ever want to join up, we get the first draft pick with you. We'd be honored to have you with us. With or without the Cat Eyes." Luke was relieved to hear that he was not serious about the "drafting" part, but felt overwhelmed to hear him say the other part, so much so that it truly crossed his mind to enlist when he got back home. It felt good to be needed and he felt the event somehow bonded him to these guys.

"What agent should I use and what benefits do you offer?" he joked back.

"Have your people, call my people and we'll put it in motion," the captain replied and smiled as he kept his eyes on the road and his surroundings.

Luke felt excited, relieved, exhausted, proud, terrified, and confident all at once. With all those emotions flowing through him, he felt truly alive for the first time in a very long time.

The next two days were a series of meetings and debriefings on what took place on the patrol and the strengths and weaknesses of the product and how it could be better used in combat. The response of those giving their reports from the patrol, as well as those observing and evaluating from afar, were in agreement that the product was effective and valuable for pre-contact use and civilian interaction. Then more intense discussions were held about its value to the field units once combat began.

Luke was brought in for several rounds of interactive questioning by the panel of men and women evaluating the product. He was amazed at how different he was being treated compared to the initial meeting, but he was even more surprised at the strong and obvious difference in respect he was given compared to Apollo. It was almost as if Apollo was not in the room during the discussions. All questions were directed at Luke and anytime Apollo would try to step in and take the lead, which he initially tried at every opportunity, they would only look toward and respond to Luke, even though Apollo had asked the questions. Toward the end, Apollo gave up trying to be "the man" and surrendered the role to Luke. But outside the room, Apollo would immediately try to re-establish and remind Luke that he was in charge and tried to coach him on how he could have better responded to, and reacted with those asking the questions.

As Luke listened to Apollo "coach" him with his self-proclaimed words of wisdom, he could not help but feel an intense lack of respect for him and a greater distance within their relationship. Luke no longer felt they were business associates, or even that he was his boss and employer. He was now more concerned about meeting the needs of the soldiers in his patrol, than with selling the product. *His patrol,* He smiled at the thought of how many times he had referenced the patrol as 'his' during the past few days. Not in a sense that he owned it, but that he was a part of it. He now understood how a soldier visiting home might feel when someone questioned them about the war. Unless you were there, you really did not understand the bond that was created in battle. That when someone tried to relate to, or to join in with these soldiers, the mutual respect and teamwork they often wanted to experience was something that was first earned, not granted. Luke knew he was a long way from earning full acceptance with this group, but that he had made some significant progress compared to Apollo.

Luke heard Apollo talking about the success of his visit and presentation, how many potential units they could sell, the production lines that would be needed and how much money it would mean to the company. Luke could see where this discussion was going and that Apollo was already trying to figure out where to spend the future millions he would make from this deal. Luke wanted no part of the discussion.

"I'm going to head back to my room for a little rest," Luke interjected as he pushed his chair away from the table and stood up. Apollo looked at him with an almost hurt feeling of not being able to finish his personal victory speech. Then he seemed to have a revelation in the middle of it.

"Luke," Apollo called out to him as he was walking down the hallway. Luke stopped, and looked back to where Apollo was sitting. "I'm going to recommend that the company give you a promotion for your hard work and assistance out here. You were an important part to our success here."

An important part? Luke thought to himself and smiled. *I nearly died as I watched men I hadn't known prior to last week fighting for their lives and for mine in a country that seemed filled with hatred and violence. I've watched men die right in front of me who I had essentially and unknowingly pointed out for execution.* A promotion? Professional counseling is what came to Luke's mind. Better yet, a sincere, heartfelt 'thank you' would go a long way. Yet for Apollo, it was always about money and he probably felt that the offer of a bonus or promotion would somehow buy Luke's support and loyalty to him. Luke felt a moment of hollowness inside as he thought back before this event and wondered what an offer of a promotion would have bought Apollo in the past with him? *Am I really that shallow?* he thought to himself. He just nodded his head as he stared at the smiling Apollo. Then he turned and headed back to his room. *I'll take your money, but you bought nothing with it.* As he turned the corner he almost ran into Cliff.

"There you are. I understand you're leaving in the morning for that comfortable job and cushy chair in the states?" he stated more than asked.

"Someone has to earn enough tax money to pay for this war," Luke said back still thinking about Apollo's offer.

"Well from the sounds of things, your company will be doing some business with Uncle Sam, so I hope you own stock in the company." Luke realized that he did not, which in some odd way made him feel better about himself and all the issues intertwined with this situation.

"Nope, just running on sheer stupidity, I'm afraid. How about you? Were you able to sell all your Uncle Sam stock before the big buy, or would that be considered insider trading?" he joked.

"Nah, only the Senators and Congressmen are allowed to benefit from insider trading. I'm already so far upside down on my stock value that I would have to pay someone to get out. I'm afraid they have me for as long as I'm needed." He smiled. There was a moment of silence, as the two seemed to have agreed without any words that the 'tit for tat' banter had gone on about as far as it could. Then Cliff looked him straight in the eyes.

"I'm happy that my instincts were right about you. You should be proud of what you accomplished out there. You took a huge risk that will probably save thousands of lives over your lifetime. Call me next time you plan to visit here on your vacation. Who knows, we might be seeing each other sooner, than later." He smiled again as if to break the seriousness of his compliment.

"Something tells me that you would know I was here long before I had a chance to call you." He smiled back. "But thanks. Coming from you, that means a lot. I appreciate you taking me under your wing and leading me down the path you wanted me to follow."

Cliff smiled at Luke's observation.

"Was it that obvious?"

"Not at first, but as they say, hindsight is 20/20." He raised an eyebrow and smirked.

"Oh come on. Deep down you know darn well you wanted to do it. I just gave you a little direction to make sure your dreams came true." Luke thought about his words and the feelings he had inside and at first thought about continuing the joke along then changed his mind. "I think you're probably right." Then he couldn't keep himself in such a serious state. "Does that mean it's my turn to buy the late night drinks?" he asked.

"I know just the place." And they both started for the mess hall for one more free soda.

Chapter 8

Although exhausted from the long flight home, when he finally touched down at LAX, Luke felt somehow reenergized by the thought of being home again. He walked past the security checkpoint and down the stairs towards the baggage claim area. Half way down, the crowd of expectant faces looking for their loved ones came into view. Then he saw her. She had blond hair and blue eyes and an incredible smile that filled the room. Apollo walked right past the two of them heading for the baggage return. She walked up slowly and coyly with her hands in her pockets.

"Need a ride soldier?" she asked, as he set his carry-on bag down beside him.

"Hmm, not sure. What's your going rate?" he asked, waiting for some sexy reply that she always had ready for him.

"How about dinner on the way home?"

That was not exactly what he was expecting, but it did sound like a good idea.

"Just dinner? Seems awfully cheap for such a long ride home," he replied hoping to open up the door to a more interesting and provocative conversation.

"Well let's start there and perhaps I'll let you buy me some dessert as well," she said almost uncomfortably as she avoided his eyes.

Houston, we have a problem. He put his heart and mind on protect mode while he tried to sort through all the feelings that were suddenly running through his mind. At just the right moment, she stepped forward and gave him a big hug and a kiss and then wiped away the lipstick that was left behind on his cheek.

"I missed you," she said as she smiled and looked into his eyes.

"Are you sure? You seem different, almost guarded. Is everything alright?" he continued as he picked up his carry-on bags and put his free hand around her and headed for the baggage carousel.

"Yes. In many ways better than ever, but definitely different." She glanced away and he followed her eyes toward Apollo standing at the front of the baggage carousel waiting for his bags. "How was your trip and the time you got to spend with Apollo?" He knew what she meant by the question as they had many discussions and laughs over drinks about how much of a pain he was to be around, as well as how selfish and cold he was toward people.

"Pretty typical all around. No, actually worse." He slid the jab in toward the end and chuckled and waited for her to join in.

"How sad for him, and you," she responded.

"How sad?" Luke questioned her response. No mean comments, or personal digs to join in with his chiseling away at Apollo and his weaknesses. There was definitely something wrong and he was feeling very uncomfortable with it. "What did you think it was going to be like spending over a week with the guy? Playing cards and some great male bonding time? We're talking about Apollo, right? Or am I the "sad" one?" he jabbed with his words. He could see that they hurt her and he immediately felt bad for letting them come out. "I'm sorry, it's been a long trip and everything seems different from when I left." She smiled as if to accept his apology and then looked back toward Apollo.

"He must be very sad inside, when he could have a friend like you and chooses not to see that."

They silently watched the bags going around the carousel. Luke's mind was motoring again. On one hand he was kind of bothered that she hadn't jumped in on the Apollo bashing moment, which was the norm, but instead took a different path. On the other hand, he liked the fact that she did not join in and instead showed compassion toward him. In the end, he was left feeling like the fool for starting the whole thing.

He saw his last bag coming around the corner and Apollo walked past him and said, "I will see you first thing in the morning."

No 'Thank you' or 'Good job' or anything that would have demonstrated that he was a human being on the inside. He didn't even acknowledge the presence of Danielle, one of his other employees. Luke glanced at Danielle and realized she was right. It was sad to see someone like that. He grabbed his bag as Danielle took one of his carry-on bags and they headed for the parking lot.

Without even a discussion on it, they stopped at their favorite Chinese restaurant. It was late enough to miss the crowds, but not too late to miss the best chefs that were on the early evening shift. The owner of the restaurant came out to meet them as soon as they were seated.

"Hello Danielle and Luke!" Luke smiled as he remembered the first time they had come here. The owner, Martin, had introduced himself to them and listened to their names. He and Danielle had come by again over a month later and he came to the table and said "Luke and Danielle, it is good to see you again." The fact that he remembered their names won their hearts and they had been coming back ever since. The additional fact that the food there was some of the best Chinese food around, didn't hurt either.

"Hello Martin," they both replied as Danielle gave him a hug then Martin shook Luke's hand.

"You look tired Luke; you need to get more rest. Would you like me to bring you your usual?" he asked with his Chinese accent.

"That would be great, Martin," Luke replied.

"But no Volcano tonight Martin, I'm driving," Danielle interjected the 'driving' part at the end as if it was an afterthought. Luke looked at Danielle and then back at Martin. "Bring it anyways; I'll drink it all if she doesn't want any," Luke said and ended with a smile toward

Martin and then raised an eyebrow toward Danielle. She only gave an odd smile back to his words.

Luke controlled the conversation and asked about how she was doing and what had happened during his absence. He was hoping to get her to reveal some nugget that would help explain why she was being different, but from what he could see and hear, he could not put his finger on anything in particular. When the food arrived and he began to eat, he relinquished control of the conversation long enough for her to take over.

"My turn!" she interjected at his pause. "So, tell me about the trip. There was some gossip going around the office that you and Apollo got shot at, true or false?" She seemed deeply concerned when she asked the question, but all he could think about was how Apollo had somehow managed to include himself in the dangerous part of the story. Not that he wanted to be the hero or glory boy, he just hated seeing someone try to take credit for something he didn't do, especially Apollo. He thought about clarifying, but thought it would only seem petty on his part, so he just responded.

"True. Bullets and bombs flying everywhere and I even had the joy of having a gun aimed right at my head." His expression changed as the vision came back in full color in his mind. "The guy died right in front of me. An American soldier saved my life." He went cold as he replayed the whole series of events in his mind. As he looked back at Danielle, she was sitting there with her mouth open in disbelief. After a brief and uncomfortable silence, she said, as if probing or failing to actually believe him,

"You're serious!" She almost shouted and put her hand over her mouth as he nodded.

"The guy even pulled the trigger, but for some reason the gun didn't fire."

She fell back into her seat and set her chopsticks next to her plate. She just stared at him and then stared back at her food.

"That must have been terrible. I'm so sorry, but I'm so happy you're safe." As if reading his face, she reached over and held his hand and smiled. "God answered my prayers. I asked him to keep you safe."

There it was again. The words "prayer" and "God" being used in a sentence by someone who previously he would have never thought to have ever uttered those words. He felt it was time to cut to the chase and sort through this issue.

"Are you planning on joining a convent or something?" he asked and then half smiled as he took another bite of Kung Pao chicken and waited for her response.

"No," she answered drawing the two letters into a long sound and raised one eyebrow before continuing. "Why, are you planning on shipping me off to one?" she replied cleverly and smiled at the end of her question.

Touché, he thought as he tried to draw out the length of time it took for him to chew his last bite while he gathered his response.

"No, it just seems that I've heard you use the word 'pray' quite often and based on our prior relationship and our activities of choice I might add, the image of a *God fearing woman* does not come to mind," he emphasized part of his words with his best fire and brimstone preacher imitation. "So what gives?" he asked and took another bite of food.

She seemed to blush for a moment and shift in her chair. She played with her food with her chopsticks, but didn't pick anything up from the plate as she pondered his question. Then she looked him straight in the eye.

"Have you ever read the Bible? I mean really looked at what was in there and wondered why it was written?" she asked.

"You mean Adam & Eve, Noah's Ark, Moses crossing the Red Sea, sweet baby Jesus and childhood stories like that?" he asked jokingly.

"No. I mean read the more important stuff, like, why those things happened and the whole purpose for the Bible in the first place. Has it ever just made you wonder why it has endured for thousands of years and why people who have read the Bible are willing to die for those words?"

"Yeah," he responded drawing the word out over a few seconds before continuing in a cold and hurtful voice. "Because some people are weak willed and need some sort of crutch to either explain away their failures, or in false humility, credit someone else for their successes. Either *the devil made me do it* or *God's will* made it happen. Both views shift the responsibilities away from them so that they can cope with their less than wonderful lives." He could see the effect his words had on her and even he felt the bite of the anger and hurtfulness that the words had as they came out of his mouth. She looked down at her plate and nodded her head as if in agreement.

"Well, this weak willed person has been studying the Bible and she hopes that she can blame her less than wonderful life on the devil instead of on the poor decisions she has made." She shot back coldly and took a bite of food.

He thought to himself and smiled, *that's the girl I remember*, he thought and felt he was finally making progress, but she interrupted his next question before he could get it out.

"I'm sorry, that was very mean of me and uncalled for." Her whole demeanor had changed in a moment, as did the prior smile on his face as she continued. "This must seem so strange to you and you even have a right to feel what you feel with the way I have changed the direction of our relationship. It's just that since I've been studying the Bible, it seems like it has filled a spot in my heart, or life, which has been empty a long time." Her sudden apology and humility definitely caught him off guard, but the words *changed the direction of our relationship* were the uppercut that put him on the canvas. The fact that she had admitted that she had changed their relationship made discussing things any further a mute point. Luke knew it was time to throw in the towel in his effort to save this relationship and simply do his best to hide the hurt.

"No. I think it's great that you want to do this. It might be just what you are looking for to make you happy," he said superficially. She just stared at him and read through to the heart of his answer.

"I was hoping that we could do it together." She hesitated and then continued, "I care a great deal about you, but this is a decision that a person needs to want to do, not feel they have to do it, or worse, to do it with the wrong motives. I don't know where it will take me when it's all said and done, I just feel I need to do this so that I can make, what could be, the most important decision in my life." She held his gaze until he pretended to look down to take another bite. There was no way he was going to get pulled into holding someone's hand while they tried to *find themselves* on their spiritual journey of enlightenment. Who sold her this crock of nonsense anyways? No, it was time to break free of this one quickly, before it gets really weird. Her words startled him out of his deep thoughts.

"I understand what you are feeling. David said that you would probably respond this way. I just hoped differently."

"David? Who's David?" he said trying to disguise his inner jealousy.

"David from work. I have been studying the Bible with his wife Susan. I told you that before you left," she said.

"You said you were going over there for dinner, not to talk religion," he snapped back as he tried to remember their discussion on the matter, but realized that he had not paid very close attention to what she had told him. The only thing he could remember about the discussion was that he was glad she was not heading out to the bars with her party friends, and thatDavid and Susan's was definitely a "safe" place. Had she really said, "To study the Bible?" He tried to think, but nothing came to his memory. He shook his head as if to clear it and decided that it didn't matter.

"I'm really not interested, but thank you for thinking of me." He half smiled and saw Martin heading toward him and Luke gave him the "check please" sign. As he looked back at Danielle, he saw a different woman sitting next to him. It almost felt as if she had moved two feet away from him, but what he was not sure about was who's heart had created that two feet of distance, his or hers. He could tell she was disappointed in his response. *Good* he thought to himself, *maybe that will help her to come to her senses and realize that I am right and she should stop this foolishness.*

As they waited for the check, Danielle kept trying to re-engage the topic, but he kept steering the discussion to work, and she eventually gave up and followed the more shallow line of conversation. The distance between them grew further and by the time she had dropped him off at his apartment, it was a simple pat on the arm from him and a "Thanks for the lift" as he got out of the car and took his bags out of the back seat. She was lovely and pleasant to him in spite of his coldness, but he knew she needed to understand that this was one thing that that he would not allow to be a part of their relationship. He had made it through the security door and had reached the stairs of the apartment complex before she finally drove off. As he walked down the hallway to his apartment, he heard the yelling coming from behind the newlyweds' door and he shook his head. His apartment seemed cold and lonely as he closed the door.

Chapter 9

Luke felt strange walking through the office on his way to his desk. Everything seemed different after his trip to Iraq. It was almost as if the people had somehow changed since the last time he was here. Thinking about it, he realized it was not them that had changed. He kept trying to determine whether something inside him had broken while he was in Iraq or if something fixed itself while he was there. *Maybe both?* He contemplated the thought as he dropped his briefcase on his desk and glanced across the tops of the cubicles scattered throughout the 'war room' as the management called it.

The same people that always came in early were the same ones there now, some busily preparing themselves for a day of doing nothing. They were the ones that seemed to enjoy the social dimensions of working at an office more than the work itself and would keep themselves 'busy as bees' but at the end of the day, accomplished little. He watched a young woman named Sarah, whom smiled as she quickly walked by him with an "I'm so busy" look on her face and a handful of papers and files clutched importantly, as if she were on a mission to hand deliver some urgent documents to someone. She was one of those that was always "swamped" if you asked them how they are doing. They would never miss an opportunity to tell you if you were kind or foolish enough to ask. "Trollers" is what Danielle and he named them, they just walked around trolling for someone to talk to.

Then there were those that sat at their desk and cranked out code, or reports, or whatever they were suppose to do. They would rarely even acknowledge the people around them unless they were spoken to. They were socially limited and unless the conversation was about code or some really abstract area of expertise that few would know about or understand, they rarely would respond with more than a few short words when engaged. When someone did ask a question within their realm of comfort, it was if a geyser had gone off at Yellowstone. The information would come gushing out of them as fast as they could share it until their pool of knowledge on the subject was exhausted, then they would slow down and go back into social dormancy.

"I had an Old Faithful moment with Stewart" is how he and Danielle would refer to such encounters. He smiled at some of the other categorizations he and Danielle had made up about people's many character quirks. Suddenly a sense of sadness came over him as he realized that those discussions with Danielle would be far fewer now that things were different between the two of them. He would miss them.

He sat down and logged into his system to pull up his calendar for the day and then checked his email to see what interoffice stuff was happening. His task list reminders started rolling in and he began to prioritize them according to what he felt was more important and who had sent them.

10:00 a.m. Cat Eyes debrief on recent field demonstration, Conference Room 3. Those scheduled to attend: Apollo, Samuel Carr, Ronald Ruhle, Jonathan Weber, and Luke Baker.
Luke knew that Apollo had written the task because he was mentioned first. In looking at the names, he felt he was in pretty good company since it included the president and the two lead developers on the Cat Eyes project.

The general consensus around the office was that the two lead developers were more like "suck ups" to Apollo than hard core developers. Their skill was more in line with testing and cleaning up code rather than creating it from scratch, which was similar to his software coding skill set. That thought humbled him a little. They followed Apollo around like puppy dogs, nodding their heads and fetching things when orders were given. They avoided everyone else in the office except the other "suck up" newbies who wanted to get in on that same promotion track. Luke hoped he would never end up like any of them.

The company did have some excellent developers working for it on the game design side, but Apollo was the only real developer on the Cat Eyes team. Knowing Apollo, it's exactly the way he wanted it. It gave him some serious job security and a lot of internal power, but based on basic business practices, it was a very dangerous way to build a company. One car wreck and they'd see their whole development team wiped out, leaving a developing project in turmoil for someone to clean up, starting from scratch to figure it all out.

With a few minutes to spare before the morning meeting, Luke quickly wrapped up his most pressing emails and either notified people of his inability to attend, or re-scheduled his meetings around the debrief time. He left his desk briefly to retrieve a file folder from Jonathan's desk and then made a quick stop at the employee lounge to get a fresh cup of coffee for the meeting. As he walked into the lounge he saw Danielle pouring herself a cup from the full strength pot. He thought about sneaking back out the door and avoiding the encounter, but felt too weird in doing so. He was more concerned about being spotted in the middle of such an action, so he just took a deep breath and headed for the pot of coffee next to where Danielle was standing.

"Good morning," he said with a smile and reached for the half empty pot that she had just set down on the hot plate in the machine. She looked surprised by his welcome, but smiled so beautifully that he partially missed his cup on the first try at filling it.

"Good morning to you, careful it's really hot!" she said, very concerned as she noticed the hot liquid just missing his hand and getting all over the folder he was carrying.

"Yeah, unless there are bullets and bombs flying around, I really have trouble holding my concentration," he quipped and she giggled.

"I could hit you over the head with a chair or something if you feel it would help calm you down?" Her smile had a mischievous look to it as she blinked her eyes and raised an eyebrow as if waiting for the invitation to do so. He realized that he had held her eyes in his too long and it had now become awkward.

"I'm afraid you're a little too anxious and willing to offer that kind of assistance for me to feel good about your motives." He raised one eyebrow and added a sarcastic smile and looked away.

They both stood there saying nothing and then as if on cue, took a sip of their coffee trying to remove the awkwardness of the silence. He wanted to speak, but his mind drew blank, something that had never been a problem with Danielle before. He wanted to talk and laugh and joke with her, but he knew he had made a decision last night to change the relationship and pull his heart back. Unfortunately, his heart must not have gotten the memo.

He did an instinctive but Oscar winning performance of looking at his watch without really reading the time.

"I'm running late for a debriefing," he told her and then shook off the remaining coffee from the file folder and headed to the door leaving her standing there in the break room. He paused briefly in the doorway and glanced back to where she still stood waiting and watching him leave. He really wanted to say something clever, but nothing came to his mind that made any sense. "The chair…" he finally said as he nodded his head toward it. She slowly looked at it and then back to him with a confused look on her face. "The chair idea… that uh… that probably would have been a good idea for a prior occasion," he stumbled through his words and then smiled. She just smiled and nodded, as she seemed to get his meaning and said,

"Maybe next time?" He grimaced, then returned her smile with a nod and left.

As he headed down the hallway toward the meeting rooms, he glanced at his watch again, this time to really read the dials. "Crud! I am late!" he mumbled to himself and picked up his pace.

When he entered the meeting room, he was asked to sign a detailed non-disclosure document that was placed in front of him. He had already signed one when he first started to work at the company, but this he guessed, was probably to tie up any loose ends missed in the first one. Looking around, he noticed that the other two developers, Jonathan and Ronald, or the "gopher twins" as the war room employees liked to call them, were also required to sign the documents. They must have come early if they had read the whole document; either that or they just blindly signed it. Luke read through the agreement and as he had guessed, it was very similar to the employee non-disclosure he had previously signed, but this one just seemed to add a lot more teeth to the agreement.

When Luke asked about it, the president of the company, Samuel Carr, said,

"I requested that the three of you be more involved with the development of this product, which requires you to be privy to more sensitive information than before." Luke had always liked Mr. Carr and had based a lot of his decision to accept his current position on his interview with him. He seemed to have a good read on people and could work effectively through issues and personalities without getting caught up in them. He looked over toward Apollo and could see from his face and posture that he was not happy about having Luke included in the "inner circle" of the product development. He glanced back over it again and looked at Mr. Carr to get one last read on him. He just returned the look with a smile. Luke was not sure how to read the last part, but he knew that everyone was waiting for him. He signed it and slid it toward the other two signed documents in front of the president. Luke had a humorous vision of Samuel grabbing the agreement and jumping into the air and yelling "Yes!" or "He's now mine!" but Samuel didn't even move to pick them up or even change his expression. He just turned to Apollo and said, "Go ahead."

Apollo wrapped up his initial overview debrief of the Iraq trip and presentation in about 50 minutes. Luke felt it was not only 30 minutes longer than it should have been, but also Apollo used way too many "I" statements where it should have been "we" and included himself in a large number of "we" statements where he was not even involved. To add to Luke's frustration, he never even used a "Luke" in his presentation. From an outsider listening in, you would have assumed that Luke's main purpose with the trip was to carry Apollo's bags.

As Apollo finished, Mr. Carr glanced over at Luke and asked,

"Since you were there, is there anything you would like to add to the overview Mr. Baker?" Apollo seemed surprised by the question and glanced over at Luke and back to the president. Luke wondered if that was nervousness that he saw flash across Apollo's face? He wished he had the Cat Eyes on to get a more accurate read on him. After a brief silence he shook his head and glanced at Apollo and back to the president of the company.

"No, that gave a good 'big picture' overview of the presentation."

The president seemed to hold his stare on Luke longer than he wanted him too as if trying to glean some hidden insight from him. Then he smiled and nodded. He looked back toward Apollo and nodded. Apollo seemed hesitant to continue, but seemed to re-gather his arrogance and proceeded to launch into the next part of the meeting. He passed out handouts and spreadsheets to everyone in the room to follow along.

The first hour of the overview spent was listening to his potential sales projections of Cat Eyes units to the military. He broke things down by military branches, divisions, battalions, platoons, and even squads to come up with potential numbers. Luke was impressed with the depth of data and wondered where he got such detailed information on the military. The final potential number of units was staggering. Luke was very excited about the numbers, not as revenue, but for how they would have a positive impact on the soldiers in the armed forces.

After a brief break, the next hour was spent discussing the production capabilities of the company and ways of ramping up production to meet various demands should they receive the anticipated contract with the government. Mr. Carr encouraged interaction and input from every member of the team. Luke talked about beefing up the field units to overcome the challenges faced by the military (heat, cold, rain, mud, dust, impact, concussion, etc.) and they decided the best solution would be to focus on creating a durable and insulated carrying case that the standard units could slide into, rather than continually redesigning the units themselves.

Luke found the whole discussion very exciting and loved the fact that he could contribute to the conversations and development of the product. The excitement level grew in the room as more and more of the potential challenges were overcome and they were able to walk through the marketing plan for the product. It was Apollo who suddenly changed the direction of the meeting.

"I would like us to also consider the many civilian markets available to us and the income potential they have." Luke knew the original product came about during Apollo's development of a game platform, so he was interested in how it could be integrated into a game.

"I thought you decided the game concept you were working on was not feasible?" Samuel responded to Apollo's statement. Apollo hesitated, then somewhat overconfidently responded, "I'm not talking about re-activating the game development side, I'm talking about the potential this holds for the local government and corporate realms." He opened his briefcase and pulled out a set of handouts that he passed around the group. "First, I want you to consider the sales potential if we were to offer it to other government services. For example, the police forces across the nation? Imagine every police officer knowing what your intent was as they approached a car window, whether you were telling the truth or not when they pulled you over, or during an interrogation. The ability to give the security teams at airports a new level of understanding as you passed through, essentially scanning your thoughts as well as your bags. Border agents, judges, the FBI, the CIA, political negotiators; the revenue potential on the government side alone would be enormous." Apollo smiled greedily when he spoke the word "revenue" and drew out the word "enormous." "The next step would be to market to the corporate and business world. Imagine the advantages it would give an employer in hiring decisions or with sales and negotiation interactions."

When Apollo first started speaking about selling the Cat Eyes to a civilian market, alarms went off in Luke's head. As Apollo continued, Luke's thoughts came so quickly that he could not process them all, but taken together, they spelled out serious danger. He glanced around the room to see everyone else's reaction and saw that the gopher twins were actually eating it up and were smiling and nodding their heads at Apollo's words, no doubt seeing their own income grow with each new market suggestion. Luke glanced over at Samuel and saw a deep concern etched across his face as well, which gave him some security that he was not the only sane person in the room. Apollo continued down a long list of potential markets and the uses the glasses could have on nearly every aspect of society, but when Luke thought about the potential misuses of them something inside Luke suddenly snapped.

"Are you nuts?" The words in his mind came out of his mouth before Luke realized it. Apollo stopped the presentation with a surprised and almost hurt look and then quickly replied with a curt "Excuse me?" Luke could see that his initial surprise had changed to anger, but Luke's dismay was in control of his better discretion and the words kept pouring out of his mouth.

"Do you understand the societal ramifications of what you are suggesting?"

"Mr. Baker, I'm very aware of the societal ramifications, as you put it. In fact I am counting on them for our marketing plan to succeed." Apollo replied coldly. Luke just shook his head in disbelief.

"No. No, I don't think you do," he stammered awkwardly, trying to control the breakneck speed of the thoughts that were forming in his mind. Luke waved his hands in a vain attempt to stop the thoughts. "The clear value of this product in the hands of American soldiers is one thing, but what you are talking about would strip away every element of personal privacy."

"No. We are talking about the ability to discern the truth in all situations," Apollo responded coldly and then continued. "Don't you hate liars? Do you realize how much time and money are wasted by individuals, companies and governments as a result of people lying to them? I'm not talking about creating a perfect world. I'm talking about a tool that will help us to at least move toward one." Luke sat with his mouth open in shock as Apollo's words came out. He shook his head in disbelief.

"No, that is a world of paranoia and fear, Mr. Walpole. Where every word and thought needs to be weighed carefully before spoken or immediate consequences will await you. You are talking about a world where emotions, good or bad, can no longer be felt or expressed or you will be immediately pulled over, arrested, and found guilty. You are talking about creating a working environment where feelings result in instant demotion or being fired because you woke up on the wrong side of the bed that day! What makes us who we are, our choices, our decisions, our innate personality, would be laid bare to everyone we'd come into contact with for the sake of a dollar!" Luke realized that although he was speaking to Apollo, he was looking directly at Samuel as if making his appeal to him, but Apollo was the one that responded, not Samuel.

"Clarity, Mr. Baker. Clarity is what it holds for the world, something that you could use at this moment! The paranoia and fear is only a consequence for those whom are guilty." Apollo's stare at the end implied that Luke's protest made it clear what he thought about Luke's view. *I walked right into that one*, Luke thought.

"You did not have any these concerns or feelings prior to today, why the sudden change of heart Mr. Baker?" Apollo smugly pointed out. Luke hated the fact that he would not call him by his first name, but responded anyways.

"I was under the impression from the beginning that we were building a unique and secret product that would help our troops in deadly situations to save lives, not a mass produced morality checking device that can be used by anyone who can afford to own it," he said in a more controlled voice and looked back toward Samuel who had said nothing during the whole interaction, almost as if he was looking for someone else to interject common sense or reason into the discussion.

"Apollo, I appreciate your creative thinking and desire to see the company prosper with this product, but I think Luke brings up some interesting points that we need to consider carefully before going down any other path except that which we currently are pursuing with the military." Samuel's calm response lowered the tension in the room.

"Sam, do you really think the rest of the world will wait around and not exploit these markets while we sit on our hands and pretend that they do not exist? Knowing the Chinese, they will probably have this copied and ready for market before we can even get the first units off the assembly line for the military. Patent protection or not, we either capture all of the markets now, or we may as well hand the whole thing over to someone else and let them take the revenue." Apollo's tone was condescending and acrid and Samuel seemed taken aback by Apollo's obvious challenge of his authority and decision.

Luke knew that the Chinese and many other countries held little regard for US or international hardware or software patents. In tech fields, hardware was all too often reversed engineered and quickly copied regardless of who invented it or had the legal rights to it. The real question was how well Apollo had encrypted the 'special' code that he had developed for the unit. Samuel and Apollo continued to look each other in the eyes, neither backing down. Finally Samuel smiled and without looking at his watch said.

"We've been at this for several hours. I think this is probably a good time for us to take a lunch break and think over the opportunities and challenges that have been presented. Great job everyone. Let's all meet back here at 2 p.m. to continue our planning session."

Apollo and the gopher twins proceeded to gather up their stuff and head out the door. Luke started to stand as well, but Samuel motioned for him to stay and so he sat back down. Luke really needed to vent his thoughts about this, but because of the confidentiality agreement that he had signed, up until now he had no one to go to. He then wondered if being open with the president of the company was such a good idea, so he held his thoughts in and waited for Samuel to start. Samuel got up and walked slowly over to the door and closed it and then walked over to the window and stood there silently for sometime.

"What's your opinion of Apollo?" he asked Luke without turning around. Luke fought to control his initial desired response before speaking.

"I think he is a good developer and big picture thinker." Those were the only positive things that he could think of at the moment that he was willing to share about him. He thought Samuel was coughing or sneezing as he watched his body gently shaking against the backdrop of the window, then he recognized the noise that followed was gentle laughter. Samuel turned around and the smile on his face was clear and real. "Good company line response. Now tell me what you really think. I mean *really* think," he said the last part without the deep smile. Luke took a deep breath before continuing.

"What I really think? Hmm. Well he's self-focused, egotistical, arrogant, emotionless, and pretty much a megalomaniac... Sir." He tossed in the "Sir" to add a little humor to his response. Samuel nodded his head and smiled.

"Yep. That's a pretty darn accurate and succinct evaluation." He walked back over and sat down in his chair. "I appreciate you telling it like it is, Luke. Not only just now, but also during this morning's discussion. I need you to always tell it like you see it. Respectfully of course, but truthfully."

He began opening his briefcase as he continued,
"The last thing I need is another Apollo worshiping "yes man" on this project." He removed a file and pulled out a several page document printed on paper with an official looking letterhead. "This is a detailed letter from a Mr. Cliff Jackson of the Government Advisory Board that I believe you met in Iraq. There is also a letter from a Captain Tillman accompanying Mr. Jackson's letter. I received them yesterday, prior to your return." Samuel glanced briefly at Luke before continuing, "I must say that the two of them paint a far different picture of how things transpired in Iraq than what Mr. Walpole described in his briefing this morning." He looked up at Luke and then continued, "Luke, they are both letters of commendation and give full credit to your actions and words for the success of the Cat Eyes presentation. In fact, they do not even mention Mr. Walpole." He smiled and chuckled softly as he slid the letters over to Luke for him to read.

As he read through the letters, he could not help but remember the feeling of camaraderie he had experienced with them and the excitement of the time he spent there. The letters accurately described the training and demonstrations, along with the danger that Luke and the patrol had been in. He felt they were more than kind when describing his actions during those events. He slid them back over to Samuel once he had finished reading them.

"Are they an accurate assessment?" he asked Luke. Luke frowned and felt uncomfortable with the question or even how to answer it. He leaned back in his chair before answering.

"Well, I'm a little disappointed that they left out the part about me defusing a nuclear device with 3 seconds left and the part where I threw my body on a live grenade to save the

President of the United States during his surprise visit. Other than that, it was pretty accurate," he said with a deadpan look toward Samuel. Samuel only laughed as he put the letters back in his folder.

"I'll be sure to add those parts in for you." Once the letters were back inside his briefcase he leaned back in his chair and looked intently at Luke. Luke felt as if Samuel was measuring him for a suit. "You don't like where this product is headed do you Luke?"

Luke shook his head. "No. Not the vision Apollo has for the glasses. The military clearly needs the product and can benefit from it. We're talking about saving hundreds, even thousands of soldier's lives with it, and perhaps tens of thousands of civilian lives." Luke hesitated before he continued, searching for how best to express his next words. "The problem is that Apollo is right. Once this product is released, the hounds of hell will be chasing after it. Where will it end? What will history show that we unleashed on the world with this product? Forget the fact that we chose to only release it to the military, once it is out there it will take on a life of its own. It may have some noble uses, but I think that there are many ways that the system will be used incorrectly or dangerously." Luke looked up at Samuel to see if he was grasping what he was saying. "Can you see what I'm saying? It's a perfect product for someone who places no value on feelings or emotions or privacy, just black or white. In the wrong people's hands, this can be a horrible tool, or worse, a weapon."

"I know. I've been trying to get my arms around this as well. It all seemed so very exciting in the beginning when Apollo first pitched his concept to me. Once he got the government involved, I started seeing not only the potential, but the dangers it held as well. Now, I'm seeing more danger than potential. What's more, I'm not sure I have the ability to stop this thing, now that it is moving forward." Luke latched onto one of the words that Samuel had just said.

"You said 'his' concept. Based on our employee agreements, this is your product and you control the destiny of it. Right?" Luke added the question because he could tell that something was not setting well with Samuel.

"I have been working with Stanley Walpole for nearly 12 years now. He originally came to me with a clever game idea, which I invested in and helped him take it to market through my company. We both made a lot of money from that idea, a lot of money. Since then we have both made even more money on other ideas our developers have created and marketed." He hesitated and took a deep breath, "I know it's terrible business leadership, but one thing I never did during all of that was to get an employee agreement signed with Stanley following our initial partnership." He shook his head before he continued, "We made so much money on the first product and we worked so well together, that it didn't seem necessary. When things are going well, you don't think of such things." He looked at Luke almost with an embarrassed expression on his face.
h

"So it really is *His* product then?" Luke asked, but it sounded more like a statement than a question.

"Not technically, but I would have a great deal of difficulty trying to fight him for it in court. My attorneys have researched it and advised me that because he has such deep personal financial pockets, that we could very likely lose the long legal battle in court should we chose to take it there, so I have avoided it."

Luke was rocking back and forth in his chair as he listened to Samuel, then he stopped suddenly.

"So, why are you taking the time to tell me all of this?" Samuel took a deep breath and looked Luke in the eyes.

"Luke, I liked you when you were first hired for this project. When I received the letters of commendation yesterday from your Iraq visit, I knew you were a man of character and courage. The reason I'm telling you all this is that I need someone I can trust on the inside, which is why I pushed to have you added to the lead team. I need someone who has the same strong feelings and concerns about the product and the dangers of it as well. Someone who is willing to stand up and say the things I cannot say about it to those that need to hear it."

"Because if you say it, he will take his pet project to another company with less scruples and they will make it happen anyway," Luke interjected.

"Yes," he replied.

"Are you sure it's not about the potential loss of money if he were to do that?" Luke asked and Samuel seemed genuinely hurt by the comment.

"No, it's about losing control of my company. He's taking me down a path I feel I cannot control."

Luke let the silence of the statement sink in as he tried to figure out what role he was supposed to play in this whole game.

"So what is it that you expect me to do?" he asked Samuel.

He just shook his head and hunched his shoulders before answering.

"The right thing. When the defining moment comes, I just want you to do the right thing and help me to do the same," he said pausing only long enough to shrug his shoulders again. "I don't know when that time will come or what it will look like, but I just ask that you do the right thing when it does."

Luke sat, waiting for some specific direction; some clear and concise guidance from Samuel, but none came. He was not sure if he should laugh, cry or storm out of the room. He just sat there, baffled and speechless, trying to figure out what to do next, and then he slowly pushed his chair away from the table.

"Well not to spoil your confidence in me, but the 'right thing' that I need to do right now is find a bathroom," Luke announced with a smile as he stood up to leave the room and then paused at the door. Without looking at Samuel he said, "I think you may have picked the wrong man to do the right thing." He then opened the door and headed down the hallway.

Chapter 10

As Luke sat down at his desk, he slowly put his face into the palms of his hands and let it sit there. He could not believe how naïve he had been or how he could have missed the clear danger that this product posed until Apollo spelled it out for him Just like Samuel had said, during the past four months that he had worked for the company, he had been focused on the potential of the product and the specific use for the military. He had either lacked the time or the maturity to recognize the risk that it posed. Was he just too busy or had he simply refused to consider the real dangers that accompanied the development of such a technology? Maybe it came down to the fact that he just didn't care enough to even consider them.

Already he could see many new uses and misuses of the product. His mind raced as he once again began running down the many dangerous paths that the development could lead to. Depending upon your perspective, it either had incredible or terrible potential. The thought of it in someone like Apollo's hands, someone who lived life almost emotionlessly. He was always calculating and analyzing from his head, and his disconnection from all people was disconcerting to say the least. The matters of the heart, which were being completely neglected was what terrified him the most.

Hearing the tap on his cubicle wall, he removed his face from the palms of his hands to see who the intruder was. David Stevens stood at the entrance of his cubicle with a concerned look on his face.

"You okay?" he asked Luke, apparently sensing from the look on his face the pain and turmoil he was going through.

"Hey. Yeah. I'm okay. What can I do for you?" Luke asked, even though he had a pretty good idea as to what was coming next.

"Danielle mentioned that you were a little upset that she had gotten together with Susan while you were gone. I thought maybe you would like to talk about it? I'd hate to have any confusion or bad blood between us." He tossed the invitation out there as if to test the waters.

Luke had so many feelings and thoughts running through his head that he was afraid he was going to lose it with someone at any moment. The fact that this guy's wife somehow coerced his girlfriend away from him while he was gone only made things more frustrating. His first reaction was to yell at him and tell him to get away from his cubicle, but he resisted the urge. The fact is he had come to really like David. He had been the first person to befriend him when he started working at the company. He liked his sense of humor, his quick wit and his level headedness during tough times. He was a great and well-respected programmer, although he was not the social animal of the office by any means. Not a social reject, just not someone that you'd go and get buzzed after work with. It was almost as if he had subliminally set his moral boundaries with Luke pretty early in their relationship and apparently, they stuck, because when it came to the party life that he and Danielle enjoyed, he knew better than to even ask. A feeling stuck in Luke's craw at the last thought. Was it guilt that they had used to sway Danielle? God, he hated religion and what it did to people.

Luke responded softly, but sternly. "Talk about it? What exactly is it that you would like us to talk about David? You mean the fact that you and your wife broke up Danielle and I with your religious perspective? If that is what you want to talk about, I'm definitely not interested."

David nodded his head as Luke let the words flow in and around his cubicle before responding in a gentle but confident voice.

"I guess it could look like that from where you are sitting. I can assure you that breaking you two up was not our purpose. It goes a lot deeper than that." Luke knew he was just being selfish and that his words to David were uncalled for and even mean, and he knew he needed to get a handle on things quickly.

"I know, David. I'm sorry for saying that. It's just been a tough day."

"Anything I can help with?" It was just like David to offer someone help right after they verbally spit on him. Luke thought that he would be a good friend if he was not so religious.

"Naw. Just work stuff." Luke turned toward his desk as if saying he needed to get back to work. David seemed to take the hint.

"Well if you change your mind on needing help or wanting to talk, or both, let me know," he said as he turned to leave the opening of his cubicle. Before he realized he had done so, Luke could not help but ask him a question,
"David, if you had to pick between freedom and truth, which one would choose?" David walked back to the opening of the cubicle. He seemed to think a moment and then answered.

"The fact that you are allowing me to choose between the two options tells me I already have freedom." He smiled cleverly, which then Luke nodded in agreement and raised an eyebrow.

"Alright wise guy, then let me ask it differently." Luke gave a joking semi-glare toward David and then continued, "If you could have the power to know the difference between what is true and what is false at every moment, would you want that power?"

David seemed at first taken aback by his question, and then he seemed to realize that Luke was dead serious. "That is an interesting question, Luke. In Genesis 2, I think verse 15, God gave man that same choice in the Garden of Eden," David said and then stopped and seemed to be waiting for Luke.
"You mean the "don't eat the apples" story?" Luke joked and waited, but David just smiled. Luke did not have the patience to play the 'who will speak first game' and wanted to get to the answer. Unfortunately he could not remember anything about the story other than Adam and Eve being naked, fig leaves and apples. "No pun intended, but which one did they pick?" he said impatiently. David just shook his head.

"You're going to have to read it for yourself. When you get home tonight, dust off that old Bible of yours and read Genesis chapters 1-3. It's the first book of the Bible." David stated. "You do have a Bible right?"

Luke at first nodded and then felt convicted by his own question on truth and shook his head no. David held up his hand as if to say, "wait" and walked away from the cubicle. Luke stood up and said,

"David, I don't need a Bi…" he stopped himself before yelling the last word across the top of the cubicle. David was already ducking into his own cubicle and dropping out of sight below the top walls. Luke looked around to see if anyone had heard him, and although no one was looking in his direction, he felt embarrassed.

David's head suddenly popped back into view and he headed back toward Luke's cubicle again. As he entered the opening, he held out a small leather book for Luke to take.

"Borrow mine and read it tonight when you get home." Luke started to shake his head no, but David continued. "Bring it back when you're done. I have several of them at home." Luke was more interested in getting David to stop talking about the issue than arguing about whether or not he would 'borrow' his Bible, so he reached out and took hold of it and gave it a quick thumb roll across the pages, quickly scanning the pages from start to end. For a Bible, it was a lot smaller than he remembered them being. The one he remembered as a kid was 5 inches thick, 20 inches high and wide and it sat on its own wooden stand at home in the living room. He could not remember seeing either of his parents ever read it; it seemed to be used as more of a decorative item.

"Thanks. I'll try to take a quick look tonight and get it back to you." He looked up at David. "You sure you don't want to just tell me and save us both some time?"

"Are you kidding? And miss the chance at telling everyone I got you to read the Bible! Never," David said in a low voice and a smile and then whispered as he looked around for some invisible spy, "I promise I won't say anything." Even though Luke knew David was kidding around, he actually believed that David would keep his word.

"If I should forget next time, remind me to never ask you a question." Luke said as David was leaving his cubicle. Luke turned back toward his computer and the leather book sitting on his desk. He did not see David stick his head back around the edge of the door so his words initially surprised him.

"I'll expect a full book report on my desk first thing in the morning." Then he ducked back out of sight before Luke could answer.

Luke glanced back at the leather book and wondered how their discussion managed to go from a question on 'truth' to reading the first several chapters of the Bible. That was probably how they got Danielle to read it as well. He had to admit that he was curious as to how his question related to the Garden of Eden, so he quickly tucked the book into his briefcase before someone saw it. He decided to postpone making the decision about whether or not to read it until later that evening.

Luke stayed in the building for lunch and just grabbed a quick snack from the lunchroom vending machine. He kept chewing on the words that Samuel had said to him and how he should respond to Apollo. He sketched some ideas down and mentally worked through the various potential endings and dangers of each strategy. He ended up deciding that the best course at present was to go back to a less aggressive approach and regain what little confidence Apollo might have in him.

At 2:00 p.m. the meeting started again and Luke noticed that Apollo was acting more distant toward Samuel than he had ever seen him. Luke asked if he could say something as they started the meeting and apologized to both Samuel and Apollo for getting a little too emotional earlier in his responses. That after his discussion with Samuel, he acknowledged and agreed that the product would be taken to the market either by us or someone else, and that it would be better financially for everyone if it was handled and controlled by their company. Samuel acted right along with the unrehearsed speech and accepted his apology. He even went as far as to issue a verbal rebuke to Luke for not keeping his emotions in check during such meetings. That the position he held was an incredible opportunity for him and one that could be taken away if he could not work effectively with the members of this key group. Even though he knew it was part of Samuel's plan, the whole rebuke did not sit well with him inside. In spite of it, Luke nodded and said that he understood, that he was grateful for another opportunity to prove himself.

Although it didn't seem to soften Apollo's rigid demeanor toward him, it did seem to change Apollo's stance toward Samuel. As the meeting continued, he could feel the initial strain between the two of them ease and return almost to a normal state. Samuel seemed to be adopting a similar strategy to Luke's and engaged more with Apollo during the rest of the afternoon. He still took on the role of 'what if' and Apollo would have a ready response lined up as if he had been waiting for that very question. Samuel would just nod his head and Apollo would move to the next topic. Luke had to fight hard not to visibly show his emotions when they touched on various topics on how the Cat Eyes in the form of a civilian product could affect various areas of privacy. Apollo saw its uses as having a great value without giving the same weight to the dangers to the freedom of people whom the glasses were to be used on.

By the time that the meeting was finally wrapped up, Luke felt even more concerned about the impact the Cat Eyes would have on the world, but he held them in and played along, towing the company line as best he could. Apollo challenged Luke to build a translation manual and training program that could be used to teach and train the end user of the product. Luke had already been working on that, but had a hunch that the main goal was to get something tangible and useful in their hands quickly in the event that Luke was no longer needed as an employee of the company.

Samuel led the way as they walked out of the conference room; he turned right and headed to his office, while Apollo, Ronald and Jonathan headed left ahead of him. As Luke stepped into the hallway behind them, he glanced to the right to see Samuel looking over his shoulder at him. He saw a brief wink and a half smile as he turned down another hallway out of sight. Luke thought that if he was to have only one ally in this mess, the president of the company was probably a good one to have, even though Samuel would not publicly acknowledge him as one.

Luke realized that it was after hours as he headed to his cubicle and that all but the hardcore programmers and support center representatives had gone home. He saw that Danielle had already left and then almost instinctively looked over to where David's desk was and saw that he too had gone for the day. He was accustomed to seeing her waiting for him to finish so that they could go and grab a bite to eat together after work. Things were definitely different now. He was not sure what the feeling was that he felt inside, was it anger, jealousy; bitterness? *Lonely* seemed to be the most accurate word to describe it. He hated that word.

On his way home, he swung by a grocery store in his neighborhood to replenish his cupboards and refrigerator after being gone so long. As he went up and down the aisles, he found himself staring at the people shopping and could not help but wonder about the impact the Cat Eyes would eventually have on each of them. One attractive lady smiled at him and he thought about Danielle and his relationship and how it had gone south. How the Cat Eyes would surely help him in the dating realm. He could determine whether his date's mindset was love or lust, he could better understand their motives, he'd even be able to know when he said the wrong thing during a conversation. He thought that next to World Peace and finding the cure for the common cold, being able to help men understand women would bring Venus and Mars a whole lot closer. There was a pain in his chest when he thought of being able to observe when someone else was more interesting or attractive to his date than he was, whether it was in the mall, at dinner or out dancing.

He let his mind race down the multitude of opportunities that would be available to him and others, but then like a cold slap on the face, the thought of someone else using them on him was horrifying. The thought of having his layers of character weakness and the social mechanism that he used to cover them up suddenly stripped away and laid bare before someone was very unnerving.

He stopped by his cell phone provider store to get a new belt case for his phone. As he waited for his turn, he watched the salespeople asking leading questions and then "up selling" the various customers toward the available products. The thought of a salesperson having the power to see the buying emotions of a prospective client was just as frightening. It would give them a powerful and overwhelming advantage over the buying client.

The "have" and the "have nots" would always be the story of the world. The advantages of possessing something before anyone else and what it gave to the individual, to the organization, or to the government turned his stomach. Weapons like rifles, cannons, tanks, missiles, and nuclear bombs, were all momentary advantages until the playing field was leveled by everyone else having the same weapon. As the advantage was slowly lost, it would be replaced by the next hig-tech advantage. It was the same for any product or service. Computers, industrial, home products, shaving blades, it was all just a big game of technology leapfrog. Why was this any different?

Luke felt himself trying to justify that the Cat Eyes was just another one of those inventions that would give someone a momentary advantage, but deep down he knew that the list he just rattled off in his head were physical and tangible items outside the realm of the human being. The Cat Eyes impacted the non-tangible element of mankind, a place that was far more secret, protected and personal. It was an area that deep down no one wanted to have exposed to anyone other than their closest friends. Yet he also knew that such power was something that everyone wanted. Apollo was right when he pointed out that Luke had not seen a problem with it when he was the only one using it.

The last part hit him like a ton of bricks. He knew that the two most important motivators for buyers are fear and greed. From a company's perspective, it was the perfect product.

Marketing programs could be designed to appeal to the greed of those wanting to have advantages over others. Or, to those wanting power, they could focus their marketing concept toward the fear of not having it when someone else does. Until the playing field was leveled, the point in time when everyone has one, the advantages to those owning Cat Eyes were almost limitless.

Luke was sure of one thing; that if everyone had the glasses, it would totally change the dynamics of human communication and interaction. He tried to imagine every feeling, or emotion, or motive he was having at any given moment being laid bare before the world. The thought terrified him. He could almost hear Apollo's voice sending out a rebuttal to his concern; "But if everyone had a pair, then the only thing that would change is that no one could lie. They would say what they meant and even if they didn't say it, you could still read the truth in their aura." But deep down, he knew otherwise.

He was so engaged in that train of thought that he didn't hear the salesman asking him if he needed any help until the more insistent,

"Sir, can I help you!" brought him back to the moment. He started to reply, but he could not clear his head enough to remember the exact reason he was in the store, so rather embarrassed by the moment, he just said,

"Uh... no thanks." Then rather sheepishly left the store. Once outside he remembered why he was there, but felt a new cell phone belt case could wait.

Chapter 11

As he sat down at his coffee table to eat the "just microwave" meal in a box and the glass of wine he had poured himself, he could not believe how quiet it was. Perhaps the best word to describe it, and he hated to use it again, was *lonely*. He absently flipped through some TV channels but could not find anything that caught his attention long enough to stay with it. He decided to put together some of his notes from work so that his next workday would be less stressful.

As he opened his briefcase and pulled out the various folders, he saw the little brown book that David had loaned him. He lifted it out and flipped through the pages. The paper was so thin and delicate, almost transparent, that he was afraid he would tear the pages as he turned them. No pictures, just words. He set it back down on the table away from his work area.

He worked on organizing his various training files and after completing each one he would glance at the little brown book on the table. By the time he was working on the third file, he found himself once again battling with the ethical questions that the use of the Cat Eyes generated. He tried to remember what chapter it was that David had said to read. Was it chapter 2? He got up for a drink of water and came back to the table. As he sipped the water, he just stared at the brown book and battled the conflicting urges to either put it away or read the chapter. He finally gave in and grabbed the book and opened it to the first chapter, or book of Genesis, as David had called it. Then he skipped ahead to chapter 2.

Almost as if he was in a hurry to get it over with, starting in verse 1 he read quickly about God creating the earth, resting on the seventh day, then about creating Adam, then about the Garden of Eden. He reread one part about the garden again in verse 8 and 9 where it said:

8 Now the LORD God had planted a garden in the east, in Eden; and there he put the man he had formed. 9 And the LORD God made all kinds of trees grow out of the ground—trees that were pleasing to the eye and good for food. In the middle of the garden were the **tree of life** *and* **the tree of the knowledge of good and evil**.

That's odd, he thought. God put 2 special trees, not just the one he remembered that everyone talked about. One was a tree of life, the other a tree of the knowledge *of good and evil*. He thought for awhile about the significance of the two trees, but decided not to spend too much time dwelling on it, as he was more concerned about finding the answer to his question. He read about rivers flowing to the garden. One was the Tigris and the other the Euphrates. He realized that those rivers flowed through Iraq. He was talking about Iraq. Was that where the Garden of Eden was located? *What a mess of a place to put a garden*, he thought as he kept reading. When he got to verse 15, he remembered that this was where David said he'd find the answer to his question about if he would want the power to know the difference between what was true and false.

15 The LORD God took the man and put him in the Garden of Eden to work it and take care of it. 16 And the LORD God commanded the man, "You are free to eat from any tree in the garden; 17 but you must not eat from the tree of the knowledge of good and evil, for when you eat of it you will surely die."

He read it several times, then went back and read verses 8 and 9 again, then back to this one. He saw that there were no rules about eating from the Tree of Life, but God told Adam not to eat from the Tree of Knowledge of good and evil. The consequence of doing so would be death. He could not help wanting to keep reading a little further even though he felt he knew the story and the ending. He read about Eve being created to be with Adam, being naked and feeling no shame in the end of Genesis 2. In Genesis 3, Satan comes as a snake to trick Eve, using the age-old tool of fear and greed. *Fear* that she was lied to by God, and *Greed* that she could become like God.

5 "For God knows that when you eat of it **your eyes will be opened**, *and you will be like God, knowing good and evil."*

He read verse 5 several times, the last time it was out loud to himself. "Your eyes will be opened, and you will be like God, knowing good and evil." He set the book down on the table and stood up and walked around the room. He could not help but relate the Cat Eyes product to this scripture. The ability to know good and evil. You will be like God.

After awhile, he went back to the book and finished reading chapter 3 where Adam and Eve's "eyes were opened" and their relationships with each other, and with God, were forever changed by choosing to eat the fruit and to know good and evil. The last 3 verses of the chapter confirmed that mankind had become like God (the knowledge of good and evil) and answered his internal question about what happened to the Tree of Life.

They gave up everything, even apparently eternal life, all for the ability to know good and evil. *Interesting story,* he thought to himself. He considered the question he asked David that started this whole thing: "If you could have the power to know the difference between what is true and what is false at every moment, would you want that power?" Luke realized that they had chosen knowledge and if you believed the story, then that is why things are the way they are today. So would choosing even "more knowledge" in this case, the ability that the Cat Eyes would provide to really know the difference between good and evil, would that make things worse, or as Apollo thinks, make things better? Perhaps a "correcting" of the problem that the world now faced as a result of the apparent choice that was made in the fairy tale story of the Garden of Eden?

He set the brown book back down on the table again and just stared off into space thinking about what he had just read. He spent a great deal of time considering and sorting through his personal perspective, as well as the big picture view of things laid out from both a religious and a humanistic perspective. His conclusion was that the tale of Genesis was a clever story, but it seemed to imply that mankind held their destiny in their own hands, and were not controlled by some higher power.

He thought through things for the hundredth time that day. The concluding vision of the future that he could see unfolding was one of everyone doing everything from behind a video screen. Since the Cat Eyes only worked when viewing a subject directly, people would do their best to mask their internal tells, hiding behind other forms of technology. All important interpersonal interactions like business deals, purchases, even dating would be guarded and played like a poker hand. Luke foresaw a very impersonal world coming, just the way Apollo liked it.

He then thought about history and how through time, things had been moving in that direction anyway. Almost all business communication had to be conducted in person until the invention of the printing press. Then the next big change in how we communicated was the invention of the phone; then radio and then TV. More recently was the advent of the Internet. He took it all in and decided that this was just the next communication technology advancement in a long line of past and future inventions. However, he continued to think through the impact of each one of those advances and tried to determine if each advance had brought people closer or driven people toward building impersonal relationships? He rubbed his brow to relieve the cramps that were beginning to form from having been wrinkled for hours.

Whether it was just to allow himself to move on from the endless loop, or a decision to give up trying to solve these questions, he decided that it still came down to the character of a person using the technology. Great writers moved the world with the printing press. Confident speakers on the phone could influence a heart or change a mind. A great writer coupled with a gifted orator on the radio or TV could sway or convince a listener or viewer to adopt a specific viewpoint or purchase a product. The internet simply allowed everyone the ability to broadcast their wisdom, or lack of, or their product, whether good or bad. He decided that people and the basic things they do have not changed; we're just using different technologies.

He put away his notes and headed to his bedroom. He fought off the routine urge to call Danielle to say good night and just crawled into bed. As he closed his eyes, the sleep he wanted did not come easily that night.

***

As he walked through the building on the way to his desk the next morning, he checked to see if David was in his cubicle. Finding that he was not, he quietly walked into it and left the brown book he had loaned him on his desk with a typed note attached to the top of it.

Thanks for the loan and perspective. I'd still like to know your own answer. I'm not signing this or even writing this with my own hand to avoid it being traced back to me. Good luck proving you got me to read it. ☺

He smiled at his cleverness as he quickly moved toward his desk and slipped quietly into his chair. In the exact place where he set the brown book on David's desk, was a paper bag with something inside it on his own desk. *Was it from Danielle?* he thought and his heart skipped a beat before he got control of his feelings and pushed it to the side as if it was no big deal. He took a moment to put things away, then slowly opened the bag. Inside was a small box wrapped in newspaper.

He removed the wrapping, revealing a box that appeared to contain a Bible. As he lifted the top off, inside was a card sitting on top of a brown leather covered book. It was the same picture of a camel in the desert that Danielle had given him on the plane. Luke set the card aside a moment and removed the book from the box and slowly opened the cover to see the same gold edged pages of soft, delicate paper. He set the book down and opened the card to see what she had written.

Even a camel needs a drink of water every now and then. This book is a canteen of living water should you choose to drink from it. I was going to have it engraved with your name, but I wanted to make sure you would have plausible deniability should someone see you with it. ☺

I hope you found the answer you were looking for in mine. I'm always available to talk if you need me.

David

David? Although he smiled at the words, his heart felt hurt to find that the gift was not from Danielle. He read the words again, and put the book back in the box and then into the paper bag. After looking at it sitting on his desk a moment, he decided to put it in his briefcase. He realized he had felt nervous with it sitting there. Was he hiding it, afraid of it, or just getting it off of his desk? He decided it was all three.

Luke spent the majority of his morning transferring and inputting his notes from the previous night into the company database. A meeting alert window popped up on his computer screen, reminding him of the morning "update" with Apollo in fifteen minutes. Apollo scheduled these meetings every day, at the same time, for the next two weeks to keep on top of each individual's progress. Luke guessed that it was more a matter of keeping an eye on him and his 'attitude' than on his overall progress.

They spent the first 20 minutes of the meeting going over the training manual and testing parameters that Luke had suggested and had begun to implement. Then Apollo spent some time firing questions at him that seemed to be more about exploring his ethical concerns than his loyalty to the company.

"Have you had any more thoughts or concerns about the project?" he asked Luke. Luke knew he needed to walk carefully here, without appearing to be too evasive. He had already played his cards and revealed his feelings during the last meeting, so suddenly jumping on board and agreeing with everything would not be believable. After careful thought on the matter, he decided to 'hide in plain sight' when it came to dealing with this issue.

"Actually I have," he responded and let it sink in for a moment as if he was still wrestling with it, then continued. "I think we would both agree that the development of the product will change not only the way in which we communicate with each other, but the clarity of it. How do you propose we address the questions of confidentiality that will be raised from the masses once its capabilities becomes public knowledge?"

Apollo seemed to be weighing his words carefully or perhaps he was weighing the person asking the question.

"Can you describe your concern in greater detail?" Apollo finally responded. Luke leaned forward as if to share a secret with Apollo.

"I was thinking last night that we're going to get pounded by a few small but influential groups that will feel it drives people further into themselves and away from each other. We need to be ready with a powerful and unified response before the media and any concerned individuals (conservatives and liberals alike) tear into it," Luke shared as if deeply concerned.

"Well how would you respond? What would you suggest?" Apollo asked.

His mental rebuttal came easy, but he needed to weigh his words carefully.

"I think there will be three types of mindsets we will need to address. I think we can win over two of the three, but the third we will not. The company will need a strong message in place to share with the media to counter their opposition." Apollo seemed surprised by Luke's candor and openness.

"Tell me about them." Apollo's request came across more as an order than a request.

"Well, there will be those like yourself that embrace the technology and the opportunity and clarity it delivers. There will be a second group that will initially resist it, or feel extremely threatened by it, but simply needs a good reason to either embrace it or to justify the use of it. The last group will fight it to the end."

"So how do you propose we handle the last group?" Apollo asked.

"By simply exposing their weakness and fears before they can voice their concerns," he responded. Luke could see that Apollo was not sure exactly what he meant, but he wanted to wait for him to raise a question before continuing. Unfortunately, it was one of his gophers that fired the question out.

"What do you mean by that?" Ronald asked.

"You qualify and discredit them before they speak," Apollo answered for Luke.

"Correct. You essentially turn the tables on them before they can fire their first rebuttal," Luke replied with a smile and nodded toward Apollo.

"I still don't understand exactly what that means," Ronald responded and waited for someone to fill him in. Luke could tell that Apollo was going to wait for him to answer, so he continued.

"For example, we might say something like this; 'We understand that this product will not be disliked and resisted strongly by those that have a lot of skeletons in their closets. We understand that there will be those that might choose to hide from the world, instead of being real and changing their ways to join with it. This product is for those that are not afraid of whom they are, with a willingness to see people get even more real with each other. You will be able to sit down with a potential business associate or employee and know if someone is lying to you or not. Can they really deliver their product on time or not. Does their product really do what they say it can do? The Cat Eyes gives them the ability to look eyeball to eyeball and know the truth." Luke finished with, "Or something to that effect."

Apollo interjected another thought, "Or perhaps it's your wife or girlfriend. Having one of those face-to-face 'moment of truth' talks on whether they are cheating on you, or whether they love you or love your money? I think it will actually drive people to each other more, not less."

Luke nodded in apparent agreement with Apollo's interjection, but inside he was wondering if his last comment was the main reason for Apollo's need of the glasses, the clarity of relationships?

"So people will think that anyone who opposes this is actually hiding something." Ronald almost looked excited about the opportunity to twist this around on someone.

"Correct," Luke said with a smile, but inside he felt ashamed.

The rest of the meeting went pretty much as planned with Apollo giving directions and advice on every matter to his two gophers, but there was a marked change in the relationship between Luke and Apollo. Not a full trust, but perhaps a level of confidence that Luke had somehow worked through his "issues" and was part of the team. Even Ronald and Jonathan treated Luke differently after the morning's discussion. He just needed to think of a way to "close the deal" on this new trust.

As they broke from the meeting, Luke asked Apollo if he had a moment to speak on a private matter. At first he seemed to hesitate, then agreed and sat back down while Ronald and Jonathan gathered their files and headed out of the conference room. Luke smiled at both of them as they left and then nodded back toward Apollo.

"Thanks for the extra time," Luke offered up to break the silence.

"What can I do for you?"

Luke seemed to hesitate before answering Apollo. "Apollo, we both know that I'm not in total agreement with how the Cat Eyes should be used, or even if they should be used at all outside of military applications," he said confidently. "But I also have come to realize that this product will be taken to market whether or not I support it and that the best place for me is to be financially and politically on board with it, not walking away from it." Luke let his words sink in a moment and took a deeper breath. "I guess what I'm trying to say in more words than are needed, is that I'm sorry for my outburst yesterday and the disrespect I displayed to both you and Mr. Carr in front of Ronald and Jonathan. I'd appreciate another opportunity to be considered and accepted by you as a valuable part of this team." He took a deep breath after finishing the last part. Apollo seemed to puff up and gave a small smirk before leaning forward to answer him.

"You did a lot of damage yesterday," Apollo hesitated before continuing, "and your impulsive behavior almost cost us the deal in Iraq, so I must say that it is hard for me to just jump at your sudden 'change of heart' and welcome you back without some deep apprehension and concern." Apollo was speaking coldly, yet his body language had a smugness about it. Luke knew that Apollo was enjoying the moment and dragging it out purposely to really drive home the point that he held all the cards there. It was pretty much what Luke had expected to see from him; no grace or humility or appreciation, just pouncing on the opportunity.

Luke was not really sure if it was his own pride kicking in, an inner desire to get out of the whole situation, or just a gut instinct, but he decided to call Apollo's bluff. He nodded his head at Apollo's word and let a frown come across his face.

"I understand. We live and learn from our mistakes and this one was obviously a big one for me." Luke pushed his chair away from the table and stood up seeing Apollo bask in the glow of Luke's humble disposition. "Thank you for the opportunity to work with you and my sincere apologies to everyone. I will have my resignation on your desk and Mr. Carr's desk this afternoon." It was only for a moment, but Luke saw that his response was a complete surprise to Apollo and not wanting to miss the opportunity; he stopped at the door and continued, "Would you prefer that I notify Mr. Carr personally or would you like to speak with him on this issue?"

Apparently the pause gave Apollo enough time to collect his response. "I… I can speak with him," Apollo responded, which was not the response Luke expected or wanted. Did Apollo just call his bluff?

"Okay, thanks." Luke gave a somewhat sad smile to Apollo. *So it ends here,* Luke thought and smiled as if grateful and headed out the door, but before the door closed behind him, Apollo spoke again.

"Why don't you…" Luke stopped at his words and looked back at Apollo, not quite sure about what he was asking. When the pause seemed longer than he wanted, he tried to clarify the situation.

"You would prefer that I speak with him?" Luke asked and Apollo seemed confused by Luke's question.

"No. Why don't you come back in and sit down a moment," Apollo said with a somewhat less than confident voice. Luke acted confused by the moment and truthfully inside he was not sure if he was excited or disappointed at the change in the direction of the situation. He knew he needed to be careful during the next few moments and that the situation was extremely fragile. One slip would end the game that he was playing.

"Uhh, sure," he replied as he closed the door and slowly sank back into the chair and waited for Apollo to start the new dialog. It took a lot longer than he expected for Apollo to begin.

"Luke, you have potential strengths that you bring to this team and I'm sure you would agree that we have invested a lot of training and time in you."

"Yes you have," he responded in agreement wondering if Apollo would go the full distance and invite him back, or if he was planning on making Luke ask for his job back.

"It would be unfortunate to have to start over with someone new."

It was not the most heart moving response, but knowing whom it was coming from, Apollo probably saw it as a huge emotional concession and it was about as good as Luke could expect. He was still not willing to give in just yet and let him off the hook.

"I'm not sure I'm following you, exactly." He put it back on Apollo hoping he had not taken their mini chess match too far.

"If you are willing to submit to some basic team rules, I would be willing to give you a second chance." Luke now felt that he pushed Apollo too far and although he got him to ask him back, it allowed him to include a set of rules to live by. Not at all what he was looking at or wanting. *Serves me right,* he thought.

"Wow, thank you for the opportunity. May I ask what the rules are that you have in mind?" As difficult as it was, Luke tried to put his best 'Thank you for the opportunity' face on as he spoke the words. Apollo seemed to be weighing his next words carefully, not wanting to miss the opportunity to gain some serious advantages.

"Well for one, I expect you to spend some time with the team outside the office," Apollo stated. Luke hesitated and waited for the bigger rule. The silence became uncomfortable for both of them as Luke realized that either no additional requirements would be set by Apollo, or that he had not formulated any just yet. Luke hoped to keep any additional rules out of the picture.

"That's a reasonable request that I can agree too." Luke was not excited about hanging with 'the team' but knowing that he was now single, he did have a lot more spare time available than before. "I also appreciate that you are keeping the 'rules' simple. Thank you for the second chance; you won't regret it." Luke knew he needed to move quickly away from the rules topic before Apollo started tossing out more of them as conditions to his reconsidered employment.

"What is on the team agenda for tonight?" he asked with a smile still trying to keep Apollo from adding additional requirements. Luke was not sure if Apollo looked surprised by the question, or disappointed, but Apollo soon stepped in and began a discourse about a sushi bar that they were going to be meeting at for dinner.

"Well if the invitation is open, I'll see you there?" Luke asked as he stood up to leave, wondering if he could get out of there before Apollo came up with further requirements. Apollo stood up and seemed to be about to speak, and then changed his mind. Finally he added, "Yes, of course. 6:30. Don't be late." The last line was delivered with an almost awkward smile, followed by Apollo gathering his briefcase and heading out the door. Luke held the door open for him as he left.

As Luke followed him out, he could not help but wonder if Apollo now classified him as one of his team, fully on board or if he simply saw Luke as an enemy that he was now keeping closer. All he knew was that he was not looking forward to an evening with Apollo, Jonathan and Ronald at some sushi bar. A trip back to Iraq somehow sounded more appealing. How in the world did he keep ending up in these situations? "I hate sushi," he mumbled to himself as he walked back to his desk.

He finished out the day laying the foundation for the user manual that Apollo had tasked him with and emailed an overview for his review and feedback. Normally he would not have done this until it was almost finished, but he decided that if he was going to play the "team game" that he was going to play it 100%. He also asked Apollo if he should also copy Mr. Carr, Ronald and Jonathan on the progress and to his surprise, Apollo replied back, "No, just me for now. They have enough on their plates at the moment."

So much for the team, Luke thought and then smiled at the vision of Apollo gathering his power base around him. Unfortunately, Luke also knew that having Apollo be the single gatekeeper of information, for all information, was a dangerous role to play within a company structure.

Luke saved the response to his encrypted portable backup disk as a "just in case" plan should things go sideways and he fell further from Apollo's grace. *You can never be too safe in these situations,* he thought.

He did his best to smile and nod at Ronald and Jonathan when they passed by each other, which seemed to somehow make their day. Unfortunately, the byproduct of that acknowledgment was that they began to 'swing by' his desk to touch bases more often than he preferred. A text chat message opened on his screen *"New best friends?"* He saw that it came from Anita, a few cubicles down. He also saw that three other individuals were included in the chat as well. She was always ready to get something started on the office 'chat line' when anything juicy was afoot. Normally he would be quick and willing to jump into the bash sessions on a moment's notice. He thought about making fun of the situation and had even typed a response, but he knew that it could get back to the wrong people, so he held back and deleted the initial response and typed; *"Big project that we are working on together."* and left it at that.

After a long pause, the computer flashed another message.

"That's it? Very disappointing 'Deep Cover 1'. I was expecting a lot more from you. ☺" Anita replied.

"Yeah! Give us the dirt on what's happening." Walt from support jumped in. He knew he had to stop this or it would steam roll into something bigger.

"Sorry, just work," he replied and tried to keep his focus and theirs on work but he knew it was too late.

"They must have some compromising pictures of him while he was in Iraq."

"Come on, your secrets are safe with us! ☺"

Before long the chat discussion had digressed into various directions and humorous conspiracy theories. Luke just minimized the dialog box and kept working.

He didn't mind being the butt of the joke for the most part, but something inside told him that this felt different. He was crossing over to the other side of the gossip club and knew that by not participating, he would soon fall out of the graces of the chat group. He looked at the names involved and did not see Danielle's name in there, which was strange as she was usually one of the leaders going 'tit for tat' with Anita's clever remarks.

Later in the day as he walked by several cubicles, he saw that chat windows were open and the office buzz persisted, but when he got back to his desk, the blank screen told him that he was not part of it. As he looked out over the tops of the cubicles, he couldn't help but wonder how much of it was about him? What were they saying? They even seemed to be treating him differently now, or at least it felt that way when he was in the break room. His mind was racing before he suddenly stopped himself.

Wow! he thought. He had never cared what anyone was typing about before, why now? Why the paranoia? Did he feel guilty about the role he was playing with Apollo? Did he feel that he had somehow betrayed the group?

He saw Jonathan walking down the aisle and he was glancing over at various cubicles as he passed them. Was he wondering the same thing? Was this how he and Ronald felt every time they walked through the area? Like an outsider? Luke slowly sat back down in his chair and contemplated whether to feel angry toward the rest of the office or guilty that he had participated in it as well. Were they really that shallow and immature? Was he?

In the middle of those thoughts, David crossed his mind. He had not thanked him for the gift. He quickly started to type a very clever, heartfelt and personal message to send to him, but he suddenly stopped as his cursor hovered over the send button. Maybe the silent treatment he was getting from the office was not about Apollo, but was about the whole Bible thing? Was David talking about it to people, or maybe Danielle?

He slowly erased the long message and simply sent over a *"Thanks for the book and for not saying anything to anyone about it."* He added a smiley face and hit send.

***

On the way to the sushi restaurant later that night, Luke continued to battle with all the feelings he had about what was unfolding around him. He could feel his heart racing, his head was spinning, he felt paranoid and his self-esteem was just about shot. It was hard enough having to deal with the whole concept of morality and the potential "world changing" results of the Cat Eyes, but adding the pressure of playing "undercover spy" for the president of the company without a clear mission or objective was nuts. Toss on top of that the break-up with Danielle because of her religious awakening, followed by the less than enviable position of becoming the target for the office chat of the week, and now having to play buddies with Apollo and his lackeys, well it was way too much for him to process. The simple, normal life that he had worked so hard to perfect these past 27 years suddenly seemed completely messed up and out of control. He felt like he was going to explode trying to hold it all together.

As he sat in the dark parking lot of the restaurant, all he could do was take a few deep breaths to help him calm down. He thought about driving away and just leaving the whole thing behind him. As he reached for the ignition switch of his car, a sudden heavy knock on the driver's window startled him. As he looked through the window he could see Jonathan smiling at him.

"Are you coming?" Jonathan asked him in a voice that sounded like a kid waiting to go into the Disneyland front gates.

Caught off guard, Luke simply sat there for a moment and collected his thoughts. "Yeah… yeah, I'm coming," he said as he pulled the keys out of the ignition and opened the door of the car and stepped out. He and Jonathan walked toward the restaurant and Luke felt a little calmer as he noticed that Jonathan seemed more nervous about being with him, than he was with being with Jonathan.

"This is the best sushi bar in the city. You like sushi right?" Jonathan asked in the same excited voice.

"Uhh, yeah, some of it's okay," Luke said, even though he didn't find uncooked fish appealing in any fashion no matter how much wasabi or ginger root he covered it with. It was the texture more than the taste that he disliked the most.

As they stepped into the restaurant, Jonathan immediately began searching for Apollo and Ronald while Luke stood at the reception desk and surveyed the room. Luke remembered why he never went there and it was not because the food wasn't cooked. It was because it was one of the best places "to be seen" in the community. Whenever he and Danielle would go there, he always felt that everyone was trying to wear "who they wanted to be" on the outside, to compensate for "who they were not" on the inside. They were "posers" as Danielle had called them, who sat around in their expensive suits and dresses sporting the latest and most stylish hairstyles, watches and cell phones. Danielle always seemed to notice the shoes, clothes and purses that the women either wore. Then there were the wannabe posers who are doing their best to fill the role, but fell short due to either a lack of money, looks, power or perhaps naïveté of the whole game. *Maybe they just didn't care what others thought?* Luke considered as he raised an eyebrow. Truthfully, it was a great place to sit back and watch people at their best or more often than not, their worst, as they played their roles in their fantasy world for all the other role players to see.

He had to smile at the thought of acting out role playing games in college, sitting around drinking beer, eating pizza and rolling dice with his buddies while they were acting out the role of a dwarf or elf based on Tolkien's Middle Earth. He smiled at how dorky he always felt about it, but truthfully, he actually had a lot of fun playing it. His overweight and less than athletic buddies seemed to always play spry elves, and his skinny and frail buddies played the stocky dwarves or big barbarians. Each pretended that he or she a hero destined to accomplish great things, and that their alter ego character was an extension of themselves and not a mere contrivance. Strangely enough, in the game, the players managed to ignore the actual appearance of the person across from them and would mentally replace them with the character they were playing.

Luke smiled as he realized that most of those in the restaurant were role playing out the same thing, the only differences were that it cost a lot more money to play this game. At least he and his buddies were real clear that the role or character they were playing was 'just a game.' But there, Luke was sadly confident that most people really believed they were who they were trying to "role-play" and had even successfully convinced many other people there of it as well.

"Found them," Jonathan announced as he came back to the reception desk to get Luke. As they walked through the restaurant, Luke saw Danielle's friend Kelly sitting at a table with two other young women dressed in style for the evening. Kelly was very beautiful, as were both her friends, and Luke knew that Kelly was the perfect fit for this place. She knew how to work her looks and could innocently sweet talk the socks off a freezing Eskimo, but based on what Danielle had said, if you crossed her, she'd rip your eyes out.

As Jonathan and Luke came near her table, Kelly seemed to do a quick scan of the two of them, almost as if determining their value, before her eyes locked in on his. At first there was no sign of recognition in her face, as she had written the two of them off, then she did a double take and smiled as she recognized him. Luke decided it would probably be a good idea to say hello, so he veered off from his current course and stopped by their table.

"Hi Kelly! Wow, you look fantastic as always," he said to her as she stood up and gave him a hug. As they separated, he briefly looked toward the other two women at the table. She seemed unsure as to what to say, so he turned to the other two women at the table.

"Hello, I'm Luke. My apologies for interrupting your evening." He was never sure if he was supposed to shake a women's hand or just nod. He chose the latter.

"O,h don't be silly, Luke. Where's Danielle?" Kelly asked as she gave him her best smile and continued to hold onto his arm. The question caught him a little off guard as he realized he had never thought about what his canned response was going to be if someone they both knew asked him that question.

"I believe she's at home," he said with a smile, wondering if she already knew the answer. He was looking for a way to change the subject; fortunately one of her friends came to the rescue.

"Hi Luke, I'm Cindy." The dark haired woman reached across the table and extended her hand, which he gently shook. She was a very strikingly beautiful Asian woman. The red haired women sitting next to her, who was even more stunning than the other two, also extended her hand. "I'm Monica." He gently shook her hand as well. During the introductions, Kelly never let go of his arm.

"Are you out having fun, or something more devious?" Kelly asked with a wry grin.

"Unfortunately, neither… it's a work meeting," he replied and saw that Cindy and Monica were no longer looking at him, but behind him. He turned to see Jonathan standing there nervously. It crossed his mind ever so briefly to just ignore him, but he knew better.

"Excuse my bad manners. Ladies, may I introduce Jonathan Weber." As they all were saying 'hello's' to each other Luke thought this might be a great time to build a few points with 'the team' and continued about Jonathan.

"Jonathan is one of the lead developers where I work. He is very brilliant and very successful, for a programmer that is." He rolled his eyes at the last part and smiled, which of course the three ladies jumped in and defended Jonathan's honor as a programmer. He was not sure if it was the brilliant, the successful, or the "very" part that he used to lead into each one that seemed to change the moment, but the women seemed to elevate their interest and friendliness toward Jonathan. It wasn't that Jonathan was unattractive, at least that is what Danielle had said, it's just that he came with a lot of ugly work history and baggage.

Jonathan had very little idea as to what was going on around him, but Luke being a "briefed" veteran (thanks to many hours of training by Danielle), knew the three women were probing for answers to important questions about him, his career, status, wealth and availability. He finally managed to break it up with a promise to invite them over after their meeting if the boss gives the okay. He directed Jonathan back to the prime objective of meeting with Apollo and Ronald. He looked at his watch, yep, late again.

As Jonathan led the way to Apollo's table, he could see that as a result of the conversation with the beautiful young women, Jonathan's whole demeanor had changed. His step was lighter and more confident, he stood straighter and taller, and he was wearing a "James Bond" smile as he sat down at the table with Apollo and Ronald.

"Hey guys!" he said energetically as he looked behind him in the direction of the group they had just left. Apollo seemed to pick up on Jonathan's new attitude as well and raised his eyebrow and then looked at Luke.

"Espresso shots or a new video game, which is it?" Apollo announced to the table, with a very dry smile and then turned to Luke. "I'm sure the team appreciates you making the time to join them." Apollo said as if he was not one of the team, but rather its spokesman.

"Sorry were a little late, but Jonathan was busy being a babe magnet," Luke answered.

"They were gorgeous! You would not believe it," Jonathan said as if he just got off a theme park ride. He turned to Luke and smiled a devilish grin and nodded his head toward Luke as he continued. "They're Luke's friends. They said they would come over after our meeting if we invited them." His statement almost sounded like a request as he looked toward Apollo. Ronald almost came out of his seat trying to spot the table where the ladies were until Jonathan turned and yanked him back down.

"Don't look so desperate!" Jonathan said in a whispered shout.

"Are you kidding? I am desperate," Ronald said with a not so innocent honesty and a face that matched his words. Luke smiled at the whole interaction.

Apollo looked at Jonathan and Ronald's anxious faces and then back at Luke.

"Well it appears you bring more to the team than just your knowledge. It looks like these guys apparently could use a little "non-virtual" feminine company for a change." He stated rather crudely to the group. Ronald and Jonathan laughed, while Luke could only bring a somewhat forced smile to his face.

"One evening with you guys and I'm already appointed the team social director. I can't imagine what my title will be after a month," Luke stated with a raised eyebrow and a smile.

"You get me hooked up on a date with any of them and you can have whatever title you want," Jonathan said trying to be cocky, but his nervous urgency was coming across much stronger.

Besides the distraction of having Jonathan and Ronald's radar constantly scanning the room to see if the three women had left, the meeting was turning out to be relatively uneventful. While the four of them drank an assortment of beverages from beer to sake martinis and nibbled on sushi, Apollo talked primarily about market shares and potential revenue rather than the product itself. He alluded that his fine-tuning of the software was pretty much completed and that the upgrading of the hardware and glasses to meet the military grade specifications was more of an afterthought that would eventually take care of itself.

There was a momentary silence as Apollo wrapped up his oratory conclusion to the group around the table. As if sensing the desire and frustration, Apollo turned to Luke.

"We'd better turn these dogs loose on those young ladies before they chew through their leashes," he said straight-faced and Jonathan and Ronald stood up from their chairs and headed toward the three ladies, then turned back toward Luke.

"Aren't you coming?" Jonathan asked Luke.

"I'd just be in your way. We'll wait for you here," he replied and smiled. Jonathan seemed to suddenly get very nervous. He came back, grabbed his martini and tipped back the last half of it. His courage seemed to return so he and Ronald headed back in the direction of the ladies.

"Do they stand a chance?" Apollo asked Luke once they had walked beyond earshot. Luke seemed to contemplate the question for a few seconds before answering.

"Yeah. Those women think they're rich and powerful, so that should give them a leg up. But, it's theirs to lose." He smiled at the end.

After a few seconds of uncomfortable silence, Luke asked the question he had wanted to ask Apollo for some time.

"So how did you come up with the idea for the Cat Eyes? Did it just come out of left field, or was it something you've been trying to create for a long while?

By the initial look on Apollo's face, you would have thought he had just been accused of cheating on a test. Guilt, fear and anger all mixed together. He then seemed to relax and recompose himself.

"I would like to tell you it was the latter, but in truth, it was more of the former." He took a sip of his drink before continuing, "I was working on a new game software and hardware module design that would imitate the old game 'Assassin' that I played in college. Not the video game, but the role-playing game where you would target other players and assassinate them. We used dart guns or kool aid filled squirt guns to kill each other. Once you had killed everyone else that was playing, you won. They of course were trying to kill you first." He took another drink. "The problem in the active game, was that carrying a realistic looking gun around campus, plastic or not, was not welcomed with open arms by the school or other students." Luke had heard about the game, but had never played it. With all the school shootings and terrorist issues in the country he knew why the game had been shut down.

"So with all that opposition, why try to build it again years later?" Luke asked.

"Because I was told I couldn't." He answered. Luke waited for the 'just kidding' part, but then realized that Apollo was dead serious.

"We have a rebel in our midst. I would have never pegged you for that," Luke replied.

"Why not?" Apollo seemed genuinely hurt by the remark.

"I guess I had you classified as more of a "don't rock the boat" type of guy. But I'm glad to hear you have a little thrill seeker in you as well." Luke smiled. "So how was the game to work if you couldn't carry guns?" Luke asked with a smile to get things back on the topic. Apollo seemed to need to think a little before continuing, and then smiled.

"It was the precursor of the Cat Eyes program." Apollo seemed to let it sink in a moment, and then continued, "I needed the ability for the players to see the other players in the game; to know which were still active, and who their target was, without anyone else even being aware of the game being played around them." Luke listened and tried to follow along as Apollo continued with his overview, "So the glasses were to meet the visual needs of the players, and the control unit was to keep the game unique to the players while tracking the hits until the game was over with one winner left standing."
Luke nodded his head as he sorted through all the info and tried to piece it together.

"So no one else would even know the game was being played." Luke stated almost as a question.

"Correct. Just like real world espionage that is being played out around us. Most of us have no clue," Apollo responded almost excited by the fact that Luke was getting the picture. He thought about his time in Iraq and how much was happening behind the scenes without him even knowing it.

"So how would you assassinate someone if you did not carry a gun?" Luke asked.

"I was planning on using a laser sensor pen attached to the control unit that would detect when an opponent had made successful contact with the target or not."

"What does successful contact mean? Shoot them or touch them?" Luke asked.

"Both. The pen would have a 30 to 50 foot range for distant shots and touch capability for point blank assassinations. You would receive more points for zero distance terminations." Apollo smiled devilishly at the last comment. Luke pondered the game as Apollo waited for a response.

"Interesting concept." Luke nodded. "From someone who never played the game, it sounds like fun. So what happened that you switched from 'assassin man' to 'cat man'?" Luke asked. Apollo almost seemed disappointed at the change of topics.

"During the R&D work and the integration of the glasses with the control unit I kept getting less than desirable results. I realized that the current operating systems available did not have the structure needed for the integration of the Cat Eyes." Apollo hesitated, "I also knew that I could not protect the code if I used them. So I wrote a whole new operating system that was very specialized and heavily encrypted to handle the Cat Eyes code." Luke was impressed with the idea that someone could write a whole new operating system from scratch that worked as well as the Cat Eyes code did.

"It's definitely impressive. Tell me you have it copyright protected," Luke added and smiled, but Apollo shook his head.

"I didn't need to," Apollo said distantly and then refocused on the conversation. "I wrote it so it could not be copied. Nobody honors a copyright anyways; they just decompile it and use it without paying the creator." Luke was surprised by the statement and felt Apollo might be a little naïve or overconfident in his ability to protect his special code and operating system. "After the specialized code was written, it opened up a whole new avenue of possibilities that were not available before," Apollo added.

"How long did it take you to write the operating system?" Luke asked and Apollo seemed to smile inwardly.

"Four weeks," Apollo said oddly with a smirk.

"You wrote a whole new operating system in four weeks?" Luke said unbelievingly, "Seriously, how long?"

"I don't care if you believe me or not. Let's just say that I was inspired. The amazing part is that the end result came out far different than expected. It allowed me to approach the hardware solutions from a whole different angle. The problem was that the sensor mechanism that was going to display and track the 'hit and contact' of the opponent kept producing rainbow colors. The more I refined the software, the more clarity I received from the color spectrum, but I didn't understand what I was seeing until I did some additional research and testing on the lens coating of the glasses. I realized that what I was seeing was not coming from the control unit, but was being generated by the individual themselves."

"So instead of the control unit generating the colors as you planned, it was actually interpreting the colors of the target," Luke stated and Apollo nodded.

"Correct. Since then, I spent the majority of my time understanding what it was that was being displayed and then fine tuning the software side of the product to get it to where it is today," Apollo explained with a sense of pride. Luke just nodded.

"What is the membrane made of that pulls in the color spectrum the way it does?" Luke asked with all sincerity. Apollo simply sat and stared at Luke for much too long to be normal hesitation.

"That is a secret, but something I am well versed on from my chemistry background and schooling," Apollo stated.

"Chemistry? I thought you were a code junkie?" Luke tried to joke back.

"Writing software is my main passion, but chemistry is a close second," he said. Luke was impressed with Apollo's credentials and academic background. They both glanced over to where Ronald and Jonathan were conversing with the three women.

"So what's next in your master plan?" Luke asked.

"As we discussed this evening, I'm working on a software upgrade that I hope will give a little more clarity in the spectrum. Other than that, it's about creating the control unit to withstand harsh environmental conditions and getting the less conspicuous design of the glasses in production. That, and a training mechanism that will get the end user up and running quickly. That's where you come in," he said dryly.

"And here I thought it was to find those two a date," Luke replied as he saw Jonathan and Ronald heading back to the table with the three ladies in tow. Apollo saw the group as well and said without looking at Luke.

"If that's the case, looks like you are no longer needed." Luke waited for the smile from Apollo, but it never came.

The rest of the evening was spent watching Jonathan and Ronald try to impress Cindy and Monica with their knowledge on drink ordering and their amazing ability of consumption. Kelly must have asked enough questions to know that Apollo was the big catch of the group because she wasted no time in flaunting her charms and interest toward Apollo. Although a little ridged at first, Apollo eventually loosened up and began his self-accentuating dialog. By the end of the night, Kelly had her arm tucked in nicely around Apollo's, while Jonathan and Cindy seemed to have either drowned their common sense or blurred their vision enough to match up. Ronald and Monica were apparently still trying to navigate the waters.

As he watched the six tablemates interact, his mind once again headed toward thoughts of Danielle. What would they be doing right now if they were still together? What would they be talking about? He felt the loneliness overcoming the drinks and creeping back into his life again. His presence at the table was beginning to feel more and more awkward and he knew if he didn't head out soon, he would be in no condition to drive. Perhaps he already was past it? He saw Monica looking across the table at him as if Ronald had just mentioned something about him, but when he looked toward Ronald, his eyes were looking past her and no words were coming from him. She smiled.

The smile caught him off-guard and he looked away, then slowly, he looked back again. She was still looking at him. He returned the smile and she seemed to suddenly light up at his returned smile. He felt awkward at not being able to at least talk with her across the table through the noise of the other two couples on both sides of her and Ronald. So he did the only thing he could think of doing in an awkward moment, he fled. He raised a hand to the group as if he was waving goodbye and stated that he was calling it a night.

There were the usual social comments from everyone exclaiming "So soon?" "Big day tomorrow?" "Don't you like us anymore?" and the like, which he navigated past diplomatically, with a little humor.

Whether it was the drinks or the beautiful woman that was hanging from his arm, Jonathan was loud and confident as he stood up and tried to give Luke a high five as he said goodbye. Luke felt like Jonathan might have tried giving him a hug if Cindy was not in between them, *lucky me,* he thought. He saw Monica speaking with Kelly and then back to Cindy in an almost rushed fashion as he shook hands with Ronald and Apollo and thanked them for the evening and the dinner. As he was finally extracting himself from the goodbyes and leaving the table, Kelly asked a question that silenced the whole group.

"Luke, if it's not too great of an inconvenience, would you be a sweetie and give Monica a ride home for me? The rest of us are having too much fun and would like to stay a little longer," she asked with a little girl's voice that sounded more like begging. He looked across the table at Monica whose expression almost mirrored Kelly's pleading voice. He waited briefly for Ronald to come to the girls rescue, but he either was not interested in the opportunity or missed it all together.

"Uh sure, of course. Where do you live Monica?" he asked. Almost ignoring his question, she quickly slid her chair back and grabbed her purse and jacket and said her 'goodbyes' to everyone. Luke was happy to see that Ronald seemed more relieved by the event than disappointed. Luke motioned for her to lead the way toward the front door of the restaurant and he followed her out.

As she walked in front of him, he was suddenly aware of how attractive her figure was and the way the short dress showed off her physical attributes. He was not sure how much of what he was seeing was a result of the alcohol in his blood and how much was the loneliness. Her red hair seemed inviting and sexy and his heart was suddenly racing. As they reached the door, he helped her put on her coat and then held the door open for her. She smiled and commented on his gentlemanlike qualities. They made small talk about the evening's events as they cross the parking lot toward his car. He opened the car door for her and watched her carefully step into the passenger seat and again, her smile disarmed him. He changed his initial perspective on her from very attractive, to extremely attractive.

As he circled around the backside of the car, his mind ran into a thought of Danielle and guilt hit him hard in the face. What was he thinking? What should he do? He knew that Kelly would say something to Danielle the next time she saw her, a casual slip of the tongue or passing comment just to see her reaction, which was just how she operated. He tried to imagine what Danielle would say or how she would respond when she found out?

He knew that Danielle had broken up with him, well sort of. Actually he thought that maybe he was the one that called it off because of her choice. Either way, the fact was that the two of them were no longer together and he was not going to support the whole *find yourself* mode that she was in. Her opinion no longer mattered.

As he slid into the driver's seat and started the car, he turned to ask Monica for directions. He realized that she was staring deeply into his eyes with a sultry and sexy look. Not being well versed on responding to a "sultry look" he simply returned the smile.

"So which direction is home?" he asked in an effort to break the moment's awkwardness. She held his gaze and then said,

"Santa Monica, please." They drove in silence the first few miles before Luke broke the quiet.

"I take it that you and Ronald did not hit it off tonight? At least not as well as Cindy and Jonathan did?" He smiled. She laughed quietly and then said,

"No, definitely not my type. What about you? You seemed content to just hang on the fringes without getting involved too deeply. No interests out there?" she asked.

He tried to determine the best way to answer her question, knowing that Kelly probably already told her that he was potentially single, so he decided that honesty was the best option. Besides, with the Cat Eyes 'coming to a store near you', he determined that he had better start practicing telling the truth in every situation.

"I did have an interest, but that seems to have gone in the wrong direction for my taste," he replied.

"What is your taste?" she asked him, almost baiting him to respond with the typical catch phrase answer of 'you'. But he held back from using it and instead remained quiet a moment, then responded truthfully again.

"I'm not sure at the moment. I thought I knew once, but too many things seem to have changed inside over the past few weeks." She at first seemed disappointed that he did not take the bait, but then seemed to use the moment to dig a little deeper.

"Since we're being so truthful," she said with an emphasis on the last word and a giggle. "I need to tell you that I have been watching you all evening. From the first time you introduced yourself to us, I can't seem to take my eyes off of you. There is something about you that is very sexy on the inside." Luke felt flattered by her words, but also embarrassed by the compliment. He never was very good at compliments.

"The 'inside'? Hmm, I feel the 'he has a great personality' sales pitch coming," he said with a laugh.

"No! That's not what I meant at all. You're sexy on the outside too, but it's what I see on the inside that is even more so. You're confident, but not cocky. You're funny, but not too deliberate or obnoxious about it," she responded and then raised her eyebrow. "Does that make sense?" she asked.

"I guess so. Thank you. Those are kind words," he said, trying to formulate the response without sounding too embarrassed. He was trying to find the words to return the compliment, but did not want to come across as fake and shallow in the effort. He tried to start a few times, but realized that he would fail in his goal, so stopped to rethink again to make sure he got it right when he finally did respond. The Cat Eyes crossed his mind again.

"Monica, I've got to be honest and tell you that my mind was far from thinking about anyone in a romantic way. I figured you and Ronald were interested in each other, so I did not even consider thinking anything other than that you were very attractive and your red hair was stunning. That is, until you smiled at me," he said with a smile as he tried to keep his eyes on the road.

"It's auburn," she said.

"What?" he replied and saw that she was smiling.

"My hair. It's auburn. Red sounds like an old woman's color." She chuckled.

Luke nodded his head a second, and then mumbled, "Note to self... never refer to an attractive woman's hair as 'red', especially sensitive younger ones." He mocked with a rolling of the eyes and then a smile. Monica at first gave a fake glare back and then giggled.

"I've never been real good at the whole expressing my feelings and emotions in relationships," he confessed out loud without taking his eyes off the road. "It seems my words always come out less than diplomatic. Generically honest, but rarely are the words as romantic as the other person would like them to be, or as you see in the movies." He frowned as she smiled.

"That's okay. I'm way over the top in that ability and will make up for the two of us. I read too many of those trashy novels as a kid." She touched her hand to her forehead and did a fake swoon then laughed.

The rest of the ride back to her house was less awkward and they joked with each other about various things. Luke found her to be very funny, but she also had moments of intense reactions about certain topics. Not scary reactions, just more honest or opinionated than he was use to people being on a first meeting.

As he pulled up to her apartment complex entrance, his mind started to race as to what he should do. He knew he would open her door and walk her to the security door of her apartment entrance, but he did not know what he should do or how to act once they got there. He played it safe and sent a non-verbal message by leaving his car running as he got out. When they arrived at the security door, she swiped her access card and opened the door and looked back at Luke.

"Thank you for the ride home," she said and waited for him to make the first move.

"My pleasure. And the 'red hair' lesson, well that will be with me the rest of my life." He smiled and gave a sad smirk. "I'll probably need professional counseling the next few years because of it, but I should be okay in the end," he said with a serious tone as he looked away and then back to her and smiled. Monica gave her best polite giggle without taking her eyes off of his. The awkward moment of silence arrived and Luke leaned forward to give her a kiss on the cheek. Monica pulled back slightly from his approach which sent a brief sense of rejection through him. She reached up with one hand to turn his face toward hers and then leaned in and kissed him on the lips. They held the embrace of their lips for several seconds before she slowly pulled away from his. That same sultry look was in her eyes as he refocused on hers.

"That's not exactly what I was hoping for this evening, but that will hold me over until next time," she told him softly, then turned and entered her building. She slowly closed the door while looking through the quickly narrowing crack, all without taking her eyes off of his.

He suddenly realized that he had not said a word following the kiss and her goodbye. His heart was pounding, his head was swimming, and his gears were turning rapidly. How did he get from 'heading home' to 'kissing a woman in front of her door' all in less than 30 minutes? He blinked and thought through the last thirty minutes of time with her and thought to himself. *Wow, she's good.* He headed back to his car and climbed in and took a deep breath. *Maybe too good.*

The drive back to his apartment went from an inner smile and pride on how the goodbye had turned out, to a slowly growing sense of guilt and regret as his mind cleared and his thoughts once again returned to Danielle. He knew that secrets in life always had a way of getting back to the ones you care the most about, the ones you want to hurt the least when you make bad choices. He knew that Monica would talk to Kelly about the ride home, and then Kelly would find a way to share it with Danielle at the first opportunity.

He shouldn't feel that he cheated on Danielle; after all, they were no longer a couple. The fact was, the event was not planned, but just happened. In spite of the justifications, he could not make himself feel good about the evening's events. His feelings for Danielle were still very strong and deep and the thought of hurting her in any way didn't sit well with him. Luke knew that the *feelings* he had for Monica were far more physical and sensual in nature and had little to do with a deep emotional connection, like the kind he had with Danielle.

On the flip side, he believed that those feelings could develop over time with someone new; he just had invested so much of his heart into Danielle and although he had the same physical and sensual feelings toward Danielle, they had developed from the inside out. It seemed like such a waste of time and great memories to start over again. He also knew from past experience that the 'physical first' approach rarely turned out the way he hoped it would. The mind gets so blinded by passion and often with alcohol, that it generally misses the obvious warnings or red flags about a person. The 'morning after' clarity you wake up to is so stunningly obvious that you are amazed how you could have been blind to it the night before. The challenge comes in trying to explain the newly acquired wisdom to the person laying next to you in a kind or diplomatic way. Luke had found this pretty much impossible, unless of course the other person had been blessed by the same sudden flash of brilliance about him?

As time passed and as his internal engines cooled down, Luke was grateful that nothing more physical happened with Monica. Thankfully, he somehow had enough wits about him to let things play out in a less physical way. He knew it would be a much better foundation to build on should he or Monica chose to let the relationship develop. She had made it clear that she wanted it to move forward, but the bigger question was, did he?

As he walked into his apartment, he felt the loneliness return and his mind battled with the tug of war of feelings between Danielle and Monica. He knew that if it were not for the whole "born again" issue with Danielle, it would not even be a consideration. He missed her very much but he knew he needed to draw a clear line in the relationship somewhere or at least set some clear boundaries. He hoped that she would come to her senses soon, before it was too late. Before they were too late.

Chapter 12

The tension levels of the team meetings during the following two weeks rose sharply as the issues of production and delivery of the system glasses to the military became the main focus of discussion. Luke was happy to see that Cliff and two other gentlemen from the legal department had flown in to supervise the signing of the final agreement that would enable the funding of the project. Luke was not privy to the funding amount, but he was required to sign a key employee agreement that was lengthy and complicated in which the consequences of breach of confidence were enough to indebt Luke to the company for more years than he cared to imagine. Although Luke understood the need for such an agreement, this one seemed overly strong in comparison to the one he signed earlier with the company. Apparently, Apollo was having a tough time with the language of the agreement and Cliff and the two legal advisors spent a great deal of time trying to placate Apollo. By the third day they apparently had found either some common ground, or one side had finally given in.

Once everyone was under an agreement, Cliff made it clear that the government would be pushing hard on a faster delivery schedule and they also wanted additional testing of the product. Luke knew the game would change now that the government had stepped in, he just didn't realize how much it would change. The new requirements and stipulations were wreaking havoc on determining delivery schedules and production timelines. The new security protocols and firewalls that were being required were very distracting to the flow of development and operations. Luke was rather surprised by the degree of security that was being implemented considering all the leaks that he had seen on the news regarding the government's closely guarded classified information. They had either learned from their prior mistakes, something he found hard to believe, or this was a whole different branch of the government directing the project. While he understood the need for the added security, it definitely created a bottleneck in the workflow.

Luke learned the following day that an additional small team of government staff members were already on their way to oversee key elements of the office and product development. Luke realized that Cliff must have pushed the Cat Eyes product and the results they witnessed in Iraq pretty hard to see this much activity so quickly. Luke was deeply concerned about the direction the government would now want to take the project, whether it would follow Apollo's plans or keep it just for military and security force use, only time would tell. Either way, he could tell that Cliff and his team had indeed grasped the full impact that the product could deliver.

With the agreement and new funding in place, Luke saw that Samuel, the president of the company, would also be allocating a lot more resources to the team. By Thursday, the human resources department was hiring additional support staff in the production and design department and transferring key employees to the Cat Eyes group. Whatever they had finally agreed to in the funding agreement must have secured Apollo's full support, for he had the lead engineers of the company running a hundred miles an hour in an effort to build a smaller and more durable system unit. He also submitted a new design and allocated the resources needed to produce a more compact and less obvious glasses design, something that had already been on the drawing board, but was waiting for the green light and revenue to justify their production. Although repressed socially and a pain in the backside managerially, Luke had to admit that Apollo was very detailed and had put in a great deal of behind the scenes work on this product that enabled them to hit the ground running once the government gave the funding for the contract.

With all the above changes being implemented, Luke was set back nearly to square one in the writing of the training manuals. With a new system unit and glasses being released, his old training processes had become antiquated before they were even completed. Luke was a little frustrated when he learned that the technical drawings of the new designs had been completed for some time but Apollo had chosen not to release them for him to work on until the last minute.

Luke found the new training manual to be a little more difficult to write than expected. Because the majority of the end users would be high school graduates, combined with the feedback and observations he had witnessed in Iraq, he felt a more hands on approach in their training would be needed than a schematic showing the functions for the various controls and color spectrum interpretation charts. He also needed to use a "train the trainer" methodology rather than just a "train the end user" approach alone. This would require two training manuals to be written, not just the one. He knew each manual needed to be short in length with simple and straightforward terminology, and tailored to a user who would be learning through a more hands-on field-testing rather than in a classroom. The fact that he had a better understanding of the needs of the field soldier from his own experience would make putting together the 'text' training part of the program much easier than usual. The 'field' training part would be a different story. Luke's plan was to personally train the trainers for that part and he would be working directly with the military personnel.

Work life had definitely changed dramatically and Luke foresaw that his typical 8 hour work days would include more overtime than he cared to think about for quite some time. On the social front, from what he could deduce from Danielle's actions, it must have been on Thursday evening of the following week that she finally heard from Kelly about his 'encounter' with Monica at the sushi bar and drop off. While she was relatively happy and quick to engage him in conversation in the lunch room or at the end of the day earlier in the week, on Friday she seemed more distant and even sad. He felt that she was actually avoiding him during the day.

When Friday evening came, he was exhausted to say the least. As he was packing up his stuff to head home after most of the office had already left, Luke was surprised to see David looking over his cubicle wall. "How's the reading coming?" David asked Luke. At first Luke was confused, but then realized what he was talking about. With his now very full 'team' schedule, office workload, and the mental battle that he was chewing on regarding Danielle and Monica; Luke realized he had not spent any time reading the book David had given him. He semi-apologetically told David so, without revealing anything about the Danielle and Monica part. Although he expected to get a strong religious scolding from him, David at first disappeared from behind the wall and then reappeared at Luke's cubicle entrance and sat on the edge of his desk.

"Well it's definitely something that a person must want to do on their own, but I promise that you'll find even a little taste now and then will not come back void of value or flavor," David stated with a smile, but Luke was uncomfortable with the idea, let alone where to even start reading. David seemed to sense his thoughts. "If you want to see God's wisdom displayed in short verses, take the time to read a few proverbs, although I would suggest reading a whole chapter at a time in Proverbs. You probably already know this but 'Proverbs' is a book in the Bible. You'll find that even reading just one or two verses every night will amaze and enlighten you. Now if instead you want to learn about whom Jesus is, read the book of John in the New Testament." He patted Luke on the shoulder and as he turned to leave his cubicle said, "It's okay to ask for help, Acts 8:26, write it down. Good night Luke." Luke nodded even though he could no longer see David on the other side of his cubicle wall.

Luke was contemplating David's suggestions. *Proverbs, John and Acts 8…* he thought to himself, but couldn't remember the last number. Well if he should ever desire to read this book that he was pushing, he'd start in Proverbs. It might not be such a bad read and a good way to kill some time before bed at night. He wondered if Danielle was reading as well. He started thinking about Danielle and wondered if she had started the same way before she lost her common sense. He felt his stomach tighten up as he thought about her, something it always seemed to do. He felt cheated and angry at her choice to pursue religion over him. *Why couldn't she do both,* he thought and then remembered that he was the one who made her chose between the two. Was she willing to do both? Did he even want to keep the relationship going if she could have pursued both?

His typical response in these frustrating moments was to shift his attention to thinking about Monica. He had spoken to her several times during the week by phone and the conversations were always, he was having trouble coming up with the word that best described them, *interesting?* Yeah, interesting was probably the best word to describe their conversations. She was very direct and even aggressive in her pursuit of him, while he was much more cautious about allowing any feelings to develop she seemed to consider it a challenge to overcome.

Monica's words were always laced with deep meanings, open expressions of feelings and often included sexual innuendoes. The former two made him nervous in his attempts to navigate those deep waters, but the latter kept his inner passions piqued and him coming back for more. He was very attracted to her directness and her desire for the relationship, which made it very easy to remain engaged in the discussions. Although Luke felt the relationship was exactly what his wounded pride needed to recover from the fading relationship with Danielle, his psychology background and past relationship experiences also raised a red flag of warning about her aggressive and extremely focused personality. He was not necessarily concerned about a 'Fatal Attraction' relationship, but he knew that hearts and feelings were at stake beyond his own and even beyond the relationship with Monica. Luke knew it was a dangerous game he was playing with Monica and that one wrong step could be costly.

He thought about the upcoming weekend and felt fortunate that Monica was going to be out of town to visit her family in San Diego. She had invited him to join her, but he felt it was way too soon for that sort of thing and when he told her so, she laughed and said she knew that was what his response would be, but she wanted to hear him say it anyway. Deep down, he was a little fearful of spending time with her and the probability that things would get physical between them if he was not careful, which was something that he was not mentally ready to deal with just yet, though his body made it clear that it was very interested in pursuing that connection.

He was grateful that after work on Friday 'the team' was already booked with other activities on their own. Luke understood that to mean that Apollo had plans that did not include the rest of them, so everyone was allowed to do their own thing. His choice was to go home and do a little testing and training work with the Cat Eyes and if the timing was right, to watch the game on TV. He signed out one of the Cat Eyes travel pack test units with security and headed for his car. He stopped briefly to grab a bite to eat at his favorite taco shop and then headed for home. He spent about two hours typing up the actual step-by-step processes for replacing the battery pack on the new system, changing out the glasses, and software upgrade installs before catching the last half of the game.

His mind was still inundated with the unresolved feelings of the week's events and as he was lying in bed struggling to sleep, he thought about David's suggestion and retrieved the brown book he had given him. *The brown book* Luke wondered why he kept calling it the brown book instead of the Bible? It just seemed strange to use that word. Luke shrugged and opened the book and checked the index to find what page 'Proverbs' was on and turned to it. His plan was to read just a few verses, but once he got started, he ended up reading the first 2 chapters of the book. The areas that stood out the most to him were the first parts of chapter 1.

<u>Proverbs 1:1-7</u>
¹ The proverbs of Solomon son of David, king of Israel:

² for attaining wisdom and discipline;
for understanding words of insight;

³ for acquiring a disciplined and prudent life,
doing what is right and just and fair;

⁴ for giving prudence to the simple,
knowledge and discretion to the young-

⁵ let the wise listen and add to their learning,
and let the discerning get guidance-

⁶ for understanding proverbs and parables,
the sayings and riddles of the wise.

⁷ The fear of the LORD is the beginning of knowledge,
but fools despise wisdom and discipline.

There it was. The "fear" of the lord seemed to be so prevalent in religion. He never understood it. It was like one of his friends growing up whose whole family feared the moment their dad would come home, never knowing what to expect from him, wrath or kindness that day. He hated seeing them live like that. He personally loved his dad, respected him and knew there were consequences for not obeying, but he always felt loved rather than fearful of him. Yet as a kid, Luke always felt that fear was the motivator with his religious friends. Like the family of his friend, they feared the consequences of their life choices and by cowering in fear, God would somehow spare them from his wrath each week at mass and confession. He kept reading, but with less depth and awe. The rest of Proverbs 1 seemed to be a simple message about, "Listening and not being stupid" Luke chuckled to himself at his personal "cliff notes". Chapter 2 suddenly caught him off guard, and he had to read it twice to get what was being said.

Proverbs 2:1-6

¹ My son, if you accept my words
and store up my commands within you,

² turning your ear to wisdom
and applying your heart to understanding,

³ and if you call out for insight
and cry aloud for understanding,

⁴ and if you look for it as for silver
and search for it as for hidden treasure,

⁵ then you will understand the fear of the LORD
and find the knowledge of God.

He struggled putting together his simple "Cliff's Notes" on this one. To understand the "fear" of the Lord, you needed to strive to understand him and his commands. He looked back at Proverbs 1 again and read that *the fear of the lord is the beginning of knowledge,* but that to understand that fear would require you to understand his words. He thought for a moment and tried to put together the Cliff's Notes in another way. He decided that it was saying, *unless there was a fear of the lord, that few would seek him. Once you feared the lord, then you had better dive in to his teachings if you were to understand why you should fear him.*

His initial thought was that this was pretty deep, but he shook off the idea of diving deeper into it. He was tired and this was way more work than he was willing to invest at that moment so he decided to call it a night again. As he slid the book away, he saw the end of verse 6 of the chapter, *but fools despise wisdom and discipline.* That verse seemed to stay with him and wove its way into his dreams.

On Saturday morning, as he was contemplating a dream that he had in which he was once again trying to run away from wolves that were chasing him, he received a call from Danielle on his cell phone. He was excited, yet nervous to see her number ID on the phone. Was she calling to say that she changed her mind and that he was more important than religion? Maybe she wanted to talk about Monica? Maybe 'talking' was not on her agenda and that she was going to give him a piece of her mind. He almost let it go to voicemail, but then decided to answer it and talk with her.

"Good morning," he said nicely and waited to hear her voice. There was a short silence before she finally spoke.

"Am I waking you?" she asked softly. He loved the sound of her voice.

"No… well, yeah, but that's okay. I was more 'thinking' than I was sleeping," he joked.

"Are you doing okay?" she asked. He was trying to guess where she was heading, as that could be a very open ended question based on what the last few weeks looked like. He decided to steer it the way he hoped she meant it to be.

"Well… not really. My life kind of got flipped upside down recently and I've been trying to reprioritizing things," he said. "How have you been?" he asked almost sarcastically.

"I know what you mean," she said softly. Her words lifted his spirits. "I miss you a great deal." His heart skipped a beat at her last words. Did she want to come back to him? He thought he would be direct and cut to the chase.

"What exactly does that mean?" he asked her and hoped for the best.

"It means exactly what I said. I miss you. I miss us." Her voice was soft and gentle as she continued, "But you made me pick between the two most important loves in my life, something I was not expecting to have to choose between." She had an edge to her voice that he rarely heard. He felt his pride and jealousy once again welling up inside him.

"So has anything changed since then?" he asked her, going for broke. The silence lasted longer than he wanted and knew what the answer would be.

"No, Luke. I still love both of you," she said, and then continued, "I know it hurts you to hear the words I'm about to say and that you do not understand that they should be positive words to your ears, not negative ones, but I love God more." Although it was good to hear that she loved him, his heart sank and his pride welled up at the thought of still being second on her list.

"Well, I would like to say that I am happy for you and your choice, but I just can't," he told her and then continued, "So why did you call me Danielle, to turn the knife?"

"No Luke. You know that I would never do that. I called to see if you would be with me today at my baptism?" she said and Luke felt knocked off balance by the question.

"Your what?"

"My baptism. I know it might not make sense to you, but I'd really like you to be there. I need you there because you mean so much to me." Luke knew from her voice that she was very sincere with her request. He thought about it in silence before finally speaking again.

"I don't know, Danielle. It's like salt in a wound, but because I care so much about you, I'll think about it. That's the best I can do right now."

"It's going to be at David and Susan's house this afternoon at 2. I hope you will make it. It would really mean a lot to me," she said, but Luke was thinking about the location.

"It's not at a church?" he asked out loud as he thought about some big religious ceremony being played out in a grand cathedral or something.

"No. It's at their pool, and dress casual or you'll look silly," she said, as if those words would help encourage him to come, she knew he hated to wear a tie and suit. "I really hope you can make it."

"No promises," was all he said, still hurt.

"I understand," she replied. After a period of silence, she ended the conversation gracefully, "Well, I need to get going. I'll be looking for you." He was not sure how to respond.

"Goodbye Danielle." There was nothing but silence on the other end of the line until it disconnected. His heart sank as he contemplated the words again. 'Goodbye?' Did he really mean 'goodbye', as in 'I will never see you again?' Was she thinking he meant goodbye in that way? Deep down, he was not sure if it was meant as a hurtful response or just an innocent reply. He knew that 'goodbye' was not a word that they ever used with each other.

He spent the next hour trying to decide if he would actually go or not. If it was not for the 'goodbye' he used at the end of their conversation, he probably would have stayed home, but he did not want her to think that he no longer had feelings for her or no longer wanted to see her. He made the decision over breakfast to go and started to rearrange his day.

As he sat down to eat his cereal, he saw the Cat Eyes unit sitting on the table next to the brown book. *The Bible.* There, he said it in his mind. As he was chewing his cereal, he just starred at the two items as if he was waiting for one of them to move. Deep down he was thinking about Danielle and her choice. In just a few short weeks did she really grow to love God more than him or was it an emotional response that was coerced out of her? Was she being pressured by David and Susan to do something that she did not want to do? Or was she looking for a way out of their relationship? He hated not knowing the answer to these important personal questions. He looked back at the Cat Eyes and a thought crossed his mind. Why not wear the Cat Eyes to the baptism? He could ask questions and watch the responses from Danielle, David and anyone else that was there.

The idea seemed like a great one until he realized that what he was considering doing was exactly what he was butting heads with Apollo about. Worse yet, he was now trying to justify the use of it because it would benefit him directly. He sat through the rest of breakfast and a second cup of coffee and battled back and forth between the two opposing thoughts. He knew it was not a fair thing to do, but these were crucial and vital questions that needed to be asked and the true answers needed to be discovered; not only for his sake, but for her protection as well. He made the decision to use the Cat Eyes just this once.

He started laying out the equipment and the clothing he would wear to the event. He knew he could not hide the wire that ran from the back of the glasses to the system unit, but he could simply use the same explanation that he gave when other people had asked him what it was during the earlier testing trials. That he was listening to the game or the radio. Few people ever asked, but Luke knew that this was a more social event than a mall, with more opportunity for nervous or curious questions to be asked from innocent bystanders.

The morning passed quickly and on more than one occasion Luke had decided to leave the Cat Eyes at home, only to end up changing his mind again. As he headed out the door with the glasses on, but turned off, he considered one more time to either not go, or leave the glasses behind. He decided that the need to know was greater than to struggle with his doubts. He felt like such a hypocrite.

As he pulled into the driveway where David and Susan lived, he was amazed by the number of cars that were parked along side the street in front of their home. Luke guessed that this must be a mass baptism where lots of people came to be baptized at the same time. He really considered just driving back home, but he found a parking spot down the street and felt that it was a sign for him to stop. He sat in the car and kept checking his watch to make sure he would spend as little time as possible at the event, then got out and headed toward the front door. The door was open and no one asked who he was there to see or even questioned his presence. He suddenly remembered the glasses and reached down and turned the system unit on.

As the power came on and the system unit booted up, the colors that he saw through the glasses began to transform from the natural, everyday colors, to the various rainbow hues that began to slowly surround the people in the home. He causally scanned the room, and saw the overlapping blue and green colors in every direction. They made finding Danielle almost impossible. He lifted his head so that he could only see through the normal part of the lens and as usual, the colors disappeared. Sensing that his head was tilted back at an angle, he remembered someone telling him that when he did this, it made him look as if he was either snooty, or that he was having trouble seeing. He was hoping just the latter part was true.

As he scanned the first room, he did not see Danielle or David but several people smiled and nodded in his direction as he walked through, doing his best to avoid eye contact and keep moving. As he headed into the next room he ran into a knot of people that he could not pass through without stopping. As he waited for an opening to occur, several people came up and introduced themselves and asked his name. When he told them who he was and who he was there to see, no one seemed surprised.

"So you're Luke," she said with a smile. "We've been praying for you," she added in a matter of fact tone. Luke seemed confused, angry and embarrassed all at the same time. He tilted his head down to see a little deeper into her words.

"About what?" he asked her. Based on her color, it apparently was her turn to suddenly feel embarrassed, but Luke could see that it was not in a malevolent way. Her colors adjusted again and she seemed to almost grow in confidence as she prepared to answer.

"Danielle asked that we pray for your safety while you were in Saudi Arabia, or Afghanistan, or wherever it was that you were. Sorry, I'm not very good at geography," she giggled at the end. He could tell from the color that there was something else that she was holding back, but it was hard to read.

"Thanks." It was all he could think to say in response, uncomfortable with the thought of strangers praying for him.

He scanned the room again and saw David in the kitchen talking and laughing with someone. Luke thought that David must be some high-ranking member of his church with so many people present at his house. Feeling awkward and looking for a friend, Luke felt the best solution was to excuse himself from the conversation and head in that direction. As he was about to pass through the door into the kitchen, he saw Danielle near the breakfast bar surrounded by at least twenty people. She was laughing and glowing and her smile and eyes were always so beautiful, but even more so today. She seemed so happy. She was wearing a burgundy t-shirt with some logo on the front that he could not make out and a pair of jean shorts and sandals. He lowered his head and saw that she was a deep blue with flashes of green, but he also could read that she was nervous. Those around her were also washed with blue and green hues. He realized that the room was almost completely void of yellows and reds except for some lone man in the corner who seemed to be checking out the women as they passed by. Not sure if the unit was working or not, just to be safe he reached down and turned the system unit off, then back on again and waited as it rebooted. It was not uncommon for him to need to clear the memory cache to correct the spectrum display, but generally it only occurred after either long use or after changing a battery unit. As it came back online, the dominant blue and green hues remained.

He looked across the room and saw another patch of yellow and red in the crowd and lifted his head to drop the colors. He was surprised to see Kelly and another woman that he knew was also a friend of Danielle's. They were talking amongst themselves and smiling as they looked around the room. Luke lowered his head and could tell that they were definitely not happy about being there. As he watched them, several young ladies came up to them and apparently introduced themselves. Kelly smiled deeply and shook their hand and responded to them. Luke could tell that based on the yellow that flashed around her, whatever she said in response was a lie. Somehow her attitude was not too big of a surprise to him.

He purposely put the living room wall between him and Kelly so that she would not see him and turned back toward Danielle. As he watched her, she looked up and scanned the room and her eyes at first passed over him then came rushing back to stop on him. Fear initially flashed in his glasses, and then she changed to a deep blue. He lifted his head to see her smiling and excusing herself from the group and she did her best to move through the crowd toward him. As she came up to him she reached out and took his hand.

"Thank you for coming," she said and continued looking at him. She suddenly frowned and reached up to touch his eyes. "When did you start wearing glasses?" she asked as if she was evaluating how they looked. Being in the moment, he had forgotten all about them and scrambled to remember the answer he had planned to give if asked.

"Too much computer work, eye fatigue," he stammered as he lied. He could tell she was not a big fan of them as the current Cat Eyes design was not going to win any fashion awards.

"It's okay," she said with a smile. "I'm just glad you came. Follow me. I want to introduce you to a few of my new friends." *New friends* seemed like a nice way to say replacements for the friends she use to have. She took him by the arm and walked him toward the group of people in the kitchen that she had left earlier.

As they headed through the people, her attitude, or lack of a bad one would be a better way to describe it, was troubling to him. He knew that she knew about Monica, yet she seemed as if it did not bother her. Definitely not the Danielle he knew from before. She would have glared an icy stare and shredded him with a few choice verbal barbs, and this Danielle was instead killing him with kindness. *Why?* was the question he kept churning over and over in his mind?

"Luke!" He heard his named being yelled from the kitchen area and turned to see David now working his way through the people to stand next to him and Danielle. "It's great to see you here," he said smiling and then frowned slightly as he looked at his face. "I didn't know you wore glasses?" But then shook off the statement before Luke could respond and said, "I know Danielle was really hoping and praying that you would be able to make it," he said as he shook his hand and patted him on the shoulder as if there was something bigger going on behind the scenes. The word 'praying' stuck in his head and made his insides clinch. Susan suddenly appeared next to him with a smile and an outstretched hand.

"Hi Luke. Thank you for coming." He waited for the praying word to follow, but instead she turned toward David and said, "I think we should get started."

"Right!" David said energetically. "Speaking of why we are here, Danielle, we need to head out toward the pool." He turned to the large crowd gathered in his house and announced that everyone should start heading outside to the pool. Susan and Danielle headed off in one direction, while Luke and David headed to the other side of the pool.

In the noise of the shuffle, David was fielding logistical questions from various people as they gathered around the pool. Luke watched as the people slowly but aggressively filled the various points along the pool's edge to secure the best places. He saw a yellow and red flash come from an area and then noticed it was Kelly and her friend standing just behind the front row of the crowds. They were both smiling, but he could tell, even without the glasses, that they were not happy about the whole situation. He chuckled as he imagined them thinking that this would be a great opportunity to meet guys. When Kelly spotted Luke standing on the other side of the pool, she smiled and waved, then looked around and raised an eyebrow and smirked as if to say 'Is this stupid or what?' He just smiled back and nodded.

David reclaimed the spot next to Luke and he held up his hand and waited until the crowd had quieted down enough to speak. Luke saw that in his other hand he held the Bible that Luke borrowed. Across the pool, Luke saw Danielle standing next to the steps with Susan and another woman he had not met. Danielle looked so happy and yet nervous from being the center of attention. David began to speak to the people gathered around.

"Thank you all for coming to be a part of this very special day for Danielle. As most of us know, this is not an event that is to be considered lightly or as an emotional response, but with a great deal of study and personal conviction." He then laughed and said, "I'm sure the sisters can confirm that based on the many days and hours of studying with Danielle, that the latter is definitely the case here." There was laughter and the young lady next to Danielle joked,

"You got that right." The crowd of people laughed as well, as if they were aware of the effort that went into those times. Luke wondered if it was just a technique to wear the person down emotionally. He was also surprised that all these people were here for Danielle alone, that there were no other baptisms scheduled.

"My wife and I have known Danielle for some time now, initially as co-workers in the same company, but more recently we have been able to build a deep friendship and a trusting relationship that has allowed us to not only share our lives with her, but more importantly

God's Word with her. All of which helped bring about this incredible event that we are all about to witness shortly." There were many shouts of 'Amen' and 'Come on Danielle' as David's words unfolded to the group. Luke wanted to let out a sarcastic 'oh yippee' but held back.

"It has been so encouraging to watch the changes in Danielle over the past four weeks as she began to read and study God's Word and his plan and purpose for her life. As she took each step on faith and put into practice His words for her life and how it never fails to deliver His promises." He suddenly lifted the book in his hands and opened it and turned to a specific spot in it. "I want to share a scripture with you in <u>Colossians 2:8-14</u>, where it reads,"

"*8See to it that no one takes you captive through hollow and deceptive philosophy, which depends on human tradition and the basic principles of this world rather than on Christ.*

9For in Christ all the fullness of the Deity lives in bodily form, 10and you have been given fullness in Christ, who is the head over every power and authority. 11In him you were also circumcised, in the putting off of the sinful nature, not with a circumcision done by the hands of men but with the circumcision done by Christ, 12having been buried with him in baptism and raised with him through your faith in the power of God, who raised him from the dead.

13When you were dead in your sins and in the uncircumcision of your sinful nature, God made you alive with Christ. He forgave us all our sins, 14having canceled the written code, with its regulations, that was against us and that stood opposed to us; he took it away, nailing it to the cross. "

"This scripture reminds me of Danielle because she has decided to no longer be held captive to the hollow and deceptive philosophies of this world. Instead, to have the fullness of Christ live in her, the putting off of her sinful nature and being made new and alive in Christ Jesus." There was applause directed toward Danielle. Luke could not help but think of the deceptive philosophies they used to get her to this point.

David raised his hand again and the group quieted down. "We want to let those of you that would like to share a little about Danielle do so at this time." To Luke's surprise, hands shot up all over the place. David pointed to one young lady and said her name.

"Danielle, I am so proud of you and the decision that you have made. I was so honored to be able to participate in some of your studies and to see what an incredible woman of God you were becoming. The difficult decisions and choices that you faced and how you handled them in faith and honoring and putting God first. I know that he will bless you for making those decisions for him. I love you and can't wait to have you as my sister in Christ." The crowd applauded as she reached out as if to take Danielle's hand from across the pool, which Danielle returned with a smile and a 'thank you'. Luke was not positive, but it looked as if Danielle was almost in tears at her words. Not sadness, but tears of joy. That seemed very strange to Luke, for Danielle was not a crying type of person, but rather tough and strong, at least with him she was. Luke then thought about the words the young woman shared. "Difficult decisions and choices" were those relating to him? He felt the growing twinge of anger and jealousy creeping into him as another person that David selected began to speak.

"Danielle, you are so much fun to be with. Your humor, your wit, and your love for people are infectious. Don't ever lose those great gifts that God has given you. I'm so excited and honored to have you as my sister." She smiled as the applause continued. For the next 15 minutes, people shared about the many qualities that they had seen in Danielle and how it related to God and his Word. Luke felt trapped between two emotions. One was happiness for Danielle and the other was jealousy mixed with doubt toward those sharing about her. Although he did not disagree with them on her qualities, they definitely did not discuss her weaknesses. It was as if they did not take the same amount of time to learn about the dark side of her character. He was surprised that they had already learned about these qualities, the same ones that he had discovered in her over time. She seemed to have opened up to these strangers sooner than she opened up to Luke.

In the hopes of seeing deception or lying from those sharing, Luke intently watched them through the Cat Eyes as they 'shared'. He saw that for every person, they were very sincere and truthful in their words and Danielle seemed to be almost glowing in the aura of love from their words. For those that did not come across as completely truthful, their color spectrum was not dangerous, but more of a people pleasing response with maybe a hint of exaggeration. As if it were some signal that the time of sharing was over, David finally pointed to Susan who read a scripture that reminded her of Danielle.

Psalm 42:1-3
"As the deer pants for streams of water, so my soul pants for you, O God.

² My soul thirsts for God, for the living God. When can I go and meet with God?

³ My tears have been my food day and night, while men say to me all day long, "Where is your God?"

"Danielle, from the first time your eyes began to read about Jesus, your soul has panted and thirsted for God and his Word. You have wanted to seek him and find him, to meet with him in prayer and listen to him in your reading of his Word. Your constant calls and requests to study the Bible in the mornings, lunch breaks and late evenings have definitely been impressive and convicting. There have also been many tears 'day and night' as we wrestled with the world's viewpoint about God and their disbelief in him. Yet you stood firm and gave your whole heart to the search and the understanding of him. You finally discovered that he was standing right next to you the whole time, just waiting to call you his own. Today your choice gets to make that happen. I love you and I'm so proud of you." Susan reached out and gave Danielle an embrace that neither of them seemed to want to let go of. Luke was very impressed with Susan and her words; he was also a little surprised to hear that it was Danielle that seemed to be the initiator of the studies. Tears flowed down Danielle's face as she pulled away from Susan and turned back toward the people circling the pool. Luke could not remember her ever crying in front of him before and could not help but feel a little more jealous seeing the close relationship that she had built with Susan and these other people.

Danielle smiled as she wiped her eyes and face. "I'm a mess right now…but it's a good mess," she said with a laugh and everyone in earshot laughed with her. Luke could not help but feel her joy and happiness. Deep down, looking past his jealousy, he was actually really happy for her. Once she had collected her thoughts, she reached out to borrow Susan's Bible, who passed it to her without hesitation.

"I'm so grateful to everyone here… for being here," she then looked up and directly at him. "Luke, thank you for coming, it means so much to see you here." He felt stunned at first by her words and special note of his presence, and he could see even without the glasses that she meant her words and it almost brought tears to his eyes. He nodded his head and smiled back to her, although he wanted to say something cute or clever in response, he was afraid to let any words leave his mouth with his throat as constricted as it was. She returned the smile. "I'm also grateful to those of you who had the misfortune to study with me at all hours," she laughed, as did those around her who apparently fell into that category, "for helping and praying for me. I would have never found what I had been looking my whole life for if it were not for you. I'm grateful for your patience." She suddenly laughed as she looked at Susan and then back at everyone else. "Susan was so kind and loving to me, even when I was such a prideful pain in the neck. I'm so embarrassed by some of the things I said to many of you in my anger and frustration. You helped me to see my sinful character from God's eyes and through his Word. But more than anything else, I'm so grateful to God and his love and mercy. Learning about him has made me learn how to fail in love all over again, and for the right reasons. I wanted to share a scripture that has become very special to me. It's in Jeremiah 29." She began turning pages. The words she had used hit Luke like a ton of bricks, "fall in love all over again, for the right reasons", his smiled dropped from his face and his heart sank. So that's it, he thought to himself. That's what changed in her so suddenly; she simply no longer loved him and even if she had, she realized that it was for the wrong reasons. Well that makes things pretty easy from here forward.

As she continued seeking the location in the book, she continued sharing her reasons for the scripture. "When I think of this scripture in the Bible, it gives me comfort that God has a plan to rescue us even in the darkest of times, even when our sin deserves his abandonment, he has already forgiven us and is working to bring us back to him. Here it is," she said as she looked down at the book, "Starting in verse 11,

"For I know the plans I have for you," declares the LORD, "plans to prosper you and not to harm you, plans to give you hope and a future. 12 Then you will call on me and come and pray to me, and I will listen to you. 13 You will seek me and find me when you seek me with all your heart. 14 I will be found by you," declares the LORD, "and will bring you back from captivity."

She closed the book and looked around at everyone. "I just feel as if God has brought me back from my captivity in a very dark world and he has given me a new purpose, a new hope, and a new future. I'm so excited about becoming his daughter for eternity and your sister in Christ. Thank you." There was a brief applause from the crowd, but it quickly went silent as Susan put her hand on Danielle's shoulder and looked Danielle in the eyes.

"Danielle, do you believe that Jesus is the Son of God, that he came down and walked the earth as a man and that he died on the cross for your sins, that he was buried and raised to life on the third day and now sits at the right hand of God?" she asked Danielle.

"Yes, I do," Danielle responded.

"What is your good confession?" Susan asked.

"Jesus is Lord!" Danielle almost shouted to the pool and the sky above. The people around the pool cheered and applauded her words and then went quiet once again as if they knew that Susan would be continuing.

"Because of your good confession, we can now baptize you in the name of the Father, the Son and the Holy Spirit, all your sins will be forgiven, you will be given the gift of the Holy Spirit and you will be added to God's family and his Kingdom," Susan shared the words as if they were rare and precious treasures. Holding hands, the three of them then slowly walked down into the shallow end of the pool together. Luke watched as words of explanation were exchanged and Danielle reached up and placed her hand over her nose as she prepared to go underwater. Susan held onto Danielle's arm with one hand while keeping the other hand behind Danielle's back. The other woman stayed near her feet and legs as Danielle slowly fell backwards and sank below the surface of the water. Susan and the other woman seemed to survey the scene before bringing Danielle back out of the water to the cheers of those gathered around the pool.

As Danielle came out of the water, to Luke's annoyance someone next to him bumped into him while clapping, more specifically into the system unit connection, causing the lenses to flash and scrambling the color spectrum. Luke, although annoyed, was too caught up in the moment to take the time to diagnose the problem. Instead, he just lifted the glasses and rested them on his head. He did raise one eyebrow and gave the person who had bumped him a brief frustrated look. In spite of the jostling, to his surprise, he felt happy and proud for Danielle and perhaps even somehow understood her better now that he saw and heard the words that were shared from the various people, but deep down he still felt sad as to how it had impacted and changed their relationship.

The next 10 minutes were about watching people work their way toward Danielle to take their turn giving her a wet hug and apparently sharing some words of wisdom or encouragement with her. As the ranks thinned out and people started to leave, he moved toward where she was standing, still wrapped in a towel as she talked with a few people. Danielle saw him and excused herself from the three people and walked toward him. Not wanting to break the apparent protocol of the group, Luke gave her a hug.

"Sorry it's taken so long to congratulate you, but I got caught up in the mosh pit and was carried outside," he joked and Danielle laughed the laugh that he missed so much. It suddenly got uncomfortable as she looked at him, or was it 'into him' as they stood together. He broke the silence by continuing, "That was a very nice... event," he said, not sure how to label her baptism. "Not surprisingly, there seem to be a lot of people, other than myself, who think very highly of you."

"I'm so happy that you were here to witness this part of my life. I somehow - I'm not sure how to explain it - I needed you to be here for it," she said as she continued to search for something inside of him.

"Why? I don't mean to be rude in saying that, but why is my presence so important when you seem to have so many people that care for you?" he asked sincerely. She seemed hurt by his words and the expression on her face seemed to confirm that she did not find what she was seeking inside of him. Shrugging her shoulders she said, "I don't know, I guess I was hoping that by being here something might change inside of you that would spark an interest in seeking God." She seemed to be waiting for what was not going to come. He tried to find the words to comfort and encourage her, but nothing came out. She smiled and took his arm, "That's okay, I'm still so happy you came." And they walked back into the house where the remaining people were hanging around.

He stayed another 30 minutes before he made his excuse to leave the remaining people. He learned that pretty much everyone was "bro" or "sis" to each other and everyone tried to give him a hug, even the guys, when they first were introduced. The hugging thing was definitely something he was not that keen about and he quickly learned to stick his hand out for a shake to preempt the uncomfortable and awkward physical embraces. The question of the day from those that seemed to take turns speaking to him, seemed to be "So what did you think?" or something close to it. "Very nice" and "I'm really proud of her" became his stock response and seemed to lessen the number of follow-up questions. Most of the people seemed to be able to read the "Let's just keep it shallow shall we?" response he put out there correctly, and did not press things any further, but there were several of the younger men in their group who apparently missed it and pressed forward with their recruiting methodology. "Are you studying the Bible with anyone?" they would ask and at first Luke tried to be cordial in his responses with "no, not at this point in time, but thanks" or "I don't think it is for me", but they were like pit bulls when hearing his answer, or maybe they were just not very smart, and instead stepped up the attack with a ton of increasingly more aggressive questions to the point that Luke had to be rude and say flat out that he was not interested and walked away from them.

After staving off the last pit bull, Luke decided he had enough and saw Danielle standing by the front door saying goodbye to someone. In his frustration, he made a break for the door to do the same. As he reached the doorway where Danielle was standing, David, who seemed to come out of nowhere, invited him to stay for the BBQ celebration. The thought of being hounded by the "pit bull brothers" was way too much for him and he said a little louder than he wanted to, "Sorry, but I have a date to get ready for". He did not mean it as a "date with a woman", but as something scheduled on his calendar. But he could see the words hit Danielle a little hard. He thought about explaining it, but after the recent encounter with the "pit bulls" something mean inside felt that it was somehow justified and he left it hanging in the air. Danielle just smiled and gave him a hug and thanked him again for coming and turned and walked into a room where Susan was sitting. Luke turned to say thanks to David, but David just motioned for the door and said he would walk him out and to his car. Seeing her response, Luke now felt horrible at his choice of words and just wanted out of there and away from everyone, but he didn't want to be rude to David so he let him follow him out. They walked the first half of the distance without any words, and then David finally spoke up to break the awkwardness of the moment.

"Not the best ending to a rather incredible day?" David said as they headed up the street.

"What do you mean?" Luke asked.

"Your choice of words seemed… well, less than encouraging to someone who cares so much about you," David replied. Luke first thought about explaining it, then shifted into anger toward David for even mentioning it. Somehow he settled on a simple response.

"I know. It was not what I meant, but it was somehow what I wanted. Does that make sense?" he asked David. David seemed to think a minute on his response before answering.

"You want to be happy for her, but you're hurt about how things are between you now," David said more as a statement than a question. Luke was amazed at how David could always cut to the chase in conversations and hit the nail on the head so quickly. Luke took a deep breath and sighed.

"You know, I was kinda hoping you'd take a lot more time talking and yammering about thoughts, ideas and personal feelings before you raised your gun and hit the mark, because I needed a whole lot more time to try to get a handle on my feeling and emotions before answering." He tried to joke the conversation off as he opened his car door and slid into the driver's seat. David smiled at his words and said,

"Yeah, I'll work on it, but no promises" He helped Luke shut the car door. Luke rolled the window down out of courtesy for them to keep talking, even though talking was the last thing he wanted to do.

"Luke, we both know she cares for you a great deal. Nothing could have hurt her more than the thought of losing your love for her. She is an incredible woman and only a fool would let her get away." David tapped the top of his car and waved as he stepped back onto the sidewalk from the car. "Drive carefully." David said as Luke started the engine and pulled away.

As Luke drove toward home, he knew that the words David shared were true. She was an incredible woman and he knew that only a fool would walk away from her. His heart felt so heavy at the thought of losing her. He let the day and all the feelings and emotions of the past few weeks roll through his mind during the next twenty minutes of the drive. Then somehow the bitterness slowly began to creep back into his heart and the idea of being a "fool" for letting her get away was replaced with the decision that it was the best thing to do. It was time to move on.

Chapter 13

The next few weeks were like a blur to Luke, and with his normally stable social life resembling one of those blender drinks, he was actually relieved to have something to occupy his mind. It was not necessarily by choice, but the sheer size of the potential civilian market that the company planned to target coupled with the demands of the military was requiring all of the resources of the team. Several branches of the military and key government officials had become aware of the project and the results of the field test in Iraq. As word of the product got out, the demand for information was developing a momentum that was at first exciting, then began to be concerning to Luke. At Apollo's insistence, all calls from government contacts were to be directed to him, but they were often redirected to Luke for specific hands-on application questions. Apollo made it clear that he wanted to be the gatekeeper of the project at all levels.

Workdays were becoming longer and longer, often with late night team meetings, planned at the last minute. Luke was constantly in the process of updating and adjusting the various user manuals to reflect the changes and updates. Luke totally immersed himself in the Cat Eyes project and Apollo seemed happy and even impressed about Luke's commitment to the project and the team. In truth, Luke's dedication was more an effort to avoid his current social woes than commitment to the team, but Luke kept that to himself.

Luke was surprised and happy to see that Cliff Jackson was assigned to lead the government's oversight team. Cliff apparently brought a lot more business related talent and experience to the table than Luke realized. Within the first few days of his second arrival, he had established a production mark three weeks away at which time they wanted to determine quantity and delivery schedules. By the end of the week, and with a great deal of pressure from Samuel, Apollo finally asked the team members to recommend the company's best employees from other game development departments who would be asked to transfer to the Cat Eyes team. As an expressed concern and added security measure, the government requested that they avoid any initial outside hires to fill these positions due to the confidentiality of the program. They felt that those that had been already working with the company would be less likely to be someone trying to infiltrate the project. The government oversight team began running thorough background and security checks on all company employees being considered.

Luke was surprised that there was such concern for security so early in the project and asked Cliff about it. Cliff just smiled and said, "Luke, it would actually surprise me to learn that our enemies did not already know about this project while you were in Iraq." Luke thought about the man who tried to kill him in the carpet store, recalling his thought the man seemed to know who he was.

"Are they that aware of such projects?" Luke asked Cliff.

"Living in an open society like America is what makes our country great, but it's also what makes us vulnerable and makes my job very difficult," he said with complete seriousness. "Between the greed and desire for power which seems to be innate in all of us, that our society encourages, it is not hard for our enemies to acquire such vital and valuable information." Luke took a sip of his coffee as he thought about Cliff's words.

"How deep does it go?" Luke asked.

"Based on similar projects, I'm guessing that the project and overview has already been leaked. That any available surface data is already being passed through our enemy's chain of command, mostly being leaked through the various government entities that are now involved with the project."

Luke just sat there trying to comprehend the resources needed to keep so much information moving up the various chains of command and how deep a network or networks would have to be to achieve it. He then decided to drop the topic. He had too many other things to worry about and felt he would leave that sort of thing to the professionals.

Friday morning was extremely busy. Apollo announced to the team that he had released the latest software upgrade and that testing would commence later that day and continue over the weekend. Luke knew that meant no play for him that weekend. On the heels of the recent software release, Apollo called a Friday morning meeting to discuss possible candidates within the company. He initially tried to not include any of the government team members, but word somehow got out about the discussion and the HR contact, Serena, requested to sit in on the meeting as an observer. Jonathan, Ronald, Apollo, Samuel, Serena and himself sat around the conference table silently going over the list of possible candidates that Apollo had put together from various departments for their review. Key individuals from programming, support, manufacturing and logistics were on the list. The goal was to have the team evaluate and rank each potential candidate, on their own and then they would discuss them in an open forum. In reviewing the list, Luke was very surprised that David Stevens was not listed. Luke felt he was the most qualified of the candidates available. He wrote down his name under the 'other suggestions' category to be discussed later.

As each person signaled that they were ready, Apollo opened by stating whom he felt should be added to the team in each department. Luke watched as Jonathan and Ronald nodded in agreement and quickly surveyed their lists and adjusted them to better reflect Apollo's choices. He just shook his head as he looked at Samuel across the table from him, who only smiled, while Serena sat silently. Luke had the feeling that this was looking more like a rubber stamp meeting than an open discussion. Luke tested his feeling by bringing up David's name and explained in detail why he was the most qualified for the position in the programming category. At first Jonathan nodded in agreement, but Apollo quickly rejected him due to his religious beliefs and tried to move away from the topic quickly. Luke thought that was a strange statement and asked Apollo what he meant by it.
"Let's just say he's a little too radical in his beliefs for my taste and is not well suited for the team. He's kind of, well you, except with more teeth," he said and Jonathan and Ronald gave a nervous laugh at the statement as if to deflect the obvious character slam to Luke. Luke could see that Samuel was watching him with a concerned face while Serena sat silent and expressionless. Luke just tilted his head at his words and tried to get a better grasp as to what he meant by 'more teeth' and how it related to him. Apollo was already entertaining other possible suggestions when Luke interrupted him again.

"I don't follow you," Luke stated and the room went silent as Jonathan and Ronald both lost their grins and glanced over at Apollo as if expecting a fight.

"Follow what?" Apollo replied sternly as if trying to bait Luke.

"The 'teeth' comment. Can you clarify that for me?" Luke asked in a polite but equally stern voice.

Apollo now seemed perturbed by the additional interruption and the need to explain his comment. He then looked over at Luke and took a deep breath and set his pen down, leaned forward and put his arms on the table.

"What I mean is that due to his religious convictions, he is more apt to hold tight to any objections that conflict with his beliefs, causing trouble and delays to the work flow," he said coldly in response. Apollo's words may have been about David, but they were also a very thinly masked public statement that Luke had betrayed his own convictions. Convictions that Apollo still believed he held and allowed his own reservations to be walked over. Luke prepared to step up and hit back with a few words of his own, but Samuel stepped in before he could respond.

"Gentlemen, I know we are all under a great deal of pressure to deliver this product on schedule, but Apollo, that comment was uncalled for and inaccurate. I have seen nothing in Luke's character or commitment to this team that should be questioned by anyone sitting here. I also agree that David is an outstanding candidate that should be considered by this group." Samuel looked hard and long at Apollo who only stared coldly back at him for several seconds before responding.

"My apologies, but I still do not wish to have Mr. Stevens on this team and that's final," Apollo said without looking at Luke. Luke felt like he was going to explode in spite of Samuel's attempt to vouch for Luke. Luke tapped his pen on his pad a moment then leaned back in his chair and tried to remember the reason he was maintaining this charade for Samuel as the so called 'team' worked their way through the remaining names on the list.

As the discussions continued, Luke was trying to determine if he was more upset by the reason for the rejection of David or the insult to his own character and convictions. He knew Apollo was right about the latter based on his compromise with the Cat Eyes for Samuel's sake, but Luke disagreed with Apollo's reason for rejecting David. What Apollo viewed as a negative, Luke considered as a strength, which he admired about David and felt compelled to defend it. Ronald was talking about the qualities of Danny Noonan, another possible candidate when Luke spoke up again.

"Perhaps his perspective is exactly what we need on this team." Ronald seemed confused by Luke's words.

"Danny's perspective?" Ronald replied.

"No, David's," Luke replied and then continued while looking at Apollo who seemed to be on the verge of throwing a fit at the subject coming up again. "You fear the religious right's response so why not put one on the team that will show us exactly what we are up against. Especially one with such 'deep' convictions." He let the words sink in a moment before finishing. "Besides, you will have him on a signed non-disclosure, so he can't hurt us." Luke smiled at the end. Luke knew he had gotten under Apollo's skin because Apollo's complexion turned a shade redder, but Samuel raised his eyebrows and nodded as if considering it. Apollo also saw Samuel's apparent agreement, but quickly jumped in before Samuel could interject any comments on the matter.

"I do not 'fear' the religious right and the answer is still 'no' and that is my final response about this." Apollo looked right at Luke as if to dare him to speak. In his anger and frustration, Luke no longer feared the consequences and responded calmly.

"So if I'm reading this 'team meeting' correctly, this meeting was meant to be just a quick approval of your hand picked people than a real desire to bring on the best talent for the team? Because we all know that David is the best developer in this company and has the best work ethic of any of these other individuals, but you're going to let your fear of the religious right keep you from doing what's best for this team and for the product as a whole." Apollo just glared at him across the table but was concerned by Luke's words with Serena watching silently. After a few more silent seconds Apollo finally responded.

"Perhaps you make a good point about my overlooking his talent. Why don't we take a quick 'team' vote to see if we all feel the same about David?" He glanced around the room and then said, "All in favor of extending an offer to David Stevens, raise your hand." Luke knew that the whole 'vote' approach was already a moot point, as Jonathan and Ronald would carry the swing vote over his and Samuel's vote, but he felt good that he at least got under Apollo's dandruff enough to force the vote. He raised his hand, he saw Samuel raise his hand, two votes to their three. Then the unthinkable happened, Jonathan slowly started to raise his hand. It was just enough to make it clear he was for David, but meek enough to show that he was fearful of opposing Apollo. Luke was stunned and Samuel mirrored his expression as they both continued to hold their hands up in support of the vote. Apollo on the other hand seemed fit to be tied shifting his glare from Luke to Jonathan. *So Jonathan was finally growing a backbone,* Luke thought. Luke knew that he would need to spend some time encouraging Jonathan if that spine were to have a chance to develop. Apollo's wrath would be quick and brutal and Jonathan would not survive it on his own.

Luke could feel Samuel looking at him, but avoided making eye contact with him until much later in the meeting. When he finally did, Samuel gently shook his head and gave a slow blink of his eyes; Luke thought he saw one corner of his mouth turn up at the end.

By the end of the meeting Danny Noonan, Gloria Peters and David Stevens were selected as the candidates they would ask to transfer to the team this week with more to follow. Luke knew that there was plenty of scuttlebutt going around the office about the new project and the resources that were being diverted to it. That alone was enough to pique the interest of any developer.

As they headed out of the meeting, Apollo gave Jonathan the cold shoulder and spoke with Ronald as if he was his new best friend. Jonathan sat there as if trying to figure out why he had just sacrificed everything with that vote. Luke stayed back and nodded to Samuel as they both looked at Jonathan trying to arrange his papers. Samuel nodded back and asked Serena to give her thoughts on the selections as well. Luke sat back down across from Jonathan, waiting for him to look up at him. When the look failed to come, Luke spoke up, "Jonathan, that took a lot of courage and a lot of character. I know you're questioning why you did what you did, but I think you know why." Luke continued to wait for some sort of acknowledgement from Jonathan. Jonathan finally looked up at him.

"It's your bloody fault," Jonathan said curtly. At first Luke was stunned at the words, but then he saw Jonathan smile and then continued, "I've never seen anyone stand up to Apollo, not even Samuel. Dude, that was awesome," he said and then his smile grew larger and added, "I guess I'm just a little tired of getting bullied around all the time and seeing you do that, well let's just say it inspired me. It's probably not the smartest career move I've made, but it sure felt good at the time," he smirked.

Luke was taken aback by the comment. Had his standing up for David really inspired Jonathan so much that he would risk his position in the team to do the same? Was it because it was the right thing to do or was it just because he stood up against a bully?

"Yep, we're probably both going to find ourselves on the street on Monday," Luke joked with Jonathan, silently fearing that the jest might have more truth to it than either of them would like. Things on the 'team' just got a lot more complicated.

As he walked back to his desk, he felt the strong urge to head over toward David's desk to let him know what might be coming his way, but realized that perhaps it was already too late as he looked up to see Apollo and Ronald standing there with David, already engaged in conversation. *What a snake,* Luke thought as he turned into his cubicle and sat down in his chair to see if he could pick up any of the conversation. He smiled at the hypocrisy of his statement since he was more upset at being beaten to the punch as he tried to tune in.

"I want you to know how grateful we are for your efforts, but I need you to put the company first in this situation." Apollo turned to leave, but then stopped again, "Please know that we will compensate you accordingly for your increase in responsibility." He then smiled and walked past Luke's desk making as if he was speaking to Ronald, "Loyalty is such a great but rare quality in these times."

Luke rocked back in his chair and ran his hands through his hair as he replayed the last hour in his mind. His pride had managed to put Jonathan in hot water, further distancing himself from Apollo and jeopardizing his commitment to help Samuel. The good news is that he apparently managed to get David a raise as a result of really ticking off Apollo. *Well at least something good came from all this,* he thought to himself as he stared blankly at his computer screen. Luke wished the day were over. He looked at his watch begrudgingly and saw that it was only 10:15 a.m. and there was still a whole day in front of him.

A synthesized ding from his computer let him know that he had a message. As he looked at it, he saw that it was from David.

"Got lunch?" was all it said. As he looked closer, he saw that David was using a different message client, not the standard office one.

"That might not be a good career move for you." He typed back. He waited only a moment before a reply came back.

"I'll risk it. ☺" Then another message followed, "Rosarita's at noon?" Luke typed back. "Sounds good. How will I recognize you? ☺"

"I'll find you," David replied with his quick wit. Luke smiled and thought that it would be good to speak with David about his discussion with Apollo and see what he was thinking about the regarding the invitation to work on the Cat Eyes development team.

He spent the next hour and a half organizing new graphic renderings to be used for the manuals. The more he thought about the whole situation, the more he was tempted to walk into Samuel's office and give his two weeks notice. Luke felt it might save everyone a lot of time to the chase of his inevitable dismissal. Whether fortunate or not, his pride would not allow Apollo such an easy victory, no matter how frustrated he was with him.

At 11:50 he locked down his computer, grabbed his cell phone and headed out the door to meet David. It was a short three-block walk down the road and some spicy Mexican food actually sounded good. David had already arrived and grabbed a table by one of the windows in the corner when Luke walked in. David watched Luke intently as he walked to the table, as if he was looking for something hidden. They skipped the typical small talk and instead sat in silence until the waitress came to the table to take their order. They each ordered without looking at the menu since everyone who worked for the company had eaten there many times. As the waitress walked away, David broke the ice.

"You've looked better," he said. and Luke nodded and tried to think of something funny, but his heart was not into it.

"So why is Apollo so insistent on me not taking that programming opportunity with the new product line you guys are working on?" Luke was not surprised that David had seen through Apollo's manipulation. David was pretty sharp.

"David, you are the best person for the job, but you do not want to take that position. Take the raise and stay right where you are," Luke said with all sincerity. David tried to try to read through Luke's words for understanding but gave up and replied, "The word around the water cooler is that the government is now involved in a big way, so whatever it is, it must be very important. It sounds like a great opportunity, so why the warning speech?" Luke tried to think through how best to word his opinion without breaking his confidentiality clause.

"Let's just say that it's a lot bigger, more complicated and more dangerous than it might appear. I just think you and your family would be better off if you stayed where you're at." Luke looked up at David and then to the waitress as she brought their food. David sat silently as they both poured extra hot sauce on their burritos, then David bowed his head and prayed for his food in silence as he always did when they had lunch together. Luke was never sure what he should do during those times, should he wait or keep eating and pretend he didn't notice the praying? The first few times they had lunch together, David asked him if he would like him to say a prayer for the food out loud. Luke said 'no thanks' so ever since, David prayed in silence.

"It sounds like you're in trouble," David said, as he took a bite and watched Luke's face for a reaction.

"Only in dealing with Apollo. The rest is just work and procedures. The project is very unique and more far reaching than it might appear, but you'd be stepping into a pool of sharks and I'd hate to see you get hurt on my account."

"What do you mean by 'on your account'? It's no secret that Apollo and I are not close friends, and sadly, to my knowledge, no one else is either, but it sounds like you stuck your neck out for me and now you're a little concerned about it," David said and Luke just blinked at his quick read on the situation.

"David, I honestly believe you are the best candidate, but my anger toward Apollo and his reasons for not wanting you on the team is what makes this a dangerous lateral move for you. If you take the position, it would be an uphill battle from the beginning to the end of your employment. Considering you will be under Apollo too, could be a very short time for both of us." David finished his burrito in silence.

"Well, it sounds like you could use some help in dealing with Apollo on the project and having a friend on the programming team could make all the difference." Luke shook his head at David's words.

"I don't know if I will be on the team much longer, so you'd end up having to fight that battle on your own and he eats guys like us for lunch." David frowned at Luke's words and then smiled.

"I doubt that. Guys like us are way too stringy and tough to eat," David said. Luke smiled and tried to determine if this was a good thing or not, but it definitely made him want to stand and fight knowing David would be there with him. As they paid their bill for lunch and headed out the door, Luke said, "You'd better work on your resume and don't say I didn't warn you."

"God has blessed Susan with a great job, so I'm not too worried about paying the bills if I get canned, but I'll freshen it up just in case."

As they walked back to the office, Luke tried to understand why David would want to take on this opportunity knowing that it would be trouble for him. As they approached the office, he found himself needing to ask.

"Why," was all he said.

"Do you want the complete truth?" David asked and Luke just nodded. "One, I tend to stand up to bullies when prudent. Two, I rarely turn away from a righteous challenge that could help a friend. And three, God believes in you and he has put it in my heart to help you find him." Luke nodded at his words yet felt uncomfortable by his honesty.

"I appreciate your second reason, but I think your third reason might be a little faulty," Luke replied. David smiled as he held the door open for Luke.

"Who says you're the friend I'm thinking about?" Luke was expecting a long religious rebuttal on his third point response, but now he was trying to figure out who the other 'friend' might be. As they stepped into the courtyard of the office complex David thanked him for lunch and excused himself to go speak with another individual across the courtyard. Luke saw him wave to the person, who smiled in return and shook his hand as they got close. Luke took the stairs up to the office instead of the elevator, something Danielle was always trying to get him to do. Danielle! Was Danielle the other friend he was talking about?

Jonathan was waiting by his desk when he returned. His face was worried, but he seemed to sit taller in spite of it.

"Hey Jonathan, what's the latest?" Luke asked knowing that something was going down. Jonathan tilted his head toward the break room and walked toward it without saying anything. Luke looked around and then followed him. Once they entered it, Jonathan surveyed the room to make sure it was clear and then turned and whispered loudly to Luke.

"Apollo and Samuel are having a blowout in Samuel's office. I was walking past and you could hear them clear out into the hallway. I'm guessing he wants us fired and Samuel is trying to talk him out of it." Luke nodded his head and raised his eyebrows as he listened to Jonathan pour out his thoughts on the matter.

"Did you hear what they said, or are you just guessing?" Luke asked.

"I heard Apollo say something about how he refuses to work with you on this. Samuel was just trying to calm him down. Later, I saw Apollo leave and then Serena left Samuel's office a little later." Luke knew Apollo held most of the cards and would play every one of them to get him removed, so he figured he should plan on getting a box to put his stuff in when he got back to his desk. Luke turned to a confused Jonathan.

"If it goes down the way you think, when I'm gone, you should try to make amends with Apollo. Tell him you're sorry about the vote, but that you did not realize how strongly he felt about David and did not realize until now how dangerous I was to have on the team. That might get you back in his graces enough to save your job. Life will suck for awhile, but it should eventually get back to where it was before," Luke said to Jonathan using his best consolatory voice. Jonathan seemed to reflect on the thought a moment; he then looked back at Luke.

"No thanks, I won't go back to that again." Luke tried to read his face and knew that by standing up to Apollo, Jonathan had gained some confidence and clarity about himself. Luke just hoped he would take that confidence with him wherever he went. He patted Jonathan on the shoulder as they turned to leave the break room.

"For what it's worth, I'm proud of you and your decision." Jonathan smiled and seemed to glow a moment from the words, but then headed down the hall toward his cubicle.

When Luke arrived back at his desk and logged back into his system, he saw that a memo from Apollo had been sent. He expected the worst when he opened it, but was surprised that it was just a partial team meeting, not his pink slip. Only Ronald, Samuel and Apollo were to meet to discuss the software upgrade. Although not surprised, Apollo made it clear that he and Jonathan were not invited. *So it begins,* he thought as he sat back in his chair. Standard protocol was to wait until the end of the day and then let the individual know they had been terminated and that they should gather their personal effects and turn in their security access card. Then they would be escorted out of the office. Luke was pretty confident that Apollo would make an example of him for the rest of the office by really putting on a show as he was being escorted out the door.

He tried to plan what he should do when they arrived. He even tried to think of what should be done prior to their arrival and what pain he could cause them. But being vindictive was not one of his strong points, so he decided to go at things from a more professional perspective. He took the rest of the day to neatly organize all his digital files and information, as well as all personal notes and research that he had done on his own time. Once completed, he burned it to several disks and added a personal note, then delivered it to Serena and asked that she deliver it to Cliff for him. She asked if this was personal or public in nature. He explained it was public, just a backup of all his work and that he wanted to make sure that his work was never left under the control of only one individual. She seemed to be concerned about the content and his words, but did not pursue the matter with him. He wished her a pleasant weekend and headed back to his desk to gather his things.

On his way he swung by Jonathan's desk to see if he had heard anything yet, but he shook his head and looked around as if expecting the same thing to happen at any moment. "It's not like Apollo to let a moment of gloating pass without rubbing our noses in it," Luke said. Jonathan smiled but the words seemed to remind him of something.

"Yeah," was all he said in reply.

As 5 p.m. came and passed, then 5:30, Luke decided that he was not going to wait around to entertain Apollo, so he grabbed his personal stuff and headed out the door with Jonathan close on his heels.

As he reached his car, he yelled across the parking lot to Jonathan, "What do you have going on tonight?" Jonathan seemed to remember he had planned, then realized that if there was something scheduled, it would have probably been with Apollo.

"Nothing, why?" He seemed truly interested. Luke debated on asking him, but felt with his taking a stand on their side today that the least he could do is invite him out for the night.

"Do you remember Monica?" Luke asked.

"Cindy's friend?" Jonathan replied with an anxious look and Luke nodded.

"She's having a small party at her apartment tonight. Care to join me?" Jonathan almost floated in the air.

"Yeah, what time and where?" he replied almost too enthusiastically.

"I can't remember the exact the time that was left on my machine, but I'll call you when I get home. I think it was 8 o'clock." Luke waved goodbye.

Luke started to get into the car and then stood up again and looked at Jonathan. "Hey, whatever happened between you and Cindy? I never asked how things turned out with the two of you." Luke was concerned that there may be some awkwardness at the party if things had not turned out well between Jonathan and Cindy. Luke kicked himself for not asking that question before inviting Jonathan. Jonathan seemed embarrassed by the question and mumbled something in response.

"What?" Luke asked.

"I never called her," Jonathan said a little louder. Luke remained silent a moment before continuing his line of questioning, still not sure if the invite was a good one or not.

Why?" Luke asked thinking perhaps the evening ended poorly between them. Jonathan looked around as if to make sure no one could hear him except Luke.

"I was too nervous. I mean the evening went well and all, but…" He just shrugged his shoulders instead of finishing the sentence. Luke was still not sure what 'went well' meant, but it did not seem to be a bad ending. Jonathan's coming should be okay, Luke thought briefly.

"Don't worry about it. I'll call you later," he said as he slid into his seat and started his engine.

Do I really want to go? he asked himself, thinking of all the possible conclusions to the evening. He would rather spend the evening with Danielle, but that was out of the question, so this seemed the best alternative to a night at home contemplating his upcoming firing on Monday. He definitely needed a distraction to take his mind off of things and Monica was very good at distracting. He put his car in gear and started to back out of his parking slot. 'Drowning his sorrows' suddenly seemed like a good idea. The blast of the horn made him jump in his seat and hit the brakes at the same time. A red sports car barely managed to avoid the back of his car as he came to a stop. It did not slow down as it left the parking lot and quickly moved to the exit. *Wow, that was close,* he thought to himself and realized that he needed to pay closer attention to his surroundings when driving. He was glad the person did not stop and chew him out for not looking. This time he glanced both ways before he pulled out of his parking spot and toward the exit. *That would have been a perfect crummy ending to an already crummy day,* he thought as he headed home.

Chapter 14

Luke sat in his car in front of Monica's apartment complex feeling uneasy and a little nervous. At home he had battled over whether or not to even go, but felt that if he didn't now, he would be condemning Jonathan to a similar fate of sitting home alone and wallowing in his thoughts and regrets of life. He called Monica earlier to make sure it was alright to bring Jonathan. Apparently, Cindy would be there and she did have an interest in Jonathan, but since he dropped off the map, she assumed he didn't like her. He explained that Jonathan was just a little shy and needed a little coaxing. She replied that it sounded a little like someone else she knew. Luke's heart skipped a beat and his stomach went into a knot again as it shifted into 'fight or flight' mode. Her giggle on the other end of the line broke the awkwardness of the uncomfortable moment and she told him that she was looking forward to seeing him and hoped the evening would end a lot differently than last time.

When he hung up the phone, his mind was conflicted between desire and guilt. He thought about the distracting possibilities with Monica, while battling the knowledge that allowing himself to be distracted by Monica would hurt Danielle when the word eventually got back to her. He just wished things were back to normal. He even thought about calling Danielle and telling her directly that things were over between them so that he could have a clear conscience. But that was not what he wanted. He would rather find a way to somehow convince her that she was heading down the wrong path and have her back the way she used to be.

He called Jonathan with the details and reminded him not to be early, so that he would not end up being the only one there. Luke decided to go dressy casual for the evening and wore a little extra of the cologne that Danielle bought him for his birthday. He was never a clothes fanatic, nor did he have great taste in men's clothes, so he wore what Danielle had recently picked out for him.

He locked his car, took a deep breath and then headed toward the front door. He decided to keep things plutonic with Monica he felt better about his status with Danielle. He was not mentally ready to deal with another relationship. Luke reached the front door, checked the directory to find her floor and then dialed the number for her to buzz him in. He could hear music and voices in the background, so he assumed the party must be in full swing. He introduced himself to the person on the other end, who just said "hi" and buzzed him past the security door. As he rode the elevator up, he reminded himself again that this would be just a 'get to know you' evening with Monica and her friends. He knocked on the door and Cindy was there to answer it.

"Hi Luke!" she said as he stepped into the apartment.

"Hi Cindy, you look great!"

"Thank you. I thought Jonathan was coming with you?" Luke suddenly understood why Cindy had answered the door instead of Monica.

"Not with me, but he is coming," Luke told her, which seemed to brighten up her face considerably. Cindy escorted him into the apartment, where he could see about twenty people, sitting, standing or moving about the living room and the patio deck that lead from it. As he looked around it seemed that, excluding himself, Monica had apparently only invited the beautiful people of Los Angeles to her party. Everyone was dressed in the best labels that money could buy and seemed to have the face and body to match. He definitely felt underdressed, and was now very happy that he had worn the outfit that Danielle had picked out for him. Monica's place was very large and the interior décor was very classy. Everything was coordinated, from the furniture and the window treatments to the paintings and designer knick-knacks. The whole place looked like a professionally staged model home in a high end housing development. He suddenly felt insecure at the idea of having Monica over for dinner.

"Monica, Luke is here!" Cindy called into the kitchen area and nearly every head turned to look in his direction. Luke got the feeling that he was sized up from head to toe by a dozen people in the space of a few seconds. Luke nodded and smiled to several nearby people. They smiled back but feigned to be too busy to engage him in conversation.

Luke's gaze moved across the room and as he looked through the open kitchen area, he saw her. She was radiant and walking towards him, her eyes fixed on his. Her auburn hair had been pulled back and slightly up, highlighting her features perfectly. She wore dark red lipstick and the perfect shade of eye shadow that brought out the green in her eyes. She was stunning. A black silk miniskirt that formed tightly around her perfect legs, hips and waist, left no doubt about her figure. Her white silk blouse was semi- transparent and revealed a matching white undergarment straight out of a Victoria's Secret catalog. A string of white pearls were around her neck and the sparkle of diamonds came from her ears. The black 'pumps,' as Danielle called them, made her look much taller than he remembered. As she walked toward him everything seemed to come together in perfect harmony and there was no doubt that anyone looking at him would know that he was smitten by her. Just when he thought that she could not get any more attractive, she smiled at him. It was one of those sultry, movie moment types of smiles that would be etched into his mind for eternity. He just stood there taking her all in.

"Well, do you like it?" She asked him and giggled that incredible giggle of hers.

He took a deep breath. "You look absolutely incredible… stunning… perfect," he almost stammered. She tucked her arm into his and walked him through the living room and toward the outside patio and every eye followed them out.

"Good answer." She squeezed his arm, "I've been dying to wear it for you since I bought it in San Diego." He kept trying to clear his head enough to be able to make some sort of intelligent conversation, but all he kept thinking was *wow*. "How was the trip?" he asked as he regained his faculties.

"You should have come, it was so much fun. We went to the Hotel Del, went out for dinner at some of the most amazing places, and obviously, we did a little shopping." She stopped at the railing and looked out over the city and what remained of the sunset. He just stood there soaking in every detail.

If there was a moment in his life when he felt things were perfect, it was that moment. He had the most beautiful woman he could imagine holding onto his arm in the most beautiful city, watching a beautiful sunset. He suddenly remembered that he never liked Los Angeles, but he had to admit that the woman on his arm definitely made it look a whole lot better.

"Stay right here, I'll get us each a drink and we will toast the evening." She turned and repeated that sultry and captivating walk back toward the kitchen. Luke could see the lights from the kitchen silhouetting her figure and reminding him of how transparent her white top was. His heart was beating fast, his head was swimming, and his stomach was tightening. He knew this feeling and where it would take him if he let himself stumble forward like a lamb being led to the slaughter. He thought about running for the door while he still had the strength to do so, but it was too late as she had gathered their drinks and was heading back toward him. She stopped briefly to speak with someone in the living room. As she did she turned slightly sideways and the lights behind her silhouetted her figure. He tried to remind himself again of his decision to remain *only friends* but the thought seemed so stupid to him now and the reasons for it even more ridiculous. He had enough presence about him to at least realize that he no longer had any control and that the gears were turning too fast to stop them. She walked toward him and handed him a drink.

"I forgot to ask what you wanted, so I made you an Iced Tea." She smiled as he took the long tall glass and took a drink. The bite of the alcohol told him that it was a Long Island or a close cousin. It didn't matter, in fact, she could have handed him a glass of poison and he probably would have drank it. The thought of Eve, handing the apple to Adam to try, and him biting it without even thinking of the consequences, suddenly made more sense. He was not match for the power of a beautiful, intelligent woman.

They spoke for another thirty minutes or more about her trip, about her week, and what she did for a living. He learned that she was the only daughter of a wealthy family and that she worked in the art industry as an interior designer. She went to school at USC, where she majored in Art History. She had done some modeling, but learned that the profession was not as glamorous as she envisioned it to be. The last three years she had worked for a leading interior design firm. It all seemed so perfect and planned and besides the modeling endeavor, the way she wanted things to turn out. From time to time, Luke would glance around the patio and interior of the apartment and watched the people that had come to her party. From the outside they all seemed about as well off and perfect as her life. He wondered briefly why his life had been so challenging. Was it the money or lack of it that allowed him to get started? Perhaps if he could find a job that would pay him more, he could live a similar life? His hearing seemed to fade for a moment as he reflected on the similar perfect people that had known in his life. They had just as many flaws and issues as anyone else. When he noticed that Monica had gone quiet, he looked back at her and saw that she was studying his face and smiling curiously.

"I'm sorry. I've been doing all the talking. What are you thinking?" she asked as he continued to reflect on the evening and everyone around him.

"Why me?" he suddenly said, in all seriousness, but with innocence in his voice. She seemed confused by the question and unsure of how to answer it. "I mean, with all these incredibly successful, handsome men around you, a life that is on a fast track to wherever your dreams may take you, why do you have an interest in me?" he asked and looked into her eyes for the answer. "I'm flattered and honored to have caught your eye and all, but I don't fit into the world that you live in nor could I compete with the lifestyle that you are accustomed to."

She seemed to understand the question and where he was coming from and she smiled then looked around the room at her guests. She took another sip of her drink and took a deep breath.

"Well, it's because you're not like everyone else at this party." She seemed to gather her thoughts again as she continued, "You're not trying to impress me, or convince me that you are someone other than who you are, nor do you tell me things just because I want to hear them. You're innocent in a special way, not jaded or hardened by wealth or social status and you're honest. You see things differently than anyone I have ever dated." She hesitated and looked away and then back into his eyes, "You're the breath of fresh air that has been missing in my empty life." It was Luke's turn to be stunned. He did not view himself in any of those ways.

"That's not me you just described and I'm afraid if you think of me in that light, you will be very disappointed when you get to know me." He hesitated long enough for her to interject.

"That's what I mean; you never try to persuade me or convince me of how wonderful you are. I always know who you are. You are so unlike anyone I have ever gone out with." He felt encouraged by her words, but also uncomfortable knowing that he was not the person she thought he was.

"Even a brief breath of fresh air eventually needs to be exhaled. I'm not sure I'm ready for that kind of pain again so soon." She held his eyes for what seemed like forever and her smile faded slightly. Then it returned suddenly.

"Then I guess I'll need to hold my breath for as long as possible," she said and put her head on his shoulder. He was on cloud nine and never felt more encouraged and confident, but as he walked around and spoke with the other people at the party, there were still faint alarms going off inside. About the time he was going to ask a few questions, Jonathan and Cindy came up to them. Cindy was also hanging on Jonathan's arm and was obviously very excited about seeing Jonathan again.

"Glad you found the place." Luke said.

"My GPS rarely fails me," Jonathan replied. Not being the most diplomatically sensitive and rather awkwardly direct, Jonathan asked Luke, "Where's Danielle?" Luke seemed embarrassed about being asked that question in front of Monica.

"Probably at home, why?" Luke responded.

"I just thought you two were an item and was surprised to see you with Monica." He said completely missing the awkwardness and insensitively of his words.

"Were no longer an item Jonathan, and she's probably at church now that she has found religion," Luke said sarcastically. His anger came out not toward Jonathan, but Danielle.

"At church?" Jonathan seemed floored by the answer. "I just can't see Danielle going to church. What church?" he asked, while Monica and Cindy seemed distantly interested, but did not want to interrupt the discussion. Luke realized he didn't know the name of it.

"The one David Stevens goes to," Luke replied. Jonathan seemed shocked at his words.

"That church is a cult and teaches false doctrine." Jonathan's words hit him like a ton of bricks. Not the "false doctrine" part, because that meant nothing to Luke, but the idea that she was in a "cult" struck a nerve.

"What do you mean by cult?" he asked, trying to gather a little more information before he let his fears and emotions run too wild.

"I mean it's a cult. David invited me to church once, so I went, but when I did a little background research on their church and what they believe, it proved to be a cult. So I never went again," Jonathan said. Luke seemed confused by his response.

"What do you mean by 'proved to be'?" Luke sounded almost upset with the vague terminology Jonathan was using.

"What I mean is that their teaching is very radical and not in line with standard Christian doctrine and teaching. They are very works oriented and they believe you must be baptized to be saved," Jonathan answered carefully.

"How do you know what standard Christian doctrine is?" Luke asked. Jonathan seemed a little taken aback by his question.

"From church." Luke was surprised by the answer.

"You go to..." Luke started to reply in shock, "I didn't know you went to church." Luke recovered and then continued. "Where do you go?" he asked.

"The same one I've gone to every Sunday for as long as I can remember," he replied and then Cindy blurted out, "I do too!" She was excited that Jonathan also went to church. "I sometimes go to a Korean church with my family, but mostly to a large downtown church." She explained. Luke smiled at their realization that they had something in common, church. Luke turned to Monica and raised an eyebrow as if asking her the same question. She smiled and said, "Almost every Sunday." She raised an eyebrow and then continued, "I go to Cloud Cathedral, a large church of over 10,000 members every Sunday."

"Really! They say that is supposed to be one of the best churches for meeting guys." Cindy giggled and then continued, "Very affluent, from what I saw. I went there once, about a year ago."

"Maybe we can all go there together on Sunday?" Jonathan chimed in. For a guy that was too scared to even call Cindy before, Jonathan seemed to have gathered enough courage to setup a date. Luke listened as the three made plans and talked about which service time to pick from. Luke could not help but think about Danielle's new church and wondered if she knew it was a cult. He thought about her baptism, the people that were there, the awkward closeness they had, and even the 'pit-bull brothers' and their aggressive tactics. Then he thought about David and Susan and what he knew about them. It just did not seem to fit, but then again, he wouldn't have guessed the three standing before him were church-goers either.

He refocused on the conversation that was unfolding and realized that they had made plans on him attending with them. At first he was very resistant to the idea, but then he thought about going to see what it was like and perhaps learning a little more about their religious beliefs. He also thought that it was a great way to perhaps catch Danielle's attention and encourage her to move away from the current church she was in, one that did not have such strict guidelines for dating and relationships.

"Well, is it a date?" Jonathan asked Luke. He thought again about it and knew he did not have much else going on.

"I'm not a big fan of religion, but I'll check it out," he said and Monica smiled and squeezed his arm.

As the night wore on, the crowd seemed to thin slowly until it appeared that there was only Monica, Cindy, Jonathan, and himself sitting on the living room couches, and two other couples that seemed to have taken up residency on the patio chairs outside.

Monica continued to bring the 'iced teas' as the night wore on and Luke could tell that not only was his mind getting foggy, but also Cindy and Jonathan were obviously well on their way to a bad hangover. Monica had continued to get more physical with him, her hand went from occasionally touching his arm or leg, to continually resting there as the four of them talked or listened to each other tell war stories about their work lives, college days, and past relationships.

Every time there was a need for a drink, she would always volunteer to get the drinks for everyone, 'I am the hostess!' she would state adamantly and then get up and gather everyone's empty glasses and head for the kitchen. At first Luke did not pick up on what she was doing, but after the second and third rounds, he realized that in spite of the already attractive silk shirt that she wore, she was purposely bending over across from him to better display her lace undergarments. The first few times, he tried to be the gentlemen and not look when the opportunity presented itself, but as the effects of the alcohol and his 'gentlemanly' defenses weakened, he started to allow himself to take in a brief glance. It was as if she knew instinctively when he started looking, for the moment he took his first look; she looked up to see where his eyes had been. He initially thought he was going to get a scolding or a frown from her, but she simply smiled and winked. The rest of the night was an obvious game that she was playing with him at every opportunity and he was fully participating. His engine was revving faster and faster, driving him out of control even, and away from his 'just friends' plan for the night. He knew the longer he let things play out, the less he would even want to stop it.

During one of Monica's drink or bathroom runs, Luke had broken free of her display of incredible physical attributes long enough to notice that Cindy and Jonathan were also getting more and more physical and they were spending less and less time talking and more and more time whispering and kissing each other. It got to the point that when Monica would leave, he felt very awkward in their presence, almost as if he was not there, but an invisible observer.

During Monica's last drink runs, Luke got up to use the restroom down the hall. As he took his first few steps toward the bathroom, he was surprised at how much the alcohol had affected him. He must have had more than he realized. He braced himself against the wall just outside the bathroom door and tried to figure out what to do when he realized that it was occupied by one of the patio people. He then remembered Monica mentioning a second bathroom in her bedroom. As he walked down the lighted hallway and toward the back bedroom, he saw pictures of her on the wall with various people. Some were with women, but mostly they were of her and various men over her lifetime. From what he could tell, they were vacation pictures, formal pictures, party pictures from college and maybe a few family photo's. There seemed to be hundreds of people that she had known in her life. He felt strange inside, almost a feeling of jealousy, as he looked at each one of them. He barely knew her, yet he felt possessive of her and her past. Was he really having such deep feelings for her that he would feel jealous of other men she had been with in the past? He knew that he had not been Danielle's first experience, nor her his, but she had never posted the evidence for the world to see. As he reached the end of the hallway and the pictures, he looked back and chuckled at the thought of his uncle's place back home, where he mounted every trophy animal he had ever shot in his life. He was an avid hunter and fisherman, but he only mounted the biggest catches on his wall. He wondered if it didn't work out between Monica and him, would he be considered worthy enough to be mounted on her wall or would he be left in a old picture album.

His urgent need to relieve himself made him glance back at the main bathroom again but saw that it was still occupied. So he turned to the bedroom and pushed open the bedroom door. As he stepped into the room, he saw that one of the patio couples had managed to slip by them in the living room and were making out on the bed; both of them were in various states of undress. His first impulse was to quickly back out of the room before he was seen, but then he saw the open door to the master bathroom right next to him. With the others occupied and his need high, he just smiled and quietly walked to the bathroom and closed the door behind him.

He turned on the light and tried to remain steady as he relieved himself. He couln't even remember the last time he was that intoxicated.

"College!" He almost shouted, but then mumbled "My junior year in the fraternity…" as the night flowed back into his mind. He frowned as he rocked back and forth and then he remembered that he woke up in his room the following morning with some sorority girl whose name he could not even remember now. She was always a very sweet girl and he remembered them drinking and laughing and then being so passionate with each other that evening. He also remembered that they both woke up feeling horrible and very embarrassed by the situation. He felt sad as he remembered that after that night, when they saw each other on campus, they were both so ashamed of their behavior that they couldn't even acknowledge each other.

He balanced himself with his legs leaning against the sink while he washed his hands. Someone must have opened a door to the bedroom or to the outside, as he felt a gentle breeze blow across his face. He looked toward the closed bathroom door to make sure it was still closed and then turned his head back toward the sink. He glanced up and was surprised to see a face in the mirror that he barely recognized. The hair was disheveled and the lips were more of a smirk than a smile, but it was the eyes that surprised him the most. The eyes seemed wild, yet sad. He saw a different man looking back at him and he did not like what he saw. He stared several seconds at the face, searching for something that seemed lost somewhere in the depths behind it.

He finally bent down and splashed water on his face in an attempt to wash it away and reflected on the situation that he was now in. There was an incredibly sexy woman in the other room who has given him every sign in the world that she wanted him to stay the night with her. Everything in his body told him to stay and enjoy the pleasures she offered. But, there was something else deep inside that was trying to remind him that there would be a cost to such a decision and it could be more than he wanted to pay. He tried his best to remember, but he could not grasp why it was that he was holding back. He shook his head and could not even believe he was trying to talk himself out of such an incredible opportunity. Another splash of water and he watched as the drops fell from his face and into the sink below him. *Friends!* He remembered, they were supposed to be just friends. So how did he get to a point of even considering spending the night with her? *The iced teas…* He remembered that he was a friend of the girl in college too; well, they were friends before that night.

In spite of his mind telling him that it wasn't, he knew that the alcohol was the agent of change. He closed his eyes and tried to think hard about what his next move should be once he stepped out of the bathroom. It was either back into her waiting arms or out the door and into his car. He didn't want their relationship to turn out like it did with the girl in college. He actually remembered now that he had really liked her before that evening. He did not want to destroy his relationship with Monica in the same way that he had destroyed that one.

He gathered up what was left of his common sense and decided that he was way too drunk to drive, so he would either need to call a taxi or sleep in his car. With his mind made up, he quietly opened the door and walked quietly past the now totally engrossed couple on the bed, shutting the door behind him, as he snuck down the trophy hallway. As he turned the corner into the living room, Monica was waiting in his spot on the couch and her face was as sultry and seductive as he could have ever imagined a woman's face to be. He glanced over to see that Jonathan and Cindy were in a deep and passionate embrace with their lips locked together, oblivious to Monica sitting across from them. He chuckled as he thought of the time his dad took a hose to two of the dogs back home that were going at it during a family gathering. As he looked back to where Monica was sitting, he saw that she had undone a button on her top and that she had put one leg under her other causing her skirt to reveal the vast majority of her long legs. She looked absolutely amazing and he was confident the moment he was now in surpassed the majority of his fantasies. Then he spoke.

"Everything inside me says that I'm insane to walk away from this moment, but I want us to still be friends tomorrow," he said with a slight slur as he tried to hang onto the memory of the girl in college that had been his friend. She blinked and seemed stunned, then angry and then sad. He stood there and watched all the expressions cross her face without moving.

"We will still be friends. Just better friends," she said and smiled seductively at him as she patted the cushion next to her. He started to buy into her words, but then managed to somehow shake them off.

"I think I like you way too much to take that risk and I want to make sure it's me that feels that way and not the alcohol. Monica, you are one of the most incredibly sexy women I have ever met, but I've been here before, and based on the pictures in the hallway, I'm guessing you have too. I just don't want to wake up tomorrow to learn those feelings were a lie and I'm just another picture for your wall." She seemed to be a bit embarrassed by his observation. Luke looked over to see that Cindy and Jonathan had stopped their kissing and were looking at the two of them. Monica slid her foot down and slowly stood up and walked toward him. Although he had missed it before, he could see clearly that the alcohol was working a number on her as well. She stood there looking at him as if trying to understand how to respond in the moment she found herself in. Luke guessed that she had never gone this far in the seduction game only to be turned down.

"Well, I'm glad you find me sexy," she said and smiled up at him. "Although I wish you would change your mind, I also find your response at my best attempts to seduce you another breath of fresh air." She reached up and kissed his cheek. "If you would like to sleep on the couch, I can run these two love puppies off and I'll sleep in my room." She said with a giggle. It sounded like a great idea and he wanted to buy into it again, but he knew better.

"One, I don't trust myself nor my will power to stay on the couch with you sleeping just a short distance away. Two, you're going to need to run two other love puppies off your bed and out of your room before that is an option for you," he said with a smile and nod toward her bedroom. She seemed flattered by his first comment and then really bothered by the thought of his second comment.

"Well that's just rude," she said and then smirked and then realized what she had said. "Not you, them. They are rude." She tried to clarify her response nodding towards her bedroom and he smiled back already knowing what she meant. His mind seemed to be clearing the more he talked.

"Shall I call you a cab?" she asked, finally accepting that victory was out of her grasp. Luke shook his head.

"No, I'll call one and just wait in my car for them to arrive." He looked back at her. "Thank you for an incredible evening. That white blouse and skirt and lace undergarments, and long legs…" His eyes followed his words to each part of her body that he mentioned and then rested back on her eyes, "And your eyes and lips and neck… Let's just say that they are forever etched into my mind." He seemed to be contemplating staying again before he caught himself. "And I gotta get out of her before I change it." He took a deep breath then leaned forward and kissed her gently on the forehead. "Thank you for an amazing evening." He stopped as he opened the door and looked back at her.

"I hope we're still friends in the morning." He smiled and she returned the smile as he closed the door behind him.

He made it down the stairs and into his car where he locked the doors knowing that he had drank too much to drive safely. He tilted the seat back and closed his eyes. He woke up about 4 hours later. It was 5 a.m. and he had a stiff neck, a terrible taste in his mouth and a headache. He dug his keys out of his pocket and headed toward home. He could still feel the alcohol in him, but he was in far better shape than when he first fell asleep. He took extra care to drive slowly and carefully all the way home to not draw any undue attention.

Chapter 15

The morning was mostly spent trying to stop the banging inside his skull and attempting to reconstruct the events from the night before. Why he had allowed himself to drink as much as he did, knowing full well what the consequences would be he had no idea. In the early part of the morning, it was all he could do to drink a great deal of water, chase it with pain relievers and stay prone. As his stomach settled, he considered the previous evenings encounter at Monica's house. As he lay on the couch, he began replaying the various discussions, observations and interactions and was surprised at how much he had missed 'in the moment' that seemed much clearer to him now.

Monica's stunning and seductive beauty was still as clear as could be, but the whole evening seemed much more staged than he remembered it being at the time. In his mind's eye he could see that she was very obvious about her intent to lure him into spending the night. He was almost embarrassment about the term 'lure', as it reminded him of fishing with his grandfather as a boy. They would change out lures depending upon the type of fish they were striving to catch, or they would switch again when they weren't catching anything. Was he just a fish chasing the specific lure Monica was using? Luke knew that guys were suckers for the 'sexy lure' and she had blatantly cast that one out in front of him all night long. Sometimes it was the funny, or clever, or confident, or shy lure that would work, but just like fishing, you would just keep swapping them out until you found the one that worked best for your prey. Monica definitely had the 'sexy lure' down and Luke was sure she had caught many stupid fish on it. How he had managed to avoid it, he was not sure, but he was grateful that in addition to his hangover, he did not have a regretful 'morning after' moment to have to deal with.

Luke wondered if Jonathan or Cindy were running for cover from the dreaded 'morning after' bullet. He had hoped Jonathan would have made the decision to leave with him, but based on how things were going between them, he doubted it. He felt like he should have said something that would have encouraged Jonathan to leave, but he seemed rather naïve when it came to such situations.

Luke vaguely remembered one of their conversations from the previous night. *Did I commit to going to church with them?* he thought. It seemed impossible, but he was pretty sure he had said something to that effect. He pondered the circumstances of the invite. *I had a very attractive women dressed way beyond sexy, enough alcohol to keep a marine platoon happy, and in the middle of it they asked me to attend church with them?* Luke shook his head as he thought about the hypocrisy of it all. He knew that did not represent every Christian he had met in his life, but it sure felt like it covered the bulk of them. Then he thought about David not really fitting that hypocrisy image. In the middle of that thought another memory hit his recall button.

"Cult!" he said the word out loud. Jonathan had said that Danielle was involved in a cult: David's church.

Luke tried to grasp the meaning of the word and how it applied to Danielle, but he was not sure how to process it in his mind. Images and thoughts of David Koresh, Jim Jones, Reverend Moon, Scientologists, and other religious groups that had very extreme beliefs or practices. Is that what Danielle was involved in? If so, how could he help her get out of it? He wondered if maybe it was as simple as telling her about his concerns since maybe she just didn't know? Would letting her know change things between them, maybe the killing of two birds with one stone would not only get her away from the group, but more importantly, bring her back into a relationship with him? He then realized that the challenge was that he did not have enough information for that conversation. Maybe Jonathan did, since he had already researched the group that David was somehow involved with. Maybe it was worth learning a little more about Christianity before talking to Danielle. He decided that the best course of action would be to go to church on Sunday with Monica, Cindy, and Jonathan. This would allow him to gain a little Christian education and to pick Jonathan's knowledge bank about David's church. He grabbed his phone and sent a quick text to Jonathan.

"Are we still going to church tomorrow with Monica and Cindy? If so, when and where?" He set his phone back down on the couch and flipped through the channels looking for something good to watch.

"I think so," Jonathan's replied a few seconds later.

"Well, let me know the details and I'll meet you all there," he texted back.

"K" Luke figured he had woken Jonathan and that he was probably in worse condition than he was earlier that morning.

As he sat there thinking more about the best strategy to help Danielle, he remembered the brown Bible that David had given him. He found his briefcase and pulled it out.

Were they all the same? he wondered to himself and thought about the Bible that he held. He turned the first few pages until he came to a liner that read *New International Version,* but he was not sure what that meant. He went online and did a search on bible versions and those who had transcribed them. When his cursory study was complete, he learned that the NIV, King James and American Standard seemed to be viewed as the best literal translations by the majority of the Christian world. The NIV was apparently written in a more easy to read format vs. the old English style of the King James version that he had heard quoted in religious movies or plays.

He opened the book and thumbed through the pages and read the titles of the various chapters. Some were long, others short. He noticed that the last third of the Bible had red printing on some of the pages. After a bit of online reading, he found that there was an Old and a New Testament. The Old Testament started at the beginning of the world and was written during and detailed, the history of the Jewish nation and the promise of a coming messiah. The New Testament was written as the fulfillment of the promised messiah, Jesus Christ, and the life he led during his time on earth. The old was written mostly by the prophets and leaders of the day, while the new was written mostly by the apostles or those who lived in the first century during the time of Jesus.

He set the book back down on the table and just stared at it a moment realizing that, although he had a better understand of the big picture of the Bible after three hours of research, he still did not know much more about what was actually written in it. He looked again at the number of pages and the idea of trying to grasp it all seemed daunting at best. There had to be a better way. What he needed was a condensed Cliff's Notes version like he used in college to prepare for an exam. He pulled out a pad and pen and wrote out a list of questions he was going to ask Jonathan about the Bible and David's church.

In the middle of writing out his questions, his cell phone rang. He assumed it was Jonathan with the details for church, but as he looked at the caller ID, it was a number that did not match any of the names in his phone's contacts list. He thought about ignoring it, but decided he had better answer it, just in case.

"Hello,"

"Luke?" the voice questioned. He thought he recognized the voice, but could not put his finger on it right away.

"Yep, how can I help?"

"It's Samuel. Sorry for calling during the weekend, but I need to speak with you," Samuel said. Luke's heart dropped when he figured out who was calling.

"I think I know what you are going to say. I'm off the team and being let go from the company," Luke replied and waited.

"Well no, but if Apollo gets his way you will be. How things unfolded yesterday definitely complicated things, and if we can't pull this back together, things between Apollo and I may become ugly. I need your thoughts on what steps would be needed to keep you in place." Luke was surprised that it was not a 'no need to come in on Monday' call and tried to reorganize his thinking.

"What's the status with David Stevens?" Luke asked, knowing that the other two candidates had accepted the new positions almost immediately.

"He let Apollo and I know Friday evening that he would accept the position, which, as you can imagine, really ticked off Apollo. Apollo is definitely on the war path right now. On top of that, his upgrade is not working as well as he hoped it would." Luke thought about the team. With the addition of David, the team now consisted of eight members. As it stood, he envisioned a possible coalition of four per side. He tried to imagine what he could do to give their position some strength, to give Samuel the power to protect Jonathan, David and himself should it turn into a divided team battle. He thought of Cliff and Serena and had an idea.

"Now that you have the agreement in place with the military and their stringent stipulations, I think you should put a call into Cliff and let him know your concerns and the possible dangers of having a development team controlled by Apollo. They won't allow him to continue on the project without a singed confidentiality agreement. It might also be a good idea to share some of Apollo's past discussions about his desired direction to take the project." Luke let the idea sink in a moment before he continued. "Samuel, my fear is that if you can't get control of things quickly, it will get real messy for everyone." Luke finished with a sigh. Luke sensed that this confrontation with Apollo was wearing Samuel out and that he lacked the energy to fight this battle with Apollo, although he knew he needed to.

Luke's read on Samuel was that although Samuel had not been afraid to fight such battles earlier in his career, he had gotten a little too comfortable to want to fight this kind of a battle again. Luke felt bad for how things turned out as a result of his actions on Friday. "Sorry about Friday, I just couldn't let Apollo walk over David. I should have kept my mouth shut."

"It turned out okay, considering. Although Jonathan was a total surprise," Samuel said and chuckled.

"Yeah, I didn't see that one coming either."

"Well, I hope you really wanted David on the team and he was not just an excuse to piss off Apollo?" Samuel's statement was more of a question. Luke thought a minute before answering.

"Well, it was probably equal parts of both."

"Thought so. Well, I'll call Cliff and let you know how things turn out. Have a good rest of the weekend," Samuel said.

"You too," Luke replied and pressed the end button on his phone. He was not sure if he felt relieved or disappointed that he had not been fired. He felt as if he had experienced enough drama on the project and just wanted some peace and quiet. He loved a good challenge, but there were limits and it was just a job after all.

Except for a visit to the health club for a workout, Luke stayed home the rest of the day and tried to let his body catch up on flushing the alcohol out of his system. Later that evening, he received a text with the directions and time from Jonathan for the Sunday service. The more Luke thought about the whole 'church visit' thing, the less he liked the idea. He was even wondering how things would be between Monica and him considering the way he had resisted the bait. The only thing that could keep church, Danielle and Monica off of his mind was trying to figure out what the political landscape was going to look like at the office on Monday. He lay there on his bed, staring at the ceiling with his mind working through all the 'what ifs' as he tried unsuccessfully to fall asleep. All he wanted was to return to the simple, boring life he had before he went to Iraq. The problem was that he could not figure out how to get back to it without creating even greater problems.

***

At 9:50 a.m., he found himself waiting just outside the doorway of the church where they had agreed to meet. He spent the time watching cars pull up to the curb to either unload or load their cargo of well-dressed occupants and then pull off toward either the parking lot or the exit. There had been an earlier service, and when he arrived, there were a large number of people leaving the building, the majority being fifty years old or older, but those entering the building at this point seemed to be a much younger crowd. *Were there different services for different age groups?* Luke wondered, but then remembered his dad and mom and how they were 'early risers' compared to most of the friends he grew up with. Although he was an early bird by nature, the weekends always seemed to find him staying up late into the night with his friends, making rising early more difficult.

As he watched for his friends to arrive, he was very impressed with the cars that were filling the parking lot. Cindy was right in that this must be a very wealthy group as the dresses and suits and 'bling' that were being worn definitely stood out. It was like a fashion show without the music, and a lot fewer skinny models; these folks definitely ate well. He smiled at the thought. As noticeable as the affluence of the people was, his eyes were drawn to the impressive architecture, landscaping and furnishings of the building that they were all converging into. Not being familiar with this part of the city, he left thirty minutes earlier than normal to compensate, but found it without any problems. So, he arrived a full thirty minutes earlier than planned. At first he had waited in his car, but after watching all the cars in the parking lot, and people coming and going, he was wondering if he had missed the start time so he headed in to see if his friends were already waiting for him. Once inside, he saw the schedule of services and the '8:00 a.m. service' that was already in progress and realized his mistake, so he took his time walking around the outside corridor of the facility, until the sound of the 8:00 a.m. sermon wrapped up and applause rumbled distantly through the building.

Almost on cue with the applause coming from the inner part of the building, the doors suddenly opened and what began as a trickle, became a stampede of well-dressed human cattle, moving toward the exit doors and out to the parking lot. Standing out of the flow, he watched as people passed by. Some were smiling, others frowning but most had an almost blank, expressionless face. As the flow slowed down, he gradually moved back outside to the agreed meeting place and continued to wait for Jonathan, Monica and Cindy. As the tide of people began to flow back with the arrivals for the next service, it struck Luke as strange that although he had been standing either in or near the building for almost thirty minutes and at least a thousand people had passed by him, no one had come up to say hello, to introduce themselves, or to welcome him to the church. He had received some courtesy smiles and nods as people passed by him, but no one actually stopped. In truth, he was unsure if he was happy that no one stopped, or disappointed by it. Here he was, surrounded by all these religious people and yet he felt all alone. Deep down he decided that he preferred being invisible.

"Luke!" He heard his name being yelled and saw Jonathan and Cindy walking up the steps toward him. Luke gave a conservative wave and smiled at them. He guessed that they must have driven together and then felt guilty about his decision to not ask Monica if she needed a ride. He had purposely made the decision not to drive her so that if things got uncomfortable or too pushy religiously, he would have the freedom to leave early. As Jonathan closed the gap, Luke reached out and shook his hand with a "good morning" and a "you look fantastic" to Cindy who smiled and returned the compliment. She definitely did look attractive in her Sunday dress and she seemed very happy to have Jonathan next to her. He had always preferred the 'classy sexy' look over the 'hot and sexy' that you would see at the bars and night clubs. The latter definitely got his attention faster and brought out the animal instincts, but the classy look seemed to produce a different kind of attraction in him that was less, well, less vulgar.

Jonathan and Cindy nervously chatted about the busy weekend and other shallow topics as they killed time. Luke thought it was funny, maybe even a little awkward, that they were purposely avoiding any 'morning after' discussions following Friday night's party. Apparently, that was not a topic to discuss on a Sunday morning in front of a church. As they continued chatting, Luke looked up to see a vision of a woman coming up the steps toward them. She was stunning. She was wearing a stylish hat, sunglasses and a dress and heels that had the visual presence of an Audrey Hepburn on fashion and beauty steroids. As she got closer, he could see auburn hair pulled back and flowing past her shoulders. As she removed her sunglasses, he was stunned to realize it was Monica. His heart skipped a beat.

"Wow." He didn't even realize he had said it out loud until she smiled.

"Thank you. Do you like it?"

"You look incredible." It was all he could think of to break the silence as she moved in close and slid her hand around his arm and leaned forward as if to tell him a secret but instead kissed him on the cheek.

"Right answer again," she whispered seductively and smiled as she reached up and wiped her lipstick from his cheek.

Her smile changed ever so slightly as she turned to Cindy and Jonathan.

"I'm sorry that I'm late. I hope you haven't been waiting long?" While they exchanged greetings, Luke was trying to subtly take in the full beauty of Monica as were the majority of the other men and women who walked past them on their way into the building. He smiled as he realized that any desire for him to remain 'invisible' had now passed with her arrival. He knew he had gone from feeling insignificant, to almost feeling like he was escorting royalty. She was that stunning. When the social niceties had ended, it was Jonathan who spoke up to change the direction of the conversation.

"Well, we probably better head in if we want to get good seats." With his hand on Cindy's back, he guided her toward the entrance of the building.

"Good seats in church? Is there such a thing?" Luke he said softly to Monica, with a faint smile, who gave him a soft elbow to the ribs. They joined the inflow of human cattle that carried them into the corridors, through the inner doors, and gradually into a spectacular auditorium filled with thousands of seats and people. There was even a balcony above that he had not even realized existed from his earlier tour. It seemed as if Monica knew everyone in the auditorium. Waves, handshakes, hugs, words and whispers were exchanged at practically every aisle as they moved toward seats that an usher was directing them to. Luke watched as all eyes flowed over Monica. Overall there was an admiration in their look, but there were also a few women who spoke with a smile but, seemed to wish ill on her once their eyes broke contact. When they passed from her to her escort, there was more of a judgment or evaluation check going on. He felt like a suit on a mannequin in a department store that was getting sized up from a distance. At first it really bothered him, but then he realized that he was doing the same to them in response; wondering if they were old boyfriends or just 'wanna be' boyfriends. *Who could blame them,* he thought as he remembered the many times he had watched an attractive women with a dorky guy walk by and wondered what she saw in him. He tried to somehow look cooler than he was, standing straight, stomach held in, chest out, smiling, but then realized the only thing that was making him look 'cool' was Monica. He nervously smiled at the thought that it felt much better to be on this side of the observation fence. Or did it?

They eventually took their seats as a huge choir dressed in burgundy robes flowed onto the stage and began to sing. This prompted everyone still standing to work a little harder at finding their seats. Monica tapped a songbook that she held out in front of her, as if trying to get Luke to read and sing along. He leaned down to whisper in her ear over the singing.

"They will escort me out if I start singing. I don't want to embarrass you in front of all your friends." He raised an eyebrow as if he was serious, but she smiled and shook her head.

"I'll risk it, now sing," she ordered sweetly with a smile. Luke noticed that her singing voice seemed to match her appearance. Was there anything that this woman was not blessed with? He found that the sound of the choir singing through the massive speakers easily drowned out his voice, so he just moved his lips to the words, but kept the singing voice at a barely audible tone for the few songs they opened with. As a man approached the podium and began to welcome everyone, Luke tried to estimate the number of people that were sitting in the room. He surmised there were over four thousand, maybe five in the room. Another man stepped forward to share a scripture on the crucifixion of Jesus and the meaning of the juice and bread, which was then passed up and down the aisles for people to take a wafer and a tiny cup with grape juice in it. Although Jonathan, Cindy and Monica each 'partook of the communion' as the man called it, he did not.

Luke tried to imagine the amount of juice and wafers and volunteers it would take to provide for all these people. Another song was sung before another man shared a brief lesson from the podium on giving to God. Although he expected some televangelist style pleading and praying for money, it was relatively simple in nature and talked about meeting the ongoing needs of the church and future plans for a new youth recreation building. At the end, the choir began to sing as trays were passed down the aisles and people would drop their checks and cash into the plate. Luke had very little cash in his wallet and no checkbook, so he felt more and more uncomfortable as the tray came closer and closer toward him. At first he decided he would put the only cash he had in the plate, a ten dollar bill, but as the plate got closer, he saw Jonathan and Cindy put much larger bills in it and he felt funny putting in just a ten, so he decided to not put anything in as the tray passed by. He wanted to explain his actions, or lack of, as he passed the tray to Monica, but once again felt it was best to hold to the age old adage and 'remain silent and be thought a fool rather than to speak up and remove all doubt.'

He was happy to have that part of the service over and glanced at the order of service card that had been handed to them when they first entered the auditorium. The lesson was next and it was titled, "No Compromise". The man leading it seemed to be a favorite, because there was loud applause as he approached the podium and tried to settle the crowd down. As he spoke, Luke found him to be very engaging and personable in his delivery. As suggested from the pulpit, Luke used a Bible that was in a holder on the back of the seat in front of him to follow along. Like the lesson title alluded, the speaker spent the next thirty minutes talking about how we can compromise not only in our lives, but more importantly with God and how these compromises can eventually bring us great pain or worse. He used an Old Testament scripture as his primary reference. Judges 2:20-23:

Then the anger of the Lord was hot against Israel; and He said, "Because this nation has transgressed My covenant which I commanded their fathers, and has not heeded My voice, I also will no longer drive out before them any of the nations which Joshua left when he died, so that through them I may test Israel, whether they will keep the ways of the Lord, to walk in them as their fathers kept them, or not." Therefore the Lord left those nations, without driving them out immediately; nor did He deliver them into the hand of Joshua.

He talked about how God can use negative things in people's lives to test them, to let them see what they are made of. Of how he uses angels to bring messages of encouragement when people are obeying God, but also messages of punishment when they turn from their obedience. The preacher used many scriptures in the Old Testament to support his statements, but Luke could not find them in time to read along. He spoke about how people will give up trying to do the right thing and give in or give up and compromise. That God does not hesitate to remove his blessings from people if their suffering will motivate them to return back to him. How God will do whatever it takes to bring them to himself and that the Devil will do whatever he can to keep them from returning to God. The final challenge was to be a man or woman who would stand up for righteousness, no compromising, and their desire should be to have a pure heart. He ended with a scripture in Psalms, which Luke was somehow able to find in time. Psalms 51:10

Create in me a clean heart, O God, and renew a steadfast spirit within me.

As the sermon was wrapping up, Luke felt pleasantly surprised that he was actually encouraged by the message that the man had delivered. He was not sure that he learned what he had hoped to learn, but he liked the conviction of the preacher delivering the message. It reminded him of his dad as a boy and how he taught him the importance of being a man of your word, even when it hurts. He heard the man speaking again and encouraging those people who felt moved by the message, who felt that they wanted a 'clean heart' so that they could have a personal relationship with God, to come down to the front of the auditorium and accept Jesus Christ as their savior. Luke watched as first a few, and then a growing number of people slowly began to move down the aisles toward the front of the auditorium. Suddenly there were several hundred people congregating and to his surprise, he saw Jonathan and Cindy walking down the aisle to join them. Remembering Danielle's baptism, Luke was looking for the baptismal or pool of water that they would be using, but could not see any. The man at the podium asked them to repeat what he called "The Sinner's Prayer for salvation," after him:

Dear God in heaven, I come to you in the name of Jesus. I acknowledge to You that I am a sinner, and I am sorry for my sins and the life that I have lived; I need your forgiveness.

I believe that your only begotten Son Jesus Christ shed His precious blood on the cross at Calvary and died for my sins, and I am now willing to turn from my sin.

You said in Your Holy Word, Romans 10:9 that if we confess the Lord our God and believe in our hearts that God raised Jesus from the dead, we shall be saved.

Right now I confess Jesus as the Lord of my soul. With my heart, I believe that God raised Jesus from the dead. This very moment I accept Jesus Christ as my own personal Savior and according to His Word, right now I am saved.

Thank you Jesus for your unlimited grace which has saved me from my sins. I thank you Jesus that your grace never leads to license, but rather it always leads to repentance. Therefore Lord Jesus transform my life so that I may bring glory and honor to you alone and not to myself.

Thank you Jesus for dying for me and giving me eternal life.
Amen.

At the end of the prayer, those repeating the words cheered and hugged each other, while those watching from the seats applauded and smiled. Luke thought that the words used were very nice and even humbling, but he was also confused. It was very different than what he had witnessed at Danielle's baptism. And although he was happy for them, he had thought that Jonathan and Cindy had said that they were already Christians.

Monica slid her hand into his and leaned her head against his shoulder as she watched them hugging below. Luke leaned down toward her.

"So what are your thoughts on what just took place with Jonathan and Cindy?" he asked her. She seemed confused by his questions, so he tried to clarify. "I mean, do you feel compelled to become a Christian as well?" he asked and she seemed to finally catch his meaning, although she smiled at him, her expression was interesting.

"I already became a Christian, silly," she replied.

"Oh." Although he was wrestling with some thoughts about her affirmation, he decided to wait until he could gather his thoughts before breaching a conversation on the subject. He watched as Cindy and Jonathan were slowly trying to work their way through the crowd toward the exits and when they saw each other, Jonathan motioned for Luke and Monica to meet them at the entrance.

They met outside and after a brief discussion, agreed to meet at a nearby hotel for a Sunday brunch that was 'to die for' according to Monica. Luke had a hard time imagining Monica at a brunch buffet, but the description of the various food choices made his stomach rumble. Luke walked Monica to her car as she waved goodbye to many of her friends and fans.

"So what did you think of Church?" she asked him in a coy voice as they approached her car. He thought a moment before answering.

"It was better than I expected, but less than I was hoping for," he replied. He could tell by the look on her face that she did not understand and was hoping for a little more feedback from him as she stood beside her car. "I'm starving, how about we talk about it over lunch?" She smiled and agreed. He watched her drive off and then looked around to see where he had parked his car, realizing that it was a big lot and he did not remember where he ended up finding a spot earlier that morning.

The hotel was nice, but the buffet spread surpassed his friend's praises and his expectations. Unfortunately, he guessed that the cost was also going to greatly exceed his expectations. He was thankful that he had his credit card on him. They were escorted to their seats and the waitress poured each of them a mimosa.

Jonathan immediately offered a toast to everyone's success and happiness. Luke took a short sip and remembered that he had never been a fan of champagne, but the orange juice made it drinkable. He ordered an iced tea and then each of them headed for their favorite foods that were laid out before them in abundance. Luke had a momentary twang of guilt as he thought about the soldiers and friends he had been with in Iraq that had a far less appetizing menu and with far fewer choices. He tried to shake the image of the chow line he experienced there, but somehow found the thought of it appealing in spite of the contrast in the quality and quantity of food that was being offered here. *It must be a lot like camping food*, he thought to himself. The way eggs and bacon and pancakes always tasted better over the fire while camping than at home or in a restaurant. His eyes wandered over the seafood table, and he put aside his thoughts and loaded his plate with a little of everything.

They ate in relative silence for the first few minutes, with the exception of an "oh my gosh, this tastes so good" or what could only be called some culinary expletive or statement of happiness. Once the initial attack on the food was over, Monica turned the topic of the conversation back to Luke's statement in the parking lot. "So what did you mean by '*it* was better than you expected, but less than you hoped for?'" she asked and Jonathan and Cindy seemed to perk up at the question. Luke took his time to finish chewing what was in his mouth and then took a drink of his iced tea as he carefully framed his response.

"Well, I guess I was hoping for a lot more clarity and teaching on doctrine, or processes of Christianity than what was offered. It was all fine, it just left me wanting," he said and waited for a reply, which no one seemed to want to deliver.

"What you need to learn about Christianity is that it's all about faith," Jonathan finally stated as if to break the uncomfortable silence that was forming. "Our salvation or justification is by faith. Well, faith and our belief in Jesus Christ." Luke was waiting for Jonathan to say more, but he realized that more was not coming.

"Yeah, but what does that mean exactly?" Luke asked.

"Faith in the blood of Jesus Christ," Cindy interjected. "He was an atonement for our sins."

"Whose sins?" Luke asked.

"Everyone's sins," she answered in a matter of fact way, as Jonathan nodded his head in agreement, he then seemed to catch himself and said, "Well, for those who believe in him."

Luke started to nod his head ever so gently, but then changed the direction from up and down to side-to-side and shrugged.

"That just seems so…" He was trying to find the right words as the 'so' dragged on until he finally continued, "Anti-climactic considering how much information there is that was written in the Bible. I mean, if I'm not mistaken, we are talking about a book that was written over a long period of time before Jesus was born, and then following his life. To just say a prayer and you're suddenly good to go, well, is that really it?" Luke shrugged again and raised his eyebrows.

"It's an amazing ending if you ask me." Monica smiled. "What would you expect or feel should happen?" Monica asked him.

"Even the main scripture that we read today had a solid requirement of *unless you keep my commands*, so to just say a prayer, well it just seems like there should be more involved," he said. There was a long silence. Longer than he wanted before Jonathan responded.

"You do need to repent, but that is the beauty of grace and mercy. We do not deserve it, nor can we earn it. It is a gift from God." Cindy and Monica both nodded their heads and smiled at the words. Luke could tell that either he did not understand their explanation, or they did not understand what he was getting at. He considered trying to explain it again in a different way, but did not want to make their lunch any more awkward than it already was. So he nodded his head.

"I guess I just need to do a little more reading on this to grasp all of it." The mood seemed to lighten at the words and he took another bite. Then another thought jumped into his mind.

"So how does David's church differ from your church and its teachings?" He could tell he just threw another wet blanket on the moment. Jonathan took a sip of his mimosa and then seemed to take on a confident air about him.

"They believe in a 'works' based salvation. They deny that belief in him alone, Jesus Christ, will save you, but that there requirements that must be met first in order to be saved." He looked up at Luke as if his words should have answered his question, but he could see that Luke was still missing the point. "Man has already been under two different 'works' systems, but both failed and left mankind condemned. One was given to Adam in the Garden of Eden and was as simple as 'don't eat from the tree'. How simple is that? But Adam failed under that system and so mankind was doomed. The second works system was the Law of Moses, which again man failed to follow and that system of laws failed to bring salvation to those who tried to follow them. Both systems were to show us that man couldn't be justified by his works, but only by God's grace." Jonathan seemed happy with his explanation and the simplicity of it.

Luke felt there were some good points brought up, but then the questions started rolling into his head. He remembered reading about the Garden of Eden and the two trees and everything that went down with Adam and Eve. He was not sure about the Law of Moses, but he remembered watching the Ten Commandments as a kid. So many questions! He tried to fight the urge to toss them out there and ruin the pleasant atmosphere of the lunch, but his nature got the best of him and, after all, this was the reason for his coming to church in the first place, to get the answers he needed.

"But wasn't it God who put those systems in place? I mean why would he do that if they were doomed to fail? Sorry, but to me such a strategy seems cruel at best, unless he wanted there to be some sort of testing measure involved that would show who were or were not his followers. I mean how would you know the difference between a Christian and a non-Christian? Or is there?" Luke asked.

Jonathan seemed uncomfortable and hard pressed to find the right answer and both Cindy and Monica seemed off balance as well. Luke knew he pushed too hard.

"I'm sorry, I'm just trying to find answers to questions I've never asked before and I'm trying to understand concepts I've never considered before. I'm grateful that you are trying to answer them for me, even though the two of you only became a Christian today," Luke said.

"I've been a Christian for 7 years," Cindy replied. Luke felt confused by her response.

"I became a Christian 14 years ago," Jonathan added. Luke started to ask a question, then stopped, but then asked it anyways.

"So why did you go forward to do the Sinner's Prayer today and accept Jesus?" He asked them both. They both seemed hesitant to answer, but Jonathan spoke up first.

"I felt it was a prayer of recommitment to the Lord." Luke nodded to his answer.

"So kind of like a Catholic confessional?" Luke asked innocently.

"No!" Jonathan and Cindy said vehemently at almost the same time. "I felt I had drifted and I wanted to recommit my heart to him," Jonathan replied in a softer voice.

"And so did I." Cindy added.

"So you were not accepting Jesus as your savior, you were just recommitting yourself to him? So why not just say a prayer to yourself?" he asked.

"We could have. We just thought it would be nice to recommit together," Jonathan answered with a look of guilt on his face.

Luke could not help but think that their extra-curricular activities on Friday night probably did not fall within Christian guidelines. He felt the response smacked a bit of guilt, but he could also appreciate their desire to mutually recommit their relationship to God. Luke started to ask another question on the matter, but then stopped. He felt he was getting more confused by the answers than he was before he asked the questions. He felt getting more specific was the best approach, rather than tackling it from a 10,000-foot view. The question he was struggling to solve was how to do that?

After a moment of silence, Monica changed the discussion topic to something travel related. Some friends of hers from the church went on a missionary journey to a tropical island in the Pacific Ocean, which opened up a flurry of questions as to where each person would want to go and how long they would want to stay? Luke just listened for the most part and smiled at each suggestion.

Lunch went pretty smoothly from that point forward and they gradually left and headed for their cars. Luke was still enamored, if not stricken, with Monica and her visual presence.

"Thank you for putting up with me today," he joked, which made her smile that amazing smile.

"You're not as difficult to be around as you think you are," she retorted and raised an eyebrow.

"Maybe, but I think I've perfected the art of knowing how to rain on a picnic better than anyone," he said, but Monica shook her head.

"No, my dad has that title hands down, but you can be a little frustrating in other areas." She smiled seductively and leaned forward and gave him a short kiss and then put her head on his chest and her arms around his waist and held him tight. He reached around and did the same as he leaned down and tried to rest his cheek on the side of her head only to catch an eye full of scratchy ribbon from her hat. It looked a lot softer than it was and he tried several times to figure out how to place his head against hers without touching the ribbon. He suddenly felt Monica's body shaking in his arms. Was she crying? Was she upset? The shaking turned into what he finally recognized as laughter as she pulled away and looked up at him.

"So much for a romantic hug," she said as she continued laughing and stepped back from him. She tried to adjust her hat, which he had managed to push out of place during the embrace, causing it to sit awkwardly on her head.

"Did you have to register that hat as a weapon when you bought it?" He kidded her as he rubbed his face. She gave him a fake glare and then smiled while trying to reposition the hat with little success.

"Oh well, I'm heading home anyways. I've got to get out of this dress and heels, they're killing me," she said, still trying to adjust her hat after their embrace. "Care to offer a damsel in distress a little help?" She once again smiled mischievously and raised an eyebrow waiting for his response. Luke nodded his head and then shook it sideways.

"Yeah… no. If you thought your hat got messed up from just an embrace…" He smiled almost red faced. "I'm afraid I'd be more like the bad guy tweaking his mustache and snickering, than the hero coming to your rescue," he said and she laughed at his words.

"If it worked better for you, we could think of it as a bad boy for a bad girl?" She gave him that look that launches fireworks and warning bells at the same time. He tried to be clever, but all he could do was blush. She suddenly laughed out loud again.

"I love making you uncomfortable." She smiled and put a finger on his chest and continued her seduction, "You know it's only a matter of time before I wear you down right?" He smiled and then got serious.

"Then what happens?" he asked.

"Do you want to hear specifics, or to be more general in nature?" she answered without losing her sultry look. Although she was amazingly attractive, he felt something inside him growing almost cold. Then the words came out before he could stop them. "I mean between us. Would the hunt be over?" She seemed as if she was trying to find the sexual context in his words, but then realized what he meant. She slowly lowered her hand from his chest and looked him in the eyes.

"Is that how you view me?" she asked and watched his eyes as if looking for the truth.

"Monica, I don't know how to view this relationship. I have this amazingly beautiful, intelligent, funny, and influential woman who could have anyone she cared to blink her eyes at, yet she has somehow set her eyes on me. Every natural urge in me says to run right into your bed and enjoy that moment with you, but something deeper inside is telling me that only pain and heartbreak waits for me afterwards." He tried to read her face for what might be hidden, but couldn't find an answer behind those eyes. "I keep thinking that I am such a fool for thinking that, but the old saying *of one cannot stare too long at the sun, or they'll go blind* comes to mind over and over. Your beauty continually blinds me to the possible reality of this relationship. I've had my share of shallow, physical attraction based relationships to know that there is very little inner joy waiting for me the morning after." He waited for her to say something. She finally spoke.

"Do you think I don't want the same thing? Do you think I haven't been through the same shallow, disgusting, humiliating moments in my life that I don't know that?" she finally answered with tears in her eyes.

"I believe you have. But don't you think there is a better way to go about it?" He took a deep breath and looked around. "One year, five years, even ten years ago I thought I knew the best and only way. But looking at past lessons, pain, regret, guilt… I can't… I… I don't want to build a relationship that way anymore." He exhaled and shook his head and scrunched his eyes, "Let me clarify that statement. Every bone in my body wants to repeat that cycle, but my heart doesn't. Maybe I'll grow out of this next week and be willing to jump right back into that kind of a relationship again. But I can't right now." He took a deep breath and reached out and touched her face. "I'm so sorry."

Monica leaned her cheek into his hand and closed her eyes. "You are the most frustrating, yet strangely attractive man I have ever met," she said and then rolled her eyes. "I don't know if it's because I cannot have you that you've captured my interest so deeply," her face then turned serious as she looked into his eyes again, "or if it's because deep down I agree with where you are trying to lead me." She took in another deep breath, a long pause before she exhaled again. "I don't think I'm ready, or perhaps I'm just unwilling to be led in that direction." She seemed to be looking for some sign of surrender in his eyes at her words. He nodded.

"I understand. I have no clue as to what is going on inside of me, but I understand your perspective and decision." He leaned forward and kissed her forehead. "Thank you for making me feel so wanted during a difficult time. I wish you all the happiness and love that you deserve." She seemed to sense the moment and the end, and gave him that sultry smile one more time.

"If you ever change your mind, call me." She stepped toward her car and Luke opened the door for her. He watched the most physically attractive women he had ever known slide into the seat and shut the door. She glanced up at him one more time, smiled and then drove off.

He stood there in silence for several minutes thinking about what he had just done. "Luke Baker, you are such an IDIOT!" he yelled the last word into the air, then remembering that he was standing in a parking lot; he looked around to see an older couple staring in his direction. He walked toward his car and started the long drive toward his apartment.

As he tried to clear his mind of Monica and the decision he had just made, in would flood the thoughts of loneliness without Danielle and getting her out of that cult became his new focus. At least until he thought about what Monday morning at the office was going to look like. Could things get any worse for him? He couldn't imagine how.

Chapter 16

Luke felt exhausted. He sat in his car in the parking lot of the company, his hands on the wheel as if he were still driving. The song "Should I stay or should I go" from the rock group *The Clash* was bouncing around in his head after hearing it on his way to work. The knock on his window made him jump as he turned to see David looking in with a curious smile on his face. Luke nodded, then pulled the keys out of the ignition, grabbed his briefcase and stepped out of the car.

"Hey," Luke said with the best smile and attitude he could muster.

"You umm… well, you look terrible," David said as Luke rolled his eye. "Sorry, just being honest." David ended and patted him on the back.

"Can I suggest not being next time?" Luke replied sarcastically as they headed toward the main door.

"I received a nice call this weekend from Apollo," David said.

"Really? And how did that go?" Luke replied and emphasized his faked happiness.

"Apparently he is very excited about having me on the team and can't wait to have me take the lead in development and training!" David matched the feigned excitement. *So it begins*, Luke thought. Luke was the training lead and it would be just like Apollo to try to pit David against Luke by offering him Luke's position.

"You must feel very special?" Luke snickered as they went through security and headed toward the elevators.

"Like a deer in the cross hairs," David replied as they stepped onto the elevator and pushed the floor button.

"Welcome to the party pal." Luke replied with a slight adjustment to his normal voice. David seemed to think a moment.

"*Die Hard*, right?" David said. Luke was a little surprised he recognized the line in the movie, but more so that he had even seen it.

"I didn't know you watched those kinds of movies. You know, with all that bad language. Tsk tsk."

"Yeah, well, I love movies, but I did watch that one was before I became a Christian," David said as the elevator door opened and they stepped into the office reception area. David turned his head toward Luke and looked him in the eyes.

"Are we in this together?" he asked Luke. Luke stared back a moment and realized that he had felt like he was heading into this all alone. But somehow David's words gave him a little comfort knowing he had a friend in this dogfight.

"Yeah. Let's do it." Luke said with an emphasis on the last three words.

"Animal House?" David replied almost unsure of his guess? Luke thought a minute and remembered that line being used in the movie he mentioned, but shook his head as he glanced back.

"No. They were the last words from Gary Gilmore before he was executed by firing squad." David seemed caught off guard at first, but then chuckled and replied.

"Wow, you really know how to motivate people before a battle."

"Just being honest," Luke replied with a sarcastic chuckle.

"Touché," David said as they stepped into the new development area.

The first thing Luke did when he reached his desk was to check his online schedule for the day's events. As he scrolled down what appeared to be a never ending list of tasks, he saw that the only meeting scheduled was an organizational meeting starting in 15 minutes. The attendees included all past and new team members, as well as Samuel, Serena and Cliff. Luke was surprised to see that Cliff was back in town so soon, unless he was planning to attend by teleconference, but regardless, he was happy to see his name on the list. Luke gathered the latest updates on the various training materials he was working on just in case he needed to demonstrate his progress. He quickly tried to second-guess what areas of his work that Apollo would be attacking in this meeting and how best to defend them. After a few moments of thinking, he felt confident that he knew all areas and felt he had gone above and beyond the standard procedures in every aspect. He knew Apollo could not make him feel guilty or concerned about any area of his work, assuming Apollo was truthful in what he was saying. As he headed to the conference room, he saw that David was standing by a cubicle near the conference room as if waiting, but when he saw Luke, he pretended to race him to the door. Luke smiled and rolled his eyes.

"I can't believe I suggested that you be added to the team," Luke whispered as he got close to David.

"You? Are you kidding, it was divine intervention," David whispered back and raised both eyebrows as he turned the handle and opened the door for the two of them to go in together. Luke knew that they were 5 minutes early to the meeting, but even with their early arrival, they were still the last ones to join the meeting.

"Luke! Good to see you," Cliff said as he worked his way across the room to shake his hand.

"You too." Luke replied and then turned toward David. "I don't believe that you've met David Stevens, one of our newest team members? David, Cliff Jackson."

"No, I haven't. It's a pleasure to meet you David. Luke speaks quite highly of you," Cliff said as he shook David's outstretched hand.

"Not true," Luke interjected and smiled.

"Luke has told me a lot about you Mr. Jackson, so the pleasure is all mine." David replied as he released Cliff's handshake.

"Well, obviously he didn't tell you everything about me, or you would never have joined the team." He said and looked toward Luke and gave a fake whisper, "Smart thinking Luke." They all chuckled at the banter. Cliff turned toward the rest of the team.

"Since everyone is here, why don't we take our seats and we can get this meeting started." As everyone found a seat, Cliff whispered to Serena, who stood and quickly passed around a single sheet to the new team members.

"We obviously need to deal with a few paperwork items before we can begin discussing the project and development side of things." She looked around to see the new team members pulling out their various agreements as she continued, "This sheet is acknowledging that you have read and understood the agreements prior to signing them."

Each person quickly reviewed the single, personalized acknowledgment form as it was passed to them. "Please review this sheet, and if you are in agreement, please sign it where stated and pass it back to me. If any of you require more time to review the prior agreements, please notify me and we can reschedule this initial meeting until all are present," she added as she sat back down, but no one seemed to require more time or had any questions. The signed papers were passed back along with the various signed agreements, which Serena verified and placed in each new team members corresponding blue folder. She then nodded toward Cliff.

"Thank you, Serena. Welcome to the Cat Eyes team," he said and let the name sink in a moment. Luke saw Gloria and Danny glance at each other and raised an eyebrow, but David seemed unfazed by it all. "You might be asking yourself, 'What are Cat Eyes?' which would be the right question to ask. Unfortunately, I'm not the best person to describe to you the ins and outs of this very special product, but I am the best person to share with you why the government has taken such an active interest in bringing this product to production so quickly. In the simplest of statements, we believe it will save countless lives in both the civilian and military sectors. It potentially could be the most powerful, non-lethal tool in our country's resources." He let the overview settle in a moment before continuing. "Although officially, the government is your employer, as your agreement's stated, we believe the best people to direct this product to its final release and supervise the ongoing enhancements are sitting in this room. This will be the core group of individuals that will take on the leadership roles of this product and who we will build the company and services around." As he finished, he smiled at everyone at the table and then turned toward Apollo. "Truthfully, we have Apollo to thank for this incredible product and he will continue to guide and lead the development team. With that said, I would like to give Apollo the floor and allow him as much time as he needs to give you an overview of the Cat Eyes product." Cliff nodded toward Apollo and then sat back in his chair and began purposely watching the people around the table.

Luke having heard the overview so many times already spent his time watching Cliff and Serena. With Apollo being appointed the lead on development, Luke surmised Samuel had either not spoken with Cliff or Serena about this concern of having Apollo lead the team, or he had and they had rejected the idea. He watched Cliff's eyes roam around the room to the various people, and glance only briefly in his direction. When they made eye contact, Cliff gave him an ever so brief nod of his head as if conveying a message. Unfortunately, Luke did not know what that message was supposed to mean.

Apollo spent the next hour and a half going over the testing and development that had gone on since the product's initial introduction. Although he mentioned himself and Ronald throughout the overview, he never mentioned Jonathan, and only mentioned Luke as someone he hired to facilitate the training process. He discussed the live testing that the company had done in Iraq and the results that were seen, again with no mention of the role that Luke had played in it. Without even looking at Cliff, he knew that Cliff was watching for his reaction to Apollo's decision to ignore the role he played there. Because he knew he was being watched, Luke did his best to hide any negative expressions or reactions.

It was during Apollo's discussion on the various uses of the Cat Eyes and its potential to reveal the truth that David gave Luke a brief glance and somehow smiled with his eyes, though his lips did not move. Luke was confident that David now understood the question he had asked him about 'knowing the truth' several weeks ago. Luke was very interested in hearing his thoughts on the matter now that he saw the full picture. Apollo finished his overview and Cliff thanked him and turned back to the group.

"Thank you, Apollo. Well, I hope you now have a better understanding of how this product can assist the country and why we are so excited about getting it in the hands of those brave men and women that serve it." He seemed to hesitate a moment, then decided to move forward. "I want to point out that Apollo and his focused development of the product has been amazing to say the least..." He hesitated as people mumbled their agreement to the words and then continued, "but one person that I think you should know had the most impact on bringing this product to reality in the eyes of the government has been Luke Baker." There were confused looks on most of the teams' faces, except for Apollo, who briefly turned red and then pretended to completely disengage from the conversation as he shuffled papers. "Where Apollo was the mind behind the product, Luke was the face of the product and he and his actions brought out the true personality of the product and breathed the needed life into it during the testing and evaluation in Iraq. Few of you realize it, but at extreme personal risk, Luke tested the product in a high security prison, face to face with high risk targets, and then personally risked his very life in order to test it in a live fire battle environment... that means with bombs and bullets flying and bad guys dying. His actions while using the Cat Eyes saved many civilian and military personnel in the process. Without that personal investment and belief in the product, it would not have won the hearts of those who were greatly opposed to it. And we would not be sitting here today." Cliff stood up and began clapping, the others following suit; everyone except Apollo and Ronald.

Luke actually felt embarrassed by the attention, but deep down he felt vindicated, maybe even proud of the words that Cliff had shared with the team. Cliff raised a hand to quiet the group.

"I cannot stress enough how incredibly important the development process of the Cat Eyes is if we are to meet the critical delivery timeline that has been established to get the final product to our end users. Apollo will be taking the lead on making sure that development stays on track as well guiding of the development team to fill its functions." Cliff looked down at his notes as Ronald mumbled his approval of Apollo's leadership. "Equally as important to understand is that we have many committees, panels, and closed door sessions that we will need to guide this product through, including navigating any potential controversy that may accompany the introduction of this technology. This is something that must be done with great care and finesse if we are to get the product into the hands of the people that need it the most, the soldiers protecting our country. This will take careful understanding, strong product knowledge, great insight, and an incredible level of people skills in order for us to navigate those waters successfully." Cliff hesitated slightly again. Luke knew that Apollo did not possess any of those people skills Cliff mentioned and got the feeling that Cliff was trying to determine the most politically correct way to announce that Samuel Carr would be taking on that role so as not to offend Apollo. "Because of the importance of that critical role, we have assigned Mr. Baker as the team lead relating to all implementation, customer/client interaction, and training." Luke was stunned at hearing his name announced as the new lead. Cliff continued, "Just for clarity, everyone except Apollo will be reporting to Mr. Baker during the next six months. Apollo and Luke will oversee their respective areas and offer assistance to each other as needed."

You could hear a pin drop. The stunned look on Apollo's face was only matched by that on Luke's, but what shone in Apollo's eyes conveyed a far different internal conversation than Luke's. David was the first to break the awkward silence.

"Without a doubt, we have the best in both categories leading the team. I'm extremely excited and look forward to working closely with Apollo and under Mr. Baker." Jonathan nodded in agreement, as did Danny and Gloria. Ronald's reaction was closer to Apollo's. Luke knew that he had better divert the conversation quickly before the new team members began to truly grasp the issue at hand.

"Well, to say this is a surprise would be an understatement," Luke said putting on his best surprised look. "I look forward to working with each of you, including our overseeing leaders, Cliff and Selena. Apollo and I have had the pleasure to not only witness together the value of the product, but to understand the potential and future that it holds and more importantly, to forge a working relationship that will allow us to deliver maximum results first for the team, then for the company, and ultimately for our clients." Apollo only smiled and nodded as people turned toward him for his reaction to Luke's response.

Seeing that Apollo was not going to respond with words, Cliff seized the moment.

"As you can imagine, our most immediate need is on the development and production side. Apollo has written some very unique and impressive code and he will transfer his knowledge to the rest of you at the earliest opportunity. God forbid, should something happen to Apollo, we'd have a devil of a time sorting through the code from scratch. With that said, we will have David and Danny support Apollo in software development. Gloria, with her extensive production experience will join Ronald in ensuring the Cat Eyes production schedule is met. All four of you will be under the guidance and direction of Apollo. Jonathan, you will be working under the guidance and direction of Luke who will initially oversee the "big picture" element of the product as well as the client presentation, training and interaction. Just to avoid any communication or leadership questions, Apollo and Luke will each have full access to all information on both sides of the product development and client implementation." Most of the individuals at the table nodded their heads in response.

Cliff glanced at Serena and then back at the group. "Why don't we take a break and allow the new team members to spend the rest of the day reading over the documentation on the Cat Eyes product in their specific areas, and for the team leads to schedule group or individual meetings to answer any questions that you have? Thank you everyone." Cliff smiled and started gathering his paperwork. As everyone was leaving the office, Cliff spoke up again.

"Luke, Apollo, can you to stay a little longer? We need to discuss a few policy and product issues with the two of you for your team. Samuel, please join us as well." Both stopped at the door and returned to their seats as everyone else slowly departed. When the door finally closed behind the last person, the room grew very quiet as Serena and Samuel sat quietly while Cliff continued to review various papers in front of him. He finally looked up as if trying to read the expressions of both men's faces.

"We need to talk about the two of you and how to proceed from here. Stanley, I know that you are not happy with Luke being given the lead contact role on the government side, but if I may be blunt, you do not have the personality nor the people skills needed to guide this product through the various channels that it will need to go through. Your individual talents are quite amazing and very valuable to the direction we are trying to take the product, but your huge ego and 'going rogue' approach to product development and your gatekeeper mindset, will seriously impeded the success of this product. Your approach may have worked nicely for you in the private sector, but it has no place in the government sector and will doom the product as well as put all of us at great risk."

Everyone sat quietly as Cliff's words echoed inside the room. "Per your agreement, you need to get Danny and David up to speed on your software immediately. Are we clear?" Cliff asked and Apollo nodded disdainfully.

Luke was very surprised at Cliff's directness and lack of concern for Apollo's ego, even referring to him by his real name. So much so, he had to fight back the urge to jump up and yell "Yes!" while doing an end zone victory dance over the verbal smack down that was just delivered, but instead he sat silently and watched Apollo's face. *A volcano waiting to erupt* was the best analogy that came to his mind.

Cliff seemed to see it as well and stepped in to keep it from happening. "I'll play the 'Apollo' game in front of your team and other employees, but please understand that in this room, the ego's get left at the door. I need you on this team. We need you on this team. But the keyword you are failing to grasp and embrace is that this is a TEAM, not a dictatorship of 'yes men'." He leaned back in his chair and picked up his pen. "Contrary to your belief, Luke had no idea that he was going to be placed in this position, nor, by the look on his face, did he even want it. But he understands the need of the moment, the hour, and the product and has demonstrated time and again his willingness to set his personal needs for the benefit of the team. That is why he was selected as our lead contact for the government." Cliff leaned forward again, putting his elbows on the table. "Trust me, when you can understand and fully embrace that concept, I will be happy to hand that role back to you and I'm sure Luke will be happy to give it back as well." Luke found himself nodding his head toward Apollo in agreement.

Luke watched as Apollo slowly gained control of his emotions and his face and body language shifted. He suddenly nodded and opened his previously clinched hands as if to say, 'I understand'.

"I need your help." Apollo said to Luke. Luke was taken aback by the words; not necessarily the words themselves, but how they were spoken. "The recent software upgrade has generated some 'ghosting' with the glasses and I need someone who knows the product spectrum to help analyze what is going on." Apollo explained and looked back toward Cliff.

"Of course. I'll take a look as soon as were done here," Luke replied as he nodded, "I know how much this product means to you and how much of your life you have poured into it. I just hope you make it easier for all of us to help you with it." He felt like he had extended a peace offering, but Luke felt a strange coldness as Apollo somehow managed to look through him without actually looking at him. At that moment, Luke knew the battle was far from over and that it had simply shifted to a far more subtle and dangerous battlefield where new weapons and tactics would be employed. Cliff once again broke the silence.

"I need you to work together on this project. This is not a 'me verses them', or a 'my team vs. your team' mindset. We are all in this together and we either succeed or fail together. If it fails, the product dies right here and is shelved and locked down tight, with no one receiving the big payoff. The government now owns this product and is the sole funding source for it. We all believe in this product, so I will not allow the ego or pride of anyone to kill it. Are we clear?" Cliff stated very sternly but professionally.

"Yes sir," Luke said with a nod. Apollo remained silent, seemingly stewing in his thoughts.

"Mr. Walpole?" Cliff asked again. Apollo snapped out of his deep thinking mode.

"Oh sorry, yes, I uhh, completely understand and agree with you Mr. Jackson," he finally replied. Luke was surprised to hear his words come out sounding as positive as they did considering the look on Apollo's face. But with his prior expression gone and he appeared to be a tamed tiger. Of course, Luke did not buy it, and he doubted that Cliff did either.

The meeting ended with a handshake between Cliff and Apollo and then one between Cliff and Luke. Apollo grabbed his stuff and headed to the door to avoid the potential handshake between him and Luke. He did stop at the door and turned toward Luke.

"Stop by my office on the way out and pick up the latest upgrade. I need to know what is happening to the spectrum side so we can correct it in the code," he said as if it was an order. Luke nodded as Apollo left the room. He turned back toward Cliff.

"Thank you," he said quietly. Cliff nodded.

"They needed to know the role you played in Iraq and how much you were willing to risk for the success of the project," he responded to Luke.

"I meant thank you for putting him in his place. It gets a little tiring on your own." Luke smiled. Cliff smiled and glanced at the closed door.

"I've wanted to do that since I first met him. I just needed the authority and the right environment for it to stick," he said in a strong whisper. Luke chuckled.

"It does feel good doesn't it?" he said as he gathered his papers and Luke headed for the door.

"Luke." Luke stopped and looked back at Cliff. "It's going to get tougher before it gets better with him, and I'm pretty sure this is far from over. I'll need you to keep an eye on him and his actions and let me know if you see or hear of anything we need to be concerned about." Luke tried to think of something clever to say in response, but he knew the situation did not warrant it, so he simply nodded his head.

As Luke headed down the hallway toward his desk, he knew he would be passing Apollo's office, but because Apollo had ordered him to 'stop by' on his way, he was considering just walking past and going to his desk first, just to tick Apollo off. But as he got to the door, he decided there was enough bad blood and that there was no need to be childish. He turned into the open door and saw Apollo sitting there with the Cat Eyes glasses on his desk waiting for him. He seemed perturbed that Luke had not arrived earlier, but apparently was going to hold back from making a comment. Luke smiled inwardly at the thought that he had somehow still gotten under Apollo's skin even though he didn't try too.

"So what's going on with the glasses?" Luke asked as he stepped into the office.

"Shut the door," Apollo interjected before Luke finished his last word. Luke fought the urge to demand that he ask nicely or say please, but instead just took a deep breath and closed the door behind him. He sat in the chair across the Apollo's desk and waited.

Apollo put the glasses on and looked around the room and then back at Luke. The thought of Apollo suddenly seeing all his feelings made him a bit apprehensive. *Was this going to be a truth or consequences discussion with the Cat Eyes being the judge and juror between them,* Luke thought? He waited for the questions as Apollo continued to scan the room and then back at Luke. He finally reached up and removed the glasses and handed them to Luke and slid the systems unit across the table to him.

"I don't understand it. The code was supposed to just sharpen the spectrums, but in doing so, it created some strange static or 'ghosting' or something in the peripheral areas. I don't see it now, but when you are in a larger area, it comes out." Luke felt a little relieved that Apollo had relinquished the glasses to him, but wondered how often Apollo wore them.

Luke left the systems unit sitting on the desk as he placed the glasses on. The first thing he noticed as he looked through the glasses was that the spectrum was much sharper and easier to read.

"Nice job on the spectrum enhancement," Luke said as he continued to look at Apollo's improved spectrum.

"I'm not interested in hearing about the new clarity. I'm only interested in knowing what is causing the ghosting," Apollo said coldly, ignoring the compliment. Luke glanced away from Apollo and around the room.

"I'm not seeing the ghosting you're talking about. Why don't I take it and do some field testing with it to try to recreate the ghosting issue," Luke said as he glanced back at Apollo. He saw a flash of anger or frustration in Apollo's spectrum at his words, then it stayed a yellowish hue. Luke was stunned by what he saw. It was fear that Apollo was showing. *Fear of what?* Luke thought in silence. Was Apollo afraid of him? Doubt it.

"Find someone else to speak with when you're wearing those." Apollo's voice brought Luke out of thoughts and back to the real world. He could see that Apollo was not happy about Luke wearing the glasses.

Luke opened his mouth to say, "How's it feel?" but stopped himself from what would have been another nasty fight with Apollo. Instead he slid them off and placed them by the systems unit on the table.

"I'll take them with me and test them around the office," Luke stated strongly and waited for an objection, a confirmation, or some other response from Apollo, but none came. Apollo just spun his chair to the right and starting working on his computer as if Luke was not even there. Luke picked up the systems unit and glasses and headed out the door.

As he walked back to his desk, he turned the glasses in his hand to look at the new Cat Eyes design from different angles. The new style was still a little crude, but less obtrusive and more closely resembled reading glasses than the previous unit. The system unit wires were less visible and would follow the neckline behind the ears better than the previous version. If you had longer hair, you could easily keep the wires hidden. He was so intent on examining the glasses that he walked right past his new cubicle. He looked up and then around to reorient himself to the new office space and remembered where to find his cubicle. As he sat down at his desk, he looked closely at the new shell of the systems unit. It was much smaller and resembled an older cell phone style. Apollo and Ronald had been busy indeed.

Luke put the glasses on. "Are those the Cat Eyes?" The familiar voice came from behind him and he turned around to see David looking over the cubicle wall at him. Luke smiled back and said.

"Yep. The latest and greatest version," Luke said and set the glasses back down onto his desk. He leaned back in his chair and they both just stared at it as if waiting for it to do a dance or something.

"Not much to look at," David said sarcastically.

"Don't let it fool you; it's a real chick magnet," Luke responded theatrically with a nodding of the head and a raised eyebrow, and then waited for the hammering he set himself up for.

"Yeah…" David said drawing out the word as he nodded his head, but he did not take the bait and go for the kill. "Well, this explains the 'truth' question you tossed out at me. It definitely is a conundrum." He said and they both nodded their heads in unison as they pondered the glasses.

"Lunch plans?" David asked as if the seriousness of the moment had somehow magically passed.

"The fate of the world is on our shoulders and all you can think about is lunch?" Luke asked over dramatically to be funny. David just nodded with a blank look on his face.

"Greasy tacos?" Luke responded blankly and joined in.

"Deal!" David said as he nodded.

"Can I bring the glasses? I need to do some field testing with them," Luke asked and David at first nodded and then tilted his head as if he saw through the real purpose and gave him the 'do you think I'm stupid' look. Luke waited for David to challenge him about wearing the glasses around him.

"You just want an excuse to pick up chicks," David said with a fake seriousness. Luke at first was caught off guard and then nodded.

"I need every advantage I can get." Luke shrugged and smiled guiltily, then shifted back to a more serious tone. "Really, no issues with me wearing them around you?" he asked David. David thought about it a moment before shaking his head and answering.

"No, I don't have any plans to lie to you, nor ulterior motives…" Then he stopped and looked as though he had been caught. "Except you buying me lunch, Susan needed to borrow all my cash this morning." Luke thought a moment before answering.

"No problem, I think I owe you at least a lunch anyways for diving into this mess with me." He replied. David continued to stare at him. Luke finally raised his hands as if to ask 'what?'

"Don't you want to verify my 'no cash' story?" David said and nodded toward the glasses.

"No, no… that would be too easy. It'll all come out eventually. And more, muhahaha," Luke said jokingly with a deeper and more sinister voice that David dutifully ignored.

"Sounds like fun. Let's say… in an hour?" David asked as he and Luke both glanced at their watches. Luke was surprised that it was almost 11 already, but nodded in agreement.

"An hour it is," Luke replied as David tapped the top of the cubicle and turned around to his desk. Luke was glad they had put David's desk so close to his and Jonathan's was on the other side of his cubicle.

As Luke logged into the system, he saw that he had been assigned new passwords and access points to the new Cat Eyes division materials. Everything was now on a separate server and he and Apollo had been granted access to almost every directory and folder. He spent thirty minutes reviewing the information that had been deemed "classified" or off limits to him prior to this morning, just to get familiar with where everything was located. Suddenly, a new system drive came online through Apollo's system where there had not been one earlier. He clicked on the drive to review its contents and saw several folders available. He opened a few files in several of the folders to briefly review their contents, but Luke was surprised to find that each of the files was written in Latin. He jotted a few notes down as to the names and locations of files as he opened them but could make very little sense out of what he was reading. The content was definitely strange from a research and development perspective, but he could see numbers and lists and dates in one spreadsheet. Then, just as quickly as it appeared, the files were suddenly gone. *Strange,* Luke thought and started to do a little more research on it, but felt he needed to stay focused on the tasks at hand and decided to would take time to review them in greater detail later.

He spent the rest of the hour going over the new security protocols and processes. He saw that all units now had to be 'checked out' and that no software or paperwork could leave the building without prior authorization. Knowing that he wanted to test the new system unit upgrade during lunch, he took a moment to go through the procedures with Serena.

Cliff was in the office with Serena as he knocked and entered. They both were silent as they waited to see who was entering.

"Luke, come on in," Cliff said and motioned to the seat next to him. "What can we do for you?"

"I saw that there are new check-out procedures for equipment. Apollo asked that I evaluate the new upgrade and the ghosting issues he is having with it. I thought I'd take it with me over lunch, I'd be with David Stevens and would like to get his thoughts during the testing," Luke mentioned to the two of them, not sure which one would make the decision. Cliff glanced back toward Serena as if highly concerned.

"Do we have any Navy Seal teams available to create a safe perimeter for their lunch meeting?" Cliff asked Serena. Luke was at first stunned by the question and was amazed by the level of security, but then saw Serena smile and then Cliff's face also broke into a smile. Luke took a breath and exhaled.

"Wow, got me. That had me very worried for a moment." Luke shook his head and smiled. Cliff laughed out loud, but Serena held her composure to just a smile.

"No problem with the check out. It's probably a good idea to have David along as well anyways, I'm sure he has lots of questions," Cliff said and then continued, "We were just going over this mornings meeting. What are your thoughts, with regards to Mr. Walpole's reaction?"

Luke took a moment to think through the question and how to best respond without seeming petty or vindictive. Cliff seemed to read through his dilemma.

"Just say it Luke. You're not going to get demoted or fired for saying what's on your mind."

"He's a hard one to read, but I know he's not one to 'play nice' when he is not in charge, or when he doesn't get his way. I think today was a shock to him." Luke hesitated and then continued, "His gears are turning, so I'm not sure where that will end up." Cliff seemed to agree.

"Well, keep your eyes open and let me or Serena know if anything seems strange," Cliff said and Luke raised an eyebrow at the strange part as he held the glasses. Cliff seemed to understand and smiled, "Stranger than normal for him, that is." Luke nodded and stood to leave, but hesitated at the door.

"How far would I get if I decided to run?" he jokingly asked Cliff. Cliff thought a moment.

"Inside a mile, which translates into the maximum range of the sniper team we have in place," he said.

"Gotcha. Note to self, no unapproved long walks." Luke closed the door as he left, but deep down he wondered how deep the security went with regards to the product and him.

On the way back to his desk, he stopped by David's. Not wanting to include anyone else in the event, he asked quietly if he was ready. David nodded and saved and closed the file he was working on. Luke swung into his cubicle only long enough to grab the systems unit and glasses. He took a moment to put the glasses on and then slid his light jacket over it to conceal the wires. He knew it was too nice of a day to wear a jacket, but he wanted to keep a low profile with the Cat Eyes. He lifted the glasses off his nose and placed them on top of his head and headed out the door with David close behind.

"You need to know that I am not trained in hand-to-hand combat, so should we be jumped, the most I can do is hang onto one of them as you run away," David joked.

"Don't worry about it, they always come in three's, so we're both doomed," Luke joked back as they headed down the stairs and through the security area to the sunny outside. Luke squinted as he walked and then remembered the Cat Eyes glasses resting on top of his head.

"Going active, so watch what you say," he warned with a smile as he slid them down and turned on the systems unit. It booted up the same as the previous model, with the same couple of quick flashes and then the rainbow splash that faded into the standard vision. As the rainbow faded, just as it had done in Apollo's office, the color spectrums initially looked clearer to him and easier to read. But then on cue with his wondering about the 'ghosting' issue, a faint shadow passed across the lens. It reminded him of a bird flying overhead with its shadow crossing over you. There one moment and gone the next.

He lifted his head for normal vision and then back down again to look through the top for the Cat Eyes vision. The clarity of color was definitely clearer and easier to read as he watched people walk by. He stood there looking around the area, taking in his surroundings.

"Is everything alright?" David asked as Luke continued to adjust to the new spectrum.

"Yeah, there is just a slight difference with the new upgrade," he replied as they stood in the middle of the parking area.

"Well, if this is what you had in mind for lunch, then I think I'm going to find someone else to eat with," David said sarcastically.

"Good luck finding someone else to buy you lunch," Luke said as he continued to shift from active to inactive with the Cat Eyes. Luke tipped his head up and said, "Okay, let's go feed you before you riot on me."

"Now we're talking," David replied as they walked the several blocks to the nearby taco stand.

David quietly watched Luke tip his head up and down as he surveyed the courtyard full of people heading to lunch. Luke kept using single word mumblings like 'hmm' and 'weird' and 'woe' to no one in particular as they continued on and eventually arrived at the taco stand.

"Care to share what's going on, or are you sworn to secrecy?" David asked Luke who turned toward David and angled his head back up as he looked at him.

"Sure, but let's get our food first," Luke replied and they placed their order, gathered their various salsas, hot sauces, napkins and drinks. Moments later, their taco plates were ready and they selected a seat outside on a concrete table that sat under a hard plastic umbrella.

Luke continued to look around as he ate his first taco. David seemed content to focus on eating his two tacos and watching Luke mumbling with the glasses. David pushed his empty plate to the center of the table and pulled his drink over to where his plate was moments before. Luke glanced back at David to see him staring at him with a 'well?' look on his face.

"Sorry. I'm just trying to understand what's going on with the upgrade," Luke stated and finished his last bite, then wiped his face and took a drink. "Apollo reported that the new upgrade had some sort of 'ghosting' going on. He's right, but I'm not sure what is causing it." Luke turned to watch a group of three women in the distance walking toward them. "See those three ladies coming toward us?" David turned to look and nodded. "Right now their reading is clear and normal, but right about… now, yep… it's like a shadow or sudden adjustment occurs as they pass a certain distance," Luke said half lost in thought.

"Everyone or just some people?" David asked. Luke thought about it a moment.

"I think everyone."

"So, it's consistent. What about distance, does it occur at the same distance each time or does it vary?" David asked.

"I'm not sure exactly."

"Then let's test it out." David stood up. "Give me a thumb up or down when I get to the place where the ghosting starts and stops. Once there, see if it's consistent." His voice faded as he headed toward the area where the three women were. As Luke watched David head off into the distance, he saw that David's color was blue spectrum dominant, which meant he was happy and not nervous.

As David approached the point where the ghosting occurred with the three women, he slowed down and walked twenty yards past the area, then turned and slowly walked back. Luke watched David's spectrum closely, but as he came back to the spot and then past it, nothing happened. No ghosting. Luke gave him a 'thumb down' signal. David glanced around and turned back toward Luke and gave a peace sign and then pointed behind him. Luke saw two men in suits heading toward David. David gave him a thumb up and down, which Luke nodded and focused on the two guys. As they approached where David was standing and watching them, one of their color spectrums was a reddish orange with dark intent, while the other seemed more yellowish orange, but as he saw David looking at them, the yellowish one shifted to dark green. Luke smiled knowing that the guy on the right had an interest in David. He was thinking about how he could torment David with that knowledge when the ghosting shadow passed from first the reddish aura, then it happened to the other guy once he passed where David stood sipping his drink. Luke gave him a 'thumb up' and David nodded and stayed where he was.

David was a good sport and continued standing in his spot as more and more people walked by him, which allowed Luke to work through his testing. He took out a piece of paper and a pen and over the next thirty minutes started jotting down notes and results based on sex, age and colors. He had roughly charted about sixty subjects when David looked at his watch and headed back toward Luke. Luke was looking at the crude spreadsheet results as David approached.

"Well, what did you learn? Is it a distance thing or something else?" David asked.

"I did learn something. It appears men find you more attractive than women." Luke said with a deep seriousness, while David shook his head and kept a straight face.

"Standing in the hot sun for half an hour, and that's all you came up with?" David stated coolly. Luke nodded as he tried to keep a straight face.

"I'm sure there is more in all this data that could be helpful, but I think that is the core value that I managed to glean from it." They both just stared at each other as if waiting to see which one would break first. Luke gave in.

"Okay, maybe that was not the most important data that I complied," Luke said as he glanced back down at the paper in front of him and smiled. "It seems that it's not a fixed distance, and it's not based on sex or age. It does appear to correlate with the color spectrum that the person has at the time they get close to the glasses. The dark reds can get a lot closer before they 'ghost', while the blues ghost further out." David nodded as if considering what that meant. Luke tapped his pen on a separate area of the paper. "I didn't see any 're-ghosting' as a person was leaving, just on the way in," he said distantly as if in deep thought. Luke saw David glance at his watch and knew what was coming.

"Lunch is over Einstein, we'd better be heading back or your leadership role with the company will be short lived," David said with a slight smile. Luke nodded and gathered the lunch trash and tossed them in the garbage as they headed back to the office.

All the way back to the office, David continually fired question after question at Luke about the Cat Eyes and the results they had given in the past and then comparing them with what was seen at lunch, which Luke would try to answer as clearly as possible. The questions David asked were not only very insightful, but he seemed deeply interested in how the glasses worked and the results they would provide to the end user.

Upon returning to the office, Luke immediately began charting the data. Although he had a good feel for the results before inputting the data, he felt by putting it into a presentable form, others would be able to assist with the analysis as well. He also wanted to keep an ongoing record of the various tests and results. Once the data was in and he collated the data into charts. The information gathered confirmed his initial thoughts from their testing during lunch. He just wasn't understanding why or how it correlated.

He took the short walk to David's desk and set the report in front of him. David looked down at the papers and back at Luke.

"Your detailed plans to overthrow the world?" David asked in his typical dry sense of humor. Luke did not respond except for a raised eyebrow and nod toward the paperwork. David shrugged as he picked it up and examined the charts. Luke realized he was not accomplishing anything by standing over him, so he turned and headed back to his desk. He wanted David's feedback before submitting it to Apollo and the rest of the team.

About twenty minutes later, the report landed back on his desk with a plop. Luke looked up to see David leaning against the cubicle entrance.

"So?" Luke asked and waited for a response. David seemed to want to share something, but then stopped just as he opened his mouth.

"I have an idea, but I'm thinking it's going to cost you another lunch or maybe even dinner before I'm willing to share it with you," David said without any expression on his face.

"You're kidding me right?" Luke asked, but David just shook his head from side to side in apparent seriousness until Luke finally said "Fine." David smiled at the response.

"I'd like to ask a few more questions on the functionality of the glasses and your prior experiences with them. How soon do you need the info?" Luke was hoping to submit it this afternoon, but felt it would be better with more data. Then a thought crossed his mind.

"Don't you have your own job to do?" he asked David, who shook his head.

"Apollo hasn't released any code for us to work on yet, so all we're doing at the moment is reading the manuals and overviews that you guys have written. So, I'm relatively free to help, well not necessarily free, as there is a meal or two that needs to be factored in."

"Just great, another bloody opportunist trying to stick it to *The Man* again," Luke replied and David tried to nod innocently in response.

"Can we meet after work?" Luke asked and watched David, as he seemed to think through his calendar in his head. David eventually nodded.

"I'm free until 7:20, well not free, as there are…"

"I know, I know, there are 'meals' that need to be factored in." Luke cut David off from repeating his prior statement. They quickly agreed upon a place and time and then both dove back into their work.

Late in the afternoon, Luke received an approval request from Apollo to pick up one of the latest versions of the carrying case so that he could update the various training manual sections. Apparently, the unit would be waiting for him to pick up at 4:00 p.m. at the production facility. He checked the time and saw that it was almost 4:00, so he headed out. He spent about thirty minutes filling out paperwork. In addition to the case, he picked up the spec sheets and current CAD designs for the manual. On his way back he decided to swing by the other office and say hello to Danielle. Her back was to him as he peeked around the entrance to her cubicle.

"Donde esta el bano?" he asked her in an altered voice as he butchered the Spanish language.

"Si'el bano esta' ahi…" Danielle started to say as she turned around to face him, only to stop and glare a moment. "You're weird," was all she said and then smiled. Her response was not what he was hoping for, but the smile she gave him was. He really missed her.

"Weird? What's weird about needing to find a bathroom?" he replied and then returned the smile. There was an awkward silence as they both tried to find the right words to keep the conversation going. He responded first.

"I was just in the area and thought I'd say hi," he said awkwardly.

"I'm glad you did," she replied softly.

"I mean I've already stopped by every other cubicle as well, you were just the last one in the row." He shrugged sarcastically and smiled.

"I doubt that," she said and called his bluff, "I'm guessing I was the first and only cubicle you stopped at," she retorted with a frown and stern look.

"If you like, I could have everyone in this office stand up to verify my story," he replied with an innocent look.

"He didn't stop by my cube," a voice from the cubicle to the right of Danielle's mumbled out loud, causing Danielle to raise an eyebrow and tilt her head.
"Well maybe not that one, but..." he started to say jokingly in response to her look but was cut off by a voice from the other direction.

"He didn't make it by mine either." Danielle's other eyebrow went up and the smirk on her face grew more pronounced.

"Now that I think about it, I may have missed this whole row. But the rest…"

"Must have missed my row as well," someone mumbled from behind him.

"Okay, okay, maybe I just stopped at your cubicle to say hi… but I'm planning on stopping at everyone else's before I leave," Luke said a little louder as he continued to play out the obvious joke.

"Don't stop by mine, I'm busy."

"Or mine."

"I don't want to see your ugly face in mine either."

The responses kept rumbling from various cubicles and Danielle laughed and Luke hung his head in mock shame as he waited for the responses to end. Luke missed the humor on this side of the office and was reminded and somewhat glad to hear that everyone still listened in on everything someone said. Deep down he was almost counting on them to interject their two cents to their ongoing joke.

"I see you still live in a tough, but very private neighborhood," he laughed and then heard others from various cubicles laugh as well.

"Your business is our business," a female voice interjected to the right of them.

Danielle slid away from her desk and walked toward Luke.

"How about we visit the break room where there are fewer ears to listen in?" she asked him.

"I heard that," the female voice from the right chimed in again. Luke just nodded and stepped clear of the cubicle entrance and then the two of them silently walked toward the break room. Once they entered, Danielle walked to the water cooler and filled a paper cup, which she handed to Luke, then turned and poured herself one as well. Danielle got a mischievous look about her.

"I hear you've started going to church?" she stated and waited for his response. Luke at first felt stunned that she knew, but then realized that she and Cindy were friends and gossip tends to spread faster than the speed of light. He was not sure if he felt embarrassed or guilty by her statement.

"Gosh, I totally forgot that I posted that on the internet," he replied sarcastically as he tapped himself on the forehead as if he just remembered something, which only seemed to encourage Danielle to press the issue further.

"Hmm, no, I saw it on a flyer being handed out in my neighborhood," she replied with a smile and then let the smile fade from her face as she continued. "I guess I just felt a little hurt that I got scolded for seeking God, then to hear that you were too…" she seemed to catch herself, "sorry, that was very selfish of me. I should be happy for you, not hurt." She let the mischievous look fade with the last part. Luke was surprised by her apology and thought about pouncing on the moment, but then realized that he actually felt embarrassed at his own hypocrisy.

"I guess I was just looking for answers," he said humbly. It was her turn to be surprised.

"Did you find the answers you were looking for?" she asked. Luke started to nod yes, and then ended up shaking his head side to side.

"I thought so, but realized I had learned very little and even walked away more confused," he said almost sadly.

"So, what were the questions you were wanting answered?" she asked, not letting the moment escape. He stood thinking a long while, struggling to find a way to answer her question without sounding stupid, but he knew she would not let go of this until he gave her something. It was one of the things he loved about her.

"Why it means everything to you, but so little to other Christians."

She seemed stunned by his pure honesty.

"By 'it' you mean?" she asked, leaving the question dangling.

"Why other Christians think nothing of having a relationship with another person and one with God, but with you it can only be one or the other," he said. She stared silently a moment and then began shaking her head.

"No. It's not one OR the other. It's actually about priority and purpose. I can't say that 'Jesus is Lord' and then let pleasing someone else be more important than pleasing God. I want that relationship with 'another person' but if it means having to compromise the one with God in order to please the other person, I just can't do that." Her voice cracked and Luke thought that she was close to tears. He took a deep breath, going over what she had just said and the conviction and pain that came through as she had spoke.
"I believe I understand your words, but I just don't get their meaning. Yet." he stated. She never took her eyes off of his as she listened and seemed to be waiting for something more.

"What can I do to help?" she asked with a quiet and sincere voice. Try as he might, he could not think of an answer or a clever remark to change the subject.

"Just... be patient." He looked at her and smiled. "I know I'm a real knucklehead at times, and you probably haven't noticed, but I'm rather... confused at the moment, trying to get my arms around everything. Just a little time and patience is what I need," he replied and tried to joke his way out of the seriousness tone of things.

"Deal," she said and then smiled that smile of hers. Her eyes drifted past his shoulder to something behind him. "You've got fifteen minutes," she said suddenly as she looked back to his eyes. He was at first confused, but then realized what she was talking about, but tried to make a joke out of the moment.

"I have only fifteen minutes to work through all this?" he replied in mock horror. Danielle, at first looked confused, and then caught what he meant.
"No, no, I mean you have fifteen minutes until the end of the work day, not fifteen minutes to make a decision," she stumbled through her words, but then saw the familiar smile and stopped trying to explain. She took a breath and then squinted her eyes in mock anger. "You're just plain mean Mr. Baker. Deals off," she announced suddenly and turned toward the counter and tossed her paper cup in the trash. She gave him a brief smile as she headed for the break room door. "Don't forget to say hello to the rest of the people you came over here to see." She then stopped. "David's a good place to start," she said. It was Luke's turn to be confused.

"David works with me in the other office," he said, thinking that she might not be aware of the new division. She just shook her head and gave a brief roll of her eyes.

"To find the answers for those troublesome questions." She waited for him to acknowledge her meaning.

"What questions?" he replied, pretending not to know what she was talking about. Then just as she seemed about to explain her words and remind him, he smiled. She just took a deep breath and headed out the door mumbling something about 'men' and 'fence posts' and their comparative intelligence.

Luke had just enough time to check back in the systems unit before he left for the day. When he reached his desk, he saw that it was not there. After checking all the other places that it could be, besides on top of the desk where he left it, he turned to the people in the cubicles near him and asked if anyone had swung by his office while he was gone.

"Apollo stopped by and asked where you were, but we told him that we didn't know. But he left right afterwards," Gloria, who had an open view to his cubicle said. There was an awkward silence as Luke continued to stare at his desk and replay in his mind all his actions since lunch.

"Ronald," David's voice suddenly interjected. Luke stood up and looked over the cubicle to where David was sitting in apparent deep thought.

"Ronald... what?" Luke asked. David looked up and then slowly stood up and looked down the walkway.

"I heard a noise from your cubicle, I thought you had returned, but when I stood up to let you know that Apollo was looking for you, you weren't there, but Ronald was walking down the aisle back toward his desk. I didn't think much about it until just now. I know the noise I heard came from inside your cubicle, but I can't be positive that it was Ronald who made it," David shared, but remained in deep thought. Luke looked toward Gloria for confirmation, but she was just shaking her head.

"Not while I was here, but I was gone for awhile at a meeting with Apollo." Luke and David glanced at each other and as Luke started to ask another question of Gloria, David interjected.

"Thanks Gloria, I'm sure this will all work itself out." He turned to Luke. "Why don't you let Cliff know and then we can head out for that dinner you owe me," he said with a smile. Luke started to object to the diversion of conversation, but David gently shook his head. Luke stared at David and tried to understand his reluctance in pursuing the questions with Gloria. He decided to hold that question until after he spoke with Cliff.

Luke glanced at his watch as he headed toward Cliff's office. It was already 5:20 and he hoped Cliff had not left yet. As he passed Apollo's office, Apollo looked up briefly and then back to his computer. Luke thought about stopping to ask Apollo if he had seen anything, but somehow felt he should start with Cliff. He knocked on the opened door and was happy to see Cliff and Serena across the table from each other.

"Hey Luke, come on in. What can I do for you?" Cliff asked. Luke spent the next ten minutes walking him through each activity and conversation that he had from the time he checked out the systems unit to the time he returned to his desk to find it missing.

"What's missing?" Apollo interjected from behind Luke.

"The system unit and glasses that I checked out this afternoon for the testing you requested," Luke replied. Apollo gave Cliff and Serena an overly concerned look and then back at Luke and then asked Luke to explain again the various activities and steps that Luke had taken since the time the unit was checked out.

"So you and David came back to the office with them," Apollo confirmed and Luke nodded. "But you then left the primary office to retrieve the new systems unit case." Again Apollo was making a statement, not asking a question.

"Yes, at 3:50," Luke replied.

"And you're sure you did not take it with you?" Apollo finally asked a question.

"Positive," Luke replied in complete confidence. Apollo seemed to be in deep thought a moment before continuing.

"You said you left it on your desk, but I stopped by at 4:20 to see if you had the case info I requested, but you were not there, nor was the system unit sitting on the desk as you described." Luke felt caught off guard by Apollo's words and tried to think through the timeline one more time to see if he had missed anything. He thought about mentioning that David had thought he'd seen Ronald at his desk, but if Apollo said it was missing before then, that point would not matter. Luke finally turned to Cliff.

"What do we do from here?" Luke asked Cliff.

"We could initiate a lock down; we could do a search on everyone leaving the office, I mean the team is not that big," Apollo suggested, "but I would guess if someone took it, they would have already removed it from the office by now."

Cliff seemed to be in deep thought as Apollo was speaking. "The security access cards will track who is leaving and coming to the office, but the fact that the bathrooms are currently still being remodeled and the only working ones are in the other office, means there is a lot of traffic back and forth and plenty of opportunity to leave with the equipment," Cliff said to the group.

"It was there when I left at 3:50, so we should only need to check from that time forward," Luke interjected the idea in order to save time in verifying security reports.

"I think it would be a good idea to start from the time the unit was initially checked out… in case Luke is mistaken about seeing it at 3:50 before he left," Apollo stated diplomatically. Luke could not help but feel slighted by the statement and the questioning of his word. He remembered needing to move the glasses off the request form in order to take it with him prior to leaving, so he knew it was there when he left. He thought about emphatically making that statement again, but felt it might sound contrite or be perceived as a guilty plea.

"Guys, I'm sorry I put us in this situation. I was trying to follow the new security rules, but did not think I would have to worry about it while in the office." Luke turned to Apollo as he continued, "I mean prior to our new partners coming on board, at any given time we had one or two of these floating outside the office. The first day we put a security net around it, someone tries to steal one from inside the office." Luke just shook his head in disbelief as he tried to grasp the situation and its ramifications. Luke was surprised to hear Cliff start to laugh at his words.

"Welcome to the world of secret government operations. No one cares about what you're doing until you put 'secret' on it, then the whole world wants to know what it is." He chuckled again. "Don't worry about it Luke, something tells me that there is another explanation for this that we've not been able to put our finger on just yet."

Luke nodded in appreciation, but tried to imagine what that explanation could be. He went through all the obvious players in his mind. Apollo had complete access to a system unit anytime he wanted and he had the code as well, so there was no need or apparent motive there. Ronald was too afraid of Apollo to ever think of stealing something from him and was tied in way too deep to him. As hard as he tried to think otherwise, he could not imagine Gloria or Danny becoming overnight spies. Both had been with the company too long and they didn't even know that they would be picked to be on the team of this product three days ago. That left David.

As the others talked through various objectives and follow-up strategies on security, Luke thought through David's actions over the past few days. Luke had tried to talk him out of the joining the team, but he was insistent. Apollo had tried to bribe him off the team, but couldn't. His fascination and determination during the testing over lunch had been very aggressive as well. It was David who had hinted at Ronald being by his desk, yet no one else remembered seeing him. But what motive would he have in stealing the product? He thought of what he knew about David and the only thing that came to mind was a possible religious-based motive. Did David feel deep down that the Cat Eyes were an abomination, or some sort of threat to religious freedom, or some other yet unknown angle? Luke himself still felt strongly about the possible ramification of the new technology, but not from a religious perspective. He refused to believe it. He realized that in all fairness, he was the most obvious person in the potential lineup, but he knew that he had not taken them. The question was would everyone else believe that?

Chapter 17

"So did you take them or not?" Luke asked David as they headed into the restaurant that they had agreed to meet at. David seemed to struggle as to what the question was about, before finally understanding.

"Wow, you go right for the jugular vein. Now common sense tells me not to answer that until after dinner, or you might change your mind and not buy," he replied with a smile and watched Luke continue to stare at him. "Well, being that you're not wearing your special Superman glasses, I'm guessing no matter what I say, you'll still question the sincerity of my response." He smiled and then saw that Luke still was not taking his eyes off of him until he answered the question, so he shook his head and looked Luke in the eyes.

"No. I did not take the glasses, nor do I know where they are." He held his stare until Luke finally nodded his head, then held open the door to the restaurant for David to enter.

"You better not have," he said back with a sarcastic smile. "I think we both know who might have been behind it, but I'm not sure why exactly."

"I can think of one. It's an embarrassing way for someone to start out as the new 'team leader.' I'm sure no one wants to see your reputation soiled," David said with a raised eyebrow. Luke thought about that perspective and nodded.

"Yeah, not a good start for me," he replied as they were escorted to their table and David set his briefcase down on the chair next to him.

"So what's this I hear about you getting all religious on me when I'm not looking?" David asked Luke. Luke knew that their web of friends was too small so he decided not to even try to deny it.

"Yeah. So, what are your secret thoughts on the Cat Eyes?" Luke asked, avoiding a need to discuss the question further. David frowned briefly.

"I'm pretty sure you would not have believed my hypothesis before, but now that you're a 'religious' man, who knows," David said, pausing as he thanked the waitress for handing him a menu.

As the waitress discussed the specials for the night, Luke wrestled with David's comment and how it related to his religious pursuit. They both ordered the special, Luke more out of taking the easy route so that he could get back to the discussion with David.

"So what does my 'religious' pursuit have to do with the Cat Eyes?" Luke asked and David seemed to ponder on how best to reply to his question.

"I think what you are seeing is more of a spiritual matter verses a physical one," he replied calmly and seemed to be finished with the matter as he looked away. Luke took a deep breath and shook his head.

"You mean to tell me you managed to finagle another free meal out of me, just to tell me that?" he asked David somewhat sarcastically, but with an element of truth mixed into his words. David faked a stunned look and then nodded his head. Luke just sat in silence for a moment before finally speaking. "That's it? That's all you're going to share with me?" he asked David, who then smiled.

"I thought you'd never ask," David replied as Luke realized he had walked into his trap.

"Okay, while you were busy losing your career ending demo unit, I was spending my afternoon reading up on the Cat Eyes and your field test reports; and by the way, when you are writing you use three times more words to say something than most people." David shook his head and then continued, "Anyway, not only how they work, but all the odd things you were experiencing and trying to figure out as you were troubleshooting the unit." He paused and took a drink. "Things like understanding the element of motives in the spectrum, why younger children do not register except for basic readings, and even what you stated you saw when the man that failed to kill you in Iraq died." David let his words settle a minute. "So, based on what I read and what I saw today, I think it's spiritually related." David declared. Luke sat quietly for a moment then slowly started nodding his head and then leaned forward as if to tell David a secret.

"First off, you are a lunatic," Luke said and then felt anger rush into him. "Secondly, I really don't appreciate you making fun of my personal spiritual pursuits outside of the office." Luke was serious about his words. David held Luke's gaze a moment as if trying to read his reaction.

"I'm not making fun of it, I'm dead serious. I just don't think you realize how serious what you are pursuing is and the eternal consequences it holds," David replied. Luke could tell that David was just as serious.

David leaned forward again as if he was going "all in" in a poker match. "Luke, we've been friends for awhile now, longer than you and Jonathan, and I would even like to think we are also better friends. So to hear that after we talked about a few spiritual things, you decided to go elsewhere for further knowledge, well I guess I'm a little surprised, maybe even hurt." He admitted. Luke just sat there quietly thinking about what he had said. He had to agree with him on many of the points mentioned, but he felt David missed one big one as he thought about Danielle.

"It hurts doesn't it?" The words came out before he realized it and David seemed stunned by them at first and then nodded.

"Fair enough. But if you think that our reaching out to Danielle and showing her the teachings of the Bible was to hurt you, then you have completely misunderstood our friendship. We care a great deal about both of you, more than you know," he said sincerely. Luke tried to read through the words and catch the deeper meanings that seemed to be implied, but could not.

"Look David, I know you are a good friend, but I just don't agree with what you're teaching Danielle," Luke replied. David seemed to be waiting for more, but realized that nothing else was coming from Luke.

"Interesting. You don't even know what we teach, yet you're confident that you don't agree with it?" he finally stated calmly to Luke. "So what is it exactly that you do not agree with?" he asked Luke. Luke tried to pull together what had been said, but realized that David was right and just shook his head and shrugged his shoulders.

"So, I'm guessing these disagreements with our teachings are not your convictions, but someone else's," David stated and waited. It took a minute, but Luke finally nodded his head.

"I don't know what it is that you teach, but how would I know if it was true or not? That's what I hate about religion, it's just one person's opinion compared to another's. What's really true?" Luke finally asked in frustration. David opened his hands as if to ask a question.

"So how far are you willing to go to find the whole truth, not just a little of it?" David countered. Luke thought about David's words and his deep Bible knowledge and then about how little he knew about it.

"Again, if I did discuss it with you, how would I know that what you are teaching me is any more accurate than someone else?" he asked David.

"By verifying that what we read is true and in context within the Bible, not something based on feelings, or snippets of scripture to support someone's ideas," David replied and then continued, "Luke, the real question you need to ask yourself is what is it exactly that you seek? Is it just knowledge or is it a relationship with God?"

Luke tried to think of what the best answer was, as if it was a trick question. "I would guess both, but initially knowledge, why?" he replied. David seemed to be in deep thought as Luke waited for his answer. David suddenly reached into his briefcase and pulled out the little brown book that Luke knew was the Bible and started thumbing through some pages. Once he found his destination, he cleared his voice and looked at Luke. Seeing his discomfort, David looked from side to side, smiled and whispered.

"I'll try to read quietly so you're not embarrassed," he said with a smile, and then spun the book around to face Luke and placed his finger on the scripture that he was going to read. Then in a normal voice he started quoting it as Luke followed along. "In Jeremiah 29, verse 11 gives us a little insight on the quest. It reads;

"For I know the plans I have for you," declares the LORD, "plans to prosper you and not to harm you, plans to give you hope and a future. Then you will call on me and come and pray to me, and I will listen to you. You will seek me and find me when you seek me with all your heart."

David was looking at Luke as if checking to see if he was listening and had understood the words in the verse. "That was the same verse that Danielle read at her baptism," Luke mumbled as he remembered her reading it. David nodded.

"You're right," David seemed impressed that Luke had remembered but wanted to stay on his purpose for reading it. "What do we see here about God and finding him?" David asked as Luke reread the scripture to himself and contemplated David's words.

"Apparently he has plans for us," Luke replied trying not to sound too uninterested.

"Plans for *you*," David replied. "Are they good or bad plans, short-term or long-term plans?" he asked Luke who kept rereading the verses to himself trying to find the answers to David's questions.

"Good, long-term plans," Luke replied without looking up from the verses.

"Do you believe what God says, or do you think he just wants to make life miserable for you?" David asked with a smile.

"I don't know," Luke replied initially and then shook his head, "I wouldn't think he would want bad things for us, but then again, things are a mess here."

"Agreed, but let's stay on target here with this verse. If you agree that God wants to do good things for you, based on this scripture, what is he looking for from us?" David asked and Luke looked back down at the verse before him.

"To pray to him," Luke replied and David nodded his head.

"Is he hiding from us?" David asked and Luke shook his head. "But God says that in order to find him what is his only requirement?" he asked Luke who stared at the last part of the verse.
"To seek him with all of your heart," Luke replied softly and tried to think through what that would entail.

"Luke, God is not looking for someone just seeking knowledge about him, he is looking for people who want to have a personal relationship with him. And he wants you to give your whole heart to that relationship, not just leftovers." David sat quietly and let it sink in. Luke at first nodded and felt a pull toward the whole concept of God, but then he felt anger at the words and what had happened with him and Danielle and started to shake his head.

"Then why all the wars and killings in the name of religion?" Luke asked as he tried to fight off the pressure of the words. David seemed caught off guard at first and then squinted.

"Is that really your objection or concern, or does it run deeper than that?" David asked. "because the horrific wars and killings you are concerned about are a direct result of men who were NOT seeking God with all of their hearts. Instead in their ignorance or selfish desires, political and religious leaders sought after what they wanted and twisted God's Word around to sway the masses that either did not know better, or chose to purposely disobey, his Word. Otherwise, they would have never done those horrible things in the name of God." David paused. "So, are the wars and killings really the reason you are unwilling to seek him?" he asked again. Luke felt a strong desire to walk away from the table, but at the same time he wanted to learn more about David and where he was going with the discussion. Perhaps he could find a weakness if he stayed a bit longer. So he tried to clear his mind to give an honest answer, not one bent with anger.

"Straight as an arrow?" he asked David, who nodded his head. "I'm totally confused about how to go about my research on the whole 'religion' thing. I don't have the time to read and memorize this whole book, nor do I know what or who to believe even if I did?" Luke ended his rant and looked at David, who just smiled and nodded his head.

"Okay, now we know where to start," he said and continued, "First off, a relationship with God is not about memorizing the whole Bible, we'd all be doomed if that was the case." He laughed. "But as we just read, it's about first seeking a relationship with him through prayer and reading his Word to understand what he desires from us." David hesitated and waited for Luke to acknowledge his words, then reached over and spun the Bible around and turned to another chapter and verse. Luke was impressed that he knew where to go in this thousand plus page book. "Now about the whole 'I don't have time' concern, we all have a busy and full life, and God understands that and even addresses that very concern in Matthew 6:25." He turned one final page and spun it around for Luke to read. "Read verses 25 thru 34." Luke read softly starting at verse 25.

"Therefore I tell you, do not worry about your life, what you will eat or drink; or about your body, what you will wear. Is not life more than food, and the body more than clothes? [26] Look at the birds of the air; they do not sow or reap or store away in barns, and yet your heavenly Father feeds them. Are you not much more valuable than they? [27] Can any one of you by worrying add a single hour to your life? [28] "And why do you worry about clothes? See how the flowers of the field grow. They do not labor or spin. [29] Yet I tell you that not even Solomon in all his splendor was dressed like one of these. [30] If that is how God clothes the grass of the field, which is here today and tomorrow is thrown into the fire, will he not much more clothe you—you of little faith? [31] So do not worry, saying, 'What shall we eat?' or 'What shall we drink?' or 'What shall we wear?' [32] For the pagans run after all these things, and your heavenly Father knows that you need them. [33] But seek first his kingdom and his righteousness, and all these things will be given to you as well. [34] Therefore do not worry about tomorrow, for tomorrow will worry about itself. Each day has enough trouble of its own."

"What do we see Jesus saying here?" David asked and Luke glanced back to the top and reread it again to make sure he understood before answering.

"Don't worry about tomorrow," Luke answered and thought about how much trouble each day seemed to hold for him.

"But based on what Jesus says, what is important for us to be concerned about?" David asked and Luke glanced back to verse 33.

"His kingdom and his righteousness," Luke replied.

"Right. Once again we are dealing with priorities, not neglect. Jesus is saying to seek him and his Kingdom first, that if we do, he'll take care of the rest," David said as the waitress stopped by to refill Luke's iced tea and David's water glass.

Luke thought about all the stuff going on in his life that he was barely able to keep under control. The thought of adding one more thing to his plate, well he knew that it would all fly apart. He shook his head. "This is nice and all, but it's just not the best timing for me," Luke replied.

"It never is," David replied. "But remember it's not about timing, it's about priority. The perfect time to seek God is always now, not later. You have time to meet with me for dinner? You have time to eat three meals a day, to work out, to watch your favorite TV programs, right? We make time for things that we love, but more importantly for people that we love," he said and then spun the Bible back around and turned to another scripture. Luke immediately thought about Danielle and how much time they would spend together, almost every night and weekend. Then he could feel the anger returning at the thought of her trading him for God.

"So is that why Danielle broke off our relationship? She needed to free up her schedule for time with God?" he said coldly and David stopped turning pages and looked up at Luke.

"No. More than almost anything, she wanted you to share that relationship with God with her, but you made her choose between you or God. She never stopped loving you, nor does she now love you less in order to love God more. But because she is seeking his kingdom and his righteousness with all her heart, she chose God." David said and seemed to wait for Luke to react or respond, but Luke said nothing and looked down at the Bible in front of David as if to say, 'go ahead'.

"In Acts 17, verses 24 thru 28, we see the desire of God again," he said and turned the Bible back around so that Luke could read where his finger was pointing.

"The God who made the world and everything in it is the Lord of heaven and earth and does not live in temples built by hands. 25 And he is not served by human hands, as if he needed anything, because he himself gives all men life and breath and everything else. 26 From one man he made every nation of men, that they should inhabit the whole earth; and he determined the times set for them and the exact places where they should live. 27 God did this so that men would seek him and perhaps reach out for him and find him, though he is not far from each one of us. 28 'For in him we live and move and have our being.' As some of your own poets have said, 'We are his offspring.'"

Luke continued to reread the words knowing that David would eventually be asking him a question.

"What do we see about God in this scripture?" David finally asked.

"That although he does not need us, he still desires that we seek him." Luke replied and David seemed surprised by his answer.

"Yeah. It's not by chance or luck that a person stumbles upon God. God has put things in motion and continues to put things in motion so that we might, 'perhaps' one day decide to seek him," David said and hesitated before continuing, "It's always our choice, our free will to seek him or not; he does not make us seek him. The bigger question is why? Why are we so important to him?" Luke reviewed the words again.

"Because we are his children," Luke answered and thought about his parents and all the things they do to stay in touch or how they desire to see him as often as possible. David nodded his head at Luke's answer and the two sat in silence.

Suddenly the waitress appeared with two plates, one in each hand.

"Who had the special?' she asked and then smiled as both of them raised their hand and realized that she was just kidding with them. After a few brief comments, and a moment of silence by David as he prayed, they ate as two hungry men generally do, until the majority of their food was gone. David was the first to speak.

"So, we know that to find God we have to rearrange our priorities and seek him with all of our hearts. That he desires a relationship as much or more than we do, but that it is our choice to act on that relationship, and that he loves us because we are his children." David took a last bite, finished chewing it and then took a drink of his water. "So what does that relationship look like?" David asked and turned the Bible around again and flipped to another section while Luke finished his last few bites. "In John chapter 4, starting in verse 23, Jesus tells us what that relationship or worship should look like." And David spun the Bible back around for Luke to read.

"Yet a time is coming and has now come when the true worshipers will worship the Father in spirit and truth, for they are the kind of worshipers the Father seeks. 24 God is spirit, and his worshipers must worship in spirit and in truth."

"While talking to a Samaritan woman who was confused about the whole 'where and how' to worship God question, Jesus takes a moment to differentiate between false and true worshipers. What does he say about true worshipers?" David asked.

"That they must worship in spirit and in truth," Luke replied and David nodded.

"What do you think that means?" David asked and waited as Luke chewed on the question.

"Truth, I'm guessing, means accurately or correctly," Luke replied and hesitated, "but as far as spirit goes, I'm not sure." David nodded.

"You're right on the truth part, like the woman who was confused about how to worship, we need to go to God's own words in the Bible to understand what 'truth' is. Understanding the other side of the worship equation, the 'spirit' part, is just as important. We know we can get the 'truth' from the Bible, but how do we get the spirit?" David waited a second and then turned to another scripture. "The verse we just read says that God is spirit. Now let's take a look at another verse that also talks about what God is. In 1 John chapter 4, in verses 8 thru 10, what does it say God is?" David asked as he spun the Bible back around for Luke to read.

"Whoever does not love does not know God, because **God is love.** *9 This is how God showed his love among us: He sent his one and only Son into the world that we might live through him. 10 This is love: not that we loved God, but that he loved us and sent his Son as an atoning sacrifice for our sins."*

"So what do we need in order to know God?" David asked and Luke just stared at the words.

"Love," Luke answered.

"Why is that important?" David asked.

"Because God is love," Luke replied with the obvious answer and David nodded.

"People can obey rules or commands, but at the same time hate them or the person who made them right?" Luke nodded. "So if God is spirit and is love, then what do you think he is seeking in his worshipers?" David asked the leading question.

"Someone who loves him and his commands." Luke gave the obvious answer to the question and David nodded.

"In verse 10 we see a gratitude and love that comes from understanding the sacrifice made on our behalf. So somehow must get the spirit of God, love, and his Word inside us," David ended and Luke could sense him looking at him as he continued to stare at the words. Luke continued to run through everything in his mind as he thought about the words being shared with him.

"I think I understand the love and spirit part regarding my motives for seeking God, but how do I know that what you are teaching me is true?" Luke finally answered.

"Great question," he replied and spun the Bible back around and started turning pages again. "Let's take a look at what God says is the answer to that question. In Acts chapter 17, starting in verse 10, we see the answer," David said and spun the Bible around for Luke to read.

"As soon as it was night, the brothers sent Paul and Silas away to Berea. On arriving there, they went to the Jewish synagogue. [11] Now the Bereans were of more noble character than the Thessalonians, for they received the message with great eagerness and examined the Scriptures every day to see if what Paul said was true. [12] Many of the Jews believed, as did also a number of prominent Greek women and many Greek men."

"So what made the character of the Bereans so noble?" David asked and Luke saw the answer before him.

"They verified that what Paul was teaching was true," Luke replied and David nodded.

"How did they verify it?"

"By examining the scriptures."

"How often?"

"Every day."

"How excited were they about doing it?" David asked and Luke smiled.

"Very."

"Can you see the heart coming out again? That is what made them different from the Thessalonians. Although it was a new teaching for the Jews in both Thessalonica and Berea, the Berean Jews weren't set in their ways, but studied out what was being taught to them." David let the words sink in a moment before continuing.

"Luke, that is my challenge to you. Before we leave, I'm going to write down every scripture we discussed tonight. What I want you to do tonight, tomorrow, or however long it takes you, is to verify that what I am teaching you is accurate," he said and Luke nodded. "Feel free to bounce anything I'm sharing with you off anyone else to get their thoughts as well. When you feel you are ready, we can dive in a little deeper and peel back a few more layers at whatever speed you desire to go at. Finding God is not the difficult part, because he promises that you will find him if you do. The hard part is making a decision to seek him with all your heart in the first place." David reached over and pulled the book back toward him and closed it, then took out a pen and started writing on the back of a napkin.

As David was writing, Luke kept sifting through the ideas that had been shared with him. He wanted to get several opinions as to what was being taught, but he was not sure where to go for answers. His first thought was to call Monica, but figured that that would probably just turn out to be a distraction. His next thought was to talk with Jonathan and get his thoughts since he was relatively neutral. The whole concept of religion seemed so strange to Luke, yet there was something comforting about it as well.

As he looked up, he scanned the room and wondered what the people sitting nearby may have overheard of their discussion. The family that was initially behind them was gone and a disheveled man was sitting at the table. There was an older couple that just ate in silence, not even looking at each other. There was an attractive, yet simple looking woman with a short, 'pixie' haircut sitting alone at a table a little ways from theirs, sipping her coffee.

As he watched David continue to write on the back of the napkin, Luke wondered what it was that he did not trust about David regarding this spiritual matter. He trusted him with almost any other aspect of work or life. Was it his overconfidence, or was it more personal in nature. Maybe out of anger at how David's brand of Christianity had affected his relationship with Danielle? Something was definitely wrong and red flags started going off right and left again now that he thought about things a little deeper. David suddenly slid the napkin over to him and Luke saw that he had written down the various scriptures that they had read.

"Promise to study them all out?" he asked Luke, who nodded and put the napkin in his pocket.
"I spent good money for an answer, but you still have not told me what you think the ghosting is from," Luke asked. David seemed surprised by the question.

"I most certainly did!" he replied and it was Luke's turn to be surprised as he looked back on their initial discussion and then shook his head as David was sliding out of the booth to go. "I told you it was 'spiritual' in nature." He waited for Luke to reply.

"Are you telling me that that's the wimpy answer you're going to stay with?" he asked and David nodded innocently. "I take it you're not going to go into more detail than that?" he asked David, who just shook his head.

"Maybe after we study the Bible a little more, then you might be able to understand and see the full meaning of it." He paused as he slid the bill over to Luke and smiled. "But I promise, next time I will buy dinner."

As he picked up the bill, Luke was not sure if he should be mad or laughing. Although he appreciated the time for the Bible study, he somehow felt he was just scratching the surface of what David had in mind with regards to studying the Bible. As he was waiting for the credit card to be run, Luke glanced out the windows of the restaurant and the people that were either leaving or coming in. He saw a brief flash as a red sports car exited the parking lot and turned right toward the freeway and an old Lincoln town car pull in right behind it. After paying and heading out the door, he turned back toward David.

"So did you take the glasses or not?" He pretended to be serious as he asked David. David suddenly seemed as if someone let the air out of him and started shaking his head.

"You are hopeless," he said and started walking toward his car across the parking lot. "See you in the morning," Luke smiled feeling better about getting under David's skin.

As he approached his car, it appeared to be sitting at a weird angle, almost as if the right front tire was on something. But as he got closer, he saw that his back left tire was flat. He took his coat off, jacked up the car, and dragged the spare out of the trunk and replaced the flat. As he placed it in the trunk of his car, the trunk light showed that he had not run over a nail, but that the sidewall of the tire had an inch and a half cut in it, about the size of a knife blade. He slammed the trunk shut. *Who would slash my tires?* he thought to himself as he climbed into the car and shut the door. He held onto the steering wheel a moment as he tried to think through the people he had seen in the restaurant that may have taken offense to their discussion, but then realized that there was no way they would know which car was his. He took a deep breath and reached over to put the key in the ignition and remembered the red sports car leaving the parking lot. He knew he had seen that car before and searched his memories to place it. He raised an eyebrow sarcastically knowing that it was not a jealous boyfriend since he wasn't dating anyone. Maybe it was someone involved with work? He remembered seeing that same car at work, almost hitting it when he was backing out. He knew most of the employees and that car was never in the parking lot. He figured he had better report it just in case. He banged his hand on the steering wheel in frustration at the thought of someone slashing his tire.

"So much for plans to prosper me and not to harm me," he mumbled as he started his car and drove toward home.

Chapter 18

As promised, Luke studied the scriptures that David and he had discussed late into the night. He found it difficult to stay on track as he was continually pulled away, thinking about the owner of the red sports car and wondering what possible reason could he or she have for slashing his tire. The first thing that he did when he pulled into the company lot the following morning was to scan the area for the red car, but there was no sign of it. He even walked out to the street and looked around that general area, but still no red car. Perhaps it was just a random act of violence that he did not need to worry about.

As he approached the entrance of the building, Luke noticed that there was a team of workers running cable and installing equipment around the building. As he entered the main office and walked toward their secure area, he saw a few more workers installing equipment. Instead of a card key entrance, there was now a real person sitting at the door area at a makeshift desk who smiled at him as he slid his card at the reader and entered the secure area. *Is all this new security because I lost a pair of the Cat Eyes glasses?* he wondered, and headed toward his desk. Luke was definitely impressed with how quickly they responded to step up security.

Luke dropped off his briefcase and jacket and headed toward Cliff's office, assuming that he was still in town.

"Come in." He heard as he knocked on the door. Cliff was sitting behind the desk and Serena was on the other side with a look on her face like she had been interrupted mid sentence. "Hey Luke," Cliff said and smiled. Luke looked at Serena and nodded and then back at Cliff.

"Do you have a second?" Luke asked and Cliff motioned with his hand to another chair sitting next to Serena.

"Are you here to confess?" Cliff asked with a serious look. "Just kidding. What's up?" Luke at first was a little stunned by the joke, but was happy to know he was just kidding, or was he?

"Last night my tire was slashed at a restaurant," he said and Cliff seemed upset to hear it.

"Sorry to hear it," Cliff replied.

"At first I considered it a random act of violence, but I have been seeing what I think is the same red sports car in different areas around the city over the past few weeks." Luke hesitated as he saw Cliff's eyebrow rise up. "The same car was leaving the parking lot of the restaurant as I was paying my bill," Luke explained and Cliff paused introspectively then looked at Serena and nodded.

"What kind of sports car was it?" Cliff asked and Luke hesitated as he answered.

"I'm not all that up on the actual years of sports cars; now jeeps or SUV's I'd have a better chance with, so I went online to try to figure out what year it was. I think it was somewhere between a 71 and a 74." Cliff looked expectantly, waiting for more.

"Maybe you could share the make of the car?" he urged with a smile after an awkward pause and Luke realized his mistake.

"Corvette. 71 to 74 Corvette. Did I say it was red?" he joked, feeling somewhat embarrassed. Cliff seemed to think a moment before speaking.

"License plate?" Cliff asked, already knowing the answer, as Luke shook his head no. "Did you get a look at the driver?"

"The side and back windows were tinted."

"You feel that it could be related?" Cliff asked and Luke nodded and then shrugged his shoulders. "I'll have our people check into it." Luke stood to leave.

"Thanks. Any luck on the lost unit?" Luke asked, but Cliff shook his head.

"We've sped up the security installations to avoid any future losses. That unit might be lost, but we'll keep an eye out for it," Cliff said and Luke nodded. Luke felt bad that he was the source of the loss and the need for all the sudden security activity. Luke at first thought about keeping it to himself, but then felt it was best to toss it out there.

"I know background checks are your specialty, but can you look into the church that David Stevens attends?" Luke asked and then felt embarrassed for asking, like he had just betrayed a friend. Cliff raised an eyebrow and looked at him.

"Is there something there that causes you concern?" Cliff asked and Luke hesitated before finally saying something. With a shrug of his shoulders he replied, "Jonathan mentioned that it was a 'cult' of some sort and I just don't know enough about it." Cliff nodded to Serena, who, apparently, was able to read his mind and excused herself from the room.

"Is this request for the programs sake or a more personal nature?" Cliff asked. Luke was surprised that Cliff knew about Danielle but then he realized that his background had probably been more thoroughly researched than anyone's at this point.

"Both I guess. It's just unknown territory for me," Luke admitted.

"We have done our due diligence in researching David's church, its leadership and its teachings," Cliff stated,. "Although they have a reputation for being more radical or staunch in their beliefs than your average church, they have never been viewed as a security risk or threat to the country, or this project. There are always a few bad apples in every group, for the most part they are very well behaved, non-violent, and despite being more conservative in nature, they are not politically organized as a group. They are very evangelistic in nature, but no more so than the Mormons or Jehovah's Witnesses." Cliff watched Luke for a reaction. "Is that what you wanted to hear, or do you still feel concerned for Danielle?"

"You guys don't miss a thing, do you?" he asked Cliff who then smiled and then shook his head.

"More than you can imagine, but we try to do the best we can with the limited information on hand."

"Is she in danger?" Luke asked trying to read Cliff's face. Cliff shrugged his shoulders.

"I can never tell what will happen when someone pursues the spiritual side of their lives. Everyone has a different response. Some go to extremes, while others go from being extreme to being passive. I can tell you that your physical relationship is probably in danger," he said and smiled.

The comment caught Luke off-guard and he did not care for the assumption that Cliff made. Was the loss of the physical side really his main concern? Looking back on it, he felt the greatest loss was his emotional connection with Danielle, not the physical. He also knew that it was no secret about how he and Danielle were before she found religion.

"Thanks," was all Luke could say as he headed out of Cliff's office.

Luke turned to head back to his desk and standing right behind him was Apollo apparently waiting his turn to speak with Cliff.

"Good morning," Luke said, but Apollo barely nodded as he stepped past and opened the door to Cliff's office.

"Good morning Cliff." He heard Apollo say in a friendly tone just before the door shut. Apollo was never friendly, unless he wanted something from you. Luke wondered what the conversation was going to be about and felt a rush of insecurity flow through him as he walked toward his desk.

Luke sat and stared at his computer screen and he could not stop feeling as though he had betrayed a friend by asking Cliff about David's church. He tipped his head back in his chair and caught a movement near his cubical opening. David was standing there shaking his head.

"Still worrying?" David said and Luke seemed confused about the question. "Matthew 6:25, the 'do not worry' part?" he said and Luke thought back to their discussion from the night before. "You did go home and study it out right?" David asked. Luke pretended to not know what he was talking about and then smiled and nodded.

"Yeah, I just found the 'plans to prosper you and not to harm you' scripture a little hard to swallow when I got to my car and found one of my tires had been slashed. How do you explain that, Mr. 'seek the kingdom' man?" Luke asked sarcastically and David frowned.

"Sorry to hear about that Luke," He replied and then raised an eyebrow. "Ephesians 6:11 says, *'Finally, be strong in the Lord and in his mighty power. [11] Put on the full armor of God, so that you can take your stand against the devil's schemes. [12] For our struggle is not against flesh and blood, but against the rulers, against the authorities, against the powers of this dark world and against the spiritual forces of evil in the heavenly realms.'*" David quoted from memory the verse and looked back at Luke. "When you seek God, you will be opposed. That is why you must seek him with all your heart, or the forces of darkness will stop you." Luke just stared at David and was reminded of a dramatic line from an old sword and sorcery movie.

"Do you have a religious answer for everything?" Luke asked with a smile and David shook his head.

"Nope. But God has a righteous response to every situation," he replied and then smiled. "So, did you think any more about our discussion from last night?"

"What discussion?" Jonathan asked as he stepped up to the cubicle next to David. David turned toward Luke, allowing him to answer the question. Luke realized that he was trying to protect the confidence of their Bible studies. Luke actually welcomed the opportunity to bring Jonathan into the discussion and wanted to see David's reaction.

"David and I were doing a Bible study last night. He gave me some scriptures to look at." Luke said and saw the flash of concern cross Jonathan's face, but coming into the open with the study did not seem to bother David. Jonathan seemed caught off balance trying to determine what to say next, but quickly regained his composure.

"Cool. Can I join you next time?" Jonathan asked. The question at first surprised Luke, but after a moment's thought he decided that it would be a great way to have additional questions from an opposing belief. Luke looked at David as if to wait to hear an answer as well.

"That is completely up to Luke, but I'm okay with it if he is," David reply and smile surprised Luke.

"Sounds good to me. So, when are we getting together next?" Luke asked, still testing David on his resolve to have Jonathan in on the study.

"I believe I'm available tonight, but let me check with Susan to make sure. Will that work for the two of you?" David asked and waited to see the response from each person. Luke had not really wanted to study again so soon, but he couldn't find a reason not to so he turned toward Jonathan to wait for his response. Jonathan looked like a kid who had just found another best friend.

"I'm open this evening," Jonathan stated enthusiastically and turned back toward Luke, waiting for him to make the final call on the matter.

"Tonight it is, let's say 5 at my place, since I live between the two of you." Jonathan nodded but David hesitated.

"Can we make it 7? I'd like to spend dinner with my wife since I missed her last night," David asked and they both assented.

"Tonight at 7 it is. I'll have the Tequila shots waiting," Luke said sarcastically and Jonathan seemed shocked by the comment.

"I don't think that would be…" Jonathan started to say, but David interrupted.

"I think Luke is trying to be funny, with a heavy emphasis on 'trying,'" David said and Luke shrugged.

"Just trying to keep it fun… you two are way too serious. Now, correct me if I'm wrong, but I think we have a great deal of work to do?" he said sarcastically and Jonathan nodded nervously as he walked away.

"Slave driver," David mumbled as he walked back to his cubicle. Luke looked at his screen again and tried to think of which of the thirty tasks he needed to accomplish was most important and then remembered the 'ghosting' issue and what David had said about it. *How did that relate?* he wondered as he reviewed the data again.

He could not get the thought of the lost unit out of his mind. He glanced around his desk again as if he had somehow missed it the last twenty times he had looked for it. He saw his notepad and the notes with the list of directories of the files he had seen on Monday morning when all the system files were made available to him. At first he pushed it aside, but then picked up the pad and read the names of the files and the directory location that they had been in. The main directory had been linked to Apollo's desk computer. He glanced at the names on the pad again: 'Pretereo' 'Circumvenio' 'Inganno' and 'Dominus.' He did not understand what any of those words meant, so he typed 'pretereo' into the internet search engine and was confused that the first 2 pages of results were about a type of wrestling shoe and where to buy them cheap. *Did Apollo wrestle?* Luke thought to himself and smiled at the idea of Apollo having to touch someone, let alone wrestle them. As he reached the third page of search results he saw one link description mention that in Latin meant 'escape'. Luke thought about the correlation of the name to wrestlers and shoes to help them escape. He tried 'circumvenio' and the first link that came up was a Latin translation definition, "to surround, to overthrow'. Luke stared at the translation and then typed in 'inganno' and read the translation of the word. It meant 'deception' in Italian. He typed in the last word 'dominus' and the translation read master or lord. He just stared at the screen and then back at the words on the pad for a moment and then turned and logged into the secure area of the server to review the file folders he had written down.

He tried to follow his notes through the folders and subfolders where the files had been located, but once again he could no longer find them. He spent the next twenty minutes doing a system search for the folders or file names, but despite his best efforts, he could not find the files in any location. They had been removed from the system. Luke leaned back in his chair and tried to think of any explanation for the files being removed or deleted and what to do with the information he had. Should he talk to Cliff about it? He was already feeling like a childish 'tattle-tale' after asking Cliff about David and now he was thinking about storming back into his office with his hands on his hips to 'tell on' Apollo? Cliff probably already knew about the files and had perhaps asked Apollo to remove them. He decided not to say anything and shook his head at how frustrating his job had become.

As he continued trying to work, a worry surrounding the mysterious files continued to build in his mind. What if something happened and Cliff asked if he had seen the files before, and if so, why he had not reported them? He could just deny knowing about it. Then the fear of the truth being revealed by the Cat Eyes hit him. What if the unit was used on him during interrogation? Maybe not now, but later, if something happened, they might be. They would know that he knew about the files and did nothing. He let out a big sigh and pushed away from the desk, stood up, grabbed the notepad and headed for Cliff's office.

As he walked past Apollo's office, he saw him look up and then call his name,
"Luke! Got a minute?" Luke hesitated and thought about just ignoring him, but knew that it might seem strange, so he stopped and walked back to his office door. Apollo smiled at him, which was an action that sent shivers down his spine. But the look on Apollo's face seemed far different. "Can you explain something for me?" he asked Luke, who just raised an eyebrow.

"I'll try." Luke replied and he watched Apollo lean back in his chair with his hands crossed behind his head and then stared at the ceiling a moment before looking at Luke and continuing, "I stumbled upon some strange files the other day and then a little later in the day I was going to do a little more research into them, but now I cannot find them. Thinking it a little strange, I created a program to keep track of anyone who might search or access such files. Your name popped up on my screen today as someone searching for them. Care to explain?" Apollo stated coldly and Luke felt like an animal that just realized it had walked into a trap. Briefly he entertained the idea that Apollo might have found the same files and had the same concerns about them as he had, but no, Apollo knew about those files and must have seen that Luke's account had touched them on Monday. Instead of acting then, Luke hesitated and now he was sure Apollo would have deleted the files. Why didn't he go to Cliff right away? He did not anticipate him laying a trap for him and he had walked right into it. He tried to think how best to react in this situation, accuse Apollo, deny it, or take it directly to Cliff.

"Let's take this to Cliff," he said calmly, trying his best not to give anything away.

"I'm sure we can keep this quiet if you prefer, I mean you've already lost a systems unit and glasses, now these strange files of your being deleted? I'm willing to be lenient if you can explain yourself," Apollo said with a touch of a sly smile. Luke felt like such a fool for walking into the trap, and knew that Apollo had probably covered all his bases up to this point, knowing that if Luke stepped back in to research those files again that he would be prepared to act first. Luke tried to think of a way out of the situation that did not include submitting to Apollo, but there seemed to be only one chance. Although the idea of reaching across the desk and beating the arrogance out of him was inviting, he knew that it would only serve to re-enforce Apollo's story.

"You're big on truth Apollo, let's take this to Cliff and let him sort it out," Luke said, calling Apollo's bluff and saw what looked like a flash of surprise in Apollo's eyes but then Apollo smiled and slid his chair away from his desk and stood up. Luke could tell that it was not what Apollo wanted, but that he was prepared for this eventuality. Luke did not wait for him, but instead walked toward Cliff's office and knocked on the door when he reached it.

As they walked into the office, Cliff was sitting behind his desk with an expectant smile. Luke thought about trying to get the first words in to explain what happened. He was planning to deny everything that Apollo was going to accuse him of, but felt it seemed childish and would have the appearance of being guilty, so he took a different course of action.

"Cliff, Apollo has something he would like to bring to your attention which could be of grave importance," Luke said and then motioned toward Apollo. Apollo had apparently assumed that Luke was going to follow his impulse to defend himself, so he found himself a little off balance in having to present his case first.

"Well," Apollo said and took a seat while Luke took another one and interrupted him.

"You might want to ask Serena to join us," Luke stated and Cliff picked up his phone and asked Serena to join them. When she came in, Luke gave her his seat since there were only two available and he moved over and sat on the credenza desk in the corner.

"You have our undivided attention, so what's up gentlemen?" Cliff asked and looked at Apollo, who took a deep breath as if deeply sad.

"When we opened our database on Monday, I took a moment to review other people's files to make sure that all personal information was removed and to notify them to clean such files off the system if such information were found." Apollo hesitated and looked at Luke a moment before continuing. "I noticed an external drive attached to Luke's computer, presumably a USB memory device, and took a quick look at its contents. There were a couple of strange file names and I opened them and briefly scanned the files." He again hesitated as if for effect, and Luke's mind suddenly realized why the mystery drive had appeared and then disappeared so quickly, it was a USB drive that he stumbled onto. "It's no great secret that Luke and I have had differing opinions on the ethics involved with the Cat Eyes product. He feels it is a danger to society, I feel it is essential to finding the truth in all situations." He again took a breath. "Although I only scanned them briefly, the files were about various plans to sabotage the project should it go active," he said and waited for Cliff to respond.

Cliff seemed to be trying to read Apollo's expression as if looking for some hidden clue behind the forced look of innocence. He then glanced at Luke for a moment, who did not respond in any way, and then back at Apollo.

"Why wait until today to come and tell me?" Cliff asked.

"Because I didn't have the proof. Moments after discovering the files, the drive was disconnected." He hesitated again. "And... well, I felt embarrassed by looking at someone else's private files." He smiled sympathetically at Luke.

Luke tried to control all the emotions that were boiling up inside him. He realized that since the files were on an external USB drive, he knew that there would be no backup files on the system to prove his case. Apollo had painted a story that was the exact replica of his, so now the best he could hope for was his word against Apollo's. The fact that he had lost the systems unit yesterday, only made him look guiltier. He felt the trap tighten. He watched as Cliff and Serena peered intently at him waiting for him to respond to Apollo's allegations.

"Well, Apollo's story seems pretty solid from my perspective except the roles are a bit different in my version. In fact, it's pretty close to the same one I was going to tell you before being stopped by Apollo on my way to your office. He let me know what he had found and tried to convince me to 'work a deal' with him for his silence." Apollo acted shocked by the words and then chuckled as he shook his head as Luke continued. "The only difference is that I did not know where the files originated from. I did not realize I was looking at a USB drive on his computer," Luke added as Apollo continued with his 'pity' smile and the shaking of his head. He felt alone and the temptation to feel completely overwhelmed by the situation grew more intense by the moment. Cliff and Serena remained silent, coldly observing him as he spoke.

Luke was feeling his temperature rise as the anger grew inside him. He was ready to release the hot anger, when suddenly a cool breeze of the air conditioner blew across his face allowing him a moment to calm down and take a breath. As he shifted his position on the credenza, he felt the piece of paper that had his notes on it in his hand and he opened it and looked at it. An idea came into his mind.

"During my brief time in the mystery 'folder' we are speaking about, I wrote down all the files I had seen in it." Luke held the paper as if reading a long list of names written on it, even though there were only four on it. "Seeing as how Apollo is claiming to have investigated these files, I wonder if he would care to list a few of the file names that were on the drive?" Luke asked and looked at Apollo. Apollo seemed rather surprised by the question and needed a moment to gather his thoughts.

"I'm not sure if… well most of my time was spent reading the info, not cataloging the names of the files," he replied, but Luke frowned at the response.

"Hmm, you told me moments ago that you wrote a program to track anyone who was looking for those files. Without knowing the names of the files, how could you know what someone might be looking for?" Luke asked and then continued, "I'm sure the program is still running on the server; maybe we can check to see what is in the program? Would that help?" Luke asked and Apollo's face flushed.

"You interrupted me before I could finish. I said I'm not sure if I can remember all of them off the top of my head," he replied shortly.

"Then 'off the top of your head' can you name the ones you do remember?" Luke replied and shrugged his shoulders. Apollo held Luke's gaze a moment as if trying to read him, but Luke's face gave him no clues, so Apollo turned toward Cliff.

"There were many files, but the ones that come to mind are…" Apollo proceeded to list about twenty file names from memory, three of the four Luke had on his list, most of which were Latin names, before turning back toward Luke. "Are those the ones you were trying to hide from us?" he suddenly asked and Luke frowned and furrowed his brow as he looked at his list again.

"Do you have any idea what those names mean?" he asked Apollo, who hesitated before answering.

"They are Latin names, most of which have less than friendly meanings attached to them."

"So you read Latin?" Luke asked and Apollo seemed frustrated by the question.

"Yes. I'm educated." He snarled back. Luke seemed perplexed and confused as he turned toward Cliff and Serena.

"I'm educated, but I don't speak Latin. Do you speak Latin?" he asked Cliff and Serena and they both shook their heads.

"I guess I just find it strange that you were able to list off twenty or more file names, in what seemed like perfect Latin, I might add, yet I don't even speak it or understand it. So why would I use Latin names for my files?" Luke asked and waited for Apollo to respond.

"Perhaps you wanted to hide it from others? But I was able to recognize the Latin names of your files and discovered your secret," he said coldly and smiled.

"When I stumbled on the mysterious files on Monday, I only wrote down four names. There were a lot more files, but I did not understand what they were or what the names meant, so I just jotted down a few." He looked at his piece of paper. "Just a little while ago, I did a search on the four words and was surprised to find out what they meant. You can actually go to the history folder on my computer to see that I did a search on the four names I have listed here. In truth, I was actually alarmed by their meanings, so much so that I did a system-wide search to try and find out if the names were saved somewhere else on the servers, but to no avail." He hesitated. "I find four names of concern and my first action is to perform a system search, yet you have a list of twenty plus names and instead of doing a systems search for the files or other dangerous files, you instead write a program to see if I was going to probe the system for those names? Does that make any sense?" Luke asked and stared at Apollo. Luke could tell Apollo's mind seemed to be running in overdrive at the moment.

"I knew where the files originated from, so there was no need to search the system," he replied smugly.

"I could have made copies?" Luke added.

"That would have been stupid of you," Apollo retorted.

"Yes it would have. So why would you create a program to see if I would search for them?" Luke asked the leading question.

"Because I know you are stupid." Apollo replied and smiled.

"Almost as stupid as not acting the moment you discovered and read these dangerous files, but instead you allow them to walk out the door that day without saying a word, only to wait until the next day to voice your concerns?" Luke shot back and Apollo bristled at the retort.

"I felt you were an important and valued member of the team and wanted to give you a chance." Apollo tried to sound sincere.

"Valued? I thought you just said I was stupid?" Luke replied and Apollo seemed to try to correct his thinking, but then just turned to Cliff.

"This discussion is a waste of everyone's time," Apollo said. "He has lost a systems unit, now he has been caught undermining the development of the product. I demand that Luke be terminated immediately as we try to determine the amount of damage he has caused."

Cliff just sat there looking at Apollo then back at Luke and frowned as he picked up his phone and pushed a button.

"This is Operations Director, Clifford Jackson. Please send security up to my office right away. Yes. Raven 03. Correct." Cliff hung up the phone and smiled at Apollo. Luke tried to read the meaning of the smile, but could not. His stomach knotted up at the thought of the embarrassment of being escorted out of the office. *Will they handcuff me?* Luke wondered.

"Thank you," Apollo said and then glared in satisfaction at Luke. While the rest of the office sat in silence awaiting the arrival of security, Apollo continued talking as if the ending of Luke's career with the company meant nothing. "I should have the final software release available this afternoon once I have tested it." The words 'tested it' seemed to remind Apollo that his 'tester' had been terminated. "I'll begin the recruiting process for another trainer immediately." He said ignoring Luke's presence completely. Luke could not believe how cold and calculated Apollo was. He deserved the credit for creating the Cat Eyes product; in fact Apollo was the poster child for it.

The knock on the door made Luke's insides jump and as the door was opened, Luke could see that there were three security guards standing outside the door. Two entered and one remained at the door entrance as they looked toward Cliff, awaiting orders. Luke slid off the credenza and was walking toward the security guard as Cliff spoke up.

"Please place Mr. Walpole under arrest for espionage and attempting to sell classified information to our enemies." And the guards walked over to where Apollo was sitting, leaving Luke standing frozen, in the center of the room. The smug smile on Apollo's face vanished as the words Cliff had spoken sunk in.

"What? Espionage... selling classified information? This is preposterous! He is the man you want!" He yelled and pointed at Luke and then turned back toward Cliff. "Cliff, Luke is the one you should arrest, not me," he yelled as one of the guards read him his rights and the guard reached down to help Apollo out of the seat and pulled his hands behind his back in order to place the handcuffs on them. Apollo seemed in total shock by what was happening around him and just kept shaking his head back and forth. Suddenly his arrogance re-emerged. "This is not over. You will hear from my attorney on this and it will get ugly. This is ridiculous," he sneered at Cliff and then at Luke across from him as he was led from the room. Luke thought about making some snide remark as he was being escorted out, but decided better of it.

"Please arrest Mr. Ruhle for the same charges on the way out as well." Cliff said and the guard nodded.

"Already underway sir," the guard replied as he shut the door behind him. Luke wondered how Ronald was involved in the whole matter as he turned back to look at Cliff and Serena, both seemed saddened by the situation that just unfolded.

The three of them sat in silence as they stared back and forth at each other. Luke could not hold it in any longer.

"How did you know it was him?" Luke asked.

"We knew all along that he had alternative plans and was trying to put in motion the sale of the product and software to an outside source, perhaps the Chinese." Cliff said and Luke was stunned.

"The Chinese? Why?" Luke asked.

"Money. From what we gather, I'm guessing Apollo felt the Chinese market was much bigger and they would have less social resistance to the idea of civilian sales," he said sadly. "And they could get it to market far faster and cheaper than we could." Luke just shook his head as he tried to grasp the big picture of what was going on around him that he had no knowledge of and then asked the obvious question. "Why wait so long to arrest him?"

"There were a couple of reasons, but one of the things we were trying to determine was, if you were involved as well," he said and waited to see Luke's response. "Now we know." Cliff ended and smiled.

"How do you know for sure that I'm not?" Luke asked and the words seemed strange coming out of his mouth and even got Cliff to blink.

"Is there something we should know about?" Cliff asked and Luke hesitated, but felt he should proceed.

"The systems unit is still missing and I was the last one who saw it," Luke replied and Cliff seemed to understand Luke's concern and smiled.

"We knew where it was the whole time." He turned toward Serena and raised an eyebrow, she hesitated, then nodded. Cliff looked back at Luke. "We installed a small tracking device in each of the system units. Ronald walked out with it, and then drove it over to Apollo's house yesterday evening. It's there right now." He said and then looked at his watch. "Well, it is probably being picked up right now."

"What was the other reason for the delay?" Luke suddenly asked, remembering Cliff's early comment.

"We had hoped that he would have trained one of the other developers to understand his software coding so that they could take over his role in support and development," Cliff replied, but then shook his head before Luke asked the obvious question.

Luke was stunned at how much had quickly happened since Cliff made the call. Luke suddenly remembered 'Raven 03' being stated by Cliff when he made the security call. Those code words must have put things in motion. He thought about his time in Iraq and how much was going on behind the scenes that he had no clue about until afterwards. If they knew that much about Apollo, what did they know about him? About everyone on the team? How deep did their search and knowledge on them go? He really felt vulnerable and exposed.

"Wow, what color underwear am I wearing right now?" he asked Cliff sarcastically, both Cliff and Serena seemed initially confused by the question, but Cliff suddenly understood and smiled.

"We don't go that deep, Luke. But we try to be as thorough as possible in our work. Too many bad guys out there, so we need to keep a close eye on the key individuals." Cliff looked at Luke.

"I imagine there is a lot going on that the average citizen never sees," Luke replied and nodded.

"You would have made a good lawyer. I mean don't quit your day job just yet, but if this does not pan out it might be a good career path for you; you really grilled Mr. Walpole," Cliff joked and Serena smiled. Luke on the other hand, sat quietly a moment as he thought through the ramifications of what just unfolded.

"So now what? What's the plan from here forward for the product now that the lead developer, who just happens to have all the secrets behind the code locked safely away in his brain, is in now in jail? You must have thought through a contingency plan if you were planning on arresting Apollo," Luke asked. Cliff contemplated his question just long enough to let Luke think he might not have thought through it all.

"David will take over as software lead and try to sort through Mr. Walpole's code structure, Gloria will continue to lead hardware development and you will keep moving forward with training and representation," he said and then seemed to remember a detail. "Oh, and you will be the team lead for both groups. Congratulations on the promotion," Cliff said and smiled. Luke on the other hand, just sat there looking like a deer caught in the headlights.

How did he manage to go from being in deep trouble one moment, to getting a promotion? He asked if he could be excused so he could get back to work and headed out the door.

"Dark blue," Cliff said just as he was about to close the door. Luke was confused about the words and looked back at Cliff. "The color of your underwear. Dark blue," he said and smiled as Luke shut the door. As he walked down the hallway back toward his office, he tried to remember what color of underwear he had put on this morning and even thought about stopping to take a quick look while he was in the hallway, but was afraid someone would see him. As he sat down, a chill went down his back as he remembered that the boxers he had put on were actually dark blue.

Chapter 19

The whole Cat Eyes department of the company was in turmoil following the arrests of Apollo and Ronald. Cliff and Serena were quick to put out the various fires that sprung up. They first met with Samuel and then scheduled a brief meeting with all the employees. Samuel had driven to the office once he heard the news from Cliff about Apollo and Ronald. Samuel looked almost sick to his stomach as he listened to Cliff explain the details of the arrests. After the discussion was over, he walked up to Luke and with a sad, but content expression; he patted Luke on the shoulder.

"I told you that you would be the one to do the right thing when the time called for it." Luke thought back to their conversation about Apollo and Luke nodded.

"I wish it would have ended differently," Luke replied. Samuel nodded and seemed to think a moment longer before interjecting, "Luke, assuming you decide to stay on with the company after this; I would like to give you my twenty-five percent of this part of the company. I've thought long and hard on this and I no longer want anything to do with it. I think this product will have huge revenue potential, but I'm content with what I already have and do not want to get tied up in the issues that it holds and more importantly, with those involved with it," he said and looked at Luke with an almost sad expression. "Something tells me this is far from over. You're in charge now, but be very careful." Samuel paused for a moment, "I will have the documents of transfer over to you first thing in the morning." Luke did not know what to say. He was torn between the greed of the moment and the desire to get out while he still could as Samuel was doing. He must have chosen the greed for he did not follow him out.

"Thank you Samuel, I think," he said. "So what are your plans now that you've freed yourself from this mess?" Luke asked.

"A long vacation, maybe I'll go back to developing games for teens and unmotivated adults to waste their time and energy on. I'm not exactly sure, but I do know that I'd like to be as far away from this project as possible," he said with all sincerity, then smiled and stepped out the door. Luke contemplated running out the door after him and never looking back, but it seemed like that would be taking the easy way out of the mess he found himself in.

Later that day, Luke found himself at his desk thinking through everything, trying to remember what there was that was actually keeping him here? Every aspect of his life was under scrutiny by the government, his boss was just arrested for espionage and trying to sell secrets to the Chinese, the owner of the company was running away from the project, and he was left in charge to navigate these dangerous waters all for a product he did not even want to come to market. This was far more than he had bargained for. He just sat silently and stared at his computer screen as if he was waiting for it to tell him what to do.

"Were you the mastermind behind this coup? If so, is the purging finished or are we next in line to be sacked?" Luke heard David's voice from behind him and turned to see him leaning against the entrance. He knew he was kidding, but Luke could not even find the energy or brain power to offer a snappy comeback. He just shook his head and shrugged his shoulders. "You're not alone Luke," David said, sensing what Luke was struggling with. Luke looked back at David and remembered one of the reasons he needed to stay. He promised

David that he would; that they would tackle this together. Luke suddenly chuckled and David raised an eyebrow.

"Care to share what's so funny?"

"The only reason I can think of to stick around this quagmire of a career just happens to also be the guy who messed up my personal life. I'm trying to figure out if the two are related or not," Luke said quietly. David started to defend himself, but then smiled.

"Yeah, you're not the smartest guy I ever met," David said, but then got serious again. "Just for the record… If you go, I go. If you stay, I stay. That was my promise," David reminded him.

"Thanks," Luke said sincerely, and then smiled as he raised an eyebrow, "but I think that makes us both stupid." David seemed to think about Luke's words a moment and then nodded his head.

"Good point." David replied.

"Can you believe this?" A voice almost yelled from behind David and then Jonathan stepped to the other side of the opening and looked at the two of them. "Luke, you rock! I can't believe you got Apollo canned!" Jonathan said and the words were like a blow to Luke.

"I didn't get Apollo fired," he shot back loudly and then calmed himself, "He managed to do that all on his own. He tried to set me up to take the fall, but fortunately for me, Cliff was way ahead of him." Jonathan seemed puzzled by Luke's response.

"I thought you'd be happy?" Jonathan said.

"We just lost the lead developer who had all the code tucked away in his head or at best hidden in some massively encrypted files. 'Happy' for me would have been to see him chill out and just appreciate those around him or at least to have taken the time to train others on his code structure," Luke replied and took a breath. "Now we have a huge, if not impossible challenge to get this to the soldiers as we promised and on schedule." Luke finished the sentence and noticed that Danny and Gloria were now also standing behind David and Jonathan looking as much in need of direction as the others.

"Why did he do it?" Danny asked Luke and everyone waited for Luke to reply.

"I don't know if it was any one thing or a bunch of little reasons. The fact is that he was working apart from the team and outside of the government's parameters and his actions have now put all of us at risk. It was stupid and selfish," Luke stated angrily as he tried to look everyone in the eyes. "We need to work together and communicate with each other if we are to get through this," he said and they all seemed to agree.

After a long silence, David was the first to speak up. "There's no longer a team 1 or team 2, or an Apollo verses Luke team. There's just one team that is looking out for the best interest of each other and the company." he said and everyone nodded in agreement. There was a long silence and suddenly Gloria looked around nervously.

"Can we talk about this in private?" Gloria asked and Luke nodded.

"Sure. Is there something that you are worrying about?" Luke asked and Gloria seemed to be glancing around nervously.

"Have you thought about the ramifications of this product? I mean really thought about it?" she asked with a whisper and everyone except Jonathan nodded as they got the meaning of her words.

"This is not the place to have such conversations," Luke interjected and thought about how thorough the government's security was.

"Can we get together this weekend to discuss it?" Gloria asked, and everyone shrugged and nodded. For Luke it felt strange that they suddenly had to be so clandestine about things that they said in the office. Should he attend or make an excuse not to? Should he tell Cliff about it? He was growing to hate everything about this product.

Luke looked around the group and decided to take a serious tone and at the same time warn them about the depth of the involvement of the government.

"I don't know about you, but this was a wakeup call for me. We all need to understand that our new employer takes the security of this project extremely seriously; the consequence of us not understanding that… well Apollo and Ronald are examples of it." There was a collective hush as the group reconsidered his words.

"Yeah, this is a whole new game," Danny said and smiled mischievously. At first no one said anything, and then Gloria turned and glared at the former game developer.

"Was that meant to be a pun?" she asked and he shrugged his shoulders pretending he didn't know what she was talking about, but she would not let it pass. "If so, that was horrible at best," she said and punched him in the arm.

"That's the kind of dumb joke that gives us programmers a bad reputation," Jonathan added and the banter picked up between them. *So much for keeping it serious*, Luke thought to himself. He watched as everyone except David slowly headed back to their own cubicles.

"We're still on for 7 p.m. at your house, right?" David asked over the partition. Luke thought about his question and was amazed to think that with their jobs and company seeming to be crumbling around them, David seemed unfazed by it. Was he really that out of touch with everything, or was he somehow involved with it all he wondered? With everything going on, the idea of 'studying the Bible' was the last thing he wanted to do and was about to cancel the meeting, but then he had an idea. Meeting might give them a chance to spend a little more time in private, talking about the product, and give Luke an opportunity to dig a little deeper into David's casual attitude about the day's events.

"Sure," Luke replied with a smile. "You're bringing the steaks right?" Luke asked. David smartly did not acknowledge the question and slowly sank below the partition as if he was on an elevator going down.

The rest of the day was spent dealing with a continuous stream of damage control issues as a result of losing Apollo and Ronald. There seemed to be one emergency meeting after another with Cliff and Serena and there were countless new individuals passing into and out of the new facility. Some were meeting with Cliff and Serena while others were going through the file cabinets and drawers in Apollo and Ronald's office and cubicle. Luke started referring to them as 'agents' since none of them would stop to discuss anything with the team members. It was eerie watching the agents circulating through the office. It was just like a movie scene after a corporate crime has been committed. Apollo's computer had been boxed up and removed from his office. All his personal effects and files had been cataloged and also removed in boxes. It was quite surreal. The only bright spot in his day was an email from Danielle that said she had heard about Apollo and Ronald and was wondering if he was okay. He reassured her that he was and appreciated her concern and tried to keep it light by joking that he still had a job and would not need the $20,000 loan right away. She replied cleverly that he "never paid back the last $20k advance, so no deal." He enjoyed seeing the emails and missed the light-hearted interaction they had.

By the end of the day, Luke was pretty confident that although he had been going a hundred miles an hour, holding meeting after meeting, he had managed to accomplish absolutely nothing in terms of the development of the product all day long. As he headed out the door with David, Jonathan confirmed that the three of them were still getting together. Luke had not realized how late it was until he passed through the old office and realized that almost everyone had gone home. He glanced over and saw that Danielle's cubicle was empty as well.

Luke grabbed a quick chicken in a box meal at the grocery store, along with some soda's and chips, and headed home. He settled down on the couch to eat his dinner and to do a little reviewing before David arrived, just in case he asked about the verses he was supposed to have reviewed. He thought about their previous study and the concept and David's challenge to him to seek God with "all you heart" if you wanted to find him and how it related to regular relationships. He gave the idea some merit as he thought about Danielle and that if someone did not love the other person with all of his or her heart, the chance of a relationship working out would be pretty slim. He thought of several of his past relationships. They had all failed because either one or the other partners had not wanted to totally commit to the relationship and they ended shortly afterwards. Danielle was a different situation, she wanted to keep the relationship going, but he had not wanted to share her love with someone else. She had chosen God.

"How can I compete with God?" he said out loud. *"Hey honey, I closed a sale today. That's nice dear, God created a new solar system for me during lunch."* He mimicked the interaction in his head and felt overwhelmed by it. Then he realized that he was here physically and that God, if he existed, was spiritual and unseen.

"You'd think that would give me some sort of an advantage," he mumbled.

At 6:10 there was a knock on the door.

"A little early," Luke mumbled to himself and opened the door. He saw Jonathan standing there with his briefcase.

"Hey Luke, I wanted to come early so we could talk about the study before David got here," he said and walked past Luke and into his apartment.

"What did you want to talk about?" he asked as he shut the door and followed him into the living room. "Can I get you a soda or water?"

"Uhh, sure. A glass of water would be great." He set his briefcase down and took a seat on the couch while Luke headed to the kitchen for the drink. "I guess I just wanted to prepare you for the study," Jonathan almost yelled his response into the kitchen area.

"Prepare me? What exactly does that mean?" Luke said as he handed Jonathan his water and sat in the chair across from him. Jonathan took a drink and then opened his briefcase.

"Well, as I shared before, these guys are a cult and what they teach is false doctrine, so I thought you might like to know more about them," he said as he took out a bunch of books and materials and laid them on the table.

"*These guys* are David and Danielle, and they're friends in case you've forgotten," Luke replied a little sarcastically. Jonathan seemed uncomfortable with the reply.

"Well, yeah but, I guess what I'm saying is that their doctrine is really messed up and there is a lot online written about what they believe that is not very... well, positive."

Luke looked down at the various printouts that were now spread across the table and picked up several of the closest items and glanced briefly at the website source and then at the words on the sheets of paper. They all talked about how the organization that apparently David and Danielle were a part of had a 'works' mindset when it came to salvation, how they believed in the false doctrine of water baptism for salvation, the denial of the gifts of the Holy Spirit, mainly speaking in tongues, their 'controlling' of members, and several other issues. The way it was presented, it read like a scary novel.

"Who are the authors of this information?" Luke asked as he continued scanning the various articles.

"Mostly, they are written by recognized religious authorities or leaders from various mainstream churches. Some are written by past members," he replied.

After about thirty minutes of further reading in silence, Luke looked up to see Jonathan sitting with an almost smug look on his face, which, for some reason, bothered Luke.

"So, the key differences or disagreements, from what I can gather here, is that they believe in water Baptism, they expect their members to adhere to their teachings, and they deny the gifts of the Holy Spirit?" he asked and raised an eyebrow.

"Yeah, pretty much. It's the 'works based' mindset that I was talking about last time."

"I still don't understand what that means, a 'works based' mindset," Luke stated and Jonathan seemed to think a moment before explaining.

"It means that you have to earn your salvation, instead of accepting it as a free gift from God," Jonathan finally answered and Luke nodded his head, still not grasping exactly what that meant, but then glanced at his watch.

"It's almost seven and David should be here any moment. Let's put this away as I don't think he would appreciate seeing it." Luke said as he gathered up the articles and handed them back to Jonathan.

"You don't want to keep these?" Jonathan asked and Luke shook his head.

"No, but I appreciate your help on this. It'll help me to know the right questions to ask."

Several minutes later there was a knock on the door and David joined them around the table in the kitchen.

"Anything new I need to know about since we left the office?" David asked and Luke and Jonathan shook their heads uncomfortably, wondering if David somehow knew about their prior discussion. "I just assumed at the pace things were unraveling, there might be some additional news on Apollo and Ronald," David replied and placed his Bible on the table and then looked at the two of them.

"Nope, nothing new to report," Luke replied relieved that he was not talking about the information Jonathan had brought. He grabbed his own Bible and placed it on the table in front of him.

"So, have you two talked about how you want to do this next study?" David asked and they once again seemed uncomfortable with the question and they both shook their heads. David seemed to pick up on the awkwardness of the moment. "Is there something I'm missing here, do I have a booger hanging from my nose, or spinach in my teeth or something?" he said and raised an eyebrow as he glanced between the two of them. They both just shook their heads. David seemed determined to try to understand what was going on that was creating the awkwardness of the moment, but finally shrugged.

"Okay, can we start with a prayer?" David asked and Jonathan nodded, which David picked up on. "Jonathan, would you care to lead us?" David asked and Jonathan's expression had that 'deer in the headlights' look about it.

"Uhh, sure…" Jonathan replied and Luke listened as Jonathan nervously tried to pull together a series of coherent, yet forced expressions of gratitude that was packed full of religious sounding words.

"Thanks Jonathan," David said when he had finished praying, apparently unfazed by the jumbled prayer. "Okay. Just to get you up to speed Jonathan, last time we talked about priorities and where our happiness comes from, Psalms 119:1-2. We read that our priority should be to seek his kingdom and his righteousness and not to let the worries of life stop us, Matthew 6:25-33. That God has incredible plans for us, Jeremiah 29:11-14, but we will need to seek him with all of our heart if we are to find him, and embrace those incredible plans he has in store for us, not half heartedly," David said from memory as he watched Jonathan and his reaction. "Do you have any questions or thoughts before we continue?" David asked Jonathan, who shook his head. "Luke, anything been on your mind since the last time we met on this?" Besides questions on the information Jonathan had brought, Luke was still chewing on the whole slashed tire issue, but felt it was best not to bring either of them up just yet.

"Nope." David seemed to hesitate a moment as if he was going to say something, but then moved on.

"Okay then. I have a question for both of you. Are you seeking God with all of your heart?" David asked and waited for each to answer.

"Yep, every day," Jonathan snapped his response back at David, while Luke really thought about the question.

"No," Luke replied and David tried to read into his response.

"Based on what you have read, do you think you will find him then?" David asked without any emotion and Luke seemed to chew on the question again before answering.

"Based on what we have read, no. But I think the bigger question I'm still struggling with is still whether or not I want to?" Luke replied. "But, assuming I did, how would I know that what we are reading is truly from God and the plan he wants us to follow?" Luke replied and felt almost clever with his response. David smiled and nodded.

"First off, I appreciate your honesty; secondly, you ask a great question. But the more important question we have to ask is, do we all agree that the Word of God is the core foundation of Christianity?" David asked but did not wait for an answer from them, "Because without that confidence, anything could be true." David looked around the table and picked up a butter knife that was lying there and held it up. "How long would you say this knife is?" He handed it to Luke, who turned it around in his hands.

"Seven inches," Luke guessed and handed it to Jonathan who guessed seven and one half inches and handed it back to David.

"Both are pretty good guesses. But without a standardized system of measurement, your seven inches would be half an inch shorter than Jonathans. Wouldn't it?" David asked Luke and Luke nodded as he thought about the concept. "Without a ruler, or standard to measure it with, the idea of accurate measurements could get really messed up if we went by what we 'guessed' the length might be, verses what it really was based on the standard." David waited to see them both agree with the concept. "In the same way, without the Bible as the agreed 'standard' that we will go by, then the idea of who God is, or even what his Word teaches, simply becomes anyone's or everyone's 'best guess'. Which as you can imagine, could get really confusing to someone trying to determine what is true or false. Would you agree?" David asked and they both nodded their heads. Luke was impressed with the analogy.

David leaned back in his chair a moment as if trying to decide which direction to go next. "Jonathan, I'm guessing that you believe that the Bible is God's Word, but Luke on the other hand is not all that sure if it was from God or from man, is that correct?" David asked and Luke thought a moment and then nodded.

"I'm not sure that there even is a God, so I'm not sure if that really messes things up or not," Luke said sincerely.

"Again, I appreciate your honesty. Belief in God takes faith, and Romans 10:17 reads, '*Consequently, faith comes from hearing the message, and the message is heard through the word about Christ.*'" David quoted off the top of his head, "So the good news, Luke, is all we have to do is spend time in God's Word to increase our faith as we learn about him."

"So basically, I'll either start to believe in God as I read about him, or I'll believe less in the idea of a God if I do not agree with what is written?" Luke asked.

"Exactly," David said and smiled. "So with that in mind, in order for us to see what it is that God wants us to learn, we have to all agree that this book, the Bible, is going to be our standard. It will be our spiritual ruler if you will, of what we will measure our 'guesses' and 'beliefs' against to discover what is true and what is false. Agreed?" They both nodded.

"Okay, turn over to John 1:1 in your Bibles." David said as he opened his Bible and waited for them to get there. "Jonathan, can you read the first verse?" He asked and Jonathan nodded.

"*In the beginning was the Word, and the Word was with God, and the Word was God.*" David waited a moment before asking a question.

"So what is the Word?" David asked and waited for a response, which Jonathan was the first to answer.

"The Bible," Jonathan said and smiled.

"Yes, but what else is the Word?" David asked.

"God," Luke said softly as he read the verse again.

"The Word was God," David replied and nodded. "Let's keep reading. Jonathan, can you read 2-5?"

"*He was with God in the beginning. Through him all things were made; without him nothing was made that has been made. In him was life, and that life was the light of men. The light shines in the darkness, but the darkness had not understood it.*"

"What else do we learn about the Word here?" David asked.

"He made everything and is the light of the world," Jonathan stated confidently, but Luke focused on the last part of the scripture.

"But we don't get it, or understand him," Luke added and David seemed a little surprised by Luke's comprehension.

"Exactly. Luke, can you read verses 10-14?" David asked and Luke let his eyes move down the page to the verse.

"He was in the world, and though the world was made through him, the world did not recognize him. He came to that which was his own, but his own did not receive him. Yet to all who did receive him, to those who believed in his name, he gave the right to become children of God— children born not of natural descent, nor of human decision or a husband's will, but born of God. The Word became flesh and made his dwelling among us. We have seen his glory, the glory of the one and only Son, who came from the Father, full of grace and truth." Luke finished reading and scanned the scriptures again for their meaning.

"The Word became flesh…" Luke said and then continued. "Is he talking about Jesus?" he asked David, who nodded.

"What does he give us?" David asked.

"The right to become his children," Luke replied.

"Okay, so the Word is God, and the Word became flesh and walked the earth to teach us. So, for the rest of the study tonight, we are going to look at how the Word is also the Bible that we hold." David said and tapped his Bible with his finger. Luke tried to get his mind wrapped around what they had just read. God is the Word, Jesus is the Word, and Jesus walked the earth. *But why?* Luke thought, staring at his Bible.

"So what purpose does the Bible have for us?" David asked and Jonathan was quick to respond.

"To teach us about Jesus."

"Yes, and what else?" David asked, but after a few moments, David answered it himself. "To teach us and others how to live the lives he desires of us," he said and then turned a few pages in his Bible. "Turn over to <u>2 Timothy 3:16-17</u>; Jonathan, would you read that for us?"

"All scripture is God-breathed and is useful for teaching, rebuking, correcting and training in righteousness, so that the man of God may be thoroughly equipped for every good work." Jonathan waited for the question he knew would be coming from David.

"Based on what we are reading here, how much of scripture, God's Word, is directly from God?" David asked.

"All of it!" Jonathan answered and smiled and David nodded.

"100% of it. What is it useful for?" David asked.

"Teaching, training, correcting and rebuking," Jonathan interjected quickly as if he was in a race to give the first answer.

"Correct. So what is the difference between teaching and training?" David asked and Jonathan hesitated long enough for Luke to squeeze a response in.

"Teaching is classroom work, while training is putting it into practice," Luke stated.

"I can teach you all about how to run a marathon, but unless you go out and train to run one, your chances of completing one, let alone winning one, would be very small," David said and they all smiled. "So how would that relate to God's Word?" David asked and there was a period of silence before Luke finally answered.

"Unless we put what is taught into practice, we'll never understand how to live by it." Luke replied.

"Good. So what's the difference between correcting and rebuking?" David asked and they both seemed hesitant to answer so David interjected. "Correcting is when someone makes a mistake and someone gently explains to them the right way, but if after showing someone repeatedly the right way and they continue to do it the wrong way, we sometimes need to get a little more stern with our correction. It is the same with God's Word." He explained and smiled and then looked back at the verse. "So why do we have the Bible?"

"To be thoroughly equipped for every good work," Jonathan replied and David nodded.

"So we learn from this scripture that the Word is from God and is useful for every aspect of our life." David started turning pages again. "Okay, turn a couple of pages to Hebrews 4:12-13. Luke, would you read that when you get there?" David asked and Luke nodded as he was turning the pages and then started reading.

"For the word of God is alive and active. Sharper than any double-edged sword, it penetrates even to dividing soul and spirit, joints and marrow; it judges the thoughts and attitudes of the heart. Nothing in all creation is hidden from God's sight. Everything is uncovered and laid bare before the eyes of him to whom we must give account."

"Have you ever thought of a book being alive and active before?" David asked. Although Jonathan was nodding his head, Luke had never really thought of one in such a way before.

"I've felt a book could make things come alive on the page and in my imagination, but I have not thought of calling one 'active' before," Luke shared as he continued thinking about the verse.

"It says it is sharp and useful for something?" David asked.

"It can judge the thoughts and attitudes of the heart," Luke said and then the words he just spoke out loud froze in his mind and mouth. *"The thoughts and attitudes of the heart,"* Luke said to himself and leaned back against his chair and thought about the Cat Eyes glasses. The glasses could see the thoughts and attitudes of the heart! Luke looked right at David and saw him smile at Luke's sudden realization.

"Nothing in all creation is hidden from God's sight. Everything is uncovered and laid bare before the eyes of him to whom we must give account." David finished the scripture from memory and held Luke's gaze a moment longer. He glanced at Jonathan, but could tell he had not drawn the same correlation, but seemed to be wrestling with something else. David broke the silence.

"Interesting how God's Word says that it, God's Word, is what is supposed to be used to address these issues, wouldn't you say Luke?" David said and smiled again. Luke just nodded and tried to get his mind wrapped around this new concept, searching for deeper correlations. Why did David ask that question? Luke thought and waited to see where things were going to go now that there seemed to be a second, underlying conversation going between the two of them. Was this the "spiritual" aspect that he was talking about with regards to the ghosting issues?

"There's a lot more that we could talk about in this scripture," David suddenly interjected, "but let's take a look at another scripture; turn over to 2 Peter 1:20-21. Jonathan, you're up," David said subtly ending their sub-conversation and brought Luke back to the Bible discussion. Luke tried to watch the direction the other two were turning their pages in order to find 2 Peter.

"Above all, you must understand that no prophecy of Scripture came about by the prophet's own interpretation. For prophecy never had its origin in the will of man, but men spoke from God as they were carried along by the Holy Spirit."

"What are we learning about God's Word in this scripture?" David asked and Luke read it again, a bit frustrated by the fact that he was still working on the previous verse.

"The Holy Spirit wrote the Bible," Jonathan answered and David nodded.

"That man wrote the words that God wanted them to write. They were the pen and ink that God held in his hand to write with," David said and looked at the two of them. "These are the exact words that he wanted us to have, not just some good ideas that were grouped together by a bunch of different good-hearted people during the first few decades of the church." David added, but Luke frowned.

"Assuming you believe that. But how would you really know that to be true? Two thousand years have passed which would give people or organizations plenty of opportunity to change what it says for their own purposes," Luke interjected and David nodded.

"There has been a lot of criticism about 'translations' and the opportunity, over the years for things to get 'adjusted' by man, in order to meet a particular groups desires or beliefs. One of the most contested books in the Old Testament was the book of Isaiah, which has many prophecies and predictions about the audiences future coming of the Messiah. It was written around 700 B.C., over 700 years before the birth and ministry of Jesus. The book of Isaiah predicted events that had not yet happened during the life of the writer. It predicted that Babylon would be a world power, the destruction of Jerusalem, even the rise of Cyrus the Great and actually naming him one hundred and fifty years before he came to power." David paused for a moment and then continued, "So the critics claimed that the prophecies, dates and names were added to later copies of Isaiah in order to 'correct' errors, while Jews and Christians held to the belief that they were the original and thus accurate prophecies." David took a drink of water and then continued, "So the battle of opinions on the matter raged for over 2,000 years until 1949, when the Dead Sea Scrolls were found in the caves near Qumran by the Dead Sea. A complete book of Isaiah, written centuries before Jesus' birth, was found there. Amazingly, the prophecies, names, dates and words were the same as the ones we hold today. It silenced many of the critics regarding the consistency of God's Word, but faith still is the final factor of belief. You either believe that the creator of the universe can protect the core of his Word, or that he can't." David then smiled. "There will always be doubters."

Luke thought about the whole idea of the Bible: Was it really the same today as it was 2,000 years ago? "So if you doubt, then you're doomed to hell?" Luke asked sarcastically.

"Turn over to <u>Matthew 28:16-17</u> and let's read about what·happens to doubters." David turned the pages in his Bible and Luke copied the direction that he was heading from their last scripture.

"For over three years, Jesus had been teaching twelve hand-picked men about what he called 'the kingdom of God', about himself, and about his Father in heaven. Jesus had performed many miracles, died on a cross right in front of them, then rose from the dead and hung out with his followers for forty days before ascending into heaven." David paused to make sure they had turned to the scripture. "Witnessing all that, let's see how they responded in these verses, '*Then the eleven disciples went to Galilee, to the mountain where Jesus had told them to go. When they saw him, they worshiped him; <u>but some doubted</u>.*'"

David looked up from reading and raised an eyebrow. "The following verse Jesus calls down lightning from heaven and cooks them in their sandals!" David raised his voice and waved his hand angrily, then smiled as he saw Luke glance back down at the verse. "Just kidding. No, our nature is to doubt, Luke, while Jesus' nature is to encourage and clarify. His Word and its truth is what removes the doubts that work their way into our minds. But when we doubt, we can either turn to God for the answers and trust and obey his commands, like these eleven men did, or we run from him, like Judas did," David said calmly. Luke knew enough about the Bible to know that Judas was the follower that had betrayed Jesus and ended up killing himself.

"These men believed in Jesus, where Judas did not," Jonathan interjected proudly and David seemed to consider the response and then raised an eyebrow.

"Jonathan, do you think that belief alone is what Jesus is looking for?" David asked Jonathan, who at first seemed to consider the question and then nodded his head.

"<u>John 3:16</u>, '*For God so loved the world that he gave his one and only Son, that whoever believes in him shall not perish but have eternal life,*'" Jonathan quoted from memory and David nodded.

"Great scripture, one of the most quoted scriptures in the Christian world, but let's take a look at another scripture about belief and then we'll come back and visit that again. Turn over to <u>John 8:30-32</u>. Jonathan, can you read that for us when we all get there?" David said as the sound of pages turning filled the room.

"*Even as he spoke, many put their faith in him. To the Jews who had believed him, Jesus said, "If you hold to my teaching, you are really my disciples. Then you will know the truth, and the truth will set you free."*"

As Jonathan finished reading, Luke could see that David was watching for Jonathan's reaction to the scripture.

"What do we see about these people that are following Jesus?" David asked Jonathan.

"They believed him and put their faith in him," Jonathan replied, but did not look up from the scripture. David nodded.

"What did Jesus tell these 'believers' about how to 'really' be his disciples?" David asked and waited, but Jonathan did not reply. David continued to wait and Jonathan continued to remain silent and the moment became awkward for Luke. He thought it was strange that Jonathan would not answer, when it was so obvious in the scripture.

"If you hold to my teaching, then you are really my disciples," Luke interjected the obvious in order to move past the moment. David nodded.

"What else did he make clear to those who 'believed' in him?" David asked without taking his eyes off of Jonathan. Luke did not wait for it to become awkward this time.

"Then you will know the truth and the truth will set you free," Luke stated and watched Jonathan remain sitting in silence.

"Jesus uses an "If – Then" statement, almost as if he was a programmer writing code," David said and smiled. "Jesus was always drawing a line in the sand to clarify what a true believer was, someone who actually holds to his teachings, from those who just profess to believe. He clarifies that unless they "hold to his teachings" they will never know the truth, and thus can not be set free." David let the words sink in. Jonathan continued to appear to be re-reading the scripture again.

"What do you think Jonathan?" Luke asked, trying to resolve this silent standoff.

"I just don't agree." Jonathan finally replied and leaned back in his chair.
"With which part?" Luke asked and Jonathan just shook is head.

"I just think you are trying to lead this lesson in a 'works based' direction, which is what Jesus did not want," Jonathan finally stated in a confrontational manner and crossed his arms. David seemed to let the moment settle before continuing.

"So what part of what we are reading is making it seem 'works' oriented?" David finally asked.

"Jesus died on a cross to take away our sins. End of story," Jonathan replied adamantly and looked at David.

"So he takes an action on our behalf, but does not require us to take an action in response?" David asked Jonathan. Luke felt a little guilty, but he was now starting to really get into the study and what he wanted to hear discussed and debated.

"John 3:16 '*For God so loved the world that he gave his one and only Son, that whoever believes in him shall not perish but have eternal life,*'" Jonathan quoted the scripture he used earlier again. David nodded and turned pages in his Bible.

"In James 2:18-19, God wrote, assuming we still agree that he is writing what the Holy Spirit wanted, '*But someone will say, "You have faith; I have deeds." Show me your faith without deeds, and I will show you my faith by what I do. You believe that there is one God. Good! Even the demons believe that—and shudder.*'"

David let the words settle before continuing. "Jonathan, Jesus does not doubt the sincerity of these people, but sincerity does not equal truth. Remember the butter knife and the guessing of its length? Likewise, unless a belief is fully supported in the Word of God, it cannot become a doctrine of salvation."

"Is this really all that important of a debate? Can't we just agree to disagree?" Luke asked, sensing the frustration level growing in the room.

"Yes it is. I know it seems minor, but it is a serious issue of faith and worth the time to dig through it." David said and waited for Luke's reaction. Luke finally shrugged and then nodded. David started turning pages again.

"Turn over to Matthew 15:1-9 and let's take a look at an example of when Jesus challenged that same type of thinking." David said and then waited for Luke and Jonathan to find the page.

"I'll give you two a break and read this, let's start in verse 1," David said with a smile.

"Then some Pharisees and teachers of the law came to Jesus from Jerusalem and asked, "Why do your disciples break the tradition of the elders? They don't wash their hands before they eat!" Jesus replied, "And why do you break the command of God for the sake of your tradition? For God said, 'Honor your father and mother' and 'Anyone who curses his father or mother must be put to death.' But you say that if a man says to his father or mother, 'Whatever help you might otherwise have received from me is a gift devoted to God,' he is not to 'honor his father' with it. Thus you nullify the word of God for the sake of your tradition. You hypocrites! Isaiah was right when he prophesied about you: "These people honor me with their lips, but their hearts are far from me. They worship me in vain; their teachings are but rules taught by men."'"

"Luke, here is a little history from this time period; the Pharisee's were the religious leaders of the Jewish people of the day. They had created an elaborate system of ceremonial traditions that they would always perform when washing their hands before eating in case the food was handled by anyone who was ceremonially unclean. Again, this was not directed by God's Word, but was a man made tradition. So when they saw that Jesus' disciples did not honor their tradition, they got upset. But Jesus took the moment to point out a glaring contradiction between one of their 'traditions' and the Word of God," David stated and tapped the Bible with his finger. "The Bible commanded that a man must take care of his mother and father, honor them, yet the Pharisees created a new tradition, a way to free a person from that responsibility by allowing a person to instead give a large, one-time gift to the Temple. It was called *Corban*. By giving a gift, which roughly amounted to about what that person would have spent in the care of their parents to the Pharisees, he or she no longer had to be responsible for taking care of them." David watched to see if Luke and Jonathan understood, and both nodded their heads. "So what did Jesus say about this tradition that they had made?" David asked and waited, but Jonathan continued to remain silent.

"It nullified God's Word." Luke replied.

"And his view on their worship as a result of it?" David asked.

"They worship in vain, just following rules taught by men," Luke paraphrased the scripture.

"Jesus was not saying that traditions were necessarily bad, only those that contradicted or compromised God's Word. That is why we have the Bible to reference. To help us determine the difference between a 'teaching of God' and a 'teaching of man.'" David waited for Jonathan to respond and looked over at Luke and waited.

As awkward as it was, David was going to wait until Jonathan responded. It was several minutes later that Jonathan finally looked up.

"I'm not as well versed in the Bible as you are, but I just know that your church is a cult and teaches false doctrine." Jonathan blurted the words out quickly and sharply. David did not seem at all phased by the statement, he simply nodded.
"False doctrine is a pretty strong statement; Can you be a little more specific as to what you mean?" David asked calmly and Jonathan looked over at Luke and then answered.

"You believe in a works-based." Jonathan stated and David exhaled.

"Jonathan, you repeatedly use 'works-based' statements, but never explain or give examples of what you mean."

"You believe that you must be baptized to be saved, which is not taught in the Bible. Jonathan blurted and then sat back nervously in his chair.

"Okay, now I understand what you are relating your 'works-based' accusation to." David replied and paused before continuing, "The study of 'works' and 'baptism' as a part of salvation are pretty deep studies. Would you like to tackle them tonight or take some time to gather your resources first and discuss them later?" David asked kindly to Jonathan who seemed a little relieved by the offer and nodded his head.

"Yeah, that would be great. Next time we can debate it," Jonathan said and David frowned slightly.

"Jonathan, I'm not big on heated debates, but I'm happy to discuss any topic with you but only under one condition, that the only resource we use to explain our position is the Bible. Are we agreed on that?" Jonathan considered the condition and then nodded in agreement.

"Jonathan, I understand that many people feel that way toward what I believe and even speak against the church I belong to. But it's really not a church issue as much as it is a doctrine issue. Every church is flawed because man is a part of it, but the doctrine a church tries to live by is what really matters," David explained and Luke seemed a little surprised by the statement. "But you need to ask yourself if what you've heard or believe is based on what you have read personally from the Bible, or if it is from what someone else is telling you? Is it a teaching of God, or a tradition of man?" David stated slowly and calmly. "If you can show to me from God's Word, not your or someone else's opinion, where I am missing a key teaching, I will be happy to admit that I was wrong and change to match what the Bible says. But I won't be swayed by an opinion or tradition that nullifies God's Word," David replied and watched for Jonathan's expression, which gradually grew more cordial.

"Do you want to keep studying or take a break?" David asked and Jonathan seemed to think about it a moment before responding.

"I don't really see the purpose in continuing at this point," Jonathan replied and David raised an eyebrow.

"Well, the 'purpose' is to find out if what the Bible is showing us is true or not," David said. "Can I give you an example from scripture of what I mean?" David asked and started turning pages and Luke could see that Jonathan was getting frustrated. "Turn over to Acts 17:10-12. Luke, would you read that for us when you get there?"

"*As soon as it was night, the brothers sent Paul and Silas away to Berea. On arriving there, they went to the Jewish synagogue. Now the Bereans were of more noble character than the Thessalonians, for they received the message with great eagerness and examined the Scriptures every day to see if what Paul said was true. Many of the Jews believed, as did also a number of prominent Greek women and many Greek men.*" Luke finished reading and glanced back to the top of the scripture again, knowing that a question was coming.

"Thanks Luke. So what do we see about the Bereans in this scripture?" David asked and waited. Luke could tell that Jonathan was not in the mood to be answering any more questions, no matter how nicely David asked them.

"They were of more noble character," Luke said and David nodded.

"What made them more 'noble' than the Thessalonians?"

"They were eager and examined the scriptures to see if what Paul said was true."

"Jonathan, I'm not upset with what you said. In fact I appreciate your concern, but I am asking that you be a Berean and examine the scriptures to see if what I'm sharing is true or not. I'm asking you to not let your emotions or preconceived ideas get the best of you like the Thessalonians did; read verses 1-9 if you want to understand what I mean by that." David waited for Jonathan to respond in some manner or another.

"I'll look when I get home, but I already know what I will find," Jonathan said smugly to David, who sat quietly a moment before turning to another scripture.

"I hope you will examine them, not just read them. As someone who professes to be a Christian, you need to understand the importance of having things on straight more than anyone. In John 12:48, Jesus tells us very clearly; '*There is a judge for the one who rejects me and does not accept my words; that very word which I spoke will condemn him at the last day.*'" David closed his Bible and held it up in front of him. "God has given us this ruler to measure our thoughts and actions by. So we either accept what God says as true, or we reject the teachings of the Bible and replace them with something else. I'm more than willing to study out any question or belief you may have and compare it to what God has written in his Word. But the Bible must be our standard, or we will just be sharing our opinions." David looked at Luke. "Sorry that we got a little sidetracked, that was not my intention for the evening." David said and Luke shrugged.

"It's all good," Luke replied.

"So are there any questions that you have about what we studied that I can answer?" David asked Luke, but Jonathan suddenly began gathering his stuff as if preparing to leave.

"Heading out?" Luke asked, delaying answering David's question.

"Yeah. Been a crazy day, so I think I'll head home," Jonathan said somewhat nervously and turned toward Luke, "Are you sticking around?" Luke raised an eyebrow and seemed confused.

"I live here, so yeah." Luke replied and smiled. Jonathan suddenly felt even more nervous.

"I uh, yeah. I'd never been here before and forgot whose house it was," he murmured and stood up and headed for the door. They all exchanged goodbyes, although Jonathan's to David's was a little icy, and Jonathan headed out the door.

As the door shut behind him, David was the first to break the silence and frowned.

"I was afraid that was how things were going to turn out," David said and sat back down at the table and started writing something on a notepad. Luke sat back down across from David and looked up.

"Do you think he'll study out tonight's scriptures?" Luke asked and David looked up.

"What scriptures did we read tonight?" David asked with a smile and waited for Luke to reply, but Luke just shook his head as he tried to remember the various books, chapters and verses.

"I don't remember," he replied sheepishly.

"Did he write them down or ask for them before he left?" David continued and Luke again shook his head. "That tells me he did not leave with the heart of a Berean, but more like one of the Thessalonians." David finished and Luke nodded.

"Can you write those down for me?" Luke suddenly asked and then smiled innocently. David hesitated and then shook his head.

"Way to cover your bases, wise guy," David said with a smile and then finished his writing and slid the piece of paper over to him. All the scriptures were listed on the sheet; at least it appeared to be all of them as far as Luke could guess. "Study them out and let me know when, or if, you want to study again." Luke nodded as he thought about the evening.

"What was that scripture you used about 'judging the thoughts and attitudes of the heart?'" Luke asked.

"I thought that one would get your attention," David said with a smile. "Hebrews 4:12-13," David replied and reached over and circled the scripture on the sheet of paper. "Kind of eerie isn't it?" David added and smirked.

"It sounds like the Cat Eyes in action," Luke replied and frowned. "So is that the spiritual insight you were talking about with the Cat Eyes and the whole ghosting problem?" Luke asked. David's brow knitted slightly as he thought deeply preparing his answer, and then shook his head.

"I think it's deeper than that." Luke watched as he started putting away his Bible.

"Don't tell me, you won't share it until our next study or after I buy you another dinner," Luke said with a disappointed and frustrated look, but David just shook his head.

"I don't think that you're ready to know, and you would not believe me if I told you," David replied and the words left Luke speechless. *What could David mean by that?* Luke thought.

"Try me," Luke said, almost as a challenge and David stared at Luke a moment before answering.

"Okay. Part of the answer is hidden in Hebrews 4:12, but another part that is more frightening is in... I think, 1 Corinthians 4:5," he said and spun Luke's Bible around and turned to the scripture. "Yeah, that's it. *'Therefore judge nothing before the appointed time; wait till the Lord comes. He will bring to light what is hidden in darkness and will expose the motives of men's hearts. At that time each will receive his praise from God.'*" David finished reading and spun it back around. Luke thought about the words he just read.

"What exactly are you saying with that scripture?" Luke asked as he glanced down to read it for himself. David just shook his head.

"I don't know just yet, I need to pray about this and read up on it more, but it is rather frightening to think about."

"Are you saying that the Cat Eyes are somehow related to God?" Luke asked incredulously and David shrugged.

"Luke, all things are related to God; he either allows it or puts it in motion. But not all things are from God. Our goal is to know his will in all things and learn to discern between what is good and what is bad, and then respond accordingly," David replied and Luke tried to grasp his meaning.

"How do you know the difference between "his will" and someone else's?" Luke asked sincerely. David spun Luke's Bible back around and turned to another scripture.

"This scripture comes to mind when I think of you and the challenges that are before you. It's Ephesians 1:17-18." *'I keep asking that the God of our Lord Jesus Christ, the glorious Father, may give you the Spirit of wisdom and revelation, so that you may know him better. I pray also that the eyes of your heart may be enlightened in order that you may know the hope to which he has called you, the riches of his glorious inheritance in the saints, and his incomparably great power for us who believe.'*" David looked up at

Luke. "Like Paul, I pray that the eyes of your heart may be enlightened. Luke, the 'eyes of your mind' work very well, better than most even, but it's with the 'eyes of the heart' that you will learn to know God and to understand the spiritual things that are happening around you." David said and looked at Luke intently, reading his changing expressions.

Luke attempted to respond several times with either questions or statements, but struggled to find the words he wanted to use.

"So your view is that the 'ghosting' is a result of the unseen spiritual world, not a software or hardware issue." Luke's sentence was formed as a statement, not a question and David nodded. Luke took a deep breath and exhaled. "Sorry, but I'm finding it all a little hard to believe," Luke replied and shook his head.

"No doubt," David replied, "which is why I need to teach you more of what the Bible says, so that you will believe and your eyes will be opened. Not just to grasp what is happening with the glasses, but more importantly, to grasp the value of a relationship with God," David said and waited. Luke was working hard to wrap his mind around what had been talked about and the interplay between David and Jonathan and the ideas they represented.

"Sorry, but my instincts tell me that this is a software or hardware problem, not a spiritual one," Luke replied, almost frustrated with the thoughts. David shrugged.

"Based on what little you know and believe about God and his Word, I completely understand your hesitancy to accept what I'm saying. But I hope you continue to study it out so that you have all the evidence to base a decision on." Luke thought about the ghostlike shadows that he had seen in the glasses and was wishing he had a key to Apollo's code structure when he realized that David was waiting for a response.

"Sorry, yes, I'm open to another study," Luke finally replied.

"Okay, how about Thursday evening?" David asked and Luke tried to think of an excuse to say that slot would not work, but he could not think of anything and he did not want to lie.

"Sure. How about 7:00 p.m. again?" Luke replied and David agreed. "Should I invite Jonathan?" Luke asked David who thought a moment and nodded.

"Yeah. I think he needs an opportunity to get all these issues off his chest in order to move forward without carrying all that baggage with him," David said as if thinking out loud and then continued, "It more than likely will be as awkward as tonight was, but it might help to answer a lot of your concerns as well," David said to Luke.

"So you're not worried about what he might point out via scripture that could challenge your beliefs?" Luke asked and David seemed surprised by the question.

"No, in fact I look forward to it. If he can show me through the scriptures where I am wrong or misguided, then I welcome that and out of a desire to be pleasing to God, will immediately follow what the Bible says," David replied. Luke was impressed with David's candor and humility.

"Sometimes I wish I was wearing the Cat Eyes when I'm speaking with you," Luke added and smiled.

"Feel free to wear them anytime you wish. I have nothing to hide," David replied and began to stand up. "I find it all very fascinating," David stated as he seemed to drift off in thought, "the whole Cat Eyes project, revealing of hidden truths, the spiritual correlations, and how our friendship and careers are all intertwined. I'm excited and honored to be a part of it, I'm just trying to understand the why this is all coming about as it is." Luke decided that he really liked David and admired his serenity and the way he had handled what had amounted to insults from Jonathan.

"Thanks for coming over tonight, it definitely was an interesting evening," Luke stated and then smiled. David nodded as he headed toward the door and then turned back toward him.

"Homework," he said and Luke frowned. "I want you to read <u>2 Kings 6:8-23</u> tonight. You'll see something very interesting in there that will help get your mind and heart in gear." He smiled as he closed the door behind him.

"2 Kings 6:8-23" Luke repeated to himself as he stood there looking at the closed door and replayed the day's events in his mind. Strangely, prior to this evening he had felt exhausted from the past wild couple of days, yet he now felt energized and even excited about how things were developing. As he walked back to the kitchen and started cleaning, he saw the page of scriptures and then remembered the homework. Luke walked to the table, picked up his Bible and turned to the index to find the page number for 2 Kings and thumbed through the Bible until he found chapter 6, verse 8, and started reading,

"Now the king of Aram was at war with Israel. After conferring with his officers, he said, "I will set up my camp in such and such a place."

The man of God sent word to the king of Israel: "Beware of passing that place, because the Arameans are going down there." So the king of Israel checked on the place indicated by the man of God. Time and again Elisha warned the king, so that he was on his guard in such places. This enraged the king of Aram. He summoned his officers and demanded of them, "Will you not tell me which of us is on the side of the king of Israel?"

"None of us, my lord the king," said one of his officers, "but Elisha, the prophet who is in Israel, tells the king of Israel the very words you speak in your bedroom."

"Go, find out where he is," the king ordered, "so I can send men and capture him." The report came back: "He is in Dothan." Then he sent horses and chariots and a strong force there. They went by night and surrounded the city.

When the servant of the man of God got up and went out early the next morning, an army with horses and chariots had surrounded the city. "Oh, my lord, what shall we do?" the servant asked.

"Don't be afraid," the prophet answered. "Those who are with us are more than those who are with them."

And Elisha prayed, "O LORD, open his eyes so he may see." Then the LORD opened the servant's eyes, and he looked and saw the hills full of horses and chariots of fire all around Elisha.

As the enemy came down toward him, Elisha prayed to the LORD, "Strike these people with blindness." So he struck them with blindness, as Elisha had asked.

Elisha told them, "This is not the road and this is not the city. Follow me, and I will lead you to the man you are looking for." And he led them to Samaria.

After they entered the city, Elisha said, "LORD, open the eyes of these men so they can see." Then the LORD opened their eyes and they looked, and there they were, inside Samaria.

When the king of Israel saw them, he asked Elisha, "Shall I kill them, my father? Shall I kill them?"

"Do not kill them," he answered. "Would you kill men you have captured with your own sword or bow? Set food and water before them so that they may eat and drink and then go back to their master." So he prepared a great feast for them, and after they had finished eating and drinking, he sent them away, and they returned to their master. So the bands from Aram stopped raiding Israel's territory."

When Luke finished, he knew exactly what David had intended him to see, *"Don't be afraid," the prophet answered. "Those who are with us are more than those who are with them." And Elisha prayed, "O LORD, **open his eyes so he may see.**" Then the LORD opened the servant's eyes, and he looked and saw the hills full of horses and chariots of fire all around Elisha."* Luke thought about the idea of invisible armies being all around that could not be seen and how it related to the Cat Eyes glasses. Then the realization struck him, "Is he saying that the 'ghosting' is the invisible forces?" Luke asked out loud and then reread the story again and chuckled at the notion. In spite of his disbelief, he took the time to go back over the scriptures again before finally heading to bed.

Chapter 20

The next morning, as Luke was eating breakfast, his mind kept returning to the discussion on the possible spiritual causes for the anomalies in the glasses' display. He reread the scriptures David had given him, but all night long he had wrestled with the concept of there being an invisible 'spiritual' world. He came to the conclusion that although he was actually willing to embrace the possibility of a spiritual world of sorts, he was not willing to believe in a God behind it. Or perhaps not in an 'all knowing' and 'all powerful' God that created the universe, but instead could believe in a 'god like' power or powers that somehow existed beyond his senses.

He liked David and appreciated his friendship, his loyalty, and his knowledge of the Bible, but somehow felt that there was another explanation behind it all that David was blind to because of his staunch reliance on religion. The challenge was how to convince him and Danielle of it.

He got to the office an hour early and saw that Cliff and Serena were already there. *Do those guys ever leave the office?* he thought as he stepped into his cubicle. Luke pulled up his schedule for the day and he saw a note from Cliff to stop by his office when he got in, so he pushed away from his desk and headed toward his office. "I wonder what disaster is waiting for me now?" Luke mumbled to himself as he knocked on Cliff's door and heard the "Come on in, Luke!" from the other side. *How did he know if was me?* Luke wondered as he opened the door to see Cliff reviewing papers that were spread out on his desk.

"Hey Luke, how was your evening?" Cliff asked looking up just briefly and motioned toward the chair across from him.

"Enlightening, I guess," Luke replied and took a seat as he wondered if there was more to his question than just a pleasant greeting. Cliff tilted his head slightly as he looked up from the papers he was over and glanced at Luke, but did not pursue it further. He then reached behind his desk and lifted a file box and sat it on the corner.

"We've gathered everything from Stanley's home and we're currently documenting everything for prosecution purposes. I was also able to authorize the release of the upgraded demo unit that was taken so you can continue testing it," Cliff said and pushed the box toward him. Luke set it on the chair next to him and opened it. Inside he could see the system unit, glasses, and a variety of folders, notebooks and paper. Luke held up one of the folders and looked questioningly at Cliff.

"The system unit won't boot up. It's asking for a password and I thought you might have it or be able to figure out what it is. I thought maybe the files and paperwork could be of some help."

"Thanks, I'll see what I can find out," Luke replied.

"I don't recognize the software version, so it might just be a failed install," Cliff added and Luke nodded and grabbed the box and stood up to leave.

"Don't lose it," Cliff said sarcastically and Luke smiled and nodded sheepishly.

"Is this for office use only, or can it be removed for outside testing?" Luke asked, knowing that it had a tracking mechanism in it.

"That one is your sole responsibility to use as you see fit," he said calmly then looked up. "If you lose it…" Cliff trailed off giving a slightly threatening look and then smiled.

"Gotcha." Luke nodded with a look of feigned fear on his face, or perhaps it was real? As Luke reached the door, he remembered Gloria's request for a private meeting this weekend with the other team developers. Luke struggled on whether or not to mention it to Cliff, but after deciding not to, he suddenly turned around in the doorway to face Cliff.

"Just a heads up, there's a lot of nervousness within the team with all the agents passing through and secret meetings going on. They wanted to schedule a time this weekend to discuss the product in private, outside the office," Luke stated and waited for a reaction from Cliff who just nodded and looked as if he was waiting for something else. "Just thought I'd let you know in case you wanted to setup your sniper team," Luke said and smiled and started to close the door.

"I trust you," Cliff said and smiled as the door closed.

As Luke sat back down at his desk, he opened the box again and rummaged through the contents. He set the Cat Eyes unit on the desk and turned it on. He saw the system unit light come on and the display panel indicated that the software was booting, the software version, 4.31 was displayed briefly, but as Cliff had indicated, the password screen popped up and the boot process halted.

We never needed a password before, so what's up with this Apollo? Luke wondered as he turned it over and examined it. This software version was three versions ahead of the one that Luke and David had worked on. If this was the same unit that Ronald had taken, Apollo must have loaded up the software at his house. Luke tried entering a few basic passwords with the keypad, but nothing worked. "Great, I have my test unit back, but I can't use it," Luke muttered and set it back down on the desk and started looking through some of the folders. One thing about Apollo, he was always very thorough when it came to paperwork.

Luke started breezing through the files, but realized that this would be a long process and felt the other day's activities were more important at that point. He powered down the unit, placed it back in the box and slid it under his desk for the time being.

He heard a noise coming from David's cubicle and then David popped his head above the divider.

"Hey Elisha, ready for another crazy day?" he asked Luke, who nodded and smirked as he remembered the name of the prophet who opened his servant's eyes.

"Cute, but you'll need to find someone else to be your prophet," Luke replied and smiled.

"Good response, that tells me you're reading your Bible. How's Jonathan doing?" David asked, but Luke just shrugged.

"Haven't seen him yet today."

"Anything new on the work front?" David asked and Luke nodded.

"Got the stolen unit back from Apollo's house today, but he password protected it, so I can't get it to boot," Luke replied and it was David's turn to frown.

"That stinks," David mumbled. "Any thoughts on the discussion we had last night?" He asked and Luke tried to think of the best way to respond.

"Yeah. I'm still not buying into the whole God the Creator concept, although I am warming up to the idea of an unseen spiritual element out there," Luke admitted and waited for the response. David just raised an eyebrow.

"Humph. Can't say that was what I was hoping to hear, but I guess a little progress is better than none," David replied, which was not the response Luke was expecting. "Was it the way I was holding my hands when I was talking, perhaps it was my nervous stutter?" David asked sarcastically, to which Luke smiled and shook his head.

"I'm afraid it was your lack of knowledge and sloppy preparation that worked against you. You need to get a better handle on your subject matter next time," Luke countered sarcastically and David pretended to nod in agreement.

"Gotcha. So are we still on for Thursday evening?" David asked, apparently ignoring Luke's earlier statement about his hesitancy to believe in God.

"And risk missing the debate of the century? Yeah, were on!" Luke replied overzealously, even though he really did not want to meet again. However, he was interested in seeing how heated things would get between two professed Christians arguing over doctrine. David looked piercingly at him and seemed to read his real intentions, but apparently decided to let it go.

"Okay, Thursday it is. Now if you don't mind, I need to brush up on my Bible reading and practice my presentation skills if I'm to stand a chance of surviving your criticism." David replied and disappeared behind the cubicle wall. Luke felt a little guilty leading David along, letting him believe that he was interested in becoming a Christian, but he also felt he had made his intentions clear from the onset.

The rest of the morning was spent coming up to speed on what Apollo and his remaining team members had been working on. He met with Gloria, David and Danny, a meeting that Serena quietly sat in on, and went over their current development projects and programming goals, and then re-adjusted their priorities to try to fill the huge hole that the loss of Apollo and Ronald had left. David and Danny both made it very clear that Apollo had not released any code for them to look at since they had started, instead, he had them working on cleaning up the various open-source supporting modules that had very little to do with the operational aspect of the product's operating code. He could tell Danny was very frustrated with the code and his lack of progress. Luke learned that Apollo had asked them to test for and ensure that the proper security measures were in place to avoid any backdoor programs from compromising or accessing the main program.

"So he was basically having you try to break through the security measures to see if anyone could get into the program without his granting access," Luke added and then shook his head and smiled and David nodded as well. "What else do we know about the main code?" Luke asked.

"It's all behind a massively encrypted security program," David said and then tried to explain in detail what made it so powerful and difficult to overcome, but most of it was well beyond Luke's knowledge.

"What's the solution in order to get to the code we need?" Luke finally interjected and those in the room looked around and then back at Luke.

"The best solution would be to ask Apollo to give us the access codes and explain his coding structure, because I've never seen anything like it," David replied and raised an eyebrow as everyone rolled their eyes at the idea of asking him, "or we can keep pounding away at it, or call in more knowledgeable resources." David waited for Luke's response.

"We could reverse engineer it," Danny interjected, but David shook his head.

"That would take months, if not years. The code that I have been able to view is," David seemed to try to gather the right words before continuing, "very unique. I've never seen the methodology before and quite frankly, it shouldn't work." He looked at Luke. Luke somehow knew that David was alluding to it being 'spiritual', but was not sure if it was true or just a ploy to pique his interest a little more.

"We already have other resources working on the code," Serena suddenly added and then went quiet again. Luke just looked at her a moment unused to her speaking up. When he thought about it, it made sense. Cliff and Serena knew about the password protection and the code before they had given the test unit to Luke. It was logical that they would have specialists working on the code.

"Why wait until now to let us in on this?" Luke asked and she calmly looked at him.

"We saw the encryption issue from the beginning, but had hoped that other members of the company would be given access. When things started going sideways with Mr. Walpole, we dug a little deeper and contacted some talent inside our government agency in case things did not turn out well," she replied and Luke seemed to be waiting for additional information to be shared.

"Any luck?" Luke finally asked and she shook her head.

"Not yet," she replied, "as Mr. Stevens shared, we have found the same code issues and irregularities that he has. We hoped that someone on your team would have been given the solution."

They sat in silence a moment as they thought through their various options. Luke finally suggested a plan.

"Well we know the current code, version 4.01, works well enough to deliver in its current state. I don't know what enhancements Apollo was working on that would take the Cat Eyes to the next level of functionality, but we can live without it until we can get past the security blocks," Luke stated and the team nodded in agreement.

"What about the ghosting problem?" David asked and Luke nodded as he thought about it.

"Good point, let's go with version 3.9, the same version we demonstrated in Iraq. There were no ghosting issues with that version and I'd hate to have anything that would confuse or distract the soldiers in the field. Or worse, generate questions that we cannot answer," Luke replied and David nodded.

"So for clarification, all programming enhancements have been placed on hold – not that we could have written any code to enhance it anyway - so instead, we will be working on…?" Danny asked and waited for the answer from Luke who had thought about that same question earlier but was not sure how well his solution was going to go over with David and Danny.

"Well, Danny, if you could continue working on understanding the 'unique' code structure that Apollo has integrated into the operating system, it would be helpful. Gloria, you're doing a great job, but I am going to assign Jonathan to assist you in keeping production moving forward." Luke turned toward David and said, "I need you to help me break through Apollo's password on the demo systems unit that has the latest upgrade. He apparently installed a Cat Eyes software version that is three revisions higher than the one we are currently working on. Perhaps if we can get past the password and launch it, we can determine if he has fixed the ghosting issue and either go with the new version, or stick with 3.9." David nodded his agreement.

"Serena, where's Cliff? I thought he would have been here." All eyes turned to Serena, who hesitated a moment.

"He's meeting with Apollo. I believe he is trying to obtain the password, the encryption code, and the software algorithm that he is using," she replied and Luke had a sudden vision of Apollo under some hot lights in a smoke filled room with some intense questioning going on. But then he dismissed the idea as being illegal.

The rest of the day was spent trying to implement the decisions of the morning's meeting. Gloria was able to add Jonathan in quickly and had him tackle the responsibilities that Ronald was previously handling. Danny was granted access to the various small pieces of Apollo's code that was not password protected and he quickly went into his "programming mode," putting on his headphones, turning on his music, and tearing into the code.

Luke set the box that had contained the systems unit and glasses on David's desk and asked him to go through the various folders and removable drives, searching for any clues that might reveal a password. David copied Luke on all communication and Luke saw that he had forwarded several additional pieces of code that he found to Danny. David spent the remainder of the afternoon writing a password generating program that would run in the background trying tens of thousands of different passwords.

Luke returned to finalizing the Cat Eyes user manuals. He wanted it ready to be printed and shipped with the first series of systems units that were scheduled to come off the line in just under two weeks.

The day went faster than he expected and besides taking a quick break for a granola bar from the vending machine in the break room, he worked right through the day and into the early evening. As he passed through the non-secure office, he saw that Danielle had already left for the evening. He was hoping to speak with her about his study with David and get her thoughts on it. More than that, he missed her and felt very alone in his new role of team leader. Stepping outside into the parking lot, he saw that his was one of the last cars there.

Famished, he swung by a little place about three blocks from his apartment that made great hot wings. He grabbed a box of wings and a soda and headed home with the idea that he would find a movie and hit the sack early. He walked up the stairs to his apartment and let himself in with one hand as he juggled the wings and soda in the other, spilling the soda on his pants and then dropping it onto the entryway floor in the process. He stood there and fought off the urge to yell as he surveyed the mess. Leaving the door open with soda spreading out everywhere, he grabbed what remained of the still draining soda and walked it into the kitchen. He tossed the empty soda cup into the sink with one hand and set the wings down on the counter with the other. He pulled off a long string of paper towels from the roll and headed back toward the front door to clean up the mess, but heard the door suddenly shut.

Had Danielle stopped by? he wondered as he turned the corner toward the front door and then froze two steps later. In the hallway was a man holding a revolver aimed at his chest. It took a moment for Luke to realize that neither of them was moving, they both just stood there, staring at each other. The man was wearing a long tan coat and a hat, which was strange for the time of year, but Luke's attention was fixed on the black hole at the end of the barrel of the revolver. It seemed very large for the size of the gun.

"What can I do for you? I mean take whatever you want," Luke stated, the higher register of his voice belying his calm exterior. However, the man just stood there and smiled a cold, hollow smile in return. As they stood in silence, Luke thought quickly about his options, but the gun aimed at his chest at such a close distance in his cramped entryway seemed to limit them dramatically.

"You don't remember me do you?" the man suddenly asked. The broken silence of his words caused Luke to jump when they first came out. Luke stared at the man's face and tried to place it, but couldn't.

"Sorry, maybe you have the wrong place?" Luke responded and tried to gather some confidence. The man was Caucasian, brown hair, middle-aged, medium height and a little chubby. The man shook his head.

"No, I have the right place," he said and motioned with the gun for Luke to backup. "Why don't you take a seat?" He said and Luke slowly stepped backwards into the living room and took a seat on the couch as the man stepped around the soda spilled on the floor.

"Look, why don't you put away the gun and we can talk about whatever it is that I've done to upset you?" Luke asked calmly, but the man kept the gun aimed at him and sat down in the chair across from him.

"I know who you are: Luke Baker, big shot computer game developer, and part-time, pro bono mall cop." As the man spoke Luke recognized his face, or perhaps it was the voice, either way, the memory of the man suddenly came rushing back into his mind. He was the man who was stalking the young boy in the mall. The pervert he confronted in the computer game store. His heart sank in his chest at the realization of the moment. "You could have just let the warning be enough, but instead you had to contact my workplace, question my co-workers, follow my car, and ruin my life." He almost spit the words out at him as he listed Luke's apparent offenses. "Now I'm going to return the favor and ruin yours," the man explained and lifted the gun a little higher.

Luke tried to understand what the man was talking about, then it suddenly hit Luke. This was the person who owned the red sports car and Cliff and his team, in their search for the culprit, must have found him and done a complete background check on the man.

"Look, I never thought of you again after I protected that boy at the mall. But if you own that red sports car, then it was you that kept following me. I didn't know who you were, but I kept seeing your red sports car everywhere I turned. When you slashed my tire, I had to report it to my employer, who just happens to be the CIA. And they were not too happy about it." The man's face seemed to confirm his guilt and then at the mention of the CIA it seemed to really rattle him. "Yeah, you stepped into a real deep pile of it this time," Luke said and tried to read the man as best he could in the moment.

Luke wanted to feel compassion for the man, trying to understand what events in his life lead him to his sickness, but the realization that he would kill for it brought Luke back to reality. A sudden wave of disgust flowed through him as he thought about the man and his twisted interest in young boys. He thought about how many young boys and families he would have damaged emotionally from his actions, the thoughts struck the same hidden nerve and generated the same angry response he had experienced the last time he encountered this man. Suddenly and without any thought to his safety, Luke leaned forward in his seat and shook his head in disgust at the man. "You know, now that I think about it, I'm happy you were stupid enough to want revenge and that we're now sitting here in this situation," Luke said and the man looked caught off guard, "because if you hadn't been such an idiot, you'd still be out there feeding your sickness and twisted passions." Luke was calm but cold. The man seemed to at first cower, but then his face went red in anger and he raised his gun and aimed it at Luke's head. "When you shoot me, you'd better immediately put a bullet in your own head, because my employer will come down on you so fast and hard that you'd wish you had," Luke said coldly to the man and waited for the sound of the explosion and the impact of the bullet. As the two of them stared at each other across the length of the barrel of the gun, time seemed to stop. Luke remembered being in this situation before. The last time he was looking down the barrel of an AK47 held by a hate filled man, this time it was the same hate, just a different man and a different gun.

A strange peace came over Luke as he realized that his life was about to end. The flash of memories rolled through his mind as he thought about his parents, his family, but strangely the image of Danielle is what stayed the longest. He would miss her and wondered if she would be okay without him. He even thought about how she would respond when she heard the news of his death. *Death*. He thought about what would happen when he was dead. Was this it, or was there a spiritual realm as David talked about. Was there really a God, was there a hereafter, or was his life just a passing tick on the evolutionary clock that had no real meaning to it? He thought about the times with David, studying the Bible, and his decision. If there was a God, he suddenly realized that he had chosen to not believe in one. Suddenly a quote came to mind that he had read from a World War II soldier. When the man was asked by the author about his belief in God, the man replied, "I don't care what someone claims, when you're sitting in your fox hole and artillery shells are exploding everywhere, when bullets are flying by and smashing into the ground next to you, and there are the sounds of people dying all around you and you know you're next. There are no atheists, everyone prays." Luke thought about the quote and looked at the gun and closed his eyes and said a prayer.

"I'm sorry for not believing," was all he said and the man seemed confused by the words. He hesitated pulling the trigger as a cool breeze moved across Luke's face.

The sound of keys sliding into the lock of the door and the familiar sound of it opening suddenly replaced the silence between the two men.

"Honey, I'm home!" Luke's eyes suddenly opened at the sound of the female voice coming from down the hall.

"*No!*" Luke's mind shouted and then panicked at the thought of Danielle coming here now. Luke knew that she was the only other person that had a key to his apartment and knew that this man would kill her also. His mind raced and relaxed momentarily as he heard her turn off into the kitchen just before entering the living room where they sat. He looked at the man sitting across from him who was nervously aiming the gun back and forth at the two different entrances into the room where they sat, the opening from the hallway, the other opening coming off the kitchen, and then back at him.

"What's for dinner?" the voice called out from the kitchen and Luke was terrified by the thought of her being harmed, but was trying to find a way to save her.

"I told you to never come here again, now get out! Now!!" he yelled angrily and looked back at the man who was still wrestling with what to do. Luke heard steps coming from the kitchen opening toward them.

"I said leave!" he yelled again hoping to stop her, but it was too late. Luke could see the silhouette of her shadow growing across the floor as she was coming into the room, followed by her body.

Luke blinked as he stared at an unknown woman with a short pixie haircut standing in the kitchen doorway holding a loaf of bread in front of her with both hands. She seemed shocked by the sight before her.

"Luke, what's going on? Who is this man and why does he have a gun," she stammered as Luke tried to grasp who this woman was. He was so relieved that it was not Danielle, but at the same time he was more confused as to who she was or why she was there. The man on the other hand was now nervously aiming the gun at her.

"Luke? I'm scared," she said, breaking the silence. The man suddenly stood up, keeping the gun aimed at her, then back at Luke.

"Sit down." Was all the man said and motioned for her to move to the couch next to Luke. The woman looked at Luke, and then back at the man. Luke suddenly recognized her as the woman who had sat at a table close to theirs in the restaurant when he and David were studying the Bible. *Why was she here?* he wondered and felt bad that she was somehow now involved in this horrible situation.

"What did you do?" she asked Luke, almost pleading but not moving from where she stood, "why is he here?" she appeared to be on the verge of tears. Luke moved to stand, but the man swung the gun back toward Luke and made a 'don't even think about it' face until Luke sat back down. Luke could see that the frustration displayed on the man's face was rapidly increasing.

"I said sit down!" The man yelled at her and then suddenly stepped toward her. He reached out to grab her right arm with his left hand, while keeping the gun aimed at Luke.

The next sequence of actions happened faster than Luke could have imagined. As the loaf of bread fell from her hands, her left hand shot out and grabbed the top of the gun, twisting it downwards toward the floor and clean out of the man's hand. At the same moment, he saw that in her right hand she held a gun that had been concealed behind the loaf of bread, which she used to first deflect the man's left hand and then moved upwards in a rapid follow through. There was a loud 'thwack' as the base of her gun impacted with the man's left eye, sending him stumbling backwards. Then the loaf of bread landed softly and quietly onto the floor.

"I'm a Federal Agent, put your hands on your head and lay facedown on the floor," she barked the order at the man, who was now holding his left eye with both hands. He at first remained standing and removed one hand from his face and saw blood in the palms of his hands.

"I'm bleeding," he said, almost pleading, yet at the same time in shock.

"I said put your hands on your head and lay face down on the floor," she yelled the order again and the man looked up to see her gun aimed directly at his head. At first he hesitated, then slowly raised his hands and placed them on his head and kneeled down. Luke could see that the man's anger had now drained from his body and was replaced by sheer terror as blood flowed steadily down his face from the cut below his eye. The man hesitated briefly as he tried to figure out how to lie facedown while keeping his hands on his head. Without a solution, he eventually just tumbled awkwardly forward onto his stomach, somehow keeping his hands on his head in the process.

"Luke." The women suddenly broke the silence of the moment and Luke, still in shock, turned to look at her. She was still aiming her gun at the man on the floor and at the same time holding the man's gun oddly in her left hand.

"Yeah?" he replied nervously.

"I need you to slowly pull the hammer back on the gun in my left hand," she said. He was confused at first, but when he looked closely at the gun she held in her left hand, he could see that the skin between her thumb and pointer finger was trapped between the hammer and firing pin of the gun, and a trickle of blood was coming from the injury. He nodded and moved close enough to reach out and take the gun in both hands and pull the hammer back until it clicked. He looked up at her for more direction.

"You can let go now," she said and he released the gun in her hand and stepped back. She deftly flipped the gun around so that she held it normally, then placing her thumb on the hammer she slowly lowered it until it was no longer ready to fire. She then placed it in her belt behind her and looked back at Luke, who was just standing and staring at her in silence as he took it all in. "Thanks. You okay?" she said and he nodded.

"Yeah. Uh, yes," he stumbled through his response. "Are you?" he suddenly asked and she nodded. She moved toward the man on the floor from the side, and then knelt down placing one knee in the center of his back. She reached behind her back again, fumbling briefly, then withdrew a pair of handcuffs and locked them on the man's wrists, behind his back. She patted the man down, looking for additional weapons and removing any items and placing them on the table. She then read him his Miranda Rights, to which she made him acknowledge that he understood.

She then stood back up and reached into her pocket and pulled out a cell phone and pushed a few numbers and placed her gun back in its holster inside her jacket.

"Client is secure; target is down, but alive. We need a team sent out as backup," she said and Luke could tell that someone was speaking on the other end of the call. She glanced briefly at Luke. "No injuries, client is just a little shaken up." There was another pause of silence and then, "Yes, Sir." She placed the phone back in her pocket. "Backup is on the way," she said to Luke and he nodded.

"How did you… know?" He tried to ask, but halted in mid-sentence as he realized another question needed answering and switched direction, "How did you get in here?" he stammered as he waited for her response. She tilted her head and glanced down at the man on the floor and shook her head.

"We can talk about this later," she said and Luke nodded as she finally took a look at her injured hand.

"I have a first aid kit," Luke said calmly, but she shook her head.

"It'll be alright," she replied, "but you should get a towel to place under his head if you don't want him bleeding all over your floor." She angled her head toward the man again. Luke went into his bathroom and came back with a towel and placed it underneath the man. He could see that for the most part, the blood had stopped flowing from the wound. He saw that she had sat down on the edge of his armchair and was examining the wound on her hand. It dawned on Luke that the man had actually pulled the trigger and would have shot him had she not placed her hand in the way of the hammer. The whole disarming and takedown scene replayed itself in his head and he shook his head at the thought.

"I must say, that was very impressive," he said as he looked toward her. "Thank you for saving my life." She smiled and nodded and they sat in silence until the backup team arrived 15 minutes later. No lights, no sirens, they just knocked on the door, flowed into the room and began securing the scene, briefly treating the man's eye wound, and then leading him away.

Ten minutes after they arrived, Cliff came walking into the now almost empty apartment. Luke sat on the couch, still a bit in shock, while the female agent was in the kitchen, casually putting away the bread that she had grabbed from the countertop on the way into the room. Luke gave Cliff a half-hearted smile as he sat down on the couch next to Luke and looked at the bloodstain on the carpet. The female agent came back into the room and sat in the chair where the man had once sat. The room was now relatively silent as the three of them sat quietly together.

"I imagine you have a lot of questions running through your head," Cliff said without looking at Luke. Luke just nodded. "Well, as you already know, he was the mystery person in the red sports car," Cliff said and Luke nodded again. "We were having trouble trying to understand why he had such a keen interest in you and just couldn't put all the pieces together," Cliff shared as if thinking out loud. "Here is this known pedophile, with a very dark history, and he's somehow connected with one of our key employees," he said and looked over at Luke. "A very concerning situation for us as I'm sure you can imagine." Luke realized that they thought he might possibly be a pedophile as well, or was involved with one in some way. Luke nodded, but sat in silence. "What are you thinking Luke?" Cliff finally asked and Luke took a deep breath.

"Well, I'm battling with gratitude, anger, fear, and confusion." Luke finally replied and Cliff nodded his head.

"Which one do you want to start with?" Cliff asked and Luke looked over at the woman in the chair across from him.

"I'm sorry, I don't even know your name, but I'm so grateful to you for saving my life. You're amazing, tough… and sneaky." He smiled and she returned the smile.

"Angela, and you're welcome. Some clients are actually even worth saving," she replied.

"What about me? No gratitude here?" Cliff asked as if he was somehow overlooked in the interaction. Luke just stared at Cliff a moment as all the thoughts worked through his mind.

"Sorry, but you fall under the 'anger' category," Luke finally said with a smirk, "and the fear and confusion part as well."

"How so?" Cliff asked trying to act innocent.

"Let's see… how about explaining how you knew he was in my apartment?" Luke asked and raised an eyebrow. "You mentioned that I already knew that this guy was the mystery red sports car person," Luke said. "The only time I mentioned that was when it was just me and him speaking. So you either are clairvoyant, or you have my apartment bugged." Cliff seemed to think about denying the accusation, but suddenly nodded.

"Got me," he replied, "We installed the bugs when we thought you might be working with Apollo. We just have not gotten around to removing them yet." He paused for a moment and then continued, "It was all done legally."

"What else?" he asked innocently.

"What else? Cliff, bugging my apartment is not a minor issue. I feel violated and angry about it," Luke replied sternly.

"Okay, I'll have them removed before we leave," Cliff replied, but Luke just shook his head.

"You don't get it. You can't just do that to someone, someone who thought you were a friend, and then expect everything to be back to normal again. I feel like some worthless pawn in your big chess game and nobody took the time to ask me if I wanted to play that role," Luke said coldly and Cliff seemed hurt by the remark and hesitated a moment before responding.

"In my job, friends are hard to come by, let alone trust. When you find one, a friend, you struggle with the dilemma of what to do. To either protect them from the whole game that is playing out in the background, or let them in on it and expose them to the dangers that can result from it. I chose to protect you. With Apollo and the unknown connection with this guy unfolding around us, I was just unsure if you were the friend I thought you were," Cliff said sincerely. "Unfortunately, we've run into several situations that have peeled back the hidden layers of protection. For the record, I never believed you were involved in either situation, but I had protocols that I had to follow."

They sat in silence for a minute while Luke thought about what Cliff had said.
"So tell me about the 'fear' part." Cliff finally asked. Luke's greatest fear was dying with regrets about Danielle, but he did not share that. Instead, he decided to make light of it the moment.

"Fear? Have you seen her in action?" Luke said sarcastically toward Angela, "She scares the life out of me." He smiled. "Can she be my assistant?" Luke suddenly added jokingly and Angela raised an eyebrow.

"I can kill him now if you want," she replied to Cliff, who gave a gentle shake of his head.

"Not yet, but stay ready," he said without smiling, which made Luke's stomach go into a knot momentarily until they both suddenly smiled. Although he knew it was all in fun, Luke wondered if there might be a little truth in the jest.

"How did you get here so fast?" Luke asked Angela, suddenly realizing that the timing was too close.

"I was following him while he was following you. He was parked down the street when you pulled in. I saw him get out and follow you to your apartment. I notified the team and when I saw him enter your apartment and shut the door, I called it in as a code red and I improvised from there," Angela replied and Luke sat in silence a moment trying to understand everything that must have been happening behind the scenes.

"You have a key to my apartment?" Luke asked suddenly and Angela looked over toward Cliff who nodded.

"What, Cliff doesn't pay you enough so you need to do part-time house cleaning?" Luke asked sarcastically. Angela just smiled and shook her head.

"No, just full-time agent."

"007, license to kill," Luke joked and she just smiled and they all sat in awkward silence for moment as Luke realized that his joke was probably not one.

"So are we good?" Cliff suddenly asked Luke, who looked over at him.

"No," Luke replied and he saw Cliff raise an eyebrow and jokingly looked toward Angela and then back at Luke as if waiting to give her a signal. "But… I'm getting there." Luke replied and saw that Cliff and Angela were smiling at the joke, but then things settled down again. "I lost a lot of trust back there," Luke said sadly and Cliff nodded.

"Well, I gained a lot more trust in you," Cliff replied and patted him on the leg and stood up. "Are you going to be alright?" Cliff asked and waited for a response, "Do you want to take the day off tomorrow?" Luke shook his head.

"I've got too much to do if I want to avoid you sending Angela after me for poor performance," Luke replied.

"Good night, Luke." Angela stated as she stepped through the door.

"Thank you again Angela and next time, go easy on my bread. That stuff's expensive," he joked and Angela at first seemed confused and then smiled. Cliff just raised an eyebrow, not sure what that meant and stepped toward the door as well.

"Ahem!" Luke cleared his throat and Cliff turned around to see what he wanted. Luke tapped his ear and then pointed at his apartment. Cliff suddenly got his meaning.

"I'll send one of my men back up to take care of that before they leave," Cliff replied. "Can't get anything past that one." Cliff mumbled to Angela as they headed down the hallway.

During the next hour he watched as one of the agents removed five different listening devices located in different areas of his apartment. Most of them he would have never spotted even if he was carefully looking for them. As he lay down to sleep, he wondered how many were still in his apartment. Then he realized he would have probably been dead now if they had not been installed.

"Dead." The word hit him again. He suddenly remembered saying the prayer right before Angela walked into the apartment. Was it a coincidence, he wondered?

"Thank you," he said, just in case.

Chapter 21

The next morning at the office, Luke was surprised to learn that no one knew a thing about the previous evening's events. The more Luke thought about it, the more he wanted it to stay that way. There had been enough distractions for the team and he had no desire to explain another event tied to the company with his name on it.

He walked into Cliff's office after knocking on the door. As usual, Cliff, with Serena on the opposite side of the desk, was sitting in discussion.

"Hey Luke, how'd you sleep?" Cliff asked and smiled; Luke frowned and nodded toward Serena.

"I figured you would already know," Luke replied sarcastically and then turned toward Serena, "Good morning, Serena," he said and Cliff chuckled.

"Still upset? Understandable," Cliff responded and held his smile. "What can we do for you?" Luke wasn't still upset about the previous night's events, but he definitely was not over it by any means and did not want Cliff to think otherwise.

"In the distraction of trying to stay alive and worrying about how to get the blood stain off my living room floor, I failed to ask how the meeting with Apollo went yesterday."

"You mean with Stanley?" Cliff emphasized the name and Luke knew that Cliff did not like using the nickname. Luke smiled and nodded. "Well, let's say we came to some agreements but I'm not sure how they will turn out just yet. I will need your services during our next meeting, which is scheduled for tomorrow," Cliff responded. Luke was not excited about having to face Stanley again for any reason. It was like opening an old wound.

"In what way?" Luke asked and waited.

"Stanley is trying desperately to work a deal, but as you can imagine, we have a strong lack of trust in anything that he says." Cliff replied and Luke somehow knew what was coming. "So he has agreed to allow us to interrogate him with the Cat Eyes in order to prove that he is telling the truth." Cliff waited for Luke's reaction. Luke took a deep breath and exhaled as he wondered if Stanley had ever dreamed he would be in this situation. It somehow made Luke feel better about being the person demonstrating his own greatest fear of such a product, to the very person who felt it was the answer to the world's problems. Luke nodded his head.

"Sounds good. Knowing Stanley, he probably thinks he can beat it," Luke replied, and Cliff nodded. Luke continued, "I assume you have the series of questions that you would like me to ask, or will you be doing the asking and I'll just being verifying the answers?"

"I think we'll handle the questions, there might be too much of an emotional involvement on your end that could interfere with the questioning, although I have to admit that you are pretty quick on your feet," Cliff replied.

"Let me know what I can do to help prepare. The meeting should be interesting." Luke excused himself and headed toward the door.

"Yes it should."

On his way back to his desk, Luke ran into Jonathan, who was apparently waiting for him to leave his meeting with Cliff.

"What's the latest with Apollo?" Jonathan asked and followed Luke to his desk.

"You mean Stanley?" Luke mimicked Cliff. "I'm guessing he's wishing he would have played nicer with everyone." Luke

"Or he's wishing he would have left no survivors before he went into negotiations with the government," Jonathan shot back and Luke had to agree with his response. "Can we chat a minute?" Jonathan asked Luke before he got to his desk. "In private?"

Luke seemed to hesitate as he tried to evaluate the importance of the need to 'chat' with and everything on his schedule. He did not have time, but he knew keeping the team unified was also very important after everything that had happened during the week.

"Sure, how about the conference room?" Luke asked and Jonathan nodded and led the way to the nearby room. As they sat down Luke smiled and motioned toward Jonathan.

"I know we're having a lot of difficulties sorting through the code that Apollo created, but I'm not sure it's even possible to sort out," Jonathan almost mumbled to Luke and then continued when Luke gave him an expectant look as he waited for more information. "When I was in Apollo's inner circle, before you came along, he always talked about some sort of divine guidance that drove him to write the code."

"Well, knowing Apollo's, ah Stanley's mindset, that does not surprise me," Luke replied, disappointed that he had wasted the time to meet with Jonathan and pushed his chair back. Jonathan seemed surprised by the response.

"No, he really believed it and referred to the fact many times that he personally did not write the code, that someone… or something else wrote the code through him," Jonathan blurted out and Luke sat back down, a little confused and unsure as to how to respond. He could see that Jonathan was serious and even scared at the thought. "It always gave me the creeps when he would say it, but the more I watched him, the more I believed it was true."

"Why wait so long to say something?" Luke asked as he tried to understand Jonathan's possible motives for saying this.

"Because it sounds pretty bizarre, but since there is a spiritual side to it, I just thought you might be interested in what he had said in the past."

Luke wondered if Jonathan really believed what he was saying or if he was somehow competing with David by playing the 'spiritual' card.

"So you're saying that God told him to write this code?" Luke asked doubtfully. Jonathan hesitated a moment and then nodded. Luke furrowed his brow and then shook his head.

"I think we're dealing with a guy with a huge ego problem that likes to play God with people, but that's where it ends," Luke finally replied, but Jonathan shook his head.

"Have you seen the code?" Jonathan asked, already knowing the answer. "It's not like anything that I have ever seen before. He'd come into the office in the morning after one of his 'upgrade nights' as he would call them and have thousands of lines of new code written that somehow compiled perfectly." Luke furrowed his brow again as he tried to come up with an explanation. "Luke, it was weird and it freaked Ronald and I out every time. Ronald worshiped him because of it, I was just afraid of him," Jonathan said nervously. "When you kept standing up to him, you gave me the courage to do the same. But based on what I saw and what he said, I still believe that he never wrote the Cat Eyes code." Jonathan could see the incredulous look on Luke's face at his suggestion. "Luke, he wrote the first version of the Cat Eyes program in one weekend. No prior discussions with us about it before, in fact the Friday before he was deep into the latest release of another game program that he was struggling to complete and was way past deadline, and that was just regular code, then Monday morning he walked in the door with a basic Cat Eyes demo unit that he had managed to crudely integrate with the game module over the weekend, with a brand new operating system that worked almost flawlessly." Jonathan stated and then looked at Luke. "He then demanded that everyone was to call him Apollo from then on."

Luke leaned back in his chair and tried to sort through the logistics of writing that much code over a weekend. He had never believed it when Apollo claimed that he had written a whole operating system so quickly, but now that Jonathan was supporting that claim, he was stupefied.

"Jonathan, he'd probably been secretly working on the code for months or years and then just decided to reveal his finished work after a hard weekend," Luke replied to Jonathan who again shook his head at the suggestion.

"We thought that too, but we had just received the new game console system unit the week prior. We couldn't get the original game code that was written specifically for it to work, let alone a whole new operating system. He installed the software onto the new system and wired up the glasses to it in one weekend," Jonathan replied and Luke tried to think through how Apollo may have accomplished such a feat. "I'm telling you, it was weird. Ronald and I talked about it for months trying to sort out how he did it, but we never could figure it out." A strange shiver passed through Luke and he tried to formulate a response, but could not come up with one that was based on sound reasoning.

"Well, I appreciate you sharing that with me. I'm sure there's a reasonable explanation for it, I just can't think of one right now without more information," Luke replied and then tried to divert the discussion. "Are you coming to the study tonight?" Luke asked, not sure if he really wanted him to come or not. Jonathan seemed to hesitate a moment, then nodded.

"Yeah. I've studied out what I want to cover. I hope I don't hurt David's feelings or his faith," Jonathan replied and seemed truly concerned.

"I'm sure David will be gracious and humble to what you have to share with him. I'm looking forward to it as well," Luke replied with a smile and Jonathan looked at him as if he was trying to read Luke's thoughts.

"Are you starting to believe in Jesus?" he asked and Luke felt very uncomfortable with the question and was unsure how best to answer it diplomatically.

"Hmm, well, I'm warming up to the idea," Luke said politely. "I feel like I'm standing in what I sense is a very big and dark cavern and I'm holding a light in my hand that is gradually getting brighter and brighter, revealing more and more of the cavern around me. I still don't know how big it is, or if there is even a way out of it, but the brighter the light gets, the more willing I am to take a few steps to search for one," Luke replied, "I just don't know which direction to go." Jonathan listened intently and nodded.

"Hopefully after tonight, you'll have a little clearer idea as to which is the right direction to go," Jonathan replied as he stood up to leave.

Luke thought about what Jonathan had said as he headed back to his desk. Was that all he was waiting for? "To know the right direction to go?" The brief research he had done showed that there were many denominations of Christian churches, each seemingly offering a different teaching or perspective on scripture, and each thinking that they had found the hidden secret within scripture that made them more right and all the others somehow more wrong. *What a confusing mess*, Luke thought. He then thought about what Jonathan said about Apollo and how he came to develop the code for the Cat Eyes product.

Luke suddenly had a strange thought enter his mind and in response, he did a quick search online to quench it. He typed in "Greek mythology Apollo" and took a look at the various results. Apollo was the Greek god of prophecy, archery, healing, light and truth and he was the god of the sun. Luke read a little more, but kept coming back to the words "prophecy, light and truth" to describe the god and thought how odd, yet appropriate for Stanley to suddenly choose Apollo as his nickname when he began the Cat Eyes project. Was it just odd, or did Stanley really buy into the whole Apollo persona as Jonathan had alluded? Did he think he was somehow fulfilling a prophecy with the Cat Eyes? Luke thought about the scripture in 1 Corinthians 4:5 that David had shared with him two nights ago that talked about "*the Lord's coming, bringing light to what is hidden and expose the motives of men's hearts*." Luke was pleasantly surprised he could even remember the scripture and had a basic grasp of what it said.

"Prophecy, light and truth," Luke mumbled. Was there some spiritual correlation or was it just someone twisting history to fit his or her ego? As he sat in silence, he suddenly realized that he had so much to do and very little time to get it done. He slid up to his computer and reviewed his schedule for the rest of the day. It was packed with one meeting after another. He took a deep breath, somewhat annoyed, as he thought what a distraction this had become for him. He thought about picking up his cell phone and sending a text message to David and Jonathan to say the he was going to cancel the Bible study for tonight and focus on work, but then remembered Jonathan telling him that he was all set for the event. Luke was looking forward to hearing the two of them battle it out over their views and prove further to Luke that Christianity, or any religion, was all a mess and a big waste of time. He thought about typing it anyways, but a message alert popped up on his screen reminding him that he had a meeting in five minutes.

Four meetings and 6 hours later, most of the major fires had been put out for the day. Cliff also let him know that they would be interviewing, well interrogating was perhaps a better word, Apollo, or "Stanley" as Cliff always corrected him, at 10 a.m. the next day at the undisclosed holding facility. Luke knew that they would have their specific questions, but he took a few mental notes of questions that he would like to ask him if time allowed.

Luke spent the rest of the afternoon preparing the two working system units and glasses, along with three battery packs, for the interview in the morning. He tested both units and made sure they were each loaded with the most stable, non-ghosting, software version. He then packed them and checked them back in with security. With all the meetings, he had missed lunch again and decided to pay a visit to the vending machine in the employee break room in the other office. As he walked through the office, he kept his eyes open for Danielle. It was too early for the day to be over, but when he got to her desk, she was not there. However, as he turned down the hallway, he saw her standing with two other people at another desk. She looked up to see him looking at her and smiling. She gave him a smile back and then held up one finger and made a questioning face, which asked if Luke could wait for a moment. He nodded and pointed to the break room and she acknowledged his unspoken response. Luke smiled as he thought about how well they had gotten to know each other and how they often kidded that they could almost read each other's minds. As he grabbed a granola bar and a cup of coffee, he sat down and started eating as he waited for Danielle. He didn't realize how hungry he was until he took the first bite and actually enjoyed the taste of the granola bar, something he normally did not prefer but would choose to eat because it was supposed to be healthier for him.

Several minutes later, she walked into the break room and sat down across from him. She was as beautiful as always, brightening the room and his heart with her smile.

"It's great to see you," she said, looking into his eyes. He nodded and fought the urge to reach out and take her hand in his.

"You're as beautiful as ever," he replied.

"Thank you, so what's been going on with you? I keep hearing all sorts of things coming from your side of the security wall. Is everything going okay?" she asked and he nodded.

"Well, even if it wasn't, I'd have to tell you it was or they'd kill me." he said seriously and then smiled.

"So, is this 'all work and no play making Luke a dull boy' or are you still managing to get out and cause some trouble?" she asked, smiling. Luke wondered if she already knew about how things turned out with Monica.

"I've discovered that I don't need to go anywhere but the office to find all the trouble I can handle," he said knowing she already knew about Apollo, but guessed she did not know about the guy that tried to kill him the night before. He suddenly remembered thinking about her in the middle of it, and how worried he had been that it was Danielle, not Angela that had walked into his house in the middle of it all. Before he realized he was speaking, it came out. "Just between you and me, a guy broke into my house and tried to kill me last night." Feeling almost embarrassed for even saying it, he watched her response. At first he could tell she was waiting for him to say he was just kidding, but when he didn't, she suddenly put her hand to her mouth in shock.

"Are you okay?" she asked in shock, and then nervously kept talking, "I mean obviously you're okay, but what happened?" She stopped and waited for him to respond. He tried to think of the best way to explain everything without mentioning the Cat Eyes product, which just happened to be what precipitated the incident.

"I saw a pedophile stalking a young boy at the mall and confronted him on it. It apparently made him mad enough to later pay me a visit at home with a gun," He explained quickly and hoped it would stop there, but somehow knew it wouldn't. Danielle seemed to hold her words in as she waited for more information, but then realized that there might not be anymore coming.

"So, you talked him out of it?" she asked and he at first thought about it and then frowned.

"Talked him out of it?" he exclaimed in a disappointed voice. "I was kind of hoping your first thought was that I had overpowered him, wrestling the gun away from him. You know, big tough, manly Luke?" he said sarcastically and acted disappointed.

"So, you did end up talking him out of it," she said sarcastically back at him, not wanting to play along. He smiled and shook his head and laughed at the thought of what really happened.

"Actually a women who I at first thought was you did all the wrestling and disarming," he said. He could tell that something struck a nerve with Danielle at his words.

"A women that you thought was me?" she asked in a rather confused way and waited. He realized that he had said too much and that it would be very difficult to explain things after making that mistake.

"Yeah. Angela, she works with the government on the new product," he said as he tried to think a way through the minefield.

"And you thought she was me because?" she asked the leading question that he knew was coming but could not think of a way to navigate through it.

"Umm, when he had the gun pointed at me, she came into the apartment and interrupted the guy," he answered quietly. "All I could think about at that moment was that you had dropped by and that he was going to hurt you as well." Luke said and waited for the "why did she have a key?" question that he knew would be coming next. There was a long silence before she spoke.

"You both ended up being okay?" she finally asked and Luke nodded.

"Yeah. She apparently is trained in martial arts," he replied and then continued, "The guy was on the floor so fast; he never saw it coming." She never asked the "elephant in the break room" questions of who was Angela, why did she have a key, and why she was at his apartment. Luke could tell she was uncomfortable with it, but refrained from asking about the obvious missing elements of the story.

"He's in jail, right. I mean he's not coming back? she asked, the concern evident in her voice. Luke nodded. She breathed a bit deeper then smiled.

"I'm just happy you're both okay," was all she said in response and then her previous demeanor returned and she changed the subject. "David tells me that the two of you have had several spiritual discussions, are you finding the answers you're looking for?" she asked and Luke remembered Danielle and his last discussion on the matter.

"David is definitely a great source of knowledge on the matter, but Jonathan has been trying to help as well," he replied and then contemplated his next response. "I'm trying to grasp what my true motives for this search are. It's all very confusing at the moment." He wondered if she understood that she had been his primary motive for pursuing the information, not to have a relationship with God. "The way David presents things seems a little extreme and a minority viewpoint in the Christian world, while Jonathan's perspective is a lot more palatable and mainstream." She seemed to be ready to say something, but then stopped. Was that doubt he saw in her eyes? Did what he say generate doubt or questions on what she believed? "Care to share what you were thinking?" he interjected and she seemed to hesitate.

"It's strange that you would say that, because I was just reading a scripture this morning in 2 Timothy 4:3-4 that for all the reading I did, for some reason God put it on my heart to take the time to memorize that verse today," she said and looked up at him strangely and then quoted the scripture from memory. *"For the time will come when men will not put up with sound doctrine. Instead, to suit their own desires, they will gather around them a great number of teachers to say what their itching ears want to hear. ⁴ They will turn their ears away from the truth and turn aside to myths."* Her response was not what he was hoping for, nor was the scripture what he wanted to hear. He thought about the words of the scripture and then why she had chosen that one to memorize today and ultimately to share it with him. He tried to find a way to joke the moment off, but couldn't come up with anything. Was he just looking for the easy path to God and for others who felt the same?

"Interesting scripture," he said rather flatly in response, but inwardly, he was still thinking about it and its implication on his perspective.

"I'm sorry. I don't want you to think I was preaching at you, it just came out," she said sincerely and smiled.

"No, it's all good," he replied. "I must admit that I was hoping for a more agreeable scripture that would have verified my deep knowledge and intellect, instead of one that put me in a time out." He said sarcastically with a smile and she rolled her eyes and smiled back.

"Trust me; you could use a lot more time outs," she joked back and he nodded in agreement.

"Well, David, Jonathan and I are getting together again tonight, so who knows, maybe I can add a few more under my belt before we see each other again?" he said sarcastically.

"A few would be a good start." she returned his sarcasm and then suddenly glanced at her watch and stood up quickly. "I told them five minutes, it's been ten and they are still waiting for me. I've got to get back to that meeting." She moved toward the door. "Thanks for the visit and the talk. I look forward to hearing how it goes tonight. And make sure you ask all the questions you need answers to," she said and then with a smile and a wave, she was out of sight.

Luke sat there thinking about their brief discussion and then about the scripture she had shared. Although it was appropriate for the moment, he was more curious as to what caused her to memorize that particular scripture today. Was it just a coincidence, or was it something else? Was there a spiritual aspect to it, or was David guiding her based on what they had been studying? Luke had a hard time believing that David was somehow orchestrating it all just to convince him of a God. He smiled as he tried to envision all of the resources and intelligence work it would take behind the scenes for that to happen. "Impossible," he said as he stood up from the table and headed back to the secure side of the building. As he passed the security check in, he thought about Cliff and all of the people working covertly for him. If they could do it, was it out of the realm of possibility to believe that David could do it too? The idea seemed ludicrous to Luke, but prior to last night's happening with Angela and the pedophile, and two days earlier with Apollo, he probably would have said the same thing about Cliff and the possibility of all the intelligence work that he now knew was taking place. As he sat back down at his desk, he resigned himself to the fact that he had very little control of what took place behind the scenes in his life and that worrying about it was not going to help.

He tried to knock off a few more items from his ever lengthening to do list and even thought about working late, but his hunger and the meeting with Jonathan and David vetoed the thought. He logged off and headed home.

Chapter 22

It felt strange to walk into his apartment after the previous night's events. It felt more like a crime scene than his home and memories would flash back into his mind at every turn. He made sure no one was following him as he walked up his steps and then quickly shut and locked the door behind him. Based on the fact that his life was saved last night because of the government "listening in", there was a small part of him that liked the idea of someone being there to make sure he was all right. Knowing that Angela, or another agent would charge through the door at just the right time to put some serious hurt on any intruder that might want to cause harm gave him a little peace, but the larger part of him still felt upset and violated by the intrusion. As he put the groceries away, he thought about a life filled with Big Brother looking over his shoulder every step of the way and then decidedly shook his head.

"No thanks," he said out loud, almost as if he was speaking to some hidden microphone that might be still listening in.

He thought about what it might be like to be the watcher instead of the watched, and liked the notion. He'd like to have the ability to know immediately if someone he loved was in trouble so that he could take action to protect him or her. A sort of super hero, but even then, he could not come to grips with the idea of someone hearing and seeing a person's every moment. Was a person the sum of their actions? What about allowing a person to change? He sat on the couch and stared at the bloodstain on the floor and thought about his life and let various scenes flash through his mind, some he was proud of, while others, not so much. Would he want to be judged by what others saw?

Would he feel the same if there was nothing he was afraid of them hearing or seeing? If he completely trusted the individual, knowing that even if he did say or do something stupid, that they would keep it confidential and just between them, would he still feel the same about it? Maybe, but he was smart enough to know that there was no such person that he would be willing to give that much trust to, except perhaps his mother. Even then, there were too many things he had done in his life that he was still too embarrassed to even talk about.

His mind returned to the Cat Eyes and realized that he once again faced the dilemma of the product and what it meant for the world. Is it just another tool for the government to use in secret to make sure their people stayed within their boundaries, or would it eventually cross over into mainstream, every day life? Could you trust any government with such power? Apollo already demonstrated that you could not trust the private sector with it. To think he was now the front man that would be ushering in this life changing, even world changing, technology to society almost made him sick to his stomach. Would his epitaph read, "*Luke Baker, he opened the eyes of the world and drove everyone into hiding.*"

Luke just sat there thinking through all the consequences for the hundredth, or was it thousandth time, since he began working on this product. He finally did what he had learned to do in the past to get past it, he tried distancing himself by ignoring his thoughts and feelings. If it weren't him standing there, it would be someone else, like Apollo, who had far less scruples. Perhaps he could have some sort of positive impact on the products use to lessen the impact that it would have on society. *Doubtful*, he thought.

Luke finished his dinner of reheated leftovers, washed and put away the dishes, and then decided to read over the notes and scriptures until Jonathan and David arrived. He wanted to be more prepared this time, to be more ready to ask the questions that needed asking, not just sit back and listen like he had done in the past. He read through the scriptures on seeking God with all your heart and once again tried to grasp the basic principles of them. From what he could gather, it came down to the basic understanding that until he was willing to seek God with all of his heart, he would never find God. Was he willing to do that? Is that what Danielle had decided to do? *All of his heart*, the words echoed in his mind as he tried to grasp what that might look like and how difficult it might be just to test that theory.

Based on the scriptures and the discussions he had with David and Jonathan, God had already done the hardest part and gave everything so that he could have a relationship with him, now he was expecting those who would seek him to have the same heart-level commitment if they were to truly find him. Luke sat back in his chair and thought about the scriptures, his response to them, and all the doubts he had about them. He thought about the Cat Eyes. Could it really have a spiritual connection with scriptures in the Bible? David kept trying to tie in the glasses to the spiritual world, a world that David believed was around them, even using scriptures to talk about it. It was all very interesting and thought provoking for Luke, but he still found it very hard to believe that there was a correlation.

"But what if there was?" Luke said out loud and then looked around the room and tried to imagine what Elisha had revealed to his servant in 2 Kings. He tried to imagine chariots of fire, unseen armies of angels and demons, all battling it out in some mysterious world around him. "Battling over what?" he mumbled and then blew out a deep breath at a concept that seemed too ethereal to grasp.

He looked over the scriptures that talked about God's Word. How it was *"God breathed,"* that it *"judges the thoughts and attitudes of the heart,"* and was *"useful for teaching, correcting, rebuking and training in righteousness."* Did he believe that about the Bible? A week ago he would have laughed at the idea, or made fun of anyone who believed it, but what about now? What was going on inside, that now there was a possibility of his believing?

He read the scripture in <u>Matthew 15:1-9</u> about how traditions can nullify God's Word, how Jesus said, *"These people honor me with their lips, but their hearts are far from me. They worship me in vain; their teachings are but rules taught by men."* Luke always thought of the Bible as a book of rules, not teachings of the heart. Had man twisted the words so much that the truth was no longer being taught, or had changed so much that all worship was in vain? He tried to grasp how upset God would be if that were the case. All his hard work and sacrifice was for nothing.

And finally he read in <u>John 8:31-33</u> where Jesus stated, *"To the Jews that had believed him, Jesus said, 'If you hold to my teaching, you are really my disciples. Then you will know the truth, and the truth will set you free.'"*

"Set free from what?" Luke mumbled the question. *From doubt, from guilt, from sin, from unbelief?* he thought and continued reading the scripture in search of the answer.

[33] They answered him, "We are Abraham's descendants and have never been slaves of anyone. How can you say that we shall be set free?" [34] Jesus replied, "I tell you the truth, everyone who sins is a slave to sin. [35] Now a slave has no permanent place in the family, but a son belongs to it forever. [36] So if the Son sets you free,

you will be free indeed. [37] I know you are Abraham's descendants. Yet you are ready to kill me, because you have no room for my word. [38] I am telling you what I have seen in the Father's presence, and you do what you have heard from your father."

[39] *"Abraham is our father," they answered.*

"If you were Abraham's children," said Jesus, "then you would do the things Abraham did. [40] As it is, you are determined to kill me, a man who has told you the truth that I heard from God. Abraham did not do such things. [41] You are doing the things your own father does."

"We are not illegitimate children," they protested. "The only Father we have is God himself." [42] Jesus said to them, "If God were your Father, you would love me, for I came from God and now am here. I have not come on my own; but he sent me. [43] Why is my language not clear to you? Because you are unable to hear what I say. [44] You belong to your father, the devil, and you want to carry out your father's desire. He was a murderer from the beginning, not holding to the truth, for there is no truth in him. When he lies, he speaks his native language, for he is a liar and the father of lies. [45] Yet because I tell the truth, you do not believe me! [46] Can any of you prove me guilty of sin? If I am telling the truth, why don't you believe me? [47] He who belongs to God hears what God says. The reason you do not hear is that you do not belong to God."

Luke read the scripture again trying to get to the heart of it. These Jewish people clearly believed in Jesus, and were very religious, but apparently they were not willing to truly believe let alone obey him. Because of that, they were still somehow slaves and not set free from their sins. They claimed that they were God's children, but Jesus said that in fact they were children of the devil.

"Wow," Luke mumbled and thought about how Jesus didn't beat around the bush with these guys. He actually admired the way that Jesus dealt with their religiousness. He read the verses again looking for more. He was surprised to see that these people went from believing, to wanting to kill Jesus when he challenged them on their obedience to his word. That they had no room for his word, and that their father, the devil, did not hold to the truth either and that "the reason they did not hear" is that they did not belong to God and remained in their sins. As Luke tried to wrap his mind around all that he just read, he realized that there must have been a lot more that lead up to this confrontation and he decided he would read the whole chapter of John 8 later that night.

The loud knock on the door made Luke jump as he flashed back to the previous night's memories, but then realized that it was just a few minutes before 7:00 p.m. and Jonathan and David should be arriving any moment. Even with that in mind, he still cautiously looked through the peephole to check who it was before opening the door, something he had never done before. As he looked, he could see Jonathan standing there, but his heart jumped when he saw another figure coming up the steps behind him. At first Luke was worried that it was someone dangerous, but then he recognized David just as Jonathan turned to converse with him. Luke closed his eyes at the realization that his whole sense of security and perhaps even his confidence had changed drastically since last night and it really upset him. He let out the deep breath that he realized he had been holding then opened the door and invited the two of them in.

They regrouped around the kitchen table where they had sat during the last study, but Luke could tell that Jonathan was holding some feelings toward David. David, on the other hand, seemed relaxed and cordial to Jonathan. Luke could also see that David was trying to get a read on Jonathan as they talked.

"Well, shall we get started?" David finally asked and everyone nodded. They started with a prayer which David led. Luke sensed through the words that David was using in the prayer, that he anticipated that the evening's discussion would be stormy and he asked for humility, patience and grace for everyone. He also focused a great deal of his prayer on letting the Bible be the standard of truth to verify what they would be studying out, not feelings or someone else's views or opinions. Luke felt it was a very encouraging and disarming prayer and instead of feeling uncomfortable about someone praying, this time he actually enjoyed listening to it.

With all the tension in the air, Luke was looking forward to the discussion, it made him think about a high school football game between two rival schools, but both of these men were his friends and was very concerned about how things might end. Did he even know what it was that he was supposed to be listening for tonight? David's words interrupted his thoughts.

"So gentlemen, so far we have studied out in the Bible what it means to "seek God" in order for us to find him. Then we studied out what God says about His Word, the Bible, and how it is exactly what God wants us to know and obey. We agreed that it, the Bible, would be the ultimate "measuring stick" that we would use to either verify or disqualify what we believe and teach. Agreed?" David asked and they all nodded. "Good. Did everyone go over the scriptures that we studied out last time?" David asked and Luke nodded and although he had only finished moments earlier and he felt a bit guilty like a kid cramming for a test. Still, he was happy to be able to say that he had. Jonathan at first hesitated, but then nodded as well.

"Okay then. Well, tonight, with those foundations firmly established, were going to take a look at what God's definition of a Christian is." David said and opened his Bible. "Turn over to Matthew 28:18-20. Jonathan, would you read that for us?" David asked and Jonathan nodded as he was turning pages.

"Then Jesus came to them and said, "All authority in heaven and on earth has been given to me. [19] *Therefore go and make disciples of all nations, baptizing them in the name of the Father and of the Son and of the Holy Spirit,* [20] *and teaching them to obey everything I have commanded you. And surely I am with you always, to the very end of the age."*

David looked up at the two men sitting across from him. "These are some of the last words that Jesus shared with his disciples before being taken up to heaven. These were the men he had been training and pouring his heart in for the past three years of his ministry. Being that these were his last words, how important do you think they were?" David asked. Luke thought about how in the movies when a dying person was held in their loved ones arms, or those of a hero just before they rode off into the sunset, or even a coach just before his team took the field, the last words were always important.

"I'm guessing pretty important," Luke said and smiled and David nodded.

"Exactly. In fact, Jesus even prefaces the moment by reminding his eleven disciples that 'all authority' had been given to him. So based on this scripture and his last words, what is it that Jesus wants everyone to become?" David asked and waited. Luke thought it was a little strange that he did not see the word Christian, but disciple as the answer.

"Christians," Jonathan answered, Luke raised an eyebrow, but David did not respond but looked at Luke.

"Disciples," Luke said and then David nodded his head, but Jonathan seemed bothered by it.

"To make 'disciples.' What is a disciple?" David asked.

"A follower or imitator of someone," Jonathan replied and David nodded.

"Correct. So who do you think he wants these guys to make disciples or followers of?" David asked.

"Jesus." Jonathan gave the obvious answer and seemed proud of it.

"So Jonathan, what is a Christian?" David asked and Jonathan seemed to contemplate the question a moment.

"Someone who believes in Jesus," Jonathan answered and David nodded.

"Is a Christian a follower of Jesus?" David asked and Jonathan hesitated a moment before answering.

"Yes."

"So what is the difference between a Christian and a disciple?" David asked and everyone remained quiet. "How many times do you think the term Christian is used in the Bible?" David asked, Luke just shook his head at first and took a guess.

"One or two hundred times?" Luke guessed and Jonathan seemed to be in agreement.

"Just three times. Even then, the first time the term Christian was used was over 7 years later in <u>Acts 11:25-26</u> where it says *"the disciples were called Christians first at Antioch."* It was a nickname of sorts, a derogatory term meaning little Christ's given to the disciples by others. For the first seven years of the young church, they called themselves disciples of Christ, but essentially, both terms refer to the same group of people," David said and Luke was surprised to hear that.

"So, there's not a difference between the two, they mean the same thing," Luke stated and David nodded and smiled.

"Exactly. So what does he want these guys to do?" David asked.

"Make disciples," Luke answered, "of all nations and to baptize them," Luke said in an attempt to answer David's next question before it was asked.

"Yep, all nations. And who is a candidate for baptism?" David asked.

"Disciples or followers of Jesus," Luke replied and David nodded.

"As you can see, these are pretty straight forward," Luke smiled and looked over at Jonathan who remained quiet and emotionless. David seemed to notice it as well.

"Jonathan, you okay?" David asked.

"Yes," Jonathan finally said rather coldly and David seemed to patiently ignore the coldness of the response and continued.

"So what is the last thing he wants these guys to do with these newly baptized disciples?" David asked.

"Teach them to obey everything that Jesus had taught them," Luke replied and David nodded.

"So if Jesus wants everyone who is to be saved to be a disciple, how important do you think it would be to know what it means to be one?" David asked and the room was at first silent. Luke could see that Jonathan was still upset about something, so he gave the obvious response.

"Very," Luke stated but he saw Jonathan suddenly begin shaking his head.

"Baptism is not part of the salvation process," Jonathan suddenly released the pent up frustration that had been building inside him. "You're trying to make it sound as if baptism is required, but it's not." He looked at David who sat quietly a moment before responding.

"For the sake of staying on course for this study, could we put the whole baptism question aside a moment? I know you're loaded and ready to have a debate over that topic, but that's not the most important concern right now," David asked.

"Then what is?" Jonathan asked and David seemed to be hesitant to answer, but then nodded.

"Helping Luke to develop faith in Jesus and his Word is my goal. What is your goal?" David asked.

"You mean faith in your false doctrine?" Jonathan shot back strongly and then glanced over at Luke.

"Have I shared anything in our studies that are not read directly from the Bible and in context?" David asked and Jonathan seemed to contemplate the question a moment.

"Have I?" David calmly asked again but very directly and Jonathan finally shook his head.

"No, not yet."

"Well please let me know when I do, because I never want you to feel as if I'm misleading you, or Luke, or anyone else for that matter from what is taught clearly in the Bible." David waited until Jonathan nodded, although Luke could tell that Jonathan was still very agitated. David continued, "So would you agree that you need to be a disciple, or follower of Jesus, before you become saved?" Jonathan seemed to be searching for the trick within the question.

"You need to believe in Jesus, so yes, you need to be a follower of him, but you do not need to be baptized," Jonathan replied curtly. David seemed to wrestle with how to continue from here.

"Okay Jonathan, it doesn't look as if were going to be able to move forward without tackling this big elephant standing in the room. But before we get started, can we agree to establish some ground rules so that it will protect our personal and working relationship with each other?" David asked Jonathan, who seemed to hesitate and then nodded his head.

"Sure," Jonathan replied curtly as David collected his thoughts and continued.

"First, no one gets mad, we stay calm and respectful to each other, second, we only use the Bible as our basis for explaining our belief, no using outside literature or opinions, unless they are supported by scripture; and finally, we do not launch into an unending soap box rant, but we allow the other person to respectfully interject their support or rebuttal during the discussion," David said and waited for Jonathan to respond. "Are we in agreement?" Luke could tell Jonathan was in deep thought before finally nodding his head.

"Agreed."

Luke was surprised at how quickly the conversation had become so intense and wondered why such strong emotions were brought out by this topic.

"Why is the baptism issue so controversial to the two of you?" Luke asked and looked at them. David motioned for Jonathan to reply if he wished.

"It's not to me, but it is to David," Jonathan replied and David seemed surprised by Jonathan's statement and then smiled. Luke was having trouble understanding the significance of the whole issue.

"If it's not important to you, why do you keep bringing it up in our Bible studies?" Luke asked Jonathan, but Jonathan did not seem to want to answer, so David finally replied.

"Because if it is a salvation issue, then it means Jonathan is either right and saved, or wrong and not saved. I think that is that the crux of the issue. Is that a correct assessment Jonathan?" David asked Jonathan.

"No, it means you're not saved if I'm right because you have missed God's grace," Jonathan snapped back at David who seemed to take a deep breath before replying.

"I'm always confused by the perspective that if someone believes in baptism as a part of salvation, then they are not saved," David said and shrugged his shoulders. "Can you please explain it to me? Because, I believe in Jesus, I believe in his Word. I also have faith that God can do anything he desires. I believe you need to repent of your old life. I believe our sins are forgiven when we become Christians. I believe that the Holy Spirit is given to Christians. I believe that you cannot earn your salvation, but that it is a gift from God." David paused a moment. "Our difference is not a 'works' based or faith based issue, it is about our understanding of when we believe our sins are forgiven and when we receive the Holy Spirit," David said and then looked at Luke. "Hopefully, by using the Bible as our ruler, either Jonathan will convince me and you of what he believes the Bible teaches, or I will convince you both as to what I believe it teaches," David added and Luke shrugged his shoulders.

"Okay then. I guess I'll let you two discuss it and see how it all unfolds," Luke replied, anxious to see why this doctrine topic seemed so important to them.

"Okay Jonathan, you're up. Why don't you share your views on baptism and any supporting scriptures and we can discuss each one as we go along," David said calmly and motioned with his hand toward Jonathan. Jonathan removed from his briefcase a thick folder filled with papers and notes, and laid it on the table and opened it. Luke recognized most of it as the material he had downloaded and brought the last time they had met. Jonathan took a moment to review his materials and to gather his thoughts, and then looked over at Luke and smiled as if asking if he was ready. Then he turned to David.

"David, with all due respect, I believe that your church is a cult, what your church teaches are false doctrines, and the evidence I present will prove that fact," Jonathan stated aggressively as if he was a trial attorney speaking to a jury. Luke smiled inwardly at Jonathan's attorney approach and somehow expected David to stand and yell, "I object!" to counter Jonathan's accusations. Instead, David waited calmly and patiently for Jonathan to continue. Luke suddenly realized that he was positioned as the jury of one that the two men who were trying to persuade.

"Baptism is a works based action that does not incorporate faith, but makes salvation something that must be earned. The Bible makes it clear that faith alone, belief in Jesus is what saves us, not baptism," Jonathan stated emphatically and waited for David to respond.

"Those are pretty strong accusations, can you now show me scriptures that support your views," David replied calmly. Jonathan nodded and started again firing out scriptures as fast as he could read them from his notes.

"Romans 10:9, *"That if you confess with your mouth, "Jesus is Lord," and believe in your heart that God raised him from the dead, you will be saved."*" Jonathan said and looked down and began reading another scripture from his notes. "Ephesians 1:13-14, *"And you also were included in Christ when you heard the word of truth, the gospel of your salvation. Having believed, you were marked in him with a seal, the promised Holy Spirit, who is a deposit guaranteeing our inheritance until the redemption of those who are God's possession—to the praise of his glory."* And then in Ephesians 4..."

"Wait, wait, Jonathan hold on!" David interrupted, "we agreed that we would allow the other person to respond along the way, not just 'rapid fire' scriptures like bullets that could be taken out of context. Right? Let's be Bereans and examine if what is being said is true." David said and Jonathan hesitated as he looked at his list before him.

"There are just a few more, then we can…" Jonathan started but David shook his head.

"That's not what we agreed to, nor does it give the whole Bible a chance to speak clearly," David interjected and Jonathan seemed perturbed at the interruption to his flow but assented.

David began turning pages in his Bible, "Why don't we start with <u>Romans 10:9</u>." He said and then looked up when he got there. Luke was still turning pages when David started again. "Jonathan, when you're writing a subprogram within a software program, can you just drop in a section of code anywhere you want to and have it work perfectly?" David asked and waited for the response.

"No," Jonathan replied.

"What do you need to do for it to work?" David asked.

"The sub-program needs to reference the source files it is using, which are generally located in the primary project folders and subfolders."

"And if you don't reference those source files in the folders and subfolders?" David continued.

"It will either break the overall program, or the sub-program won't run in conjunction with the source code."

"Exactly," David stated and then tapped his Bible. "Just like with software code, the Bible has core source files, or core principles, and all the books and letters to the churches are written with those core principles in mind. It allows us to always go back to the "source code" so to speak, to see if what is being taught is true." Jonathan and Luke both nodded in agreement with the analogy. "Now each book or letter that was written to the first century churches in the New Testament is essentially a subprogram of the primary source code. Like a subprogram, it acts as its own letter as well; referencing its key points and purpose, but it is also there because it is built to support the main purpose of the Bible." David added and hesitated a moment and smiled, "Did I lose anyone?" Both of them shook their head.

"Since we're talking about code, would this be considered overtime that we could bill the company for?" Luke joked to try and lighten the moment and everyone smiled.

"Sorry, we're off the clock," David replied. "Okay Jonathan, with that in mind, let's go back to the first scripture you read. Who is the letter to the Romans written to?"

"To the Romans." Luke answered confidently and David nodded slightly.

"Yes, but specifically to which residents of Rome?" David asked.

"To the Christians living there," Jonathan replied.

"Exactly. So these Christians are already clear on what the foundations of their beliefs are, since they are already Christian's right?" David asked and they both nodded. "So would Paul need to re-explain every aspect of the core teachings of Christianity each time he wrote a letter?" he asked and they seemed to both think about it. "I mean, it would be like me having to explain to my wife, each time I wrote her a letter, exactly who I was, how we met, and even describe what I looked like?" David stated and then continued, "There are just obvious facts that each of us knows in our relationship that do not need to be mentioned each time I write to her, right?" David asked and they both agreed.

"So what does this have to do with Romans 10:9?" Jonathan asked.

"Well, using our analogy, you're referencing a scripture without acknowledging the source code or core principles," David replied.

"I don't understand what you mean by that," Jonathan responded a little annoyed.

"Jonathan, I totally agree with Romans 10:9, *that if you confess with your mouth "Jesus is Lord" and believe in your heart that God raised him from the dead that you will be saved.* But that scripture follows what Paul the apostle stated earlier in his letter and is not meant as an exclusive teaching, but one that is in conjunction with what he stated in Romans 6:1-7, where he talks about when we make that statement of faith or belief, *"What shall we say, then? Shall we go on sinning so that grace may increase? By no means! We died to sin; how can we live in it any longer? Or don't you know that all of us who were baptized into Christ Jesus were baptized into his death? We were therefore buried with him through baptism into death in order that, just as Christ was raised from the dead through the glory of the Father, we too may live a new life. If we have been united with him like this in his death, we will certainly also be united with him in his resurrection. For we know that our old self was crucified with him so that the body of sin might be done away with, that we should no longer be slaves to sin— because anyone who has died has been freed from sin."* He talks about "us" and "we" in this verse, laying the groundwork for what he will be adding later. So you can't profess one statement at the end of a letter as proof of a belief, while ignoring a statement that was written earlier in the letter that the latter verse was built on." David waited for Jonathan's reaction.

"I disagree, but what about Ephesians 1:13-14?" Jonathan challenged and David furrowed his brow at the response.

"Let's stay focused on our current scripture a moment longer. You disagree with which part? That the two verses in the letter do not support each other, or that because you do not believe in baptism, it makes the point irrelevant?" David asked.

"I just do not see the supporting relationship of the two verses," Jonathan replied and Luke was surprised at Jonathan's response. Luke understood David's explanation and how the prior scripture would support the latter one, although he was not sure exactly what each explanation in the verses meant. "So what are your thoughts on Ephesians 1:13-14?" Jonathan said and steered away from the earlier scripture. David appeared to want to continue the initial discussion, but then resigned to addressing the next scripture and read it to himself.

"Again, I totally agree with the teaching of the scripture. In it he talks about *being marked in him with a seal, the promised Holy Spirit, who is a deposit guaranteeing our inheritance.* But again it is not an exclusive verse, but one that is inclusive with the rest of the core teachings of the Bible. The real question we need to understand is "when do you receive the Holy Spirit?" Can you show me, in the scriptures, when that occurs?" David asked and Jonathan sat quietly a moment before answering.

"When you believe, not when you are baptized," Jonathan answered without using a scripture and held David's gaze.

"Alright, so do you believe a person needs to be baptized?" David asked and waited.

"Not to receive the Holy Spirit or to have his or her sins forgiven. Baptism is a response to your belief, but not necessary for salvation," Jonathan stated.

"So do you even need to be baptized?" David asked.

"No, it is simply an outward sign of an inward grace. I mean you can be baptized if you wish, but it is not required in order to be saved," Jonathan replied and David leaned back in his chair a moment in apparent thought, and then leaned forward and turned a few pages in his Bible.

"In Acts 2:36-41, Peter is speaking at Pentecost, and the the words he is about to use launches the start of God's church, his earthly kingdom. Peter not only tells us exactly when we receive the Holy Spirit, but I also want you to notice that what he teaches does not match your professed doctrine. *"Therefore let all Israel be assured of this: God has made this Jesus, whom you crucified, both Lord and Christ." When the people heard this, they were cut to the heart and said to Peter and the other apostles, "Brothers, what shall we do?" Peter replied, "Repent and be baptized, every one of you, in the name of Jesus Christ for the forgiveness of your sins. And you will receive the gift of the Holy Spirit. The promise is for you and your children and for all who are far off—for all whom the Lord our God will call." With many other words he warned them; and he pleaded with them, "Save yourselves from this corrupt generation." Those who accepted his message were baptized, and about three thousand were added to their number that day."*" David leaned back in his chair again and looked at Jonathan. "So Peter is speaking to a group of non-Christians, who, after learning who Jesus was, are now asking Peter to tell them what they should do to be right with God. What was his response to them?" David asked and Jonathan did not even look at the scripture.

"I know this is the scripture that your church uses to support your teaching on baptism," Jonathan stated curtly and David seemed to frown at the words.

"I'm not talking about churches. I'm talking about what it says in God's Word, which we both have in front of us and it says the same thing," David said and the room was silent. "So that means you're saying that we either changed the meaning of the scripture or that we are taking it out of context?" David asked and waited for Jonathan to answer.

"Out of context." Jonathan finally answered.

"Okay, so walk me through the scripture and show me where it has been taken out of context," David said and pointed to his Bible. Jonathan looked down and stared at the verses, but did not reply. After several minutes, seeing that Jonathan was not going to answer, David finally interrupted the awkward silence.

"Luke, according to this passage, what was Peter's response to those people that were "cut to the heart" and wanted to know "what shall we do?" What were the steps he had them take?" David asked and Luke read through the scripture again.

"First repent then be baptized…" Luke started but was interrupted by David.

"Who did he say should be baptized?"

"Every one of them." Luke replied.

"No mention of belief?" David asked, but Luke did not see any and shook his head.

"Do you think they believed?" David asked Luke.

"I would think so. It would be pretty silly to go through all of that if they didn't," Luke said.

"So why did Peter say they needed to be baptized?" David prodded.

"To have their sins forgiven," Luke replied.

"Their sins had already been forgiven," Jonathan interjected. "They are baptized *because* they already have their sins forgiven, not *for* the forgiveness of sins." Jonathan stated and smiled proudly.

"I actually have studied that very same question when I was first studying the Bible. It was confusing to me too until I looked that specific word up in Thayer's Lexicon," David said calmly in response and then continued, "The "for" that you state means "because of" is the Greek word **eis**, which means "entrance into, towards, for" but not one time in the thousand plus times that **eis** is used in the King James Version is it translated "because of." Jonathan, I strongly suggest that you study that out in greater depth, not just believe what someone tells you," Jonathan frowned at David's response.

"So, as this Bible translation writes, as well as every other translation, that at baptism their sins are forgiven. And what would they receive when they were baptized?" David asked.

"The gift of the Holy Spirit," Luke replied and looked over at Jonathan as he thought about the scripture Jonathan used in Ephesians 1:13.

"Is this just for those standing there?" David asked and Luke scanned the scripture again for the answer.

"Nope, it was not only for them, but for their children and their future generations as well if I'm reading it right."

"So would you say this is a perpetual command, a core teaching?" Luke nodded.

"So did everyone listen and obey?"

"No, it sounds like he had to do a lot more talking and pleading to convince them," Luke replied and kept reading knowing that another question was coming.

"So who got baptized?"

"Only those who accepted Peter's message."

"Were those that did not get baptized considered to be one of their number?" David asked and Luke just shook his head. "So we don't see Peter telling them to just believe, but to act on that belief in order to have their sins forgiven and to receive the Holy Spirit."

During the whole interaction with Luke, Jonathan sat quietly, but was slowly rocking back and forth in his chair as he stared at his notes in front of him.

"Jonathan, I'm not discounting belief in Jesus, or faith in his Word. I'm fully embracing it. The only difference between what we believe is that you choose to disregard his teaching that baptism is the point in time when a person's sins are forgiven and when they receive the indwelling of the Holy Spirit and when they become children of God." David sat quietly a moment.

"I just don't agree," Jonathan finally replied without looking up from his notes.

"I get that. Let me ask you, when were you born?" David asked and Jonathan replied.

"July 12, 1983."

"When did you become saved?" David asked Jonathan, who seemed to think a moment before answering.

"When I was fourteen, I prayed Jesus into my heart," Jonathan replied.

"Summer, fall… do you remember the date?" David asked, but Jonathan at first just shook his head, then finally replied.

"I think it was during the summer. What's your point?" Jonathan replied curtly again.

"If you know the exact date that you were born physically, don't you think the date that you became a child of God would be even more memorable in your mind?" David asked.

"Maybe," Was all Jonathan said in reply and Luke could tell he was uncomfortable with where things were going.

"The reason I ask is in Romans 6:1-7 we read that our baptism is the actual participation in the death, burial and resurrection of Jesus, so that we too may live a new life."

"I was born again when I believed." Jonathan stated confidently.

"The "born again" scripture you are referencing is in John 3:1-8 where Jesus talks about being "born again" in order for a person to enter the kingdom of God. In verse 5 it says, "*Jesus answered, "I tell you the truth, no one can enter the kingdom of God unless he is born of water and the Spirit.*" What do you think Jesus was thinking of when he said water and spirit?" David asked.

"The baptism of the Holy Spirit," Jonathan answered.

"And the water part?" David asked.

"Living water flowing out of us," Jonathan replied, but David frowned at the response.

"Living water? So you see no correlation between the water encountered at our baptism and the Holy Spirit in Acts 2:38?" David asked and Jonathan shook his head.

Luke could tell that Jonathan had shut down emotionally and perhaps even mentally, even though David was trying to work through the discussion. David tried to come at the discussion from another angle.

"Okay. Then let me ask you this, when we are "born again', whose son or daughter, whose family do we get to be a part of?" David asked.

"God's," Jonathan replied.

"Did this "sonship" apply to Jesus as well?" David asked and Jonathan raised an eyebrow and then shrugged.

"He already was God's son." Jonathan replied.

"Correct, but what about when he walked the earth as Jesus the man?" David asked and Jonathan did not know how to respond.

"Again, what is your point?" Jonathan responded curtly and David raised his hands as if to say "take it easy".

"Okay, let's cut to the chase. When Jesus was born of Mary, was he God's son?" David asked.

"Yes, the Holy Spirit came upon her and she became pregnant," Jonathan replied.

"Correct, but did God announce that Jesus was his son when he was born?" David asked and Jonathan nodded, but David shook his head. "Actually, he didn't. He had the angels announce that a savior was born, Luke 2:9-12, but God the Father did not speak," David stated and then continued. "What about at 12 years old? In Luke 2:41-51 we see Jesus state that he was in his Father's house. Jesus is well aware of whose son he was, but God remained silent," David stated and based on Jonathan's response, David could tell that Jonathan was getting frustrated with the dialog.

"Okay, last scripture, let's read Matthew 3:13-17." They turned over to the chapter and verse. "Luke can you read that for us?"

"Then Jesus came from Galilee to the Jordan to be baptized by John. But John tried to deter him, saying, "I need to be baptized by you, and do you come to me?" Jesus replied, "Let it be so now; it is proper for us to do this to fulfill all righteousness." Then John consented. As soon as Jesus was baptized, he went up out of the water. At that moment heaven was opened, and he saw the Spirit of God descending like a dove and lighting on him. And a voice from heaven said, "This is my Son, whom I love; with him I am well pleased."

"So we see that Jesus was on a very clear mission to be baptized. Did Jesus need to have his sins forgiven?" David asked and Jonathan shook his head.

"Jesus was sinless." Jonathan replied.

"So why was he there?" David asked again and Luke saw the verse that held the answer, but Jonathan did not respond.

"To fulfill all righteousness," Luke replied in order to keep things moving forward.

"Correct. We see that he was fully immersed, not sprinkled, since it says he came up out of the water. But what is really amazing, is what happened the moment he came up out of the waters of baptism," David stated and waited for a response.

"The Holy Spirit came down on him," Luke replied and David nodded.

"What else?"

"God speaks," Luke replied.

"After thirty years of silence in Jesus' life, God picks this particular moment in time, after he comes out of the waters of baptism, to not only send the Holy Spirit to land upon Jesus, but to announce from Heaven that Jesus is his son! So with this in mind, do you think this 'new birth' was just an outward sign of an inward grace, or was it part of God's design for salvation for everyone? Was it a particular moment in time that you become a son or daughter of God, the moment in time when you fulfill all righteousness? This simple act of obedience, yes Jonathan, your *baptism*, puts things in motion that forever changes our destinies, just like it changed Jesus'."

"How did it change Jesus' destiny?" Luke asked curiously.

"It was at this point in time that Jesus started his ministry and when he performed the first of many miracles." David explained, "Born of water and spirit: his baptism is what Jesus was talking about in order for us to be "born again" to enter his Kingdom. He was talking from experience." David looked to Luke and then Jonathan. "Do you think it is just a coincidence that the direction that Peter gives to those who asked him "what shall we do" in Acts 2:37-41 just happens to be the exact steps that unfolded for Jesus at his baptism?" David asked.

"You said that we wouldn't launch into any soap box rants without giving the other person a chance to respond," Jonathan snapped at David without answering his question. David shrugged.

"I've paused many times to allow you an opportunity to respond or to share scriptures, but you never said anything, so I kept going with my points. Sorry about that. Would you like to back up and address or discuss each scripture that I shared?" David replied sincerely.

Luke, ignoring Jonathan's response, was actually excited about what David had been saying. When he weighed the two presentations, he felt strongly that David had indeed made the case that the questions was not to be baptized or not, the real issue was more a matter of why you get baptized, when you get your sins forgiven, and when you receive the Holy Spirit. In spite of now understanding this, Luke was still undecided as to whether he even believed that God existed and what he should do with this new information.

Luke decided to try to help move the conversation along. "So Jonathan, you believe you are saved because you believe. David, you believe you are saved because you believe and are baptized?" Jonathan nodded, but David shook his head.

"I believe I am saved by the grace and love of God, I did not earn it, or work for it. But based on God's Word, I believe that gift of forgiveness and the Holy Spirit comes from obeying his Word and fulfilling all righteousness," David replied and Luke worked his way through the multi-faceted answer.

"It seems like such a small point, I mean, going under water, I mean I do that all the time. In the big scheme of things, is it really that big of a difference?" Luke asked, trying to find common ground for the two to land on. David looked toward Jonathan allowing him the chance to respond to the question, but Jonathan remained silent. Luke could see that David was gathering his thoughts before finally responding.

"Luke, you make a good point. This is either the most ridiculous argument that professed Christians have battled over these past few hundred years, or it's the most grievous false doctrine that could be designed," David stated.

"How so?" Luke replied.

"For me the most frightening scripture in the Bible is not in the book of Revelation, with the plagues, four horsemen, and such, but it is in the words that Jesus spoke in the gospel of Matthew. In Matthew 7:21-23, Jesus tells those listening to him the following;

'Not everyone who says to me, 'Lord, Lord,' will enter the kingdom of heaven, but only he who does the will of my Father who is in heaven. Many will say to me on that day, 'Lord, Lord, did we not prophesy in your name, and in your name drive out demons and perform many miracles?' Then I will tell them plainly, 'I never knew you. Away from me, you evildoers!'

"This scripture frightens me because it talks about religious people, people that truly believed in Jesus enough that they called him Lord, who even did amazing things in his name. But Jesus drew a line in the sand and said that only those that do the will of the Father in heaven will enter his Kingdom. Because they didn't, he tells them that he never knew them. The all-knowing God of the universe never knew them? Or did it mean they remained in their sins and could not approach him on a relationship level? These people were going about their lives thinking that they were good to go with Jesus, only to find out that they were still unsaved, not a part of his family, never having the indwelling of the Holy Spirit with their sins remaining unforgiven." David stopped and let the words sink in. "I just know that on that day I do not want to be one of those people. It is more than a technicality Luke, it is an act of faith expressed in obedience to God's command to be baptized for the forgiveness of sins. I don't want that fate for me, my family, or for my friends."

"God is not that cruel, he wants everyone to find him. He's not going to base it on whether we were baptized or not," Jonathan finally responded and David nodded.

"I think God has done everything he could to make it clear, God even wrote it down for us to read in case we forget, or are misled. But Jesus makes it very clear in <u>John 12:48</u> on what will judge us. *"There is a judge for the one who rejects me and does not accept my words; that very word which I spoke will condemn him at the last day."* His Word, what he taught and lived out as an example for us to follow, will judge us," David ended and took a breath.

Jonathan just shook his head back and forth and started gathering his notes and folders and putting them away. "I know you're wrong, but I just don't know enough of the Bible to prove it," he said.

"Then for everyone's sake, study it out and find what is true. I'm not asking you to believe me; I'm asking you to believe what God says in His Word," David replied and then smiled, "Jonathan, you're as stubborn as Naaman in the Old Testament in <u>2 Kings 5:1-18</u>. Simple obedience was all that was asked of him, but because it was not the way he wanted it to be, in fact it was easier, he refused to obey. Look it up if you feel up to it." Jonathan did not write down the scripture reference, but Luke did.

Luke and David watched as Jonathan finished putting away the last of his notes and pushed his chair away from the table and stood up. "I'll see you guys tomorrow?" Jonathan said with little emotion. The two of them nodded and said their goodbyes again and watched as the door closed behind him.

"That went well." David said sarcastically after a few moments and Luke smiled.

"You think?" Luke replied and then chuckled, "Tomorrow should be a blast." He ended and then let the seriousness of the subject matter revert the conversation to its earlier tone. "I know this will generate an obvious answer, but do you really believe there is a heaven and a hell?" Luke asked David. "I mean, with forces of good and evil fighting each other in some invisible realm, all while we are totally oblivious to it?" David weighed his words carefully before responding as he glanced past Luke and into the living room.

"Well, I've never had the opportunity to be Elisha's servant, so I can't tell you based on what I've seen that one exists, nor can I show you that there are invisible armies of good and evil fighting over our very souls. But I do know what I have seen happen in people's lives who pray, or who pray for others, and the improbable and impossible outcomes that have resulted from it. Could it be a mere coincidence? It could be, but the odds of such things happening on their own, without outside influence, are too great to believe in them being just a random accident," David replied and looked into the living room again and raised an eyebrow. Luke thought that maybe David was playing a joke on him.

"See an angel or something?" he asked David without turning around and falling for the joke. David looked back at Luke and shook his head.

"Is that a blood stain on the floor?" he replied with deep concern and Luke remembered the evening before and turned to look at the stain on the floor. He had called a carpet cleaning company and set up an appointment to have it cleaned, but now he was kicking himself for not covering it up.

"Uh, yeah," Luke finally replied trying to figure out how much to tell David about what happened. Luke thought through the events and then remembered that he had prayed just before the door opened and Angela came to the rescue. Was it God responding to his prayer, or was it just coincidental timing? As he thought about it, he could argue both sides of the perspective. But if she had arrived even one second later, it would not have mattered to Luke which perspective was correct. He would have been dead. "Someone tried to kill me last night," he said almost distantly in reply. David laughed and then stopped when he saw that Luke was not laughing.

"You're not kidding are you?" David more stated than asked. Luke shook his head, still wrestling with the whole prayer or coincidence debate. "What happened?" David pressed the point, seeing that Luke was still deep in thought. Luke tried to think of something clever, or heroic to say, but nothing came to mind.

"The guy who slashed my tire came into my apartment with a gun, but one of Cliff's agents had discovered who he was and followed him to my place. He was in the process of shooting me in the head, when the agent came in and stopped him," Luke said distantly as the words came out of his mouth and David sat silently and tried to read Luke's face.

"Wow. That's crazy. I take it someone got hurt?" David asked as he looked back at the bloodstain on the floor and Luke nodded. "That must have been very…"

"I prayed," Luke interrupted David and then looked at him. "I said a prayer, an apology to God, as the man aimed the gun at my head," Luke continued to stare at David, "and the agent walked in that very moment." Luke waited for a response from David, who just sat silently observing Luke and then took a deep breath.

"Well, apparently God accepted your apology," David replied with a smile and then continued, "I imagine there are a lot of thoughts going through your head based on where you were before and where you are now?" David guessed correctly at what Luke was feeling.

"I don't know what to think or what to believe," Luke said and took a deep breath. "I feel confused, excited, grateful, terrified, even amazed by everything, but I'm not sure which one is going to win out."

"Maybe you should just focus on gratitude for awhile and pray that everything will become clearer as time passes," David replied and Luke thought he could handle that. They both stared at the stain. "Want some help cleaning that?" David asked and Luke tilted his head and then shook it.

"I think I'll just slide the recliner over the spot," Luke replied and David nodded in appreciation.

"Ingenious solution! The incredible problem solving mind of a man, who can match it?" David replied sarcastically and Luke nodded and smiled at his jest. "Yeah, kind of like this baptism thing, just pull a chair over it and pretend it isn't there."

They sat around a few more minutes, but David could tell that Luke was on the verge of passing out from exhaustion. It had been a very trying twenty four hour. Luke thanked him for coming and for the study and his friendship as he closed the door. It had been a good day and a good study. He tried to think of the next step he should take spiritually. Things were starting to become clearer to him. He decided that he wanted to learn more, then turned and walked to his room and sprawled on his bed. He was asleep as soon as his head hit the pillow.

Chapter 23

One fumble, one drop of the ball at a critical moment can change the whole game. Strange, Luke thought, *how quickly things can flip flop.* Luke sat in the room preparing for the interview with Apollo. He could not help but think about how things had turned so dramatically. Less than a month ago, he was wondering if he could even hold on to his job, based on the rocky relationship he had with Apollo. Now, he basically had his job. He pushed the carrying case under the table and tested the Cat Eyes for the third time and then finally nodded to the man at the door. Cliff had introduced the man to Luke when he arrived that morning, but after a series of names and handshakes, his recollection of his name faded. He was happy to see Angela and took a moment to kid around with her before going into the secure room to set up for the interview. *Interview, is that what he should call it?* Luke wondered, knowing that it was more of an interrogation, but with the help of the glasses, he imagined there would be less need for 'water boarding' to extract the answers they were looking for. Perhaps there were more positives to this product than he cared to admit.

Luke slid the glasses off his head and onto the bridge of his nose and verified the color spectrums and waited. A few minutes later the door opened and Cliff motioned for someone, who was just out of sight, to enter the room ahead of him. As Apollo walked in, he saw Luke and gave a cold, dark smile. Luke immediately saw the color spectrum change to a dark red, then further darken to black, before it lightened again to dark red. Apollo did not say a word. Neither did Luke. Apollo, following Cliff's direction, took the chair across from Luke. Luke could see the hue that corresponded with deep fear in the color spectrum, still the dark red hue indicating hatred toward him was the most prominent of the colors.

"Stanley, I hope you've been treated well during your stay with us," Cliff stated, but did not look up for a response as he took a chair to Luke's right and opened up a thick folder that he had carried with him. "Now you told us that you would like to cooperate to the fullest extent possible in order to potentially have your sentence reduced, is that correct?" Cliff asked and Apollo nodded. "Please verbally answer all the questions that are asked."

"Yes. I would like to explore that option further," Apollo replied and Luke could see that he was being truthful. Cliff and Luke had prearranged a signal under the table as to whether or not Apollo was telling the truth when answering Cliff's questions. When Cliff sat down, he slid his foot next to Luke's. The signal was simple, if Apollo was not telling the truth, Luke was to bump his foot against Cliff's, if he was being truthful, he would do nothing. If Luke got mixed signals, he was to tap Cliff twice to signal him to explore the line of questioning further.

Cliff took the first twenty minutes to do a summary of Apollo's history. Luke was amazed at the detail of the information that had been gathered by Cliff's team. Operatives had apparently been watching Apollo immediately following the Iraq trip and had compiled a great deal of dirt on Apollo. It appeared that much of the code that he had written in the past, not only with Samuel, but prior employers, he had attempted to sell to other game companies. Luke felt almost ashamed for Apollo as more and more information was revealed about his unethical practices. The more he learned, the more he disliked him. He would have thought that Apollo would have felt the same sense of shame or at least some embarrassment as his ugly past was paraded in front of everyone, but he instead almost acted proud of it. Luke found it was disconcerting how much information they either had on file or could dig up, on a person.

Cliff then focused his questioning on trying to determine who was involved with Apollo's plan to sell the product to which buyers. Although Apollo was being truthful in his answers, Luke could tell from the color spectrum that Apollo was having a great deal of difficulty answering them truthfully. In addition, each time Cliff mentioned or referred to "the buyer" Apollo's fear level would jump dramatically and Luke could see that Apollo wanted and intended to lie, but would then shift back and answer truthfully.

Although resistant at first, they eventually learned, much to everyone's surprise, that Apollo had not initiated the search for a buyer, but was instead approached by an outside entity who had heard about the product. The entity, although interested in the functionality of the current version of the Cat Eyes operating system, was more interested in having Apollo develop an enhanced version of the software.

"They weren't interested in the current version?" Cliff asked and Apollo just shook his head truthfully. Cliff seemed perplexed by the new discovery and Luke could see from his color spectrum, that Cliff was having trouble deciding what direction to take the questioning.

"For what purpose?" Cliff asked and Apollo shook his head and then answered after he saw Luke write something down and slide over to Cliff after he had signaled him.

"They wanted the ability to separate the sheep from the goats," Apollo replied, and they all frowned and raised an eyebrow at the response.

"Sheep from the goats? What exactly does that mean?" Cliff pressed Apollo for more details, but Apollo became more agitated as he tried to find a way to answer. Luke watched the level of fear grow dramatically within him.

"I want you to ensure that I will be protected. If I tell you everything, I want a whole new anonymous start," Apollo waited for confirmation from Cliff, who shrugged and motioned with his hands.

"It all depends on the value and detail of what you have to share with us," he replied and Apollo hesitated a moment, then nodded.

"They wanted the ability to identify those who would oppose their plans," Apollo finally stated and seemed to shake internally with fear.
"You mean a deeper understanding of people's motives? I thought the glasses already did that," Cliff asked and Apollo furrowed his brow and then looked over at Luke, then back to Cliff.

"They wanted the ability to identify the spiritual allegiance of individuals," Apollo said and the room went silent.

"You mean religious affiliations?" Cliff asked and Apollo shook his head.

"I don't know. They just directed me to write the code for them."

"Did they share why knowing that information was so important?"

"No."

"That's some serious profiling," Cliff replied and looked over at Luke and raised an eyebrow. Offering no response, Cliff sat back in his chair and ran his hands through his hair as if thinking.

"Okay, so tell me a little more about who you were working for. What were they offering to pay you for this enhancement?" Cliff asked and Apollo's spectrum seemed to shake with fear again as he struggled to answer the new question.

"Power and position," Apollo finally answered and actually blushed. Cliff started to ask another question, but then hesitated.

"In what? The company, with them?" Cliff asked incredulously.

"In their new order of things," Apollo replied and looked down and the hue of fear was evident again. Cliff exhaled and then started laughing.

"In their new order of things? And you bought into that story?" Cliff said as he continued laughing, "Stanley, I took you as being a lot smarter than that," and shook his head.

"You don't understand, there was a lot more going on," Apollo replied and his fear level shot up again. Luke knew that he was supposed to remain silent, but he could see Cliff was trying to pursue the greed side of Apollo's motives, but Luke knew that the fear was the motivation.

"Why are you so afraid?" Luke interjected and Cliff glanced over at Luke as if to say something, but then remained silent as he turned back to Apollo and waited for the answer. Luke could see that Apollo was afraid to answer the question, but at the same time desperately wanted to. "Apollo, you've never been afraid of anyone, yet this organization that you were working with has you scared to your core. Why?" Luke pressed the question. Apollo's spectrum previously had been flashing so many dangerous colors, but changed when Luke asked him the second time.

"They are powerful and dangerous and have connections in very dark places," Apollo finally said and a relief seemed to come over him as his hue lightened to yellow.

"And the power and connections is what drew you to them?" Cliff interjected and Apollo nodded. "So why come clean now?" Cliff asked.

"Because they promised to protect me, yet here I am and time is running out," Apollo replied.

"What do you mean time is running out?" Cliff asked and Apollo looked to the clock on the wall and shook his head.

"Apparently, my usefulness to them has run out," Apollo replied and then shifted in his seat.

"So, you've already delivered the software?"

"It's been written, but it has not been delivered yet."

"So where are you keeping it?" Cliff asked and Luke could see that Apollo was getting very uncomfortable.

"That's my negotiation piece," Apollo replied and Cliff and Apollo sat quietly staring at each other, until Cliff called for a brief break and asked Luke to join him outside the room. He picked up the folder and stepped outside.

Leaving two agents by the interrogation room's door, they walked down a hallway, and then stepped into a small office. Cliff asked Luke his thoughts on Apollo's story and responses.

"From the spectrum response, I believe he is telling the truth and has not delivered the software to the buyer yet." Luke replied nervously and Cliff nodded and then looked back at Luke with a concerned eye.

"How are you feeling about everything?" Cliff asked and Luke thought a moment about the last hour of questioning.

"Truthfully, it's a little unnerving to know how much you know about people," Luke admitted.

"On Wednesday evening you asked for transparency and truth since we're friends, so contrary to what my colleagues felt, I'm letting you in on the whole enchilada. No more secrets," Cliff said and Luke nodded.

"I appreciate the trust, although I'm not sure I knew what that would end up looking like. I hope I can keep your secrets," Luke said and smiled.

"No worries, that's why I have Angela," Cliff replied and smiled back and patted Luke on the shoulder. "Relax, I'm just kidding. Besides, no one would believe you anyway." Luke thought about it a moment and then agreed that he was probably right.

Cliff looked through his folder again and then back at Luke, "I've gotten most of the answers I needed, are there any questions you would like to ask?" Luke was surprised by Cliff's willingness to end the interview at this point.

"You're not going to pursue who this entity is who approached him?" Luke asked and Cliff seemed a little uncomfortable.

"Not with you present. If it is, who I think it is, you don't want to end up on the wrong side of this group," Cliff said with all seriousness.

"So you're just going to drop it?" Luke asked in shock.

"No, but I don't want you involved," Cliff replied.

"Do you know why they would want to identify, or profile, a particular group?" Luke finally asked and he could tell that Cliff wanted to answer the question.

"I think I have an idea, but again, you don't want to know," Cliff responded, "Any last questions you'd like to ask Stanley?"

"I would like to ask a few questions about the password protection on the demo unit you acquired from Apollo's place," Luke said.

"Okay, let's get back in there, but avoid the 'entity' line of questioning," Cliff stated firmly and Luke nodded.

As they sat back down around the table, Luke could tell that Apollo had relaxed a lot and that he was not as fearful.

"I know that there's bad blood between the two of you, but Luke has some questions he would like to ask about the product's software," Cliff stated and motioned for Luke to proceed. Luke was not ready for things to get bounced his way so quickly and Apollo could see it on Luke's face.

"Having problems with the code, Luke?" Apollo sneered. Luke wanted to fire some snide remark back at Apollo, but he knew that's what Apollo wanted so he took a different approach. Luke nodded his head.

"Very much so. That is some amazingly complicated code that you wrote," Luke said and then continued, "You did write it didn't you?" he said and watched for his spectrum colors.

"Yes, beautiful isn't it?" Apollo answered and Luke was surprised to see in his spectrum that he had not written the code. Or more correctly, based on the color spectrum, he had not written all of it by himself.

"I don't know. I've not been able to take a look at all of it." Luke replied.

"Good encryption is a bitch, isn't it? You'll never access it without me," Apollo said arrogantly and smiled, which really bothered Luke. He decided he would call Apollo's bluff.

"Let's be honest with each other, I know you didn't write the code, so that makes me think that someone else already has the data, which means your negotiation for early release, or a reduced sentence, or even a "new start" just ended," Luke said and Apollo was shocked at the statement and his spectrum turned to fear.

"I did too!" Apollo almost yelled back and looked at Cliff and pointed at Luke. "He's lying. He's trying to get revenge by destroying our arrangement," Cliff just shook his head and remained silent.

"You may have played a part in it, but someone else wrote the code," Luke pressed forward, playing out his hunch. Apollo seemed to shift in his chair a moment as he shook his head.

"*I* wrote it," he said emphatically. Luke saw that he was now telling the truth and now he was confused by the spectrum.

"You said it yourself. Time is running out in order to reach a deal with the government. Contrary to your belief, I'm here to try and help you, but unless you tell us the truth, then I doubt you will get the deal you hoped for," Luke replied and saw Apollo's spectrum change enough to be more receptive. "So, did you write all of the code, with no outside help?" Luke asked again and Apollo's spectrum started changing colors as he wrestled with his response. He finally decided to answer.

"I wrote it, but was guided by someone," Apollo started and then changed his wording, "something else." The spectrum showed it was a true response and both Cliff and Luke were confused by it.

"What exactly do you mean by someone, or something else? Did someone send you the code?" Cliff interjected. Apollo seemed to wrestle with how best to respond to Cliff's question, he then looked back at Luke and the glasses and took a deep breath.

"I know this will sound strange, but the code would come to me through meditation. I would meditate and go into a trance-like state at my computer, where I would write code based on what I desired to accomplish. When I came out of the trance, the code was written." In the strangeness of the explanation, Luke almost forgot to read the color spectrum, but remembered the colors had stayed strong in support of this statement. The room remained silent as everyone wrestled with the statement and Cliff started laughing. Cliff's foot tapped Luke's and Luke realized that Cliff was looking for a false response, but there was none to report.

"So you're telling me that you close your eyes and someone else writes the code?" Cliff asked, but Apollo shook his head and tried to formulate the words he wanted to use.

"No, I'm saying that I write the physical code, but it's as if someone else is writing the code through me," Apollo stated. Luke immediately thought about the scripture that David read about the writers of the Bible being carried along by the Holy Spirit, saying just what God wanted them to write. Could this be the same thing?

"Look Stanley, I don't have the time or the patience to play your games. I need to know who this source is that is providing you the code," Cliff asked.

"I don't know," he replied truthfully, based on the spectrum reading. Luke felt a chill run through him at the thought of what Apollo just said.

"I don't believe you," Cliff replied and Apollo raised his hands.

"I don't know what to tell you," Apollo replied and Cliff listened disdainfully.

"The deal is off, Stanley. If someone else has the code and for whatever reason they are providing it to you, and you don't know who it is or how we can reclaim it, then you have nothing to negotiate with." Apollo seemed stunned by Cliff's words and his anger and intent spectrum sudden grew dramatically.

"You don't understand! It's not a country or a person, but an invisible entity!" Apollo nearly shouted. "For some reason, they can't write the code without me."

"This is such a pile of nonsense you're trying to feed us. Do we look that stupid?" Cliff demanded. "I know the group you're dealing with and if they had you write the code, then they already have it," Cliff said and Apollo shook his head.

"No, the buyers are not telling me what to write, the invisible entity is. I never gave the buyers the upgraded code that they want," he pleaded truthfully. Luke again sat silently as he watched Cliff's spectrum jump into the reds. Cliff shook his head.

"The source Stanley, or no deal."

Apollo seemed to stew in his thoughts before responding. Luke could tell that he was telling the truth, or at least strongly believed in what he was saying. His spectrum was jumping in all directions before finally resting on a single hue of dark red with heavy black tones as he looked at the clock on the wall behind them. Luke could tell trouble was coming.

"I knew you would not work a deal. Do you know why I wanted to meet today and at this time?" Apollo suddenly stated coldly, but no one responded. "Because I know something that you don't and that if we ended up here, I could give you advanced notice of an event that will shock you into listening and helping me." His colors went even darker, and Luke could see Apollo's threat was true.

"No deal without revealing the source Stanley," Cliff replied. Apollo sat quietly a few moments, glanced at the clock again then smiled and looked over at Luke.

"How're the glasses, Luke? Everything working as the master intended them to?" His words had a sinister tone to them. *Master?* Was Apollo referring to himself as the master, or someone else?

"Fine. Good enough to know that you have something up your sleeve Apollo. What gives?" Luke asked, knowing that something was in motion somewhere for Apollo to suddenly have such inner confidence. Apollo smiled and turned back to Cliff.

"I could have helped save some code, but I'm not sure it would have mattered in the end," Apollo stated and let the smile fade from his face as he glanced at the clock again. Cliff shook his head and leaned back in his chair.

At that very moment, the spectrum on the glasses flashed once, then a second time, then went blank. The system unit had shut down. Luke glanced down to check the connections and the battery levels, and tried to reboot, but to no avail. He suddenly heard the laughter coming from Apollo. Luke looked up to see Apollo staring at him.

"Is something wrong, Luke?" Apollo asked sarcastically and Luke ignored him and looked at Cliff.

"The glasses just shut down and won't reboot," Luke said to Cliff who looked back over at Apollo.

"You just lengthened your stay with us dramatically," Cliff said, trying to regain the upper hand on Apollo.

"I figured my chances weren't that great anyways, but I knew I had this as my backup plan just in case," he replied and smiled. "Are we ready to talk about a full pardon now?"

"I don't negotiate with liars," Cliff replied and Apollo laughed.

"I didn't lie. But with no Cat Eyes, how will you know if I'm lying or not from here forward?" Apollo said smugly, "I guess without the glasses, we will all need to rely on our own talents and skills."

As Apollo and Cliff verbally sparred with each other, Luke tried to think through what had just happened. Apollo knew the exact time that the glasses would fail, so it was something scheduled. The software code, or perhaps even the operating system, must have had some shut down, delete or reformat code built into it to launch at a specific time. He glanced down at his spare unit and could not get it to load either.

"Cliff, I'm guessing that any software that is currently active, will have generated the time triggers to launch the protection program," Luke stated. Cliff nodded and slid back from the table and exited the room, closing the door behind him.

At first the two of them sat in silence, staring at each other. Then Apollo leaned forward. "I must say that of all the employees, I underestimated you the most," he stated and continued staring at Luke.

"You and I both know that with a little time and effort, there's always a way to break through code," Luke replied, ignoring Apollo's comment. Apollo just shook his head.

"Not this code. It was one of the concerns I had as well. They gave me the code to accomplish exactly what just occurred. But it's still available and I will give it to you for the right deal, or I can give it to them," Apollo said with a smile.

"Who are the invisible *they* that you keep referring to?" Luke asked.

"I told you, I don't know. At first I thought it was one of the many parts of our brain that we never use kicking in and I was just the first person that learned how to access it," he said and smiled again, "But, now, I don't think so."

"So how does it work exactly? How do you access it, or them?" Luke asked, trying to keep the discussion moving forward.

"I would just think about what I needed, and then meditate on it, and eventually I would fall into a deep trance," Apollo said.

"So why do you think that it was someone else writing the code?" Luke asked, getting more curious.

"Because when I was in the trance, I would hear voices. They would tell me what to type. As they spoke, my fingers worked, even though I had no control over them," Apollo said and then qualified his statement with, "I know it sounds strange, even bizarre, but if it was not for the code and functionality, I would not have believed it either."

Luke wrestled with the whole concept and the unbelievable story that Apollo was claiming as true. If it were not for his time studying with David, Luke would have classified Apollo as a complete nutcase. Now, he found himself starting to draw all sorts of correlations while at the same time trying to discount them.

"When did it start?" Luke asked, "These visions or trances?" Luke could see Apollo trying to think through the various events and timelines before answering.

"I got this vision of 'truth' stuck in my mind and spent a great deal of time thinking about the idea of a product that could deliver it. I sat up one evening and just meditated on the idea for hours and what I would be willing to give to have it and fell into a deep, altered mental state." He hesitated and then continued, "The next morning, after spending all night in the trance, I woke up and discovered that I had formulated the general overview of the product and even down to the sources and materials on which to build it with." There was an almost mystically quality to the way he was speaking. "It was incredible. After that, I would meditate almost every night and each time I would wake up with more answers and more code."

"Do you even understand the code that you have written?" Luke asked. His intuition told him that Apollo wanted to take credit for it, but chose not to.

"No," He finally replied. "Strange isn't it? I mean why me?" Apollo asked and Luke nodded and tried to think of ways to probe for more answers when he heard him mumble.

"I'm sorry?" Luke asked hoping to get Apollo to speak up.

"They called me Apollo," he said and then continued, "actually it was another name, but it meant the same thing." Apollo then seemed to drift off in thought momentarily, "I would be a 'hero of old" they said, like Apollo. Can you imagine it?" Apollo said excitedly.

"A hero of old?" Luke asked and Apollo nodded.

"Yeah, I got the feeling from them that there are other such hero's all over the world as well," Apollo said in all seriousness. Luke just wished he had the glasses to see if what Apollo said was true or if he was just toying with him.

"You said 'Master' earlier. Were you talking about yourself?" Luke asked casually and saw Apollo shake his head.

"No. There was one who had greater influence. He was leading the rest of those that were helping me. He was amazing," Apollo said distantly and Luke was starting to feel really uncomfortable by the conversation, but pressed on.

"Amazing? How so?" Luke asked.

"There was just something about him that makes you feel at peace. I felt drawn to him and his willingness to help," Apollo said.

"What do you mean?"

"When I saw him, I just…" Apollo suddenly stopped.

"You saw him?" Luke probed harder, but Apollo just shook his head.

"It just seemed like I could see him," Apollo replied and went quiet.

Luke tried to grasp whom these people were and how it was that they were able to interact with Apollo. Was this the spiritual issue that David had been alluding to since he came on board, or had Apollo truly lost his mind? Aside from this far reaching story, Apollo's responses seemed sane enough. Luke thought about the scripture that talked about the Word of God, how it will judge the thoughts and attitudes of the heart. Was this person Jesus? Could Apollo be speaking with Jesus and his angels in some invisible spiritual realm? The thought really worried Luke, but all he could do is shake his head.

"You don't believe me do you?" Apollo eventually interjected, obviously seeing Luke's head shake.

"I don't know. I think I'm more concerned with the idea that you're telling the truth," Luke replied. The door suddenly opened and Cliff walked in and looked at Luke and then at Apollo.

"Well Stanley, you've now added destruction of highly sensitive government property to your charges. Any additional charges we should expect to add?" Cliff asked and Apollo just shook his head.

"There was nothing I could do about that."

"More of a warning would have helped," Cliff shot back with a scowl.

"The only way you will get the code now and your Cat Eyes software active again is by pardoning my charges," Apollo said.

"Fat chance. You may have delayed the project, but we'll break the encryption code and figure out the software language. You, on the other hand, will be rotting away inside a high security prison with some very nasty roommates, who I will make sure have some very unsavory recreational pursuits," Cliff said and motioned to the door.

"He told me that would happen, but he also said to be patient and that help might be in the room with you," Apollo said and turned to look at Luke.

"Who told you?" Cliff asked and Apollo looked back at Luke again.

"You just shut down my job and cancelled my product, now your contact expects me to help you?" Luke stated.

"He said you might, but he said you still had a decision to make first," Apollo said and Luke's head swam and a chill went down his spine.

"Who's he?" Cliff interjected, seeming a little confused, but Apollo just held his stare with Luke.

"The 'he' is the entity that tells him what code to write," Luke answered and Cliff just shook his head.

"Luke, contrary to what Stanley is trying to sell you, that entity is nothing more than a covert group who drugged or hypnotized Apollo and either erased his memory, or replaced it with something that he believes to be true. They use key words to either activate or deactivate a scenario of their choice, at their set time. It's an old espionage trick that never worked real well, unless the person's character was weak or greedy, those people are very susceptible to such tricks," Cliff replied and Apollo suddenly turned back to Cliff when he heard the last part of his statement. Luke could see Apollo struggling with the idea or concept that he had been tricked, instead of being in direct contact with some powerful being.

"No. You're wrong," Apollo replied nervously, "I saw him."

"No. Unfortunately for you, I'm not. Your contact is now off in another country preparing to launch the code and the product, ignoring any agreement you may have had with them. They will launch it on their own, dump it on the market, sell millions of units, and you will never see a dime of it. Nor the power and prestige they promised and that you so desired that you would sell out to the highest bidder." Cliff spat out the words.

"Stanley, I would even venture to guess that having you locked up, removing you from the corporate world was all part of their end-game. They had you work out all the software details, build the prototype and even had you program in this "cover our tracks" shutdown on all the software, and then set you up to take the fall." Cliff paused to let that soak in.

"Sorry, but it's a very common process that less than friendly governments use on gullible and greedy people," Cliff said and shook his head sadly. Luke could see in Apollo's face that he was wrestling with the possibility that what Cliff had just shared could be true. "It might seem real, but the truth is, everyone but your 'spooky' friend loses in this scenario. The only pleasure I get from this is that you lose more than any of us." Cliff motioned for Luke to come with him and walked to the door. Luke gathered his gear and materials and joined Cliff at the door entrance. Luke took one more look back as Cliff spoke to Apollo, "If you think of anything else about your contact, or the product, or anything that might help your cause, have your guards contact me." Cliff stepped out of the door. The last thing Luke saw before the door shut, was Apollo still wrestling with the idea that he had been tricked by this unknown foreign agent, but then shook his head confidently as he stared back at Luke.

Cliff, Luke and about a dozen other agents and experts, spent the next three hours around a large conference table reviewing the video of the interview and discussing their various options. Interacting with other resources by teleconference and webcam, they proceeded to test various ideas on how to work around the fact that all online Cat Eyes related software had self-destructed at the exact same time, even live storage backups had been wiped clean. From a programming stand point this should have been impossible and it defied the logic of all who were working on the code.

They tried loading various offsite backups on new date changed systems, as well as many other processes that would make the date and time irrelevant, but the moment the code went live, or even simply powered on, the destruct code would launch and delete the file. All of the experts in the room had never seen anything like it. In their ongoing efforts to recover the software using standard processes, they were compromising many of their remaining backups. They decided to cease trying to recover the software on the remaining sources until a strategy was available that could succeed without destroying the source original. Their bigger concern was trying to determine the threat that the destruct code posed for the rest of their systems. Until they could find a way to break apart the code, they felt it was the highest security risk that the nation currently faced. One of the webcam agents interjected, "Any chance we're dealing with the *Dominus* group?" The agent on the web cam link asked and Cliff seemed to prickle at the question as did several of the other agents in the room.

"Maintain security protocol please," Cliff replied. Luke could tell the word was on the minds of other agents as well, but it was not something to talk about. *Dominus*, that was one of Apollo's file names that Luke had stumbled upon.

"One of the files I saw on Apollo's USB drive was named *Dominus*," Luke said but was quickly silenced by Cliff.

"I know." The room was suddenly quiet and no one seemed to know how to proceed until Cliff spoke again. "Focus on the code people. Don't waste our time chasing ghosts."

As they closed out the day and Luke was preparing to head home, Cliff was obviously frustrated at the repeated failures that they had encountered that day.

"I must be getting old, because I've never been out maneuvered as completely as I was today. Those behind this operation just set the espionage bar a whole lot higher than I've seen it set before." Cliff stated and shook his head again as Luke listened. "I don't know if it's the Russians, the Chinese or the Israelis behind this one, but we definitely need to retool and retrain if we expect to keep up with them, let alone avoid having our entire digital infrastructure completely destroyed by them." Cliff seemed to shift his thinking, "If they manage to attach this destruct code to other key resources, then they can wipe out every key data and security file we have or hold us hostage with the threat of it." Luke could tell that Cliff had nearly completely shifted his focus from Apollo and the Cat Eyes product to the imminent danger that the embedded destruct code represented.

"Dominus?" Luke stated the word quietly, knowing that Cliff was expecting it.

"An organization that has never been proven to exist, but we have encountered what can only be described as traces of it attached to various operations that we have broken up over the years. They either are a ghost, or perhaps the most sophisticated group we have ever encountered at foiling our attempts to ascertain their existence."

"So you've tried?" Luke asked and Cliff smiled.

"Yes, Luke, many have tried to gather some concrete intel on them. Hear me on this, you need to stay away from drawing their attention. I mean any at all. Those that have made it on their radar are now dead." Cliff stated and then looked at Luke, "Are we clear about that?" Luke nodded.

"What's our next step?" Luke asked.

"All we can do is to wait and see if Stanley is going to give up his source, or bargain a solution to the destruct code. If this destruct code is as dangerous as it appears, and Mr. Walpole decides not to cooperate, then we'll need to adopt more persuasive methods to find what we need," Cliff replied and Luke nodded, and then shook his head.

"I don't believe he knows. For whatever reason, or whatever it is that they have done to him, he does not believe he understands how the code works either," Luke stated.

"For his sake, he better figure it out. We need to know how to break the encryption in order to defeat it," Cliff looked at Luke.

"What do you want me to do with the Cat Eyes development team?" Luke asked and waited for Cliff.

"Luke, I'm sorry to tell you this, but getting the Cat Eyes product to market is no longer even on the agenda. This new security threat will take top priority until further notice," Cliff replied and could see Luke's disappointment. "We'll be pouring every available resource into this. I'll be happy to keep Danny, David and you on the payroll if anyone thinks they can assist in breaking this code, but Jonathan and Gloria should return to the game development side of the company. If Danny and David are not interested, we'll need to get them back to the game development side as well," Cliff stated and Luke nodded.

"I'll handle it when I get there, so you can focus on this issue," Luke stated.

"Aren't you going to ask about your job?" Cliff asked a little surprised.

"I was hired by the company to write a training manual for a product they are no longer selling. I think once we wrap things up, I'll be on the market for a more exciting job." Luke replied and smiled.

"Not interested in coming to work for me?" Cliff asked and Luke was surprised by the question.

"Cliff, I'm way out of my league with your group, you'd just be a dragging anchor behind you. I appreciate the offer, but I don't think I'd fill a need," Luke replied.

"I could use a trusted friend," Cliff said.

"I don't need a paycheck to be a friend," Luke replied and smiled and Cliff nodded.

"Thanks. Luke, I'm really sorry about all this. I know this means no stock option or bonus structure for you, but I appreciate your help."

"Oh gee, you mean I have to return to a simple, stress free life where no one is trying to kill me? How will I ever adjust?" Luke pantomimed sarcastically and Cliff smiled. Inwardly, Luke suspected that because he was privy to the existence of the ultra secret group *Dominus* and knew about a destruct code that was now at the top of the national defense threat list, the level of stress in his life would still be high.

They walked towards the exit of the building and Cliff halted at the door, "I'm curious, what do you think Apollo meant when he said *help might be in the room with you?*" Cliff asked, "Do you think he was talking about you or someone else?"

"It sure seemed like he was alluding to me, but I don't know how or why I would even be considered helpful," Luke replied and Cliff nodded.

"It has been a very strange day. We'll be pulling resources and backups from the office today, so I'm not sure if other than the Internet, they'll be anything left working there," Cliff added and waited for a response from Luke, who eventually nodded his head.

"I'll let them know when I get there."

"We'll be in touch." Cliff said and Luke agreed.

Chapter 24

Luke left the two, now disabled, Cat Eyes units and glasses with Cliff and his team, and then headed back to the office. Serena and a small army of agents had already left, taking with them a great deal of hardware and software from the office.

As Luke stepped into the main office, David and Danny were waiting for him. Luke just motioned for them to follow him and headed into the conference room. As Luke closed the door behind him, Danny immediately launched into a flurry of questions.

"What's up with the primary code? I'm in the middle of testing it and "poof!" it's gone! The same thing happened with every backup that I tried to access as well. Is the government shutting this down or something?" Danny asked and Luke held up his hand as if to ask him to slow down.

"At exactly 11:00 a.m. today, a powerful and very comprehensive destruct program that was embedded in the Cat Eyes code, activated and deleted all the code within the source files. No one knows how the program did it, only that any code that is accessed and activated, immediately launches the destruct program." David and Danny were both speechless.

"That explains why every time I tried to access anything, moments later it was gone." Danny finally replied. "So what do we do?"

"First off, don't access anymore backups, as were running low on them. Cliff is giving us the option to either return to the game development side of the company, or we can aid in cracking the destruct code," Luke stated and watched David and Danny look at each other and then back at him.

"Will we get paid to work on it?" Danny asked and Luke nodded.

"Yes, but I'm not sure how long they will keep us on payroll. It appears as if they are shutting down the Cat Eyes division, since there is no longer a product to deliver," Luke explained.

"Well if they'll pay us, then I'd like to take a whack at the code and try and make a name for myself," Danny said with a smile.

"What's your plan Luke?" David asked.

"If you guys did not want to stick around, I was supposed to shut things down and turn out the lights."

"Well, that would have been the shortest lived company that I ever worked for," David said and smiled. "If we can reach the two weeks mark, I might actually feel better about my career decision," David added sarcastically and everyone laughed.

"Okay, then. We do this for David's sake," Luke replied. "Do we have any pieces of the code that the destruct program did not destroy?" Luke asked and Danny nodded. "That's what we need to focus on for now. We should put whatever code we have on a computer with a formatted hard drive and freshly loaded programs. Keep it isolated from the network and the internet. Set up password protected access limited to the three of us and remove any chance of remote access tampering or triggering. Let's keep trying to understand how this code works so that we can either write a program to stop the destruct, or to access the destruct code to disable it. Other than that, the whole project is dead in the water." They all agreed to the new plan of attack. "Danny, can you get on that immediately while David and I talk about another project that I want him to tackle?" Danny nodded and headed out the door.

Luke ran his fingers through his hair as if he were going to pull it out. He looked up at David, who had taken a seat across from him.

"So what's really up?" David finally asked, insightful as always.

"Just before the Cat Eyes software shut down, Apollo told me that he did not write the code. He said he would enter into some sort of self induced trance, then be told by outside sources, what to write to create the Cat Eyes code." Luke looked at David for his reaction then added, "I would not have believed him, except during his response the Cat Eyes spectrum results showed that he was telling the truth." David raised his eyebrows.

"Well that's interesting, to say the least," David replied. "What does Cliff think about all this?"

"Cliff's theory is that Apollo was hypnotized by a foreign agency and subliminally made to believe what he said. He believes – even though Apollo does not - that Apollo actually wrote all the code and these agents, through repeated hypnosis or by activating trigger words, would then get Apollo to give them the new pieces of code with each new release," Luke stated.

"Wow, that's some deep spy stuff," David replied.

"Cliff feels that if these foreign agents had written it, then they would not have needed Apollo," Luke explained. David nodded at the suggestion.

"Money laundering," David mumbled.

"Money laundering, what do you mean?" Luke asked.

"Illegal organizations try to 'launder' their money through legal channels so that they can spend it without drawing attention to themselves. Perhaps this is a form of "code laundering" to get what they want built without letting people know who they are. It's just a thought," David said and then turned to Luke. "So what do you think is going on?" Luke was thinking about the code laundering idea that David had tossed out, but finally responded.

"I don't know what to believe. If Cliff says this is a common technique, then it makes sense. But if what Apollo says is true, then that is a whole different conspiracy to try to wrap my mind around. What you've said didn't make things any clearer," Luke replied dejectedly before continuing, "If I had not been checking out all this Bible stuff with you this past week, there is no way I would even consider anything other than what Cliff said as the only explanation." Luke looked at David and frowned. "But now that you've poisoned my reasoning with your spiritual mumbo jumbo, I'm having to consider the alternatives," Luke said with a smirk.

"Spiritual mumbo jumbo? After hours of teaching and reading, that is the analogy you chose to use?" David replied sarcastically.

"You even said yourself that this whole thing is spiritually freaky and there are too many correlations between the scriptures we read and this product to be coincidental." Luke stated and shook his shoulders as if he had a chill. "I'd like to go back to my old, familiar way of thinking, but you've totally messed me up," Luke replied.

"What makes you think I'm not the guy behind the hypnotizing and you are just one of my invisible agents?" David said and started moving his hand in a strange circle. Luke at first smiled, but then thought about the statement just as David said, "These are not the droids you are searching for." David started chuckling as Luke remembered the classic use of the "force" scene from the original Star Wars movie.

"Not funny David," Luke replied and shook his head.

"Sorry, you just seemed so intense about all of this. I just knew you were vulnerable." David smiled. "So what do we do from here forward? I mean, what do you want me to do?"

"I guess, just help Danny out as much as you can. Maybe you can think of some way to get by the destruct code."

"Okay, what's your plan?"

"I think I'm out of a job, or I'm the soon to be scapegoat that all the blame will fall on. It's a mess, no matter how you look at it."

"Maybe it's for the best?" David stated and seemed to watch for Luke's reaction.

"Do you think I had something to do with it?" Luke asked defensively, but David shook his head.

"No, but I'm curious as to how truly upset you are that it's been halted," David asked. Luke actually had not answered this question himself. When Cliff said that things were shutting down, he had been disappointed. Why was that? He still did not like the product, but being part of the team, even getting to lead it for a week had reminded him of the camaraderie that he had tasted in Iraq with the troops. In truth, he was not looking forward to losing that.

"I guess there is an inner satisfaction that it's been stopped. I just don't like the idea of some foreign power or spooky organization having the technology and using it against us. I also don't like the idea of someone causing the project to fail on my watch. That really gets me riled," Luke replied.

"So do we fight or flee in this situation?" David asked. Luke thought about the *Dominus* group and involving David any more than he already was.

"David, this is not your fight anymore. There is no need for you to get caught in the backlash of this mess. If I were you, I'd bow out gracefully and quietly head back over to the gaming side of the company," Luke replied.

"I asked you before if we were in this together or not, you said yes, so where you go, I go," David replied. Luke stared at David trying to read his expression and gauge the depth of their friendship.

"This could get ugly fast, especially when the blame starts falling around here."

"Are you saying that it could actually get worse than it already is?" David asked.

"Probably not. But then again," Luke replied and they both smiled.

"Let's get back to work, while we still have a job. I need to get to that two week mark," David said and they both headed back to their desks.

Luke spent the last part of the day meeting with Jonathan and Gloria and then arranging with Serena and the HR department that they get transferred back to the game development side of the company. Luke could feel that Jonathan still had a chip on his shoulder about the study from the prior evening, but he remained professional about the lateral move. Gloria was happy to be out of the Cat Eyes debacle. *I guess there will be no need for the weekend meeting that Gloria wanted,* Luke thought. What little remained of the day was spent documenting the interview with Apollo, writing an update on the status of the current staff, and then sending the status report electronically to Cliff and Serena.

As with most Friday evenings, everyone had left by the time Luke looked up from his computer. He realized that he had nothing else to do and no one else to see for the evening, so he decided to head home as well. As he slid back from his desk he saw the box of materials they had taken from Apollo's house still sitting under his desk. *Was it empty?* he wondered. He pushed the box with his foot and felt weight still in it. Luke remembered that the third systems unit and glasses were in the box the last time he had looked, so he pulled it out and saw that everything was still as he left it. He was surprised that they had left and knew that each copy of the code would be valuable to Cliff's code breaking team. He walked it over to give the box to security, but all the agents had already left. Apparently, since they had boxed and hauled everything else off earlier in the day, they felt there was nothing left that needed protecting in the office. Luke was surprised at how fast they could shut down an operation.

As he walked back to his desk, he thought about what he should do with the unit and glasses. The idea of leaving everything in the box on the floor of the office seemed risky and irresponsible, so he decided to at least place it in his desk, behind his folders and let Cliff know to have an agent come by and pick it up. As he picked up the systems unit, his heart sank as he saw that the Cat Eyes unit had not been shut down, but had been operating in energy saver mode. That meant the software destruct program had launched and destroyed the software.

He looked at the systems unit and touched the screen to confirm that it was no longer working, but to his surprise, he saw the request password challenge still visible. His heart jumped at the sight and he tried to calm his mind into understanding what that meant. He saw that the low battery notification was red, so using the charger cord; he plugged the unit into a wall socket and saw the low battery indicator switch to charging. His heart was racing as he expected to see the system shut down each time he moved or touched the screen, but the password challenge remained. *Did that mean the destruct code had not been installed on this unit?* Luke thought to himself. He set it on his desk and stared at it as he thought through what his next course of action should be.

If what Luke suspected was true, then the fact that the password challenge was still active, meant that he held the only working copy of the operating system and source code of the software. He reached to pick up the phone to call Cliff, but then stopped. The two lines of thinking finally collided in his mind. If Cliff was right about foreign agents directing Apollo, then the software needed to be brought to the market to equalize any advantage that the enemy would have gained. But if Apollo was right about a spiritual force guiding him to create the Cat Eyes for some sort of sinister profiling, then the whole product could come to an end right here and now by simply deleting the software and destroying the backup drive.

As he contemplated his dilemma, Luke realized that this was a multi-million dollar decision for him. With his stock options, twenty-five percent ownership, and position as team leader, he would be set for life. He would be like one of the perfect people at Monica's party. He also realized that his decision would affect the entire world, not just himself. Did he really want to see the whole world change by the emergence of this technology? He thought about Adam and Eve standing in the garden deciding whether or not to eat the fruit offered. *To know good and evil,* he thought. Did he want to take their decision, and perhaps the consequences, to the next level? What was even more difficult for him to get a handle on and perhaps the crux of the whole debate, was who was behind it all? Was it Jesus? Had he made this whole thing happen? Was it some kind of final punishment for the bad choices made by Adam and Eve? If so, would he be going against God's desires by destroying the product?

Luke spent the next thirty minutes wrestling with what he should do. He was surprised that he was even considering ending the life of the product and the legal consequences of doing so. Such an action would be no different than what Apollo had done with the destruct code and he knew the same penalty would await him. He thought about calling David to get his opinion, but realized that David would then be implicated if he decided to destroy the unit, so he changed his mind.

Quite contrary to his normal stance, personality and core beliefs, he decided to put it into the hands of fate. Instead of making a decision right now, he would make a few attempts at getting past the password challenge. If he failed, no harm done, and he would just send it over to Cliff and let his team deal with it. *What if I succeed?* he thought and decided that he would cross that bridge should he come to it.

As he held the system unit, he realized that all of David's efforts at overcoming the password had failed, but he also knew that David was trying to get around it, or break into it, by using outside software programs and code. Luke decided to avoid that approach and instead try a few relational passwords to see how this test of fate treated him.

He sat back and thought about Apollo and what his interests were. Luke typed in a variety of things that came to mind that related to Apollo, but no success. He then thought about their last discussion and what Apollo had said about those that were influencing him. *What was it that he had said?* Luke wondered as he tried to recall the conversation. "THEY called me Apollo." Apollo had said. "A hero of old" was the term he had used. Luke got an idea and did an Internet search on the words "hero of old" and scrolled through hundreds of topics, but did not find anything of interest. On a hunch, he typed in "Bible hero of old" and the first search result came up with <u>Genesis 6:4</u>, which read;

"The Nephilim were on the earth in those days—and also afterward—when the sons of God went to the daughters of men and had children by them. They were the heroes of old, men of renown."

Luke finished reading the scripture and then sat back, almost stunned.. The sons of God and daughters of men had children? That surprised him. Their offspring were the heroes of old, men of renown. He did a quick search on the "sons of god" and "nephilim" and found that the verse viewed them as fallen angels. The whole idea seemed strange to Luke. "So angels married earthly women and they bore them children." Luke let his mind race down the path of thought. *"So were the Greek gods the heroes of renown? Were they actually the offspring of angels and humans?"* Luke wondered. It would explain why they might have been viewed as such great warriors, or even godlike, if they had the blood of angels coursing through their veins. There were so many trains of thought he could travel with this, but Luke forced himself to stay focused on cracking the password.

After several moments of thought, he reached over and typed in "nephilim" and various alternatives with capitalizations as the password, but all of them were rejected. He then tried "sons of god" with no success. He thought about how hopeless it seemed to find the correct combination of characters, and the millions of variations they could form, but something kept pressing him forward. He shifted directions and did a search on the Greek god Apollo and began reading various accounts and histories about Apollo. He saw one obscure line from older Greek history, that explained why Apollo was called "Helios." One section of information caught Luke's eye. *"Helios sees everything that happens during the day, so he acts as tale-bearer to the gods. He knew when Hades abducted Persephone. He was also the one to reveal to Hephaestus the affair between Hephaestus' wife Aphrodite and Ares."*

"So Helios was a snitch," Luke said out loud and smiled. Somehow Helios could tell what was going on around him, or maybe he just knew the questions to ask, and then based on the answers, was able to discern what was true or not? Luke found the whole exercise of the research and the correlation very intriguing. He reached over and typed "Helios" into the password request and hit the enter button. The screen blinked once and then proceeded to launch the software on the unit. He had found the password.

Luke just stared at the screen as it loaded the software. A brief message was displayed.

Cat Eyes - Masters License

Then, the screen cleared and continued loading. He kept expecting to see it suddenly launch the destruct code and go blank, it didn't. When it finished, it displayed a touch screen option that he had never seen before. Luke thought about the prior message that had just been displayed on the screen. If proper grammar was used, it should have said *Cat Eyes - Master License*, but instead it had an "s" added to the end of Master. Luke remembered Apollo referring to either himself or his contact as *master*. A chill went up his spine as he wondered if that was whom this unit was created for. The thought left his mind as he saw the next option screen displayed.

**Please select your access
level**

| Level
1 |

| Level
2 |

| Level
3 |

What was this about? Luke thought to himself and took a deep breath. He had never heard Apollo speak about different levels of the software. Maybe it was just the latest versions so that he could compare them?

After a brief pause, he pulled out the glasses from the box and plugged them into the unit. The system unit acknowledged the connection and Luke placed them on his head and looked down at the display screen and the three options. He fought the urge to select Level 3, but his analytical side told him to take everything with a step-by-step approach and work his way through it, comparing the differences of each level.

He touched the *Level 1* button and a brief message flashed on the display screen, *Cat Eyes - Version 3.9* and then the glasses flashed the familiar rainbow hue in the lens as it loaded. He looked around the office and recognized the version, although he knew that there would be no colors displayed without a person to view. He glanced down and saw the *Main Menu* button at the bottom right corner of the screen and touched it. Moments later, he was back at the *Please select you access level* screen again. He touched the *Level 2* button and *Cat Eyes – Version 4.1* displayed briefly on the screen. Luke had never seen a Version 4.1; the latest version he had seen was 4.01, the one with the ghosting problem. The glasses flashed again as the new software loaded, but there was no rainbow spectrum as with Version 3.9. He looked around the office, but besides a faint yellow hue, he could not see any difference than looking through normal glasses.

Luke touched the *Main Menu* button again and tried to understand the purpose of the other two versions. He guessed that just like with Version 3.9, the other two versions would need a people populated environment for him to evaluate the differences of the versions. When it returned to the menu page, he selected *Level 3* and waited for the software to load. *Cat Eyes – Version 4.3* displayed briefly. He could tell immediately that there were problems with this upgrade, as there was a misty, almost fog-like tint being generated as he looked through the glasses. He held up his hands and looked across his desk and still saw the mist traces. He grabbed the unit with one hand and stood up to look over his cubicle to get a bigger and longer distance view.

As Luke turned to face the entrance of his cubicle, he yelled and instinctively jumped backwards, tumbling over his chair and crashing onto the floor from the surprised sight of a person standing there facing him. As he laid face down on the floor, he realized how stupid he must have looked and started chuckling as he worked on extracting himself from the chair that was lying on top of him. He reached over and picked up the glasses that had fallen off of his face, fearing he might step on them accidentally.

"Sorry about that, I didn't think anyone else was in the office," Luke said as he got to his feet and turned to face the person, but there was no one there. Luke stood on his toes and glanced over the top of the cubicle to see if the person was walking away, but again, he saw no one.

"Hello?" Luke called out as he stepped to the opening and looked both ways. He thought about the man, and remembered him being very tall. Luke glanced at the top of the cubicle and at 6'1", his eyes just barely cleared it. Yet the shoulders of the man he had just seen standing there were well above the cubicle. His heart suddenly went cold and a chill ran up his spine. He turned back towards his computer and the words he had just researched. He then glanced down at the glasses he held in his hand. With his hands trembling wildly, and his head tilted down, he slowly placed them back on and turned to look back at the entrance again, but there was no one there.

Chapter 25

Luke closed his eyes and tried to recreate the image of the man whom he had seen standing before him, in his mind's eye. At first there was nothing, but as he slowed his heart rate down and concentrated, the image came to him. The man was massive, easily over seven feet tall. His clothes were more like wispy robes, and he thought the man was shoeless, or at best wore sandals and a thick belt with a... could there really have been a sword hanging at his waist? Yes, the man's hand had been resting on the hilt of the sword as he stared at Luke.

Luke just stood there shaking for several minutes trying to understand what he had just witnessed. He somehow knew what he might have seen, but refused to acknowledge it. He glanced around the office, looking for anything that was out of place, but everything was as it should be. He finally sat back down in his chair and tried to calm himself down enough to figure out what he should do. He reached for the phone, but could not think of whom he should call. Did that really just happen or was he worked to the point of exhaustion and experiencing hallucinations based on the suggestions of Apollo and David? He felt his head, looking for some sort of bump or pain that would explain everything, but he knew there would not be any. Was that the entity that had been guiding Apollo in writing the code? Had Luke somehow just summoned him or infringed on their schemes, and if so, what consequences did it now hold for him?

Luke took the glasses off and put them on the desk and stared at them. He felt silly at the thought that just because he was not wearing the glasses and could no longer see the man, didn't mean he wasn't still around, like a little child who thinks that by covering his eyes, no one can see him. He kept reaching for the phone as if he was going to call someone, but everyone he thought to call, except Apollo and David, would think he was crazy, and he did not want to involve David in this should he decide to destroy the system unit and glasses.

Should I destroy it? he asked himself. What were the consequences of the world having the knowledge of truth? Of knowing "good and evil" as Adam and Eve had. Luke knew it was potentially within his power to put an end to what remained of the project. Were the other two levels any more dangerous than the original version? He could not help but wondered what, or whom it was that he had seen? Was it some sort of dimensional space aliens that were all around, that no one had a clue about, or was it truly spiritual? If the latter, what would be the consequences of sharing it with the world? Did he even truly know what it was that he was seeing? He felt as if there was a terrible battle being fought over his very mind as he contemplated each direction that he could take. One thing was sure, he did not want to be in this room all alone with a seven foot tall guy carrying a huge sword.

He reached over and gathered up the system unit, charger and glasses, wrapped them in his jacket and headed out the opening of his cubicle and towards the exit. He continued to nervously look around and behind him as he left the office, desperately trying to be as calm as he could. He waved at the front desk security guard who worked for the game side of the company on his way out the door.

As Luke got into his car, he thought about putting the glasses on again, but guessed that wearing them while he was driving might not be a good idea. The fact that it was dark outside did not make him feel any easier. So, he left the bundle on the passenger seat and headed towards home. He felt scared, alone, and on the verge of curling up in a corner and totally losing it. *Get a grip Luke*, he told himself. He took a few deep breaths. *You are not carrying the fate of the world on your shoulders*. His mind immediately went to the Greek god of Atlas, or was he a Titan? Luke couldn't remember, but he wondered how all of that played into history. Was all of it true? Were the gods of old, simply the fallen angels playing games with mankind? If so, why would the Christian God that David spoke about even allow it? If they were supposed to be immortal, were they still around today?

As he drove, he decided that he was afraid to go home, or more honestly, he was afraid to be alone. Taking the next exit, he decided to stop at the mall that was near his place. Arriving in the parking lot, he sat in his car a few moments trying to decide what to do. He finally got out, with the system unit and glasses in his pocket, and walked into the mall.

He spent the first thirty minutes walking around trying to decide if he really wanted to put the glasses on in order to test for what he believed and feared he would see. After tiring of the mental wrestling match, he finally stopped walking in circles and sat down at a bench. He held the glasses in his hands as he watched people walk by, knowing that they were totally oblivious to what he held and the impact it would have on their lives.

After putting on the glasses, he touched *Level 1* and looked around. The familiar rainbow hue came into view and an overwhelming display of thoughts and attitudes of the heart of people were displayed in the lens. It was as he remembered version 3.9 being, perhaps a little clearer. He touched the main menu and then selected *Level 2* and waited for the glasses to load. As version 4.1 loaded, besides the yellow hue, everything looked normal as he scanned the people nearby, but then a gold-like glow could be seen coming out of a store. The strong glow, or aura, was wrapped around an older woman as she walked gingerly down the mall. Other than the golden aura, she looked like any other person in the mall. A short time later, Luke watched as a couple holding hands came through the crowded mall, both were encased in the same gold aura. What was so different about these three compared to the rest of the people walking through the mall? Luke stood up and looked down the long corridors of the mall. With his height, he could see several hundred yards in both directions and of the hundreds of people, there were just a few who had the golden aura about them. As he watched the people carefully, Luke noticed that the golden auras on some were bright and strong, while others were faint or barely present. All of which were different ages, races and gender.

Luke sat back down to try and understand what he was seeing. Apollo had stated that his buyers wanted to be able to separate the sheep from the goats. Was that really the functionality of this level of the software, to be able to identify a certain type of person? Why were they so worried about this particular group? He looked up as a young woman walked right in front of him. She was covered in a golden aura, and was holding onto the hand of her little boy. Seeing Luke staring at her, she nodded and gave a brief smile as she passed by. *What were they planning to do with these people once they had identified them?* Luke wondered and thought about the little boy holding his mother's hand.

Luke's mind suddenly turned toward history and the Nazi's effort to exterminate the Jews during World War II and wondered if their plan was any different for this group. Then it suddenly occurred to Luke the potential need for the glasses. The Nazi's had names, birth records, even racial characteristics to identify their Jewish targets, but this group was made up of all colors, nationalities, and even political affiliations. There was very little that could be used to identify one from another. The last thought made Luke look up again. But why were there so few to be seen with the glasses? From the large test group Luke had before him, the "golden aura" people in the glasses made up less than 1% of the population in the mall. *Not much of a threat,* Luke thought to himself.

Luke really wanted to solve the *Level 2* issue before moving forward, but deep down he knew that he was using it as an excuse to delay testing the *Level 3*. He deeply feared what might be waiting for him once he touched the button. Even more, he worried about what it would mean if his fear turned out to be true. What better place to face his fears than in the safety of a crowded mall?

He touched the *Level 3* button and waited for the software to load. He looked down at the floor as the lenses flashed once, then changed to the misty-gray hue he had seen in the office. He sat there looking at the floor trying to figure out what to do, or what he would do, if he saw what he feared he would see. Then he tilted his head back.

The walkways of the mall that had been somewhat crowded just moments ago, now were filled, except the new additions were not people, at least not your mall going crowd. There were hundreds of men, or beings, dressed similarly to the one he had seen at the office with a wispy, almost ethereal look to them. Some were as large as and some were smaller than the humans nearby. Even ignoring their clothing and weapons, their wispy appearance made them easily recognizable. In spite of their various sizes, they all seemed perfect in appearance.

As Luke continued to observe the various crowds of people and ethereal creatures intermixed, he saw that some of them were walking normally nearby, some were grouped in an area or around a particular person, and others seemed more distant and unengaged. He realized that he had been sitting there on the bench in utter shock, with his mouth agape, and that people were staring at him, almost sympathetically as if he were mentally challenged. In spite of everything he was seeing, he closed his mouth, sat up straight again and tried to control his expressions. He realized his hands were shaking, but there was not much he could do to change that.

He tried reason away what he was seeing but he could not come up with any other explanation except that he was going mad. Excluding the "going mad" concept, he was trying to understand if he was witnessing some sort of extra dimensional beings, or a spiritual realm that he had never imagined could exist? *Why were they there?* Luke wondered again. How would the common person react if they knew that such creatures existed? Luke imagined a mass panic of the population, hysteria and mental breakdowns, or maybe just a simple denial of what he could see was clearly there. Maybe that was the best solution, denial and ignorance. He held the systems unit and took a deep breath. *What should I do with this terrible weapon?* He was once again faced to ask himself.

He slowly and methodically watched these ethereal "beings" as they moved about the people in the mall; all of the people were completely oblivious to them. They each appeared to be either following, or resting near specific groups or individuals as they moved about. Were they trying to guide or influence them, and if so, why?

Luke initially thought that they were in turn oblivious to him, but as he scanned the area to his left, he was surprised and even terrified to see one staring back at him. At first he thought it might be a coincidence, but just like the one he had seen in his office, it tilted its head, with a curious look on its face. A chill went up Luke's spine as it held his eyes. Luke could almost feel it try to enter his mind as if reading his thoughts. Luke suddenly realized that this was no game that he was playing. These were real creatures with real purposes, and he was no longer viewed as an innocent bystander. At that very moment, Luke made a decision that he needed to destroy the last Cat Eyes unit. As he thought through what he needed to do to bring about their destruction, the eyes and expression of the creature staring at him suddenly changed to a stern determination.

If I destroy the glasses, no one would believe me, Luke thought, and he cleared the thought of destroying them from his mind. He needed to get this to someone who would understand and help him through it. He needed to get this to Cliff's team right away. He knew it was after hours, but he could call and leave a message. As Luke ended that thought and reached for his cell phone, he watched, as the creature's face seemed to relax. As he started to dial the number to Cliff's office, he saw the woman and little boy pass by in front of him again. Although the golden aura was now missing from her, he recognized them. He also remembered the fear he had felt for her and her little boy should the glasses be used in a sinister way. With renewed courage, he put his phone away and made a mental decision to destroy the Cat Eyes and nervously looked back to see if the creature was still staring at him. Immediately the expression on its face changed and Luke once again felt a strong urge to call Cliff's office to let him know he had the Cat Eyes unit. Once again as he embraced that mental decision, the face on the creature relaxed. Trying to stay calm, Luke wrestled with the two conflicting thoughts as he and the creature continued to stare at each other across the distance. He realized the creature was purposely influencing his thinking.

Luke tried to clear his mind, not wanting the creature to realize that he had discovered its attempts to influence his thoughts, but he could feel the inner struggle as he wrestled with the idea of just relaxing and calling the office, or destroying the unit. He hated the idea that something outside his own mind was trying to influence him and with all his will, pushed back against that influence until it left his mind. As he regained control of his own thoughts and decision-making process, in his personal triumph or pride, he inadvertently smiled at the creature.

The response from the creature was immediate and terrifying. Instead of surrendering and leaving Luke alone, its face flashed with anger and it started moving directly toward him. To Luke's surprise, it passed through objects and people as it came. Luke suddenly realized how very large it was. That same feeling of paralysis that Luke had experienced in Iraq when his bedroom window was blown out from the exploding bomb threatened to completely take over his mind. He sat transfixed as the creature rapidly covered the unobstructed distance between them.

From an inner part of his mind, Luke somehow understood that his very life was in danger, much like the moment in his apartment when the man was about to pull the trigger, except this time there was no sense of peace or resolve, only a dark, bottomless fear. As it engulfed him, he felt the creature once again trying to reach into his mind to tear the remaining shreds of his sanity to pieces, but somehow, something was holding it back, something invisible was shielding Luke, allowing him to hold onto his composure. Whatever it was, he could see the frustration on the creatures face. Luke felt nothing short of absolute terror as the enormous figure reached out for him. It was at that moment that his mind flashed to his apartment just before the gunman fired and what had rescued him from the bullet. He prayed.

"God, help me." Was all he could get out before a figure stepped in front of Luke, halting the other creatures advance. It was the same large man he had seen in his office. Although he was not as big as the creature across from him, he was huge in Luke's eyes. Luke could not hear anything except the people and noises of the shopping mall, but he could see that the two of them were in a very heated discussion. The interaction was not unnoticed by the other creatures in the mall. Initially one, then another joined the frightening creature, and soon there were four standing behind and to the sides of the larger one. With the others joining it, its courage was renewed, and it suddenly drew its massive weapon from its sheath as did the other four creatures with it. The lone creature standing between Luke and the other five drew its weapon and prepared for the attack. Those that had gathered to support the larger one began to move to flank the one in front of him, who simply stepped back and stood in the middle of the bench where Luke sat, as if the creature was using its own body to shield Luke.

Luke could not believe what was happening around him; the creatures appeared intent on reaching Luke even if they had to fight their way through the large man get to him. The five suddenly halted their advance as another creature stepped from behind Luke and stood next to him; its sword was also drawn, and it took a defensive position next to the one defending him.

The whole moment seemed surreal as the seven creatures prepared for battle in this spiritual world that only he and they could see, while the people in the mall continued shopping, completely unaware of what was happening around them. *Is this how it was?* Luke wondered as he formed his final thoughts, somehow knowing that his two defenders were no match for the five coming against them. *Why had these two stepped in to protect me?* he wondered.

Suddenly, two of the attacking creatures to his left darted out of the way in a panic as a single, and very impressive looking creature walked through the middle of them and stopped in front of Luke.

"Luke?" Luke was stunned to hear the new creature suddenly speak, but realized that it had not moved its lips. Luke was about to reply when a body passed through the creature and stood before him. "Luke! Are you okay?" Luke pulled his eyes away from the creature and looked into the familiar and beautiful eyes of Danielle standing before him. "Luke, what's wrong, you look… terrified," she said almost pleadingly and sat down on the bench next to him and placed her hand on his check and turned his face towards her. Her touch managed to release him from the debilitating fear that had gripped him.

"Danielle, you've got to get away from me. Bad things are about to happen," he stammered and then looked back at the creatures preparing for battle. The new one that arrived with Danielle had not drawn its sword, but seemed to be waiting for something.

"What do you mean? Does it have to do with the guy that tried to kill you two nights ago?" she asked and looked around as if trying to discover what was causing Luke so much fear, but Luke shook his head.

"No, it's spiritual. I don't want you to get hurt," he said and she looked at Luke strangely and then took his hand.

"What do you mean 'spiritual' Luke?" she asked and he knew she would think he was crazy, but he did not have time to explain.

"You don't understand but there are spiritual forces that want to kill me, you've got to leave now!" he pleaded and tried to physically push her away from him and away from the creatures moving in for the attack. She at first seemed hurt by his actions, but then got that familiar and determined look on her face and slid back next to him and placed her hand on his cheek and smiled.

"Luke, if it's a spiritual battle you're fighting, then I'm not going anywhere," she said and leaned into him and put her arm around him. At that very moment, Luke saw the creature that came with her pull his sword, then turned and stood next to the other two that were already guarding Luke. Luke heard Danielle mumbling something and realized that she was praying. As her words poured out, it seemed as if the three creatures protecting him grew more fearsome in appearance. Luke was not the only one to notice the change, as the larger creature that had come after him, along with the four that had joined him, began to slowly withdraw from the impending battle. Their faces were still reflecting their anger towards Luke and toward those protecting him.

Luke felt the horror and fear leave him as the attempts to reach into his mind lessened then finally stopped and were replaced with a sense of inner peace. He watched as the three defenders put their swords back into their scabbards yet remained ready. Luke nodded towards the three of them.

"Thank you," he said softly, not sure if they understood, or even who it was he was thanking. They seemed to acknowledge the words, but little else. Luke turned to look at Danielle, who was still praying as her head was against his chest.

"It's okay Danielle. I think everything is alright now," he whispered and pulled her close and rested his head on hers. "I'm not sure how, or why, but your arrival made all the difference," he said and she slowly pulled her head back and looked into his eyes. He was surprised to see tears flowing down her cheeks.

"Luke, you scared me. What was that all about? Why were you so afraid?" She fired the questions out as he wiped the tears from her face. She suddenly looked deep into his eyes. "Are you loosing your mind?" she finally asked.

"Almost." Was all he could think to say and thought about how to explain it. The idea of letting her look through the glasses crossed his mind. "Let me show you," Luke said and reached for the glasses, but to his surprise and terror, all three creatures put their hands on their sword hilts and shook their heads. He withdrew his hands and they in turn withdrew their hands from their swords. *Why do they allow me to look through them but not Danielle? Would they have killed me if I had let her look through them?* he wondered. For whatever reason he was being allowed to use them, but he apparently was not allowed to let others.

"Show me what?" Danielle interrupted his thoughts. Luke just shook his head as he tried to figure out how to explain what was going on around him without actually showing her. Would she think he was totally insane? Maybe he was? "Luke, are you going to tell me what's going on with you or leave me in the dark?" she said and waited for his response. He finally nodded and looked back at her.

"Danielle, I've been wrestling over whether or not to believe if there actually is a spiritual world around us or if life can be explained purely by science and evolution," he said as she continued to try to read his face. "David has been trying to help me see and understand it, but I've been resisting the truth." He was having difficulty concentrating on the discussion while ignoring the creatures as they walked past and around them, especially the one with her who purposely stepped behind Danielle and into his line of vision.

"Luke, I'm listening," Danielle said drawing his attention back to her.

"Danielle, part of that resistance is pride. I know that, but another part just wanted to understand. I needed to feel like I was making the right decision, not just the easy decision."

"What do you need to make that 'right' decision?" she asked. He took a deep breath and looked around again at the various creatures and the three that continued to stand guard by them.

"Trust me when I say this: I now believe, with all my heart, that there is a spiritual world around us," he stated nervously while trying not to look at the creatures walking behind her. "My challenge, or what I view as the decision before me now, is to try and understand how we fit in to that spiritual world," he said and he could tell that she seemed a little confused.

"I'm not following you," Danielle stated cautiously and Luke nodded and tried to think of how best to explain it.

"I know you believe in a spiritual world, but are you completely sure that they are servants of the omnipotent creator that you believe in?" he asked. She just stared at him a moment before finally answering.
"Yes, I am sure." She said confidently.
"How do you know? I mean, how do you know you're not being tricked or fooled into believing something that is not exactly what you think it is?" He asked with all sincerity. She seemed to contemplate the question and then smiled.

"Faith combined with truth," she said and Luke raised an eyebrow and she smiled. "I believe that everything God says is true and that the promises he makes he keeps. Some of that belief comes from personal experience from seeing God work in my life. Some comes from seeing God work in other people's lives," she said and could see the doubt on his face. "Luke, when I have put in motion the things that God has said "trust me in this" he's never let me down. But when I doubt that trust and belief in him and instead, put my belief in myself or someone else, I'm always left disappointed," she said and smiled faintly and Luke nodded, not necessarily in agreement, but more as stating that he understood what she had said.

"Trust is not my strongest character trait," Luke said and Danielle raised an eyebrow. "Not that I have a strong character trait," he said trying to get in front of the joke he figured was coming from her.

"They say you have to use a muscle in order for it to get stronger. Maybe it's time to start using that wimpy 'trust muscle' of yours?" She elbowed him gently in the side and smiled. He was still finding it difficult to concentrate on what she was saying as these large creatures marched past his vision. A word suddenly came to his mind.

"Wimpy?" he exclaimed, "I almost have a nervous breakdown and your way to console me it to call me wimpy?" He pretended to be hurt by her words, but she knew he was kidding.

They both sat there on the bench, Danielle leaning against Luke and him resting his cheek on the top of her head as he watched the creature that had come with her. Having her near him felt right. There was no nervous chatter, no awkward silences, just a sense of peace and comfort. He missed holding her, touching her, and the thought of kissing her forehead came to mind, but the moment the thought did, the creature glanced at Luke, stopping him in his tracks. *Was he her personal protector?* Luke wondered. He thought about a time when they were together physically, but the moment the thought entered his mind, the creature turned around to face Luke and then glared at him, almost daring him to let the memory continue down the path he was thinking. *Yes, he is,* Luke thought and quickly closed the door to that memory. The creature seemed to roll its eyes and shook his head as he turned back around to scan the area for trouble.

Luke sat there, not wanting the moment with Danielle to end. In spite of all the horror and strangeness that he was witnessing, being with her grounded him. His sanity, perhaps his very life, had almost been lost only moments before, but she stayed and prayed for him. She was willing to fight with him in the battle, rather than leave him to fight it alone. Luke thought about the creature that was with her that was also willing to go to battle for him, but then realized that it was not for him, but for her and her decision.

"Are you okay?" a woman's voice asked softly. Luke looked up to see the familiar figures of the woman and her little boy standing in front of him. Luke just stared back at her in silence. "I don't mean to intrude, but you didn't look well earlier and I was very concerned," she explained and Luke nodded.

"Yeah, it was a tough moment. I'm better, but thank you for asking," Luke replied slightly embarrassed at the thought of what he must have looked like from her perspective and smiled.

"I hope you don't mind and it will probably sound strange, but I felt I needed to pray for you," she said and Luke sat stunned as he remembered her passing by as the creature was trying to control his mind. He thought about the creature from his office that had initial stepped in, then the second creature, followed by the one that came with Danielle. Luke realized that the second creature had come from her, as a result of her prayers. He was shocked by his revelation of what had transpired.

"Thank you. It made a huge difference," Luke replied and then turned towards Danielle and then back towards the woman before him. "I'm Luke, this is Danielle," Luke interjected and Danielle held out her hand.

"I'm Sandy and this is my son Joseph, he's five," she replied as she shook Danielle's hand.

"Nice to meet you Sandy, and it's nice to meet you too, Joseph. Thank you for your prayers," Danielle stated as the boy shyly stepped behind his mother's leg. "What part of town do you live in?" Danielle asked and the two of them started exchanging stories and information. Luke was always amazed how Danielle could talk with anyone.

As he watched and listened to them interact, a thought crossed his mind. He reached down and selected the "main menu" button, exiting the *Level 3* version, and then selected the *Level 2* version. Danielle glanced over curiously as he navigated through the menus on the system unit. As the software came online and the yellow hue flashed in the lens, he slowly turned to confirm what he already knew. Danielle was also surrounded by the golden aura, almost as if flames were dancing across her. The woman before him had the same golden aura surrounding her as well.

"I'm surprised you two don't know each other," Luke said.

"Were working on it," Danielle said jokingly and Sandy smiled.

"I figured you went to the same church," Luke asked.

"Why is that?" Sandy asked curiously and Luke shrugged.

"I guess because you both care for people and you're willing to pray for them," Luke replied and they both nodded.

"That's what Christians do," Danielle replied and Sandy nodded.

"I see that," Luke responded and allowed the women to interact again. He reached down and reloaded the *Level 3* version while they exchanged phone numbers and said their goodbyes. Luke shook Sandy's hand and thanked her again for her prayers. As she walked away with her son, Luke could see that the second creature that had defended him walked with her.

He knew there was a spiritual realm around him. He could see it with his own eyes. He also knew that there were opposing forces at work within that spiritual world. Luke realized that there were no innocent bystanders, no neutral parties in the eyes of this spiritual world. You either choose to ignore it and remain blind and ignorant to the influence it holds over you, or you choose to acknowledge it, which requires you to choose the side you will fight for. It was the eternal choice that each person has been required to make since the beginning of mankind. And like all those before him, he had to choose Jesus and join his small, outnumbered, yet powerful group, rather than to choose those in this spiritual world who oppose Jesus.

He thought of Danielle, Sandy, David and the deep conviction displayed in each of them. They were willing to take a stand and he respected them for it. Even Apollo respected David and his convictions. He thought about all of the information that was out there attacking their beliefs, their churches, even them individually. Luke knew that taking such a stand must have cost them relationships and resulted in a difficult life filled with persecution and distain from those who rejected the Lord they served. He thought about those he had met at Danielle's baptism, even the "pit bull brothers" and their willingness to take a stand. *What were the costs they had counted when they made their choice?* Luke wondered. What hope would those who chose not to take a stand have? Danielle had taken such a stand, choosing Jesus over him, yet here he was.

He sat there and relived all that had happened to him these past few weeks and how prideful and arrogant he had been toward God and toward those that had tried to help him find God. He looked into Danielle's eyes and smiled.

"I now believe there is a God, that he protects those that he loves, those that are his children, and those that are willing to seek him," he said and tears filled her eyes, except this time he could see that they were tears of happiness, not sadness or fear. He held her tight and she embraced him tightly as well.

As Luke looked around, he expected to see some spiritual celebration in response to his claim of faith or belief. He was expecting to see them "high fiving" each other, or nodding towards him and maybe pumping their fists in the air, but although they were observing, they seemed less interested in the interaction than Luke had hoped.

"What do you want to do now?" she asked as she tried to clean the tears from her face and fix her makeup. Luke thought about it for a moment as he looked around the mall at the people and the creatures intermingling. He could not tell who the creatures were that moments ago had wanted to see him killed, but he could see the larger one still sitting off in the distance, as if waiting.

"I'd like to pay a visit to David," he said and she smiled. They stood up and started walking towards the exit together. She glanced up at Luke and shook her head.

"We need to get you a better pair of glasses," she said and Luke smiled at the thought.

"I agree," he said and thought about her being here this evening. "What were you shopping for anyways?"

"I don't know, I just felt like coming to the mall," she replied and Luke nodded and wondered how much influence God had in that decision.

Chapter 26

Danielle held his arm as they walked out towards his car in the mall parking lot. Not wanting the constant distractions of the creatures passing by as he walked or drove, Luke removed the glasses and placed them with the system unit in his jacket pocket. It felt good to have Danielle next to him again, not just the physical touch of her, but more the renewed bond that they had shared before. This time it somehow seemed better, even stronger than before. He felt that nothing could go wrong with her by his side. At that very moment he looked up and saw Cliff standing by his car in the crowded, but dimly lit parking lot. Luke's heart sank and he was suddenly deeply concerned for Danielle.

"Why don't you drive your car to David's and I'll meet you there?" Luke stopped and looked at Danielle. She felt the sudden change in him.

"Can you at least drop me off at my car? I parked on the other side of the mall," she said. Luke looked over her shoulder and saw Angela walking towards them, she apparently had been following them, and his heart sank even deeper in his chest.

"I need you to head back into the mall, it's very important," he said and Danielle shook her head.

"I told you I'm not leaving you." She could see the concern in Luke's eyes again and Luke knew that it was too late as Angela was now standing behind Danielle.

"Hi Luke," Angela said and Danielle turned around to see a woman standing behind her.

"Hi Angela," Luke said nervously and felt Danielle shudder slightly at the name. She looked at Luke and back at Angela.

"Are you the Angela that saved Luke the other night?" Danielle asked Angela, who shrugged and then nodded.

"I guess you could say that. You must be Danielle," Angela replied and an icy fear crept into Luke with the knowledge that Angela knew Danielle. *It doesn't surprise me*, Luke thought, *she probably knows more details about Danielle than I do. But why was she here? Why were she and Cliff here?* he wondered as Danielle let go of his arm and reached over to shake Angela's hand.

"Careful, she'll do an atomic elbow drop on you if you're not careful," Luke joked as the two shook hands.

"She's safe, there's no bread around," Angela kidded back, which made Luke relax a little and Danielle raise an eyebrow at the response, not privy to the inside joke. *If someone were going to kill you, would they joke?* he wondered. "Luke, I think Cliff wants to speak with you," Angela said and nodded toward Luke's car where Cliff was waiting. Danielle looked over to where Cliff was standing and then back at Angela. Understanding finally struck her, and Danielle realized that Luke had been trying to protect her in some way from the waiting pair. She looked up at Luke as if looking for guidance. "It's okay Luke. Danielle and I will be right here," Angela stated and Danielle nodded towards Luke. Luke leaned down and kissed Danielle on the forehead and smiled.

"I'll be right back," he said and walked towards his car.

"How's the code breaking coming?" Luke asked Cliff as he stopped next to him. Cliff just looked at Luke a moment and smiled. Cliff's face looked haggard and Luke thought he saw sadness in his eyes. *Is he sad that he has to take me in or worse?* Luke thought.

"Well, we've learned enough to know that it's not a virus that is transferring to other servers or systems. Its purpose is unique to the code that it was written for. It only affects the Cat Eyes software," Cliff stated. Luke nodded and looked back at Danielle and Angela, who seemed to be in a deep conversation.

"That's great news," Luke replied, distracted by his concern for Danielle.

"We still can't access any aspect of the software without it self-destructing, and the few pieces of code that we do have left, well, we still can't even understand how the code works. It's like it's from a different planet," Cliff said and raised an eyebrow towards Luke.

"So what brings you here?" Luke asked and motioned to the parking lot around him. "You must have better things to do than cruise the malls on a Friday night?" Luke joked.

"No, we were just very worried about you," Cliff stated and looked at Luke with a very serious expression. Even in the low light of the parking lot, Luke could see that Cliff was tired. "It's become very clear that my team has been compromised by the *Dominus* group. They seem to be desperate to acquire the software that they worked so hard to have created," Cliff said and Luke felt the sudden weight of the system unit in his pocket. Fear slowly started to rise within him.

"How do you know your team has been compromised?" Luke asked and Cliff hesitated.

"This afternoon Apollo agreed to tell us how to access the software. He wanted the deal in writing from the top echelons. In the time it took to have the agreement written up and signed, he was killed," Cliff said. The words were like a slap in the face.

"What! How?" Luke asked, almost too afraid to know the answer.

"It appears to be the result of a drug induced brain aneurism. Every small blood vessel in his brain ruptured," Cliff said and Luke swallowed. "Two of my trusted agents who were in the field at the time, were also killed within hours of his death and an attempt was made on a third agent, but that attempt failed." Cliff nodded towards Angela. "It was one of our other agents that tried to kill her. All three of the agents were working solely on the Cat Eyes project at the time," Cliff said and Luke swallowed and then a name came to mind.

"Serena?" he asked and Cliff seemed surprised by the mention of the name, and then nodded.

"Yeah. We found her in her car. Another agent was assigned to eliminate Apollo," Cliff replied and Luke could see the hurt in his eyes and knew the friendship that he and Serena shared.

"What happened with Angela, is she okay?" Luke asked, now feeling the fear of her replaced by concerned. Cliff nodded as he looked back at where she was talking with Danielle.

"She is definitely shaken up by the attack. The agent was a close friend of hers, or she thought he was. He tried to inject the same drug that was used on Apollo into her. She felt the pressure of the injection, and watched a man who she thought was a friend wait coldly for her to die. Apparently it was a very fast acting poison," Cliff said.

"I don't understand, how did she…" Luke started to ask and Cliff interrupted him.

"The needle tip caught the nylon shoulder strap on her holster and bent over." Cliff suddenly smiled, "Needless to say, he was surprised when she stuck her gun in his face. That's how we found out about the drug they were using. I've never seen anything like it before."

"Did he say who he was working for?" Luke asked and Cliff shrugged.

"Never got the chance to ask. He injected himself with the same needle and died moments later," Cliff stated and Luke just stared silently as he tried to visualize the man taking his own life instead of surrendering. He could not believe that all this had happened in the few short hours since their meeting with Apollo.

"I'm glad Angela's okay. I'm so sorry to hear about Serena. I know the two of you were close," Luke stated and Cliff nodded.

"Angela was very fortunate. Someone was definitely looking out for her," Cliff stated and then turned back to Luke. "Luke, I told you that I was worried that if you got in too deep, that you could be at risk. Hindsight, I should have never brought you in on the Apollo interrogation." Cliff hesitated, "Luke, I want you, David and Danny to close down the Cat Eyes office and find new employment immediately. I want to distance you and the rest of your team from this project and from my staff," Cliff ordered and Luke nodded, his mind still lost in the events that Cliff had just revealed.

"Why would they want to kill Apollo if he was working for them?" Luke asked and Cliff thought about the questions before answering.

"I think their greatest fear was what would happen to their network if we had the use of the glasses to probe those involved yet they needed it to achieve their goals. Apollo had no idea how dangerous *Dominus* is and once he demonstrated that he was willing to change sides, he was no longer needed, but more importantly to them, they could not allow him to give us the Cat Eyes code," Cliff replied.

"Are you still working on breaking the code?" Luke asked, at the same time feeling the weight of the systems unit in his pocket.

"No. With the depth of the security breach still unknown, we have moved all software and hardware modules into secure storage and scheduled it for destruction. For one, even though it appears to be exclusive to the host software, we want to avoid any chance of that nasty piece of destruction code cross infecting other systems. More importantly, we cannot allow it to fall into the hands of those who were willing to kill for it," Cliff stated and Luke felt guilty for not telling him sooner.

"Cliff, you don't have all…" Luke started to say, but Cliff interrupted him.

"I said I had ALL of the systems units and software secured and they will all be destroyed," Cliff stated and stared at Luke and then raised an eyebrow. "Are we clear?" Cliff asked and Luke nodded but tilted his head as if looking for more information.

"Yeah," Luke replied and Cliff smiled.

"With everything destroyed, it should put all active parties desiring to implement the software, no matter how deeply infiltrated they might be, to rest and bring the killing to an end. Once it's all destroyed there will be nothing left for anyone to build on. I'm not sure if the issue will ever be re-explored," Cliff said and then he slowly reached over and put his hand into Luke's jacket pocket and pulled out the Cat Eyes unit. Luke at first felt a sense of guilt, but he knew that Cliff was obviously aware that he had it. As Cliff turned it over in his hand, Luke tried to understand what Cliff was up to; did Cliff want the unit for himself, or for some other purpose? Should he try to stop him from taking it?

Luke watched as Cliff removed the back panel of the systems unit, reached into his own pocket and withdrew a small pair of needle nosed pliers. With the tip of the pliers, he removed a small plastic nodule from the inside of the unit. He then replaced the back cover on the systems unit and then returned the pliers, along with the plastic nodule, into his own pocket.

"Now you know how I found you. Let's not give anyone else that ability," Cliff said with a smile and then reached over and placed the system unit back into Luke's pocket. Luke was confused and tried to understand why he was being allowed to keep the Cat Eyes unit after what Cliff just shared with him.

"I don't understand." Luke replied.

"When Apollo looked at you during the interrogation and said help was nearby, I knew he meant you. I knew that meant that you would somehow figure it all out. Call it destiny, luck, or perhaps even *divine intervention*, but how I knew really doesn't matter," Cliff said and smiled. "What does matter is what you decide to do from here forward." Cliff put his hands back in his pockets and looked around and took a deep breath.

"That's a whole lot of control that you're giving away. That's not the Cliff I've come to know," Luke said and Cliff nodded.

"Luke, the truth of the matter is that I'm drawn to the incredible power and abilities of the Cat Eyes system as much as anyone else would be. I can see endless applications on how it can be used for good; at least I can justify it in my mind as good. But I also recognize the incredible dangers and loss of personal freedoms that that would surely ensue if we allow this technology to exist. To have it mass-produced and floating around in the hands of the government or private sector is a very scary concept. As more and more potential uses were discussed and more requests for the unit from out side the office came in, the more afraid I became of it. There was a defining moment when I finally understood your deep fear of it." Luke tried to guess what that moment was. *Was it when they were in his apartment after the man tried to kill him?* he wondered.

"So why don't you destroy it?" Luke asked.

"It's not in my job description and the penalty of doing so would not be great for my career and the truth eventually, always comes out. Besides, it's already a dead product as far as everyone else is aware."

"So what would you like to see happen from here?" Luke asked, still confused by the events that had just unfolded. Cliff took a deep breath.

"I think the best person to decide that is you. If I never see the product again, I'd be fine with it. My greatest fear is not what you would do with it, but what I would do with it if I had it. Luke, I know the evil that I'm capable of in the name of doing good and I know that others are capable of even greater evil than me. So I'm going to leave it in your hands, literally speaking, to decide its fate," Cliff said and smiled at Luke. "If you suddenly show up at my office in the morning with it, then I will know that our world is about to change. If not, then life returns to normal... or as normal as this messed up world can be. It's a difficult decision and one that a man of my limited character should not be allowed to make." Cliff shook his head. "Luke, I trust you. In fact, you are one of the few people left in this world that I do trust and that I know will make the right decision." Cliff smiled and then extended his hand for Luke to take. Luke slowly reached out and grasped it.

"Aren't you worried that they will track it back to me and they will once again have it in their possession?" Luke asked and Cliff nodded.

"Like I said, I wouldn't wait too long to make your decision. I only bought you enough time to make your choice. I would suggest that you either bring it to me tomorrow morning, or you destroy it," Cliff stated and Luke realized that as long as he had it in his possession, he would be a target.

Luke stood there in silence shaking Cliff's hand as the two men stared at each other. He thought about the burden that was now placed on him. He thought about all the words that Cliff had shared with him. He thought about Serena's death because of this product, about the other agent that was killed that he never knew, the attempt on Angela's life, and finally, the death of Apollo. A shudder ran through him as Cliff relaxed his grip on Luke's hand, but Luke suddenly held tight to it and looked at Cliff.

"You need to know what the upgrade does, what it is supposed to be used for," Luke stated and Cliff seemed to hesitate before answering.

"I already know," Cliff replied, "It's to be used to separate the sheep from the goats, the David's from the Jonathan's." Cliff said and Luke tried to understand why Cliff paralleled the analogy with David and Jonathan. "It's a cruel weapon Luke, a powerful one, but very cruel. The standard software has incredible potential, but that upgrade is a poisonous snake to those who oppose it." Cliff added.

"What do you mean by 'the David's from the Jonathan's' analogy?" Luke asked and Cliff smiled.

"You know the answer, but if you don't, it will come to you. I saw it when I looked at Angela and knowing her background, I was able to put the pieces of the puzzle together quickly," Cliff said and then saw that Luke did not understand. What did he mean by *when I looked at Angela*, Luke wondered.

"After understanding everything, my personal advice would be to either run as far away from David and what he is teaching you, or to keep studying with him. The first is the easier path, but it also has a short future," Cliff said with all seriousness. Although Luke nodded he was still trying to understand Cliff's meaning.

"Why would *Dominus* want such a tool?" Luke asked.

"I don't know, nor do I want to try to imagine the horror of how it could be used. But I do know that mankind is capable of just about any horrors we can imagine. Luke, although you and most of the people in this world are oblivious to what goes on in the hidden darkness, I see it every day. This is a horribly evil world that we live in. A world filled with venomous snakes that can slither silently into our lives and poison us before we ever know it. If I can offer any advice, it is that the only way to deal with such evil is to quickly cut the head off the snake before it can slither out to destroy others," Cliff said and looked for a reaction from Luke.

Luke thought about the Garden of Eden and the serpent that had managed to convince Eve and Adam that what they were about to eat was good for them, not deadly. Had Adam just cut off the snake's head, or simply said no, would things be far different today? Was that what Cliff was relating his analogy too? Luke nodded and released Cliff's hand. Luke realized that Cliff was somehow aware of the *Level 2* version, but wondered if he knew about the *Level 3* release. Luke struggled with whether or not to tell him.

"There's more." Luke started to say.

"Sometimes secrets are best kept that way," Cliff interjected as if reading Luke's mind and patted him on the shoulder. It finally dawned on Luke.

"You looked through the glasses," Luke said as he watched for Cliff's reaction. Cliff eventually nodded.

"When we picked up the missing unit from Apollo's house, Apollo had left it on and the menu screen was visible. I put them on to see if they were still working and tested the various software levels. When I had seen enough, I shut it down to take it to the office to do more testing with it. Unfortunately, when I went to turn it back on to show Serena, the password protect screen was blocking me. I could not figure it out, so I passed it over to you and your team," Cliff said and Luke remembered Cliff's words *when I saw Angela*.

"You saw a glow around Angela." Cliff hesitated a moment and then nodded at the realization that Luke was putting the pieces together.

"You purposely left it in my office," Luke stated and Cliff nodded again.

"When we cleared the office, I saw the box under your desk and took a quick look to verify that the destruct software had destroyed the code on that unit as it had on the other units, but it hadn't. The more I thought about what I had seen and what the software could do, the more I wanted to see this whole project come to an end. I wrestled with the concept of what I should do, but for whatever reason, I came to the conclusion that I would leave it in your hands." Cliff hesitated as he saw Luke's confused expression.

"That's not at all like you Cliff," Luke said and smiled and Cliff shrugged.

"Don't get me wrong, I attached a lot of "if/then" scenarios to the decision. I decided that "if" you called to say you had it or that you had gotten it to work, there would be a strong chance that others were listening and would know as well. That meant the "then," I would have had no choice but to come and get it. "If" you were unable to get it to work, or "if" you had just left it in the office, "then" I was going to pick it up once you left," Cliff said and then stopped and waited for Luke to process it all.

"That was a whole lot of if and then options. It's not like you to leave that much to fate," Luke stated and Cliff shrugged and continued to stare at Luke and raised an eyebrow as if expecting a question. Luke took the bait.

"*Level 3*, did you…" Luke started to ask and Cliff nodded.

"Seeing that will mess you up real good," Cliff replied and Luke felt an inner relief or a verbal confirmation that he was not going crazy. "Someday when this all settles down, I'd like to know what you think you saw. But right now, I just want to go back to my clueless world and somehow pretend that we are all alone in it." Cliff turned toward Angela and nodded as if stating the topic of conversation was over. The nod made Luke nervous and he turned to check on Danielle again and saw Angela shake her hand, hesitate, then release it as the two of them began to walk toward he and Cliff. Luke gave a sigh of relief and saw Angela smile and he smiled back.

"Danielle, this is Cliff. Cliff, Danielle," Luke said as Danielle and Angela stopped at his side. Danielle shook Cliff's hand.

"Nice to meet you, Cliff. I hear you have been busy keeping an eye on Luke?" Danielle stated and Cliff nodded.

"More like six eyes, lots of ears, and maybe even a video or two," Luke interjected with a raised eyebrow and Cliff and Angela both smiled uncomfortably.

"Yes, he's a slippery one. We needed to use all of our resources to keep him out of trouble. But he's all yours now," Cliff replied.

"Mine? Well, I guess that wouldn't be so bad," Danielle said with a smile and Luke was encouraged to hear her statement. "Luke, Angela was just telling me that you tried to save her when that man tried to kill you," Danielle stated and Luke at first nodded and then shook his head.

"Not exactly. I thought I was trying to save you, but I think the only thing I managed to save was my loaf of bread." Angela laughed at Luke's joke but he could see that Danielle and Cliff seemed confused.

"Again with the bread comment. I don't understand," Danielle stated.

"Yeah, what exactly is that all about?" Cliff interjected and Angela just laughed.

"Sorry, that's a secret and if I told you I'd have to kill you," Angela said with a grin.

"I'm your boss, you can't kill your boss. We have rules and protocols that all good agents must follow," Cliff said sternly and they all laughed.

"Such assumptions can prove deadly," Angela replied and then the smiles faded as the wording brought events of the day back to mind. Danielle seemed to pick up on the change in attitude.

"Well, secret or not, it was a pleasure meeting you Angela," Danielle said with a smile and leaned against Luke. "Maybe the four of us can have dinner sometime?"

"That would be nice, but I'm afraid we will be headed back to Washington now that our work here is completed," Cliff said and Angela smiled. "Perhaps we can all meet again the next time we're out this way," Cliff said as Angela stepped forward and gave Luke and Danielle an embrace and a smile.

"Please be safe and keep an eye on him," Luke said to Angela and cocked his head toward Cliff.

As they walked away, Luke heard Cliff say, "Since when did you start giving hugs to people?" Luke saw Angela shake her head, but did not hear her response.

Danielle and Luke stood in silence watching Cliff and Angela walk towards the mall, exchanging words as they walked, and then they split up, each heading in different directions. Luke wondered what the life of an agent would be like, especially one that witnessed betrayal and death from within its own circles.

"Is everything alright, or do you still want me to drive there by myself?" Danielle asked with a little sarcasm. Luke smiled and shook his head.

"I was worried when I saw Cliff standing by my car. I didn't want to see you get hurt if there was a problem," Luke said and Danielle nodded.

"I know," she replied and smiled. "Is everything alright?" she asked again. Luke started to nod and then shook his head.

"No. I still have a very big decision to make," Luke replied and Danielle smiled.

"Are we still going to see David, or have you changed your mind?" Danielle asked. Luke knew she was thinking about spiritual decisions, while he was thinking more about the decision on what to do with the Cat Eyes. Both seemed to lead to David's house and counsel. The more he thought about it, the more he realized that both had spiritual implications.

"No, in fact for the first time, I'm actually looking forward to it," Luke replied with a smile.

Chapter 27

As he walked around back of his car after opening the passenger door for Danielle, Luke began to question the idea of involving David and Danielle in this decision. Could agents of *Dominus* be following them right now, waiting to kill all those involved and take the Cat Eyes glasses? They had no qualms about killing Selena and the other agent, nor did they hesitate to kill Apollo, someone who worked directly for them. Was he putting Danielle and the people that he cared for in grave danger even by meeting with them? Luke remembered that his house was under audio surveillance so David's and Danielle's could be too? If so, anything said there would be overheard. He wondered just how much information they had about his involvement in the project and how deep their surveillance went. As he slid into the driver's seat and reached for the ignition, he wondered if his car was bugged. Then an even more horrendous thought occurred to him. *What if his car was rigged with explosives?* He pulled his hand away from the ignition and looked over at Danielle.

"She seemed very nice," Danielle stated and Luke raised an eyebrow, "Angela, she seemed very nice." And Luke, still struggling with what he should do next nodded. He knew that Cliff had been waiting by his car when they came out. Had he been protecting it, or planting a bomb in it? Should they take Danielle's car? As he wrestled with the idea of Cliff or Angela planning his demise, he realized that if they wanted him dead, that they could have killed both of them at any moment. They had been following him, and probably were still following him until they knew the final fate of the last Cat Eyes unit. Was this what the rest of his life was going to look like, wondering and fearing if at any moment an agent of *Dominus* would take either him or someone he cares out?

"What's wrong?" Danielle asked, jarring him out of his deep thoughts. All that had happened and all that he had learned was welling up inside him. He he wanted to just let it burst and tell her everything, but the fear of her being involved and at risk was too great.

"Are you afraid of dying?" The words suddenly came pouring out of him and he could tell that she was surprised by them. Danielle seemed to grimace and then smile.

"I think everyone is afraid of not knowing what waits on the other side. But I can honestly say that after becoming a Christian, I now have a sense of peace that has removed that fear."

"But are you sure of that belief?" Luke asked and Danielle nodded without hesitation.

"With all my heart," she replied and Luke could see that she meant it.

"I wish I had your same confidence," he replied.

"That confidence does not come from me, but from my faith in God and his promises," she stated.

"So what is faith?" he asked and she seemed to think a moment.

Danielle reached into her purse and pulled out a small Bible and as she turned towards the back of the book, Luke reached up and flipped the dome light on for her to read. "This helps me; in Hebrews 11, starting in verse 1 it reads, "*Now faith is being sure of what we hope for and certain of what we do not see. ² This is what the ancients were commended for. ³ By faith we understand that the universe was formed at God's command, so that what is seen was not made out of what was visible. ⁴ By faith Abel offered God a better sacrifice than Cain did. By faith he was commended as a righteous man, when God spoke well of his offerings. And by faith he still speaks, even though he is dead. ⁵ By faith Enoch was taken from this life, so that he did not experience death; he could not be found, because God had taken him away. For before he was taken, he was commended as one who pleased God. ⁶ And without faith it is impossible to please God, because anyone who comes to him must believe that he exists and that he rewards those who earnestly seek him. ⁷ By faith Noah, when warned about things not yet seen, in holy fear built an ark to save his family. By his faith he condemned the world and became heir of the righteousness that comes by faith. ⁸ By faith Abraham, when called to go to a place he would later receive as his inheritance, obeyed and went, even though he did not know where he was going. ⁹ By faith he made his home in the promised land like a stranger in a foreign country; he lived in tents, as did Isaac and Jacob, who were heirs with him of the same promise. ¹⁰ For he was looking forward to the city with foundations, whose architect and builder is God. ¹¹ By faith Abraham, even though he was past age—and Sarah herself was barren—was enabled to become a father because he considered him faithful who had made the promise. ¹² And so from this one man, and he as good as dead, came descendants as numerous as the stars in the sky and as countless as the sand on the seashore. ¹³ All these people were still living by faith when they died. They did not receive the things promised; they only saw them and welcomed them from a distance. And they admitted that they were aliens and strangers on earth. ¹⁴ People who say such things show that they are looking for a country of their own. ¹⁵ If they had been thinking of the country they had left, they would have had opportunity to return. ¹⁶ Instead, they were longing for a better country—a heavenly one. Therefore God is not ashamed to be called their God, for he has prepared a city for them.*" She finished reading and then smiled and looked at Luke. "I've learned that faith is moving forward in the face of fear or doubt, focusing on God and his present and future promises. You were my greatest fear and doubt," she said.

"Me? How so?" he asked in surprise.

"I was afraid that you would leave me if I chose to become a Christian. The very thought of it broke my heart. And when you did, my greatest fear became a reality," she said and he could see that her eyes had tears in them.

"I'm so sorry for hurting you," Luke replied and touched her cheek and she suddenly giggled.

"What's so funny?" he asked.

"When you turned away from me, I prayed that God would do something crazy and amazing, 'whatever it took' I had prayed, in order for you to find him." She sniffed as she tried to keep the tears from messing up her makeup and then laughed. "I'm sorry, I didn't think he would send someone to shoot you. Although you are pretty stubborn," she smiled and then laughed again.

Luke thought about her words and the prayer she had prayed. *Whatever it took.* If her words were accurate, God had to send two men to try and shoot him and after that didn't work; he then went as far as to peel back the fabric of the hidden spiritual world for him to see and believe. *Am I that hard hearted?* Luke wondered and then nodded as he realized that he had been. He thought about the car, the ignition, and the dangers that could be waiting for him at every turn of his life. *God is greater than all of these fears and if that is the ending God has in store for me, then there is nothing I can do about it anyway,* he thought to himself. It was like what Danielle had just read, *Faith is being sure of what we hope for and certain of what we do not see.* Luke nodded, then reached over and turned the ignition and the car started. He smiled as he put it in gear and backed out of the parking lot and drove towards David's. Faith felt good.

The drive to David's was filled with repeated apologies for how he had acted towards her and towards God. Luke wanted Danielle to know about everything that had happened between Monica and him. He was so sorry for hurting her and asked for her forgiveness, which she gave quickly, without conditions. It was as if a myriad of evil barriers were crumbling down the more they spoke, opening the way to not only the past relationship that they had shared, but to new areas of openness where they had not gone before. As they pulled into the driveway of David's house, Luke looked at Danielle.

"Thank you for not compromising for me and for praying that God would do *whatever it took* for me to find him. I know I have a long way to go on this journey, but I'm glad I get to travel it with you," he told her and she smiled and held his hand and squeezed it.

"I'm with you, heart and soul, Luke Baker. I always have been," she replied and smiled.

David, who read the conflicting expressions of joy on Danielle's face and the worry on Luke's, greeted them at the door. After accepting a glass of tea, Luke could feel David staring at him as Danielle told her perspective as to what happened at the mall and how they ended up at their house. David knew too much about what was happening behind the scenes to think that Luke was just having some sort of mental breakdown. The fact that Luke was being somewhat evasive about the exact details further deepened David's concerns.

"Can David and I speak in private about work?" Luke suddenly interjected as Susan was preparing to ask a question of Luke. Susan looked toward David and he nodded and smiled.

"How about the guys take the den and the ladies the living room?" David offered and Susan and Danielle headed off towards the living room and David motioned toward the den. Luke shook his head as he thought about the potential of David's house being bugged.

"Can we get some fresh air instead?" Luke asked and David looked intently at Luke and then nodded as if understanding the purpose of the request and motioned toward the patio door. Luke smiled as he saw David grab his Bible off the table as they walked toward the door.

As they stepped outside, David flipped on a switch that turned on the pool lights, giving the area a blue glow, and then he motioned toward the far side where there was a gas fire pit surrounded by chairs. As they took a seat across from each other David bent down and turned a knob then flipped a switch and with a "whompf" the gas ignited and the yellow blue flame jumped to life in the fire pit.

"Nice place you have here," Luke commented and David nodded.

"It's Susan's mother's place. She rents the place to us for almost nothing. It's an incredible blessing, with the pool and all. We definitely feel spoiled and blessed at the same time," David said with a smile and Luke nodded. "So what's up Luke? What's going on that's got you so tight lipped?" David asked and waited for Luke to reply.

"Apollo's dead," Luke said and David's jaw actually dropped, his mouth framing the silent word "What?"

"How?" David replied.

"It was someone in the government, actually within Cliff's team who was working for some spooky organization. They poisoned him. They also killed Serena and another agent, and tried to kill a third agent. All three were assigned to the Cat Eyes product." When David heard Serena's name he glanced around the area and shook his head.

"This is not good," David replied. "Have they caught the killers?" David suddenly asked.

"One for sure, but there could be more of them. The one they did catch killed himself with the same poison," Luke replied and David just kept shaking his head in disbelief.

"So how much danger are the rest of us that were on the team in?" David asked and Luke just shook his head and shrugged.

"I don't know, but that's not why I'm here. I'm sorry for getting you involved in all of this; I had no idea. But, I need your advice on something," Luke said and reached in his pocket and pulled out the Cat Eyes unit and glasses and sat them on the chair next to him. "I discovered Apollo's password to the demo unit. The destruct code was not installed on this unit," Luke said and David looked very surprised.

"The last active unit that has the working software," David stated. "That makes that unit pretty valuable to all parties, good and bad."

"There's more to this than just the software version we knew about. This unit has two additional versions on it that perform two vastly different and dangerous functions," Luke said and then waited.

"I'm guessing it has to do with the ghosting issue," David stated and Luke nodded. Luke reached over and turned on the system unit and turned it around for David to see.

"Are you alright with me wearing the glasses?" Luke asked and David nodded.

"I told you before I have nothing to hide."

"I know, but I need to make sure it is alright with someone else for me to talk more about this," Luke stated and David raised an eyebrow in reply as Luke placed the glasses on and pressed the *Level 3* button.

"Care to explain the last comment?" David asked with deep concern.

"I'll let you know in a moment if I can or not," Luke replied as he waited for the software to finish loading.

As the gray mist filled the lens, Luke instinctively jumped at the sight of the ethereal creature standing behind David, which caused David to turn quickly around to see what Luke was looking at, but Luke knew that there was nothing that David could see. As Luke looked at this creature, he knew he had not seen this one before, but it looked every bit as formidable and perfect as the others that he had seen. He looked to his right and there was the one that he had seen in the office and that had defended him in the mall staring back at him as if waiting. Luke turned back towards David, but a motion caught his eye and he looked past the one standing behind David and saw that there was another one standing at the edge of the yard. Luke turned to his right and left and saw that there were actually multiple creatures that had formed a large circle around the area, each facing outward as if anticipating trouble.

"What is it Luke, what are you seeing," David asked, causing Luke to regain his focus. Luke looked at the one next to him.

"It would be a lot easier if I showed you..." Luke said and reached for his glasses, but the one behind David held up his had to signal "stop" and glared at Luke. "...but, that apparently is not going to be allowed to happen," Luke ended and moved his hands away from the glasses and tried to think of how to proceed.

"Maybe you can just tell me what you're seeing?" David replied and Luke glanced back at the two creatures standing nearby.

"This version of the glasses allows me to see..." Luke hesitated, waiting for the creatures to once again raise their hands or reach for their swords, but neither moved. "... yes, that is okay for me to talk about," Luke said and sighed. "The glasses allow me to see the spiritual world around us." Luke waited for David to laugh at the thought of him losing his mind, but he sat in silence as if trying to read Luke's face. "I'm talking about the 'Elisha's servant' type vision that you had me read about in 2 Kings," Luke added and David took a deep breath and exhaled, then nodded.

"Okay," David finally replied.

"Okay? I expected to be offered a straight jacket, a 911 call, or a nice pat on the head as a response," Luke stated and David shook his head.

"I knew from the start that those glasses had a connection to the spiritual realm. So what are you seeing?" David asked and Luke glanced at the two creatures and neither threatened him as he hesitated.

"There is a large ethereal creature, big and beautiful, standing behind you as if guarding you. There is another that is next to me that seems to have a similar purpose," he said and hesitated. "And there are many more that have formed a large circle around us, as if protecting us," Luke stated and watched David expression.

"Wow. So this is what Danielle saw you going through at the mall?" David asked and Luke nodded.

"But worse. There were creatures that were intent on killing me at the mall," Luke stated and David raised an eyebrow again.

"Why?" David asked and Luke tried to think of how best to explain it.

"Because I resisted calling Cliff to tell him that I had found the password and that I had the last working system in my possession. The creature was somehow trying to coerce my mind into calling Cliff, but because I wanted to destroy the Cat Eyes unit I kept resisting it. Apparently, when it realized that I knew what he was doing, its alternative plan was to kill me," Luke said and David seemed shocked.

"How did you know it wanted to kill you?" David asked.

"I don't know exactly, I just knew that it did by the feelings in my heart," Luke replied and David nodded.

"So how did you survive?" Luke hesitated before answering.

"I prayed. The moment I prayed, the creature standing next to me here…" Luke pointed toward it and then remembered, "the one you can't see, stepped in between me and the other creature. The other one seemed pretty intent on killing me and called in some of his friends to help it defeat the one protecting me."

"Angel," David interrupted.

"What?" Luke replied.

"The *creature* protecting you is an angel. Those that were intent on killing you are demons. Although I'm guessing they look similar," David said and Luke at first wanted to argue for some other explanation, but relented.

"I know. It's just hard for me to embrace the idea. The fact is, it's impossible to tell them apart. They all look perfect and beautiful. I guess I expected to see profound differences in their appearances," Luke stated.

"I'm sorry for interrupting; you were saying the demon brought in some help?" David brought the conversation back to where they had left off.

"Yeah, it did not look good for the uh… the angel or me. But then two additional angels arrived to help it. One came from a woman who had seen me kind of freaking out on the bench and prayed for me, the other was with Danielle who sat with me and prayed. Apparently, the three of them were more than the demons were willing to confront and they withdrew." Luke finished and David continued to look at him.

"I wish I could show you, but the angels won't let me," Luke stated and nodded his head toward his right.

"I don't need to see it to believe it," David stated with a smile. "Although it would be kind of cool to take a peek, but I can wait."

"Wait for what?" Luke asked.

"For heaven. And the good news is that I won't have to worry about seeing the demons," David said with a smirk and they sat starring at each other.

"So what's your plan now?" David suddenly asked, breaking the silence.

"There's more," Luke stated. "The Level 2 version was designed with a profiling purpose in mind. To tell the "sheep from the goats" is what Apollo said." Luke stated and the statement seemed to pique David interest.

"What do you mean?"

"I believe it is designed to identify a Christian from a non-Christian," Luke said and watched as David raised an eyebrow.

"The sheep from the goats…" David mumbled and then opened his bible and started to turn the pages in it. After a few moments of back and forth searching, he apparently found what he was looking for. "<u>Matthew 25:31-33</u> reads, "*When the Son of Man comes in his glory, and all the angels with him, he will sit on his glorious throne. ³² All the nations will be gathered before him, and he will separate the people one from another as a shepherd separates the sheep from the goats. ³³ He will put the sheep on his right and the goats on his left.*" There was a silence as each thought about the verse.

"It sounds like Jesus is the one wanting to separate the sheep from the goats, not Satan," Luke stated, wondering if he had misunderstood the scripture. David suddenly shook his head.

"God knows his own, and Satan knows who are his and who belongs to God. This is not for God or Satan to use. They don't need it, this is for man to use to identify those that belong to God and eliminate them," David said coldly.

"Why? I mean from what I was able to see in the mall, there are so few that are Christians. So why would they need to identify such a small threat?" Luke asked and David took a deep breath.

"Think about it Luke. Based on what we have studied out these past weeks, what is the purpose of a Christian?" David asked and Luke wrestled with what they had studied and the last words Jesus had shared and commanded of his disciples at the end of Matthew.

"To go and make disciples…" he said as he tried to remember the exact words of the verse and David nodded.

"The only threat to Satan and his purpose of turning those from seeking God are Christians teaching the truth. Satan can't touch a child of God, but man can. If you give the physical forces of Satan the tools to identify and remove them, then the threat to them ends," David said and Luke nodded.

"That seems really twisted and hard to fathom." Luke replied.

"Tell that to the Jews during World War II," David responded and Luke nodded, remembering thinking the same thing. David then tilted his head as if remembering something and turned the pages in his Bible until he found what he was looking for.

"The beast was given a mouth to utter proud words and blasphemies and to exercise its authority for forty-two months. ⁶ It opened its mouth to blaspheme God, and to slander his name and his dwelling place and those who live in heaven. ⁷ It was given power to wage war against God's holy people and to conquer them. And it was given authority over every tribe, people, language and nation. ⁸ All inhabitants of the earth will worship the beast—all whose names have not been written in the Lamb's book of life, the Lamb who was slain from the creation of the world." That was <u>Revelation 13:5-8</u>." David looked at Luke. "It was given power to wage war against God's holy people and conquer them." David repeated the section adding emphasis.

"Are you saying this is how it is supposed to happen? The glasses will give the beast the ability to wage war against God's people?" Luke asked incredulously, but David just sat in silence and deep thought.

"I don't know," he finally replied and looked at Luke.

Luke thought about the idea of this beast, or man, or creature wandering the world, killing Christians. One by one, hunting them down and killing David, Susan and Danielle. Wherever this beast or those who were working with him went, they would have the ability to identify those that belonged to God and destroy them. Luke thought about the woman and her young son, the older couple he had seen, and the other Christians he had seen in the mall that he knew nothing about, each being hunted down and killed by the agents of evil all of them, wearing the Cat Eyes product wherever they went to help them fulfill their horrible purpose. Had Cliff came to this same conclusion? Is that why he had left this horrible decision in Luke's hands, knowing that he had a dog in the fight on both sides, with Danielle and David in one and greed and power in the other. Luke could see David staring across the fire from him, trying to understand what he was thinking and what his ultimate decision might be.

"I don't want anyone's blood on my hands. If this is God's will, then he will have another system unit out there to fulfill his purpose, if not, then it will end here," Luke said and pulled the glasses off of his head and tossed them and the systems unit into the fire in front of him. David didn't move to stop him or reach in to take it out of the fire; they both just stared at it sitting on top of the flames. At first it appeared, as if by a miracle, that the systems unit was not going to burn, but then the plastic slowly started to melt and then catch fire. The glasses began to bend and twist from the heat and the coating over the lens began to peel back. It was not long before thick black smoke and flames began to pour out of the fire and fill the area with the chemical stench of burning plastic. They continued to stare at the twisted, melted shape and what remained of the metal parts within the systems unit. Luke knew that no code could have survived on a hard drive exposed to such heat, even so, he nudged the unit that was glowing red from the continued heat of the gas flames burning under it closer to the center of the flames.

"Well, I guess that brings that attempt to stop God's people to an end. That means I gotta get back to work saving souls," David said with a smile. "Which brings us to you, seeing as how you are a believer in the spiritual world, are you ready to tackle the matter of salvation?" David said and smiled. After everything that had just happened, David was still about his purpose.

"What makes you think you've convinced me of a spiritual world?" Luke replied with a smirk?

"Danielle was right, you are hard hearted and it would take an act of God to soften that hard rock sitting in your chest," David replied and smiled.

"There's water," Luke nodded toward the pool. "Why can't I be baptized?"

"Wow, the Ethiopian Eunuch of Acts 8:26. Glad to see you're reading your Bible," David stated, but Luke had no idea what he meant. "We covered the hearing the Word, and believing, but we need to talk about the repentance of sin first. Are you game?" David asked and Luke smiled and nodded.

"With all my heart," Luke replied and David stood up and motioned toward the house.

"Then let's get you a Bible," David replied and walked toward the house. Luke looked back to make sure the systems unit was still sitting in the middle of the flames as he followed David into the house.

Chapter 28

As they sat at the kitchen table, David passed Luke a spare Bible that he had pulled off the shelf. It was not as nice as the one David had given to him, but Luke imagined that it had the same words in it. David said a prayer to start the study, praying specifically about what they had talked about outside, the dangers around them, for the protection of those that they loved, and to truly understand the purpose and power of a relationship with God. He ended it by asking God to reveal those that are lost so that they might know Jesus as well. Luke thought about his prayer and wondered about the people he had seen with the golden aura at the mall.

"How do you know?" Luke asked.

"How do I know what?"

"How do you know who is saved or not? I could be doing this all just to get close to Danielle, so how would you know whether I was sincere or not?"

"It's not for me to know who is saved or lost; only God knows who are truly his. My sole purpose as a disciple of Jesus is to bring the good news to those who have not heard it and let them choose to either obey it or turn away from it," David replied. "I don't judge anyone. Jesus said that his Word would be the judge, so I hold it up as a mirror for people to look into and compare the reflection," David replied as he opened his Bible and turned the pages. "Luke, I know it's going to be difficult for both of us to concentrate after everything that has happened, but understanding when we become God's children is extremely important," David said.

"When we're baptized," Luke replied confidently, but David hesitated.

"Yes, but our reasons for doing so need to be clear, like you mentioned, otherwise we are just getting wet," David stated. "I want you to turn to 1 Peter 2, we're going to read verses 6-10. For in scripture it says: ""See, I lay a stone in Zion, a chosen and precious cornerstone, and the one who trusts in him will never be put to shame." 7 Now to you who believe, this stone is precious. But to those who do not believe, "The stone the builders rejected has become the cornerstone," 8 and, "A stone that causes people to stumble and a rock that makes them fall." They stumble because they disobey the message—which is also what they were destined for. 9 But you are a chosen people, a royal priesthood, a holy nation, God's special possession, that you may declare the praises of him who called you out of darkness into his wonderful light. 10 Once you were not a people, but now you are the people of God; once you had not received mercy, but now you have received mercy." What do we see in this scripture Luke?" David asked at the end and gave Luke a moment to grasp everything he read.

"I'm pretty sure they are talking about Jesus and his message. That those who obey it are a special people that belong to God," Luke replied and David nodded.

"Yes. But we see that at one point in their lives, these special people were not a people of God, that they did not receive mercy, and that they were in darkness. They were called from the darkness into the light, they were given mercy, and they became a people of God. They were once lost, but now they are saved." David said and Luke nodded. "Is there any middle ground or neutral zone that we see between these two conditions?" David asked.

"No. You are either one or the other." Luke replied and David nodded.

"Here's a tough question for you. Which condition do you think you are in at this point?" David asked. Luke took a deep breath and wanted to explain that he wanted to be in the light, but knew there was no middle ground.

"One of those standing in the darkness."

"Why do you think that is?"

"Because I'm... I don't know exactly how to say it."

"Okay, let me see if I can explain it for you with scripture. Turn over to Isaiah 59:1-2," David said as he turned the pages towards what Luke knew was the Old Testament and he followed the direction. "In this chapter of the book of Isaiah, we see the author talking about sin, confession and redemption per the title. Go ahead and read verses 1-2 for us," David said without looking up.

"Surely the arm of the LORD is not too short to save, nor his ear too dull to hear. ² But your iniquities have separated you from your God; your sins have hidden his face from you, so that he will not hear."

"What do we see is the problem with an imperfect person having a relationship with a perfect God?" David asked.

"Our sins separate us from God," Luke stated and David nodded.

"Exactly. This wall of sin is blocking us from God. We are on one side in the darkness and God is on the other side in the light. For us to have a relationship with God, we have to somehow tear down that wall of sin in order to be forgiven. Unfortunately, there is nothing that we can do to remove that barrier," David said and Luke nodded.

"Do you think there are good people and bad people in this world?" David asked and Luke nodded as he thought about the many people that had influenced his life. "Turn over to Romans 3, starting in verse 23. *"for all have sinned and fall short of the glory of God, ²⁴ and all are justified freely by his grace through the redemption that came by Christ Jesus. ²⁵ God presented Christ as a sacrifice of atonement, through the shedding of his blood—to be received by faith. He did this to demonstrate his righteousness, because in his forbearance he had left the sins committed beforehand unpunished."* So who has sinned?" David asked.

"Everyone has," Luke replied.

"So if one person has sinned a thousand times more than another, are they any further away from God because of their sin?" David asked Luke, who wanted to say yes, but somehow knew otherwise.

"So whether they're Scarface or Forrest Gump, without God they are both lost," Luke replied and David smiled.

"The point is, a good moral life does not save you Luke, nor can you earn your salvation by your good works, only faith in the blood of Jesus saves you," David said and Luke understood where he was going with the point. "Remember the *repent* and be baptized part of the salvation plan?" David asked and Luke nodded. "What is it that God is wanting us to repent of?"

"Our sinful life," Luke answered.

"So what is sin? I mean if repentance of it is required, how important would you say it is to understand what sin in God's eyes is?" David asked and Luke tried to think of what would fall under the sin category. Some came to mind easily enough, but where do you draw the line?

"Fortunately, God does not leave us guessing on such matters. Turn over to <u>Galatians 5</u>, starting in verse 19." David said and started turning pages again. "*The acts of the sinful nature are obvious: sexual immorality, impurity and debauchery;* ²⁰ *idolatry and witchcraft; hatred, discord, jealousy, fits of rage, selfish ambition, dissensions, factions* ²¹ *and envy; drunkenness, orgies, and the like. I warn you, as I did before, that those who live like this will not inherit the kingdom of God.*" It says the acts of the sinful nature are obvious. As we read this list, did any of them surprise you?" David asked Luke, who thought through each one and how he had either participated in them at various points in his life, or wanted to, and then shook his head.

"I can't think of a single time I participated in any of the above that good came from it. So no, nothing on the list surprises me," Luke replied.

"No matter how we try to repackage it or redefine it in our minds, or in our society, we know deep down what is right in God's eyes and what is not, and we are without excuse," David said and turned over to another scripture. "I want to read you a few verses in <u>2 Timothy 3:1-5</u> and tell me what time period this sounds like to you," David said and waited for Luke to find the page as well before reading. "*But mark this: There will be terrible times in the last days.* ² *People will be lovers of themselves, lovers of money, boastful, proud, abusive, disobedient to their parents, ungrateful, unholy,* ³ *without love, unforgiving, slanderous, without self-control, brutal, not lovers of the good,* ⁴ *treacherous, rash, conceited, lovers of pleasure rather than lovers of God—* ⁵ *having a form of godliness but denying its power. Have nothing to do with them.*"" David finished reading and looked up at Luke.

"It sounds like today… it sounds a lot like Apollo," Luke said and hesitated. "And, if I am truthful, a little like me, if not in what I do, but what I sometimes want to do," Luke ended and David nodded.

"What is the difference between wages and a gift?" David suddenly asked Luke, who thought about it a moment and then answered.

"Wages are something you earn, while a gift is something you are given out of love or kindness," Luke replied and David smiled and nodded his head.

"In <u>Romans 6:23</u>, Paul writes that…" David said and waited for Luke to find the verse. "*For the wages of sin is death, but the gift of God is eternal life in Christ Jesus our Lord.*" Our sinful life has earned us death; in fact we've worked hard to get it. But God's gift for us is eternal life with him. What we need to urgently find out, is how do we get that gift?" David said and Luke smiled at David's passion and how fun he made studying the scriptures.

"Turn over to John 3:1-7. We've read this one before, it's about Nicodemus and being born again," he said as Luke finally found the page. *"Now there was a man of the Pharisees named Nicodemus, a member of the Jewish ruling council. ² He came to Jesus at night and said, "Rabbi, we know you are a teacher who has come from God. For no one could perform the miraculous signs you are doing if God were not with him." ³ In reply Jesus declared, "I tell you the truth, no one can see the kingdom of God unless he is born again." ⁴ "How can a man be born when he is old?" Nicodemus asked. "Surely he cannot enter a second time into his mother's womb to be born!" ⁵ Jesus answered, "I tell you the truth, no one can enter the kingdom of God unless he is born of water and the Spirit. ⁶ Flesh gives birth to flesh, but the Spirit gives birth to spirit. ⁷ You should not be surprised at my saying, 'You must be born again.'"* So Jesus tells us twice that 'no one' can enter the kingdom of God unless what happens?" David asked.

"Unless you are born again of water and the spirit." Luke replied, remembering the discussion David had with Jonathan on this topic.

"So is this something that just happens when you're not looking, or is it by decision?" David asked Luke, who looked back over the scripture. "According to what we read in the last paragraph of Matthew, it's something that Jesus is making very clear that it needs to happen, so it must be something that a person chooses to either obey or ignore," Luke replied.

"In Acts 2:22-24, Peter shows us that a person must believe that Jesus is from God, verse 22, that he was raised physically from the dead, verse 24, and that everyone is responsible for his crucifixion of Jesus, verse 23," David said while Luke read along as each verse was pointed out. "The important question is, when is the wall of sin removed, and how and when does this gift come?"

Luke read silently through Acts 2 until he reached the part where the Jews who were cut to the heart said, *what shall we do?* Luke read out loud without David's prompting. *"Peter replied, "Repent and be **baptized**, every one of you, in the name of Jesus Christ for the **forgiveness of your sins**. And you will receive the **gift** of the Holy Spirit. ³⁹ The promise is for you and your children and for all who are far off—for all whom the Lord our God will call." ⁴⁰ With many other words he warned them; and he pleaded with them, "**Save** yourselves from this corrupt generation." ⁴¹ **Those who accepted his message were baptized**, and about three thousand were added to their number that day."* Luke finished and looked back on the words he had purposely stated louder as he read. David just smiled and nodded.

"You got this don't you?" David said and Luke smiled.

"I'd like to think I'm pretty smart, but it's not that tough to grasp," Luke said and smiled.

"Okay smart guy, turn over to Romans 6:1-4 and tell me what it means," David said as Luke nodded and turned to the scripture and started reading.

"What shall we say, then? Shall we go on sinning so that grace may increase? ² By no means! We died to sin; how can we live in it any longer? ³ Or don't you know that all of us who were baptized into Christ Jesus were baptized into his death? ⁴ We were therefore buried with him through baptism into death in order that, just as Christ was raised from the dead through the glory of the Father, we too may live a new life." Luke finished and then looked back over the scripture for the answer to David's questions.

"Baptism is the point in time when we participate in the death, burial and resurrection of Jesus," Luke finally answered and David nodded.

"We repent of our old life, we are then buried with Jesus through baptism, and then we are raised to live a new life, the point in time when we are 'born again' and become a member of God's family," David said. "How much faith would you say it takes to believe that the act of baptism is when God unites you with Christ in his death burial and resurrection as Romans 6 states?" David asked and Luke shook his head.

"Apparently enough," Luke replied and smiled and a thought crossed his mind. "What exactly did you mean by me being a eunuch?" Luke asked inquisitively, yet nervously. "Are you implying something with that?" David at first furrowed his brow and then smiled as he remembered what he was talking about.

"I said your words were the same… let me show you. Turn over to <u>Acts 8:26</u>." David said and Luke turned to the chapter and verse and started reading. *"Now an angel of the Lord said to Philip, "Go south to the road—the desert road—that goes down from Jerusalem to Gaza." [27] So he started out, and on his way he met an Ethiopian eunuch, an important official in charge of all the treasury of Candace, queen of the Ethiopians. This man had gone to Jerusalem to worship, [28] and on his way home was sitting in his chariot reading the book of Isaiah the prophet. [29] The Spirit told Philip, "Go to that chariot and stay near it." [30] Then Philip ran up to the chariot and heard the man reading Isaiah the prophet. "Do you understand what you are reading?" Philip asked. [31] "How can I," he said, "unless someone explains it to me?" So he invited Philip to come up and sit with him. [32] The eunuch was reading this passage of Scripture: "He was led like a sheep to the slaughter, and as a lamb before the shearer is silent, so he did not open his mouth. [33] In his humiliation he was deprived of justice. Who can speak of his descendants? For his life was taken from the earth." [34] The eunuch asked Philip, "Tell me, please, who is the prophet talking about, himself or someone else?" [35] Then Philip began with that very passage of Scripture and told him the good news about Jesus. [36] As they traveled along the road, they came to some water and the eunuch said, "***Look, here is water. Why shouldn't I be baptized?***" [38] And he gave orders to stop the chariot. Then both Philip and the eunuch went down into the water and Philip baptized him. [39] When they came up out of the water, the Spirit of the Lord suddenly took Philip away, and the eunuch did not see him again, but went on his way rejoicing."* Luke smiled as he saw that he had said the same words the Ethiopian Eunuch stated.

"So after hearing about the "good news" about Jesus, what was the one thing that the man got out of this incredible piece of *good news*?" David asked Luke.

"Well, after finding out who Jesus was and what Philip had taught him, he knew that he needed to be baptized," Luke said and David nodded.

"So what would you like to do next?" David asked Luke, who just smiled and said. "Imitate my Eunuch friend, minus the *eunuch* part," David rolled his eyes and then nodded.

"If it's okay with you, I'd like to call some of the brothers and sisters from the church to come over to participate in your baptism. Would that be alright?" David asked and Luke smiled.

"Make sure you invite the pit bull brothers, I owe them an apology," Luke said and smiled, then realized by the returned look on David's face that he had no idea who he meant.

"Never mind." David headed to the living room to ask Danielle and Susan to help make a few calls.

Luke stood up and walked to the patio door and stepped outside. He looked at the pool and thought about the freedom and forgiveness that awaited him in those waters. He then looked over and saw the fire still burning and could see that there was only the husk of the metal pieces left of the systems unit still sitting on top of the flames. He was happy that it was no longer a threat to mankind, or more importantly, to his future brothers and sisters. He wondered what Cliff would say when he did not show up at the office tomorrow. Would he be happy or disappointed by it? Knowing Cliff, he would probably be feeling both. He looked around at the darkness beyond the lights of the pool. Now that the systems unit had been destroyed, he wondered if his protecting angel was still nearby watching his every move. Were the other angels still standing guard around the area? He looked up to see what few stars could be seen through the glow created by the bright lights of Los Angeles and smiled.

"Thank you father, I'm sorry it took so long and so much effort on your part for me to find you. I don't know what you expect of me in this relationship yet, but I look forward to seeing whatever you have in store for me," he said out loud and then turned and saw Danielle standing in the patio doorway. She was smiling as she walked towards him.

"You, Luke Baker, are my impossible, but answered prayer," Danielle said and shook her head in disbelief. "I told you that I prayed that God would do whatever it took to have you find him, but what I did not tell you was that I also prayed that he would open your eyes and do amazing things through you," she said in all seriousness. "He has answered the first part of my prayer, now I can't wait to see how he answers the second part of that prayer," Danielle stated and smiled thoughtfully. Luke thought about the Cat Eyes and all the incredible things that had happened as a result of it. *Was that really a result of Danielle's prayer?* Luke wondered. All he knew was that he was so happy to be with her during this moment and he remembered her wanting him to be there for her baptism. He suddenly smiled.

"What's so funny," she asked, seeing his smile.

"You'll be an older women," Luke said and Danielle raised an eyebrow in confusion. "As a new creation, you're several weeks older than me. That makes you an older women. I've never dated a woman that was older than me before," Luke chuckled and she smiled and shook her head.

"I've never dated a man that was younger than me, so I guess everything will be new," she chided back and smiled and he nodded.

"I imagine so."

It was less than fifteen minutes later when people began to show up at the house. What was at first a trickle became a rushing flow as people, most of whom he had never met, came into the house and greeted Luke with the traditional hug that he knew he would need to get used to. He did not mind it from the women, but there was still something about a guy giving him a hug that made him uncomfortable.

Luke tried to evaluate the people that would soon be considered his brother and sisters in Christ and he knew down deep that they would be fighting a very difficult battle against the forces of darkness that he had seen and knew were working diligently to stop them. He thought of the soldiers in Iraq that he had built a camaraderie with during the testing of the Cat Eyes. Would he bond with these spiritual soldiers the same as he had with the Marines in Iraq? He saw the pit bull brothers moving aggressively towards him and smiled at the thought of Boots and how even though they did not get along, they were still on the same team and were willing to die for each other. Luke survived a ten minute grilling from the two of them and learned that they were two single brothers named John and Bruce. He thought he knew why they were single and thought about Ronald and Jonathan and their challenges. Perhaps Danielle could set them up on a date with some other sisters in the church? *Did they allow dating in the church?* Luke wondered and then shrugged, Susan and David were married, he was sure they must have some sort of dating structure. He was just happy to be on speaking terms with Danielle again. She would swing by with a person in tow and quickly introduce them to Luke and then slip away to gather up another person.

Luke was completely surprised to see the woman from the mall, Sandy, standing uncomfortably in the doorway. Luke waved and she saw him and waved back and he made his way over to where she was standing.

"Hi Sandy, what brought you…" Luke started to ask but could not think of the words he wanted to use.

"Danielle called me. I had given her my number at the mall and she called to say that you were getting baptized and wanted to know if I would like to celebrate the occasion. I was so excited for you and grateful that she called," she said and smiled.

"Thank you for coming and thank you for your prayers tonight. I don't think you realize how much that meant to me," Luke said and she nodded.

"Prayer always makes a difference," she replied and suddenly Danielle was there to welcome her with a warm hug and tell her how grateful she was that she came. It all seemed surreal to Luke as he looked around at the people that had come to celebrate his baptism.

"Can we chat a minute?" David asked and Luke turned to see him standing beside him as if he was also taking in the crowd. Luke nodded and David motioned for him to follow him into the den where it wasn't so noisy.

"Are you sure this is what you want to do?" David asked and Luke looked around.

"And disappoint all these people? Not on your life," he replied and David tilted his head and glared at him.

"I'm dead serious." David asked and Luke nodded.

"I have no idea of what I'm getting into, but I've never been surer about something in my whole life," Luke replied and David smiled.

"I realized that we have moved a little quickly, but with all that's happened, I think it would be best to go with the "what are you waiting for' approach in this case. I don't want anything terrible to happen to you should you wait," David said and Luke thought about the demon that had tried to kill him. David said that as a Christian, he would be safe from demons, but still at the mercy of the actions of mankind.

"I think it's the best approach also. Thank you for organizing this," Luke replied and patted David on the shoulder. "You have been a very good friend to me. I hope I can return the same quality of friendship to you."

"You have been a good friend, whether you realize it or not. I'm even more excited about being able to call you my brother though," David said and Luke nodded. "I have a pair of swimming trunks and a shirt in the bedroom for you to wear, unless you want to get your clothes wet?" David asked and Luke thought about it and decided on the swim trunks. David walked him to the room and pointed to the items on the bed for him to wear.

"Before we go into the pool, I'm going to ask you the same two questions that Susan asked Danielle at her baptism. Do you believe that Jesus is the son of God, that he rose from the dead, and that he now sits at the right of the Father in Heaven?" David asked and Luke nodded, remembering Danielle's words at her baptism.

"Yes."

"Then I will ask you, 'what is your good confession?'"

"Jesus is Lord," Luke replied and David nodded.

"After that, we will walk down into the water and you will be immersed, your sins will be forgiven, you will receive the gift of the Holy Spirit, and you will be raised to a new life and added to God's family," David stated and Luke nodded.

"What will happen? Will I feel anything when I'm baptized?" Luke asked curiously and David shrugged.

"You will feel and know that you are forgiven, there is the peace and joy that comes from that, but if you are asking will there be sparks or fireworks going off inside, the answer is probably no. It will just be the joyful cheering and singing of your brothers and sisters and the angels in Heaven," David replied and smiled.

Twenty minutes later, they were standing beside the pool with the guests crowded around. Susan, Danielle, and a few people he recognized but could not name, and even Sandy shared about him, saying things like he had increased her faith by his decision or been an answer to a prayer. Then David closed out the sharing and Luke took a moment to share his appreciation for everyone that had come, for their prayers, and for God's patience and mercy. Then David asked Luke those two important questions; the gathering cheered at his confident profession of *Jesus is Lord*!

"Because of your good confession, I can now baptize you in the name of the Father, the Son and the Holy Spirit, all you sins will be forgiven, and you will receive the gift of the Holy

Spirit, and be added to God's family," David proclaimed with a smile and motioned toward the pool.

As they walked down into the water, Luke smiled at the people and looked across the pool near the fire pit and was surprised to see Angela staring back at him with a smile on her face. Luke almost waved, but just smiled at her. *Danielle must have called her,* he thought as Angela nodded her head and smiled. Luke stopped and looked around a moment. Danielle was holding Susan's hand, with tears flowing down her face. *What an incredibly beautiful face to see,* he thought, as he held his nose with one hand and let David slowly tip him back and then push him under the water.

There was the whooshing sound of water going past his ears, then the muffled cheering of people coming through the water. It felt good to be under the water, it was quiet and peaceful. Then there was a sudden flash of light in his eyes. *Was it the flash of a camera going off?* Luke wondered, but the flash of light was quickly replaced by with a growing darkness and then he was suspended in a deathly silence.

Chapter 29

After collecting his fishing pole and reattached the stringer of fish to his belt, he looked around the small clearing that he was standing in. The wolves that had attacked moments ago were now in full flight, howling in pain and frustration at having come so close to their goal. He shook his head and thought, *they should have known better*, but he knew that their rage and hatred blinded them and when opportunity presented itself, they could rarely resist.

He continued his walk alongside the river, following the dirt path toward the remote fishing hole that he knew held the treasures he had yet to catch. He looked up at the two sides of the gorge, past the sage and into quaking aspen and juniper trees that climbed the three thousand feet of near vertical cliffs on both sides. He looked a little higher and let his eyes scale the steep rock ledges that eventually disappeared into the blue sky above it. He looked back toward the river and saw that it was now flowing clear and steady and the sound of a small rapid could be heard just ahead. The warm sun sparkled off the water and the smell of sage filled his nose. The Steens Mountain was one of the most beautiful places that he knew of and he loved fishing the Little Blitzen River. Sadly, his fishing trip was almost over. It had been a long, hard trek to reach the end of the gorge. Not much further along the confines of the valley would open up and spill out into the plains. This last fishing hole was an important one and he smiled as it came into view. Today he would try again with his whole heart, because this would be his last time here and the last chance at the fish he had, for so long, patiently sought after.

He looked around at the insects that hovered over the small purple and white wildflowers trying to decide which type of fly he should use to catch the fish he had come here for. As he looked at the rod that he held in his hand, a grasshopper landed on his sleeve and then quickly launched itself off again toward the river. He took that as the sign he was looking for and pulled out a beautiful replica of a brown grasshopper from his fly box and tied it to his line. He glanced up in time to see the small surface of the deep hole suddenly erupt as the large trout, the treasure he had came for, broke the surface to claim the wild grasshopper that had left his sleeve moments ago, and land with a slap on the surface of the river. He took a deep breath and hoped that today was the day that they would finally meet.

Checking his surroundings for anything that could interfere with his cast, he moved to the best position, just upstream from the hole and slowly played out the line, lifting and dropping his arm in a slow and steady loop. He watched the line float downstream, but his attention was focused on the leader as it passed back and forth over his head until he sensed that it had reached the length he needed for the fly to reach the hole out in front of him. This fish had always proved to be cautious in the past, so he knew it would take a perfect cast to clear the nearby trees and brush in order to place it exactly where he needed it on the river if he were to have a chance of getting the bait in place without exposing his position. He held his last forward motion and watched as the line played out, dropping the grasshopper perfectly at the head of the deep pool. He tightened the line by raising the tip of his fly pole and held his breath as it floated into the flow of the surface current. A little flick of his wrist and the fake grasshopper on the end of his line twitched just enough to look real. It was the perfect place, the perfect day, the perfect cast, the perfect moment in time. He realized that this was his last chance if he were to ever catch this elusive prey.

The sudden splash brought the tip of his pole to life and once more he and the fish began their battle. The big trout, realizing that something was wrong, launched itself out of the water in an effort to shake the hook from its mouth, the same way it had successfully done so many times in the past. But this time he held the line taunt and the barbless hook held its place. When its first attempt failed, the fish dove deep and tried to wrap the line around the rocks and logs along the bottom of the river. But he held the line high and tight, keeping the head of the fish looking up instead of down. With its usual trick proving fruitless, the fish sensed it was in serious danger. It turned and bolted as fast as it could swim, in an effort to run out the floating leader line in the reel and into the reserve line. But he had learned a great deal about this fish over the years of pursuing it and although he allowed it to run, he did something different this time, he stepped into the river and waded downstream after it, all while keeping pressure on the reel with his thumb in order to make its efforts to flee exhausting for the fish.

The fish with the fisherman now in tow passed one, then another, bend in the river. He struggled to keep pace with the big fish, wading and floating down the river after it. As he approached the third bend in the river, he could feel the big fish beginning to tire. Although exhausted, it turned and began to swim upstream towards him as fast as it could. Seeing the tactic used before, he began to quickly wade backwards as he pulled and reeled in the line as fast as he could, thwarting the fish's efforts, managing to keep the line tight and the hook in place as it launched itself out of the water one last time, furiously shaking from side to side. Then it seemed as if the long battle was over as the big fish seemed to relax and allowed itself to be reeled in. But he had been here before with this fish; he knew this fish like he knew no other, and as it waited for the victor to reach down for it, hoping to catch him with the tip of his pole down and his line tight and ready to snap when it suddenly would run again. Knowing this, he instead just took a step back toward the riverbank and slowly pulled the big fish toward it. With its last trick now foiled, it instead made its last dash down the river, pouring every last bit of energy it had into this final escape attempt, but once again, the fisherman followed it down the river. Then it was over. With no energy left to fight and sensing the inevitability of capture before it, the big fish stopped resisting his efforts to bring it close and instead turned and swam toward him as if surrendering to the master.

He was tired and exhausted, but very happy. He had never fought so long or so hard for a fish before. He had caught bigger fish before, and more beautiful fish before, but he had rarely tried so many times as he had for this one. As he reached down and slowly slid his hands behind the fish in the water, he smiled knowing that he could now walk the banks of this beautiful river knowing that this fish belonged to him. He slid his hand forward and slipped the barbless hook out of the corner of the fish's mouth and faced it upstream as he held it. The fish did not try to escape from his hands; instead it lay on its side in his hands as if waiting for its fate to be decided.

He smiled down at the fish that he held in his hands, but suddenly his perspective as that of the fisherman began to change, shifting from him looking down at the fish in the water, to that of the fish, looking up through the water to where he had been moments before. The flowing water was distorting the face and the sun silhouetted the giant figure that now held him in its hands.

"This is my river, these are my mountains, the food you eat is mine, and I placed you in this river when you were born. What you have not realized is that I have been fishing for you your entire life, but in your stubbornness, your pride and your fear, you have never allowed me to catch you." The voice of the fisherman said to Luke, firmly held in the man's hands. "Now that I have, know that your place with me is now safe and secure. But also know that while you remain in this river that your purpose has changed, and how you look at things will also have changed." The fisherman said and then looked up at the sky above him and then back at Luke in his hands. "The wolves will come for you again, even more ferociously than before, just as they have come for so many of my children in the past. A storm is building on the horizon, one that none will survive without your help. It is time for you to leave the comfort and familiarity of this little river and follow it down to where it joins other larger streams. Warn your brothers and sisters that you meet along the way of the danger that is coming," The man said and then warmth came over Luke as he lay nervously in the huge fisherman's hands looking up at him. "Do not worry Luke. You will not be alone, help will always be present if you remain with me. Learn to see with the eyes of your heart, love those whom I love. Remember love always protects so use your sight to protect those I love. But be careful how you use your eyes or they will lead you down a dangerous and deadly path for not only you, but for those that you and I love." The fisherman slowly lowered him into the river. A peace and joy filled Luke as he watched the blue sky behind the figure fade and turn black. Then he felt the hands that held him suddenly lift him once more out of the depths of the water.

Luke heard cheering and applause as his face broke the surface of the water and felt the cool air on his skin. He opened his eyes expecting to see the giant fisherman still holding him, but instead, the hands that held him now were David's helping to right himself in the blue pool that he had entered moments ago at his baptism. He realized that the cheering and applause had come from the crowd of people that had come to watch. The thought of the fishing dream receded quickly from his mind replaced by the joyful commotion around him. Once Luke's feet were underneath him again and he was able to stand up, David reached over and gave Luke a bear hug, which Luke returned and held longer than he ever had with another man except his father. Suddenly, a song erupted from the crowd around him, almost startling him. David let go and the two of them climbed the steps out of the pool toward the waiting crowd of people, his new brothers and sisters.

Song leader
"I've been redeemed."
Group response
"I've been redeemed."
Song leader
"By the blood of the lamb."
Group response
"By the blood of the lamb."
All together
"I've been redeemed, by the blood of the lamb. I've been redeemed by the blood of the lamb, filled with the Holy Ghost I am, all my sins are washed away I've been redeemed."

As the song leader continued the call and response, a towel was wrapped around Luke and one by one, smiling people stepped forward to embrace Luke and congratulate him calling him brother. Luke kept scanning the area for Danielle, but he could see that she was purposely holding back, allowing the others to have their moment to congratulate him, but deep down, he looked forward to that embrace most of all. Susan, who had given him the towel, embraced him. Then Sandy was there to give him a hug, followed by the pit bull brothers, John and

Bruce, and so many others. It was several minutes before he was able to move to where Danielle was waiting patiently, but even as he stepped next to her, Angela was suddenly at her side and smiled.

"May I?" she asked Danielle, who smiled and nodded.

"I guess I can wait a little longer," Danielle replied and Angela stepped forward.

"No loaf of bread, so I guess you being here is a good sign." Luke stated and embraced Angela as she chuckled.

"Good choice Luke," Angela whispered and then pulled back from the embrace, but still held his arms.

"You saw it in the fire pit?" Luke replied, but she frowned and then seemed to understand.

"I meant becoming a Christian. But yeah, I saw it in the fire. I already knew you would do the right thing there. This was the decision I was most concerned about," she said with all seriousness.

"Why does everyone know me better than I do?" Luke chuckled and then thought about her statement and raised an eyebrow toward her. "I just realized that you have probably been listening in on almost all of my studies," Luke stated in all seriousness and Angela at first hesitated, but then nodded.

"In truth, it helped deepen, and in many ways even reestablish many of my past convictions. I hope you understand that it was part of my job."

"Are you kidding, Cliff's nosiness saved my life," he replied and smiled. "Let him know about the other decision would you?"

"Call me if there is ever any trouble relating to that issue," she said and Luke nodded. "I need to get back to work, be safe and know that you will always be in my prayers."

"You too, and likewise," Luke replied as Angela turned and gave Danielle a hug and then moved through the crowd towards the side of the house.

Luke looked at Danielle who stood across from him and smiled. She tilted her head and smiled that incredible smile back at him.

"Sorry it took so long for me to give you a hug. I got caught up in the mosh pit and couldn't get to you," she said reminding him of what he had said at her baptism. "It was nice of Angela to come," she said.

"Yeah. Thanks for inviting her," Luke said and she raised an eyebrow and shook her head.

"I thought you had invited her?" Danielle replied and it was his turn to raise an eyebrow. Luke suddenly realized that her need to 'get back to work' meant that *he* was her work at the moment. She had probably watched the two of them burn the systems unit as well. *Cliff is definitely thorough*, Luke thought to himself.

"I'm just glad she was here. It's not very often that you get to have the two women who saved your life, one physically and the other spiritually, both together in the same place," he joked. "Danielle, I'm so grateful for you and I promise to protect you and will never ask you to put me before God again. I mean it won't be easy to be the number two man in your life, but I understand now that it is not a competition, but a partnership," Luke said and smiled, "I'm definitely the lesser partner, but would still like to be considered a partner." She laughed and stepped forward and the two embraced each other. For Luke, it was not a sensual or selfish embrace, but a grateful and protective embrace stemming from a selfless love for someone. He thanked God for this moment in time.

As he held her in the peaceful moment, Luke remembered the dream or vision he had during his baptism and it all came rushing back to his mind. Fishing that little river had been so real to him, the images were so vivid. However, the transition to him being the fish at the end of it and God being the fisherman had really caught him off guard. He smiled as he realized how many times God had reached out to him in his lifetime, and how many times he had avoided him. He evaded and even fought against God his whole life. The meeting was so beautiful and joyful, why had he feared it so much? Luke wondered what would have happened if he had broken free this last time. *Last time.* Was this really, as the fisherman said, God's last attempt at reaching out to him? Luke realized that with everything that had happened in the past few months that God had pulled out all the stops to get his attention. He had to admit that if he had turned away at this point, that he would really be without excuse. He took a deep breath and was glad he had finally surrendered to him. But what did the rest of the dream mean? *A storm was building*, the fisherman had said, *one that none would survive without your help.* What storm? How could he help? Did he mean to make other disciples, his new purpose as a Christian? But the fisherman had said *to follow the little river down to where it meets other streams to warn your brothers and sisters of the danger that is coming.* What danger? Why him and not David or the other disciples that had far more knowledge and wisdom than he had? What could he do that they could not do a hundred times better? Luke took a deep breath as he wrestled with the thoughts flowing through his mind. *Don't worry Luke; you will not be alone, help will always be present if you remain with me*, the fisherman had said. What was it that he needed to learn to do? He needed to *learn to use the eyes of your heart*, the fisherman had said, but to *be careful how you use them or they will lead you down a dangerous and deadly path for not only you, but for those that you and I love*, the fisherman had warned.

He knew he loved Danielle, and somehow knew that he would grow to love the new brothers and sisters in his life. But how could he possibly help them? He felt Danielle relax her embrace.

"Are you okay?" she asked as she pulled away and he opened his eyes to once again look into her beautiful eyes. Luke caught his breath as he looked at her. He blinked several times in an effort to clear his eyes, but the faint gold aura circling her face did not disappear. He glanced around the area and saw the golden aura surround almost all of those present. One of the few that did not have the golden aura was a young man in a t-shirt standing twenty feet away. "What's wrong?" Danielle asked again, sensing his emotional change.

"Who's that guy in the yellow t-shirt?" Luke asked Danielle, ignoring her question. She turned to find the person he was looking at.

"His name is Josh, he's a college student that is studying the Bible. Why?" Danielle asked. Luke shook his head as he remembered the fisherman's warning and swallowed.

"I'm glad to hear it," Luke replied and took a deep breath again. Now he knew how he was different, but he did not understand why God had chosen him for this role. Why had he selected a man that was not even one his children, someone who did not even believe in him, to make such an important choice that could have had such horrible ramifications for his people? The same man that he used to thwart the Cat Eyes product from being used by the dark forces against the Christians of the world, was now given that same ability to use to protect his people. Having the very weapon that you intended to use on an enemy suddenly taken away and used against you, well, that must have really angered Satan. *Did Satan and his demons know?* Luke suddenly wondered. *Be careful how you use them*, the words from the fisherman entered his mind again.

This new gift needed to remain a secret for as long as possible. He looked back at a concerned Danielle, who was still waiting for an answer.

"I'm alright. I'm just happy to know that I get to spend the rest of eternity with you," he smiled and hugged her again and then worried about how he was supposed to protect her and the others from the coming storm.

Coming in 2013!

A Heart of Stone
(The 2nd book in *The Eyes of the Heart* series)

For more information on the author and future novels,
you can visit the author's website at:

www.rhackettjr.com

Follow us also on **facebook**!

Also from the Author!

The Black Dragons
(Historical Fiction/Adventure)

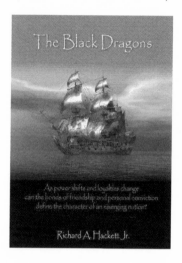

North Carolina -1775

Growing up on a tobacco plantation should be a simple life, predictable as the changing seasons, but when unlikely friends become entangled in the politics and shifting loyalties of nations, life is anything but simple. What starts as a plan to protect the families living on one small plantation, captures the attention of world powers vying for control of the American Colonies and the Islands of the Caribbean.

With few options available, untried heroes find themselves caught in a deadly struggle to protect their ideals, their freedoms and their lives. At every turn their friendship and loyalty to each other and to those brave men they come to lead, is tested. Can the innocent companionship of childhood stand in the face of hatred, prejudice, and war between world powers? Will the ideals that they embody become a testimony to a new world vision for an emerging nation?

www.rhackettjr.com

14105330R00189

Made in the USA
Charleston, SC
21 August 2012